Blue

By

Sarah Jayne Carr

Published by
Crushing Hearts and Black Butterfly, LLC.
Novi, Michigan 48374

Blue
Copyright © 2018 by Sarah Jayne Carr

This is a work of fiction. Names, characters, businesses, places, events and incidents are either the products of the author's imagination or used in a fictitious manner. Any resemblance to actual persons, living or dead, or actual events is purely coincidental.

Cover Artist:
Pretty AF Designs

Edited by:
EAL Editing Services

Published by:
CHBB Publishing LLC.

Dedication

There are two angels who leave pocket change in random places to remind me they're around. This book is for you.

It's also for the angel (who may still be alive and thriving) in Georgia. May you be carrying your trusty hatchet, eating a questionable bowl of Borscht, and speeding down residential streets in your blue convertible.

Piper, this one's for you too. Without you, there wouldn't be a Trixie.

Oh! That's right! Hey, Christine? I'm going to borrow your words for three seconds: **#sorrynotsorry**

One

Cash Jensen was a lousy lay at best, which was exactly how I wanted it. There was no doubt a dictionary existed in a corner of the world with his headshot next to the words: vain, arrogant, and hot-headed jerk. That laundry list of craptastic behaviors, along with being robbed of my third orgasm that week, helped keep my attachment to him at a bare minimum. It was perfect—a less than lukewarm connection, at least from my perspective. I called it my "five fingers" plan. As long as someone had a constancy of five or more shitty qualities, emotional investment was impossible. However, Cash was a special breed of asshole. He exceled at being part of my elite "ten fingers and ten toes" plan.

"Oh, Cash." Each pelvic thrust was monotonous as I rolled my eyes behind closed lids. The words I spoke were forced and detached. "Don't. Stop." I did my best to make it sound like "don't stop", more of a command than two separate sentences. But I failed. As usual, he was too wrapped up in himself to notice. Let's call a dick a dick here. Cash was a speed fucker, a two-pump chump, a cock sneeze.

Some girls would argue I settled for dating Cash and his silicone personality. Okay, I'll be honest. Most girls wouldn't even qualify what we did as "dating". Any details I offered about my arrangement with him were vague and his identity kept under wraps. The responses I received were usually greeted with a disapproving head bob, a wince, or a consoling pat on the shoulder. Sometimes, I'd even get all three at the same time. I called that combination the She Has an Asshole

Trifecta or SHAT. I'd lost count of how many times I'd been "SHAT" on, thanks to Cash Jensen. It was so bad, shots of alcohol were even offered my way at a bar one night by a nun who'd overheard one of my lame sauce stories. Now, if a bar-hopping nun's pitying your sex life, something's wrong. Really wrong. Why did I stick around? It was minimal effort because relationships were overrated. Every single one of them.

"More." I began creating a grocery list in my head as he grunted, pounding me into the mattress like a caffeinated jackhammer with a thirty-second battery life. *Bread. Milk. Eggs. Tampons.*

Cash was good enough, a warm body for me to sleep next to a couple of nights per week, and he served as someone to give off the illusion of the R-word. Relationship. Yuck. I swear, those four syllables teamed up together gave me a case of hives. But it kept sleazy men at bay from asking me on dates, and it discouraged the few people from my pathetic excuse of an inner circle from playing matchmaker. Knowing there was "someone" in my life seemed to be the ticket, even though I could've bought an inflatable doll and passed it off as a significant other. Oh, wait. That was the equivalent of Cash.

I shuddered at the thought of that stupid R-word. *Never again.*

"Damn, I'm a motherfuckin' stallion." Cash growled as he rolled off my body, both sweaty and spent. He folded his hands behind his head and looked at the ceiling with a satisfied smile. I knew that look all too well. His next words would be a confident, *'"Wasn't I incredible?"'.* He wasn't asking for my opinion. He was informing me he'd scored his performance an A-plus grade.

I parted my lips slightly and mouthed the phrase as he spoke it aloud.

"Wasn't I incredible?" he asked.

I knitted my brow and pushed a stray lock of dark hair out of my face. "Yep. You're a raging sex god."

My monotone response wasn't lost on him, but don't go thinking he was tuned in to my emotions on a regular basis or any similar bullshit. That wasn't his style. Getting any level of sensitivity out of him was rare and only happened when pigs took flight. On most days, I was able to mask my dissatisfaction to stroke his ego. In turn, Cash was usually too focused on himself to notice.

Rolling onto his side, he propped his head up with his hand, his elbow resting on the pillow. "C'mon, baby. You were good too. I could tell by the way you moaned my name at the end." He paused for a fraction of a second. "Seriously though. What was your favorite part? Was it the thrusting to the beat while I sang the chorus of *Mambo Number 5*? That was great, wasn't it?" There was no room for a response. "Either way, you were one lucky lady to be part of it." He winked, made a clicking sound, and formed his thumb and index finger into a gun shape. Then, he offered me a cheesy grin while pulling the imaginary trigger.

Be still my beating heart. *Did he really do that? And if he did, why haven't I noticed it before?* I thought to myself as I opened my mouth to unleash a snarky comment, but Cash cut me off again.

"It's okay. If I were you, I probably wouldn't be able to choose the numero uno momento either. See? Those Spanish courses from the late-night infomercial you made fun of are starting to pay off. Olé!"

I withheld my glare, but it was my own fault I stayed with Cash; I knew that. Plus, faking my climax again didn't help my mood. It hadn't always been that way, or so I tried to convince my libido on multiple occasions. Call it lying to myself. Call it some masochistic form of self-punishment. Call me a martyr. Any way you looked at it, Cash's ego had gone into overdrive and his sexual stamina into underdrive. I couldn't break it off though. My life was complicated.

He was Cash Jensen, what many would consider a trophy boyfriend. Yet, I felt like the loser. Irony at its finest. There was no secret; he was gorgeous. Anyone could see that. Piercing blue eyes. Tousled blond hair that looked great at any time of day. Dimples complementing a strong jaw. Tanned skin that made every suntan model in America jealous. Not to mention a muscular physique requiring few trips to the gym. It was enough to make most women's ovaries swoon with excitement—but not mine. That's where the vision faded. Skin deep. Cash was like a latex balloon. Thin-skinned. Empty up top. Full of hot air. Ready to pop at the first hint of penetration. It was transparent and shallow companionship. The greatest perk was it couldn't lead anywhere serious.

I was convinced our mediocre partnership was better than being alone where awful memories would hunt me down, screaming for my attention. And that same level of mediocre was more desirable than a healthy and stable relationship where I'd be emotionally invested. Mediocre was my theme, my safe zone, and that was okay. It was where I was protected, and I could never be broken again.

Surfacing to the present, I shoved Cash's egotistical behavior and his hand aside while looking at the clock. "Shit!" I sat upright in bed, tossing back the European down comforter. The damn thing was worth three months of my salary. For that price, I joked it had been stitched by unicorns and enchanted fairies. "It's almost seven. I'm gonna be late."

As I hurried around the bedroom, rifling through the aftermath of the clothing tornado, Cash grabbed my waist and pulled me against him. The skin-to-skin contact made me cringe. "It's fortunate you have an in with your boss." He waggled his eyebrows.

"Just because you sign my paycheck doesn't mean there isn't talk around the water cooler. I have to be on my A-game to avoid the whispers and the looks. Everyone's so fucking nosy around there. Plus, your brother would nail my ass to the wall if he knew we—"

"Whispering? Someone giving you grief at the office, baby?" A muscle clenched along Cash's jaw. He was always looking for a reason to exercise his authority. "I'll fire them. Give me names."

"Relax. I can fight my own lunchroom battles. Workplace relationships are frowned upon by—"

Cash stifled a fake yawn. "What did you do? Memorize the employee handbook? It's not very becoming on you." He rolled his eyes before turning over to graze his fingertips along my thigh. "Now, if I were on you, I'd *be coming—*"

I swatted his exploratory fingers away as they made a sudden grab for my tit. "Late. Remember?"

"Besides, don't forget I own half of that company."

"Forty-nine percent, if you want to be technical about it, Cash."

He held up his index finger to correct me. "Dr. Cash."

"I already told you I'm not roleplaying and calling you 'Dr. Cash'."

He sighed and crossed his beefy arms.

"Look, your brother still outranks you by one percent, so he makes the final decisions around there. Case closed."

"Can we not talk about Price after the award-winning performance that occurred in this bed? Remember, I'm a sex god. Thanks to me, the star. And you, Blue, were my supporting role." He ran his fingers through his hair.

My cell phone buzzed on the nightstand, interrupting our conversation. I was thankful. Scratch that. I was only appreciative until I saw who was calling.

I glanced at the screen while Daveigh's name flashed in bold red letters. "Ugh. Not today, drama queen," I mumbled.

"Problem?" Cash nibbled my shoulder, his facial stubble abrasive against my skin.

I wriggled away from him. "I'll deal with it later."

An envelope blinked in the upper corner. New voicemail. A few seconds later, a text message popped up in the center of the display.

"For the love of...leave me alone." I sighed.

"Wait." Cash grabbed the phone as he examined the screen. Who's Davey, and why is *he* texting you this early in the morning?"

I snatched it from his grip. "Stop pissing on me to mark your territory. Her name is Daveigh, and it's pronounced Duh-VAY. She's my sister. I've mentioned her to you a thousand times."

"Sister. Right," he echoed, and I could almost see the mental sticky note he made for future reference. I was willing to bet it would flutter to the floor of his overinflated brain within a matter of minutes and we'd have a repeat of the same conversation within the next week.

I jammed the phone into my purse and grabbed a thin sweater from the smallest drawer in the bureau. It was Cash's birthday gift to me. The drawer. Not the sweater. I was less than impressed with the gesture, especially considering he'd only given me half the space while he acted as if he'd presented me with the Holy Grail.

"Will I see you tonight?" Cash flashed me his abnormally white smile, the text message already lost in his mind.

I worked my waves of black hair up into a sloppy ponytail while pinning a thick rubber band between my teeth. "Maybe."

"Cash Jensen doesn't do maybe," he replied.

"Well, Blue Brennan doesn't do conversations where Cash Jensen talks in third person. You know it creeps me out."

"Oh, come on, baby." He smiled. "That new sushi restaurant opened downtown, and I've been dying to try it. Plus, that dirty art exhibit unveiled at The Miriah. Rumor has it there's a sea of cock sockets dangling from the ceiling. Each one is suspended by fishing line. It's like they're floating. Think about it. Sushi. Vaginas. It'd be considered a theme night."

Although I was impressed Cash finally used the word "theme" correctly in a sentence, my heart hesitated as the morning took a sudden nosedive. "P...public? Cash, we can't—"

"Shhhh." He held a finger up to my lips. "Maybe it's time we take our relationship out from under the sheets and into the real world."

My stomach sank to the floor as I headed toward the kitchen with Cash in tow. *Whoa, cowboy. Relationship?* My mind whirled while I questioned what pivotal point made him think we'd achieved that status. I banked on it being second-rate sex and meaningless dinner conversation. To me, he was a placeholder for a void I vowed to never permanently fill. It was my worst nightmare come true. Keeping what Cash and I had hidden was where I wanted it—swept under the rug. Maybe under a dozen rugs. Thick ones. Oh! And a cement floor. Six feet under. Having people see us together would make what we had real. Work had always been the perfect excuse for secrecy.

Why was he changing the rules on me?

"You don't have to tell me, I already know what you're going to say. The restaurant is ritzy, out of the way, and you don't like sushi. I get it. None of it's your style or your comfort zone, but that's all fine with me. I promise it'll be worth your while when we get back to my place." He ran his tongue over his teeth before gesturing at his crotch. "Mini Cash will make sure of it."

Mini Cash? I was speechless, and perhaps that was for the best.

"Shhhh...." He held up his index finger to my lips again, squashing them flat this time. "I can see it on your face. You're going to say, 'We always go to your place. Why can't we go to mine?' I've been thinking about it. Yours is a little too crummy for me."

"Crummy?" I felt nauseated as I filled my travel mug with coffee and stuffed a giant blueberry muffin in my purse. I wasn't sure if it were because of the impending date, Cash's words, or his sleazy mouth gesture. Maybe it was all three, and I'd been SHAT on yet again.

Cash nodded toward my purse. "You sure that's a good idea?"

Considering the conversation that morning, I began questioning every choice I'd made since meeting him. "Is what a good idea?" I snapped.

"An entire muffin. Every day you're here, you take one for breakfast. Do you have any idea how many carbs and grams of sugar are in those?" He reached for a bottle of low-sugar, low-fat, low-calorie, low-flavored protein shake from the fridge and extended his hand out to me. "Here. This won't cling to your ass, requiring me to lipo it later."

Anger didn't begin to describe what I felt. I wrinkled my nose at the wildly-colored label with misspellings, recalling the flavor and consistency were both comparable to lawn clippings. The bottle showed a picture of a cartoon peach with ridiculously large biceps, but it lied like a sack of potatoes. Nothing about it tasted like fruit...or French fries for that matter. "Not interested in the shitty shakes your cousin sells out of his garage. He's had five lawsuits slapped against him from customers who've gotten sick."

"Suit yourself," he let out a condescending sigh and put the bottle back in the refrigerator, "but don't come crying to me when you can't button your jeans. Remember, your metabolism is going to slow down in a few years."

"I'm perfectly happy with my pant size. If I want a blueberry muffin, I'm going to eat a fucking blueberry muffin."

Cash gripped my shoulders in a possessive gesture and spun me around in a circle slowly, taking inventory of my frame from head to toe. "I'm just saying, I'd honor the employee discount to do some work on you. Call it a perk of sleeping with a plastic surgeon. A little tightening here." He lightly squeezed my upper arms and then palmed my ass. "A little lift back here. And maybe some breast implants to boost the twins up another cup size. Don't get me wrong, it'll take some definite work on my end, but I'd have you flawless eventually."

I narrowed my eyes and moved out of his reach. "I've turned you down hundreds of times for nipping and tucking. That's not gonna change. Even though I work for you, we both know I'm not interested in the services you provide."

"What *we* both know is you *are* interested in *some* of my services you haven't turned down." He winked. "How many months have we been sleeping together?"

There wasn't time to fight with him. I was already late for work. From any angle, I didn't know what more to say, so I merely sagged my shoulders in defeat. Arguing or coming up with every excuse imaginable in the situation would be pointless. Headache? He'd take me to an acupuncturist before dinner. Emergency root canal? He'd call his dentist at three in the morning if it meant dragging me to an art museum where vagina artwork was on display. Brushing my goldfish's hair? He'd call in a favor from a salon to appease me. One fact was certain. Cash Jensen was known for not taking "no" for an answer.

two

I headed downstairs to the basement of the extravagant condo complex, taking two steps at a time in heels when my cell buzzed again. "What now?" It was another mystery text from Daveigh that demanded an immediate call. With a sigh, I dropped the phone in my purse for a second time and hurried toward the underground parking level. "Sorry, 'Veigh. Now's not a good time," I mumbled to myself.

The double doors of the massive garage shut, smacking my rear from behind while the familiar smell of old motor oil and exhaust greeted me. It was reminiscent of an established mechanic's shop. My high heels clacked against the concrete floor as I descended the ramps, the sound echoing against the acoustics of the wide-open space. I'd become familiar with parking slot 34 over the past ten months. It was another self-serving gift from Cash to ensure my vagina visited him on a regular basis. In the beginning, I was terrified of doing the walk of shame alone through the empty garage. Shadows loomed in every nook and cranny of the dimly lit area. Over time, I realized it wasn't such a lonely place.

"Hey, Otis," I said as I turned the corner of a gray, concrete pillar.

An old man poked his head out from the top of a faded sleeping bag and looked at me with bloodshot eyes. Tufts of fuzzy, white hair stuck up from his tanned scalp. "Good mornin', Miss Blue," he said with a near-toothless smile.

"I'm late for work today, so I can't chat. But I brought you breakfast." I reached into my purse and grabbed the muffin.

Truth be told, I'd never eaten a single one of the gummy pastries I'd taken from Cash's kitchen. Every single one had gone to Otis. Go 'head, make me 'flawless eventually', Cash-hole. "Blueberry today. I know. Not your favorite, but it's all that was left."

Otis looked at the muffin wide eyed and gave my hand a gentle squeeze before taking the plastic bag from my grip. "That's okay. I'll take blueberry over a hungry belly any day." His lips trembled, and he looked like he already envisioned how it'd taste. "Thank you, Miss Blue!"

"You're welcome. And here's some coffee. Two sugars. No cream. Just how you like it. You know the drill."

He nodded and reached out to take the travel mug from me with shaky hands, like I'd gifted him with a million dollars. "I'll leave the cup in the corner of your space. Number 34. By the wall."

"I'm not sure if I'm staying here tonight or not, but I'll pick it up when I'm back next. Don't let the side door latch, so you can get in tonight."

He smiled and took a giant bite of muffin, a few stray crumbs falling from his lips as he groaned with delight. "Oh, I know, and I don't expect these handouts." He swallowed. "But it's people like you who make the world a little bit better for someone who's down on their luck like me. I'll never forget the way you took pity on me when I nearly froze to death on that park bench down the street last winter. You're a diamond in the rough for feedin' me when you're around and lettin' me into this garage for a warm sleep."

My heart sank a little, my smile wilting into a frown. I wished I could believe the kind words he spoke about me. Knowing what I did in the past left me wondering if Otis would feel the same way if he understood the truth. "Have a good one, buddy." I gave the sleeping bag a pat before I hurried halfway across the garage to my car.

Looking at my watch, I cursed every swear word I knew into one drawn-out sentence. The big hand crept closer to the twelve, and that meant time was running out. I got into my aged hatchback and started the engine when I noticed a crumpled piece of paper tucked underneath the left windshield wiper.

"I don't have time for this." I got out and tugged it free from the rubber strip. A string of glittery, purple letters conveyed a one-lined message, complete with lower-case I's made into frowny faces.

i hit your ride. it's shitty, so i doubt you'll notice. Sorry.

"Fuck." I walked around the car and saw a smashed tail light and two round dents. It looked like the giant, who lived at the top of the beanstalk, sat their oversized ass cheeks down into my bumper. There wasn't time to analyze who could've done it. All I could do was pray I wouldn't get pulled over on the way to the office. Slamming the shifter into drive, I raced toward the exit of the garage.

The thick layer of smog mixed with sunlight stung my eyes as I flipped the blinker. It was late fall, my least favorite time of year—and for good reason. Across the way, the clock affixed to the spinning bank sign read quarter 'til eight in giant orange numbers. "Fifteen. Awesome." I fumbled for my day-old bottle of water in the cup holder before easing into traffic. I'd achieved the speed limit when the unexpected happened. The car in front of me slammed on their brakes and swerved halfway into my lane, forcing me to skid to a stop. I dropped the bottle and gripped the steering wheel with both hands, cold liquid spilling down the front of my sweater and soaking into my cream-colored dress pants. "Well, fuck you too, gravity! I only have fifteen minutes until Gloria'll eat me alive with a side of chocolate cake."

Great. I'm talking to myself now.

* * *

Seventeen minutes later, I strode through the circular revolving doors of Jensen & Jensen, one of the top plastic surgery offices in Northern California. Celebrities, criminals, and anyone seeking exclusivity went to the clinic. Some of the procedures and practices were legal, but most of them weren't. Due to privacy laws, I couldn't discuss any of the details outside of work. Marvin McGreen, a local and cutthroat lawyer, was known for having one client who kept him busy year-round—Jensen & Jensen.

Ornate marble pillars were perched on either side of the grandiose entryway. Their contrasting black and blue swirls on white reminded me of a sickly bruise. Ironic, considering the tasks performed behind closed doors. The floor-to-ceiling windows brought in an obscene amount of lighting, which enhanced the environment. Every imperfection was showcased.

For nearly two years, I'd worked at the surgery office, specializing in every procedure under the sun...knife. Muffin tops. Bat wings. Banana rolls. Nose jobs. Lipo. Cuntstruction. You name it. If someone could complain, Cash and Price Jensen would fix it, along with nipping and tucking wallets for every available penny.

As much as I wanted to, I couldn't complain. The funds kept food on my table and a roof over my head. My salary wasn't much considering I was "just office help" as Price Jensen had so-kindly put it on more than one occasion. Most of the Jensens' dollars padded their own pockets. The most important part was the grueling hours at Augmentation Nation, as I'd deemed it. Not many would consider that a perk, but I did. It alone was worth the meager pay because it kept me far away from Steele Falls.

When it came to cosmetic reasons, I wasn't a believer in plastic surgery. Enhancing my ass cheeks, suctioning fat off of my stomach, or tightening my vag wasn't a priority in my life. That's what gyms, diets, and Kegels were for. But when I moved into town, I needed money badly. Jobs were scarce in Sacramento. With my savings account running low, I risked living in my car during one of the coldest Novembers on record. Usually, the area had mild weather late in the year, but leave the winds to change when Blue Brennan entered the equation.

Jensen & Jensen was the first place to offer me a job with

bennies. And I'm not talking about Cash's version of benefits. So, I snatched it up and swallowed my high-calorie pride, unsure of when another opportunity would arise. Truth be told, my D-cup boobs got me the position and not my résumé. Cash'd ogled them forty-two times during my interview. I counted. Nearly a year later and after a million and twelve of his advances, I somehow ended up in bed with the dickfizzle. Thanks for nothin', education.

My heels sounded against the glossy cement flooring of the reception area, the grandiose acoustics announcing my lateness. *Why didn't I wear flats today?*

"Well, well, well...what do we have here? Is that Blue? It's so nice of you to grace us with your smile." A round, female face peered at me. She flashed a sneer from behind a computer screen at the reception desk.

"Morning, Gloria." I refused to preface the phrase with a 'good' to her. Any morning involving Gloria wasn't pleasant. My eyes flicked toward the clock. Two minutes late. *Fuck my life.*

Her eyes scanned me from head to feet, hesitating on my torso. "Did you piss yourself?"

"It'll greatly disappoint you to know I spilled a cup of water in the car."

"Mmmhmmm. Do you know what time it is?" Gloria clicked her tongue against the roof of her mouth three times, her heavily-rouged and saggy cheeks jiggling over her robust bone structure. She slid a cheap pair of reading glasses off her face, allowing them to dangle on a beaded, metal chain around her neck. The smell of gardenia perfume burned my nose. It was enough to make me gag. *Did she roll around in a flower shop this morning?*

"The time? Sure do," I said as I punched my employee code into the clock behind the desk. "You see, when the big hand is on the—"

"I know how to tell time," Gloria snapped. "You're two minutes late."

"And?"

"Where were you?" Gloria growled, her demeanor

turning immediately sweet as one of the medical assistants walked past the desk. "Hey, Justine?"

A woman clutching a clipboard approached. Red scribbles covered most of it. She wore scrubs covered in cartoon cats holding scalpels with crazed expressions on their faces. "Huh? Sorry, Gloria. Just studying up on the nine o'clock. Oh. Hey, Blue." She offered me a smile.

"Good morning," I replied. You see, Justine was worthy of a "good" before "morning", much unlike Gloria.

"Right. Tony," Gloria beamed matter-of-factly.

I almost asked if she wanted a cookie for memorizing the appointment book. Almost.

"Yeah." Justine puffed her cheeks and the let air out slowly. "I don't know how many of these procedures he's gonna have before the guy's happy. His dick's gonna be long enough to wear as a scarf soon."

"He called and wanted me to let you know he and his '100% all-beef thermometer' are going to be ten minutes late for his next cock talk."

"'All beef'? Are you kidding me? Some of that *meat* came from grafts on his arm, chest, thigh... Ugh. I think a pig was even offered as sacrifice at one point."

Gloria held up her pudgy hands in a gesture of defeat. "Don't shoot the messenger."

"I know. These experimental surgeries are getting ridiculous though." Justine groaned. "Plus, the man has a million names for his penis. Steamin' semen roadway. Pocket rocket. Yogurt slinger. Trouser snake. I've lost count. Only a matter of time until he sprains some poor girl's vagina. If he can even get the damn thing up without hoisting it by crane." She looked around and lowered her voice. "And he talks to his dick like it's a person. It's so weird."

Suddenly, I had flashbacks of Cash's references to Mini Cash and shuddered.

Gloria snorted. "Well, I'll let you know when Tony and his bologna pony arrive."

Justine looked up at the ceiling and sighed before walking away. "As always, can't wait."

Gloria's resting bitch face sprang to life again when the door leading to the exam rooms clicked shut. "So, you never answered me. Where were you this morning?"

"I don't remember you signing my paychecks, so I don't think I owe you an explanation." I headed toward the doorway leading to a cluster of business offices. It was my poor attempt at a swift getaway. Unfortunately, proximity wasn't on my side.

She stood up and blocked my path while she tried to cross her arms but couldn't. More and more, Gloria reminded me of a female bouncer at a shady nightclub. "Well, if you'd stop chasing Cash's beaver cleaver, maybe you'd be on time for a change, Brennan."

"Chasing? Cash?" I blurted the words more loudly than I'd intended as I scanned the room to make sure we were alone. If anything, Cash was the one pursuing me. End of story. I wasn't about to let Gloria get under my skin though.

For months, she'd been sniffing out Cash's crotch for a scrap of hope at getting laid, but he avoided her like a bad case of syphilis. In turn, she'd decided to make my life miserable. Total fairness.

I wanted to take a twenty out of my purse, slap it on the counter, and tell Gloria to put it toward a vibrator so she could clear the cobwebs out of her stench trench. Instead, I proudly took the high road. I bit back my retort and balled my fists, elbowing her out of the way as I walked down the hall to my office. Home away from home...or more like hideout from Gloria Peterson.

I tossed my purse on the cheap, metal desk and flopped into the uneven chair. One wheel was permanently an inch off the floor, a stock feature which drove me bat shit crazy. Twin spreadsheets loomed on the flickering screen from the night prior. It was part of a tedious project set forth by Price Jensen himself. Three days later with a condescending tone, he'd likely tell me he wanted the information rearranged, written in hieroglyphics, or presented on a platter with a gold-plated garnish. He had the ability to shat on me too. It was standard Price and a Jensen specialty. Any way I looked at it, I could never win with the roadblocks he built.

My purse buzzed. *I need to think about changing my number again.* I had a weak moment and gave Daveigh my new digits after I'd moved to Sacramento. At that moment, I regretted it.

Looking between the monitor and my purse, I wasn't sure which was the lesser of the two evils. "Ugh. She's not going to give up." I threw my arms in the air. "Fine. You win!"

Reading the most recent text message, it was Daveigh's style—vague and dramatic.

'Veigh

BLUE ANN BRENNAN! CALL ME ASAP. 911. PRONTO. NOW. URGENT. I DON'T CARE IF YOU'RE FUCKING YOUR CELEBRITY CRUSH, WHETHER YOU'RE ON THE POT, OR IF YOU'RE HAVING A BEER WITH THE PRESIDENT.

Pursing my lips, I held the phone in my hand, the weight of the impending conversation heavy. All caps with Daveigh wasn't a good situation. It was too late though. My mistake was opening the text message, so a time stamp proved I'd read more than the preview. Pandora's Box was about to open if I gave in. Tapping my index finger on the keyboard, I contemplated my options one last time before dialing my sister's number. If I didn't get it over with, she wouldn't stop, and I'd end up in a straitjacket by dinnertime.

One ring.

Daveigh's definition of "urgent" was likely a shoe crisis, details on her latest male conquest, or whether or not a dress made her ass look fat. Most of the time, I was a pro at evading her, but I'm not sure what made me buckle so quickly. Maybe I was getting soft. *Nah.*

After two more rings, much to my dismay, the line opened.

"Blue! It's about fucking time. Where the hell have you been?" a female voice reprimanded. "I've texted you a hundred times now. For hours."

I glanced at the three text messages on my phone and rolled my eyes. It was an exaggeration, but I remained calm. "Nice to hear from you too, Daveigh. It's been what? Six months? Maybe seven since we last spoke?"

She ignored my question and sighed. "You never answer. Ever. Let's not do this. Not today."

"Let's not do what?" I asked. "Our usual avoid-each-other dance? But we're so good at it, even though I'm not sure who leads and who follows anymore."

"Please don't pick a fight. This is important."

"Obviously. I can tell by your parental tone and use of capital letters in text, little sister." I paused. "Well? What is it? I stopped fucking my favorite movie star while on the porcelain throne. You should've been there. It was pretty impressive since the president and I were about to toast with our beers, and—"

"Stop," Daveigh demanded.

"What is so damn important?" I snapped. "Do you need me to tell you which pair of shoes matches your outfit better? Did the bikini barista stand fire you again for hooking up with that rent-a-cop? Did Steele Falls go up in flames? What? What is it?"

"His name is Gene, and he's a private security guard. We broke up a long time ago."

"Whatever." I huffed. "There's no doubt in my mind a new man in uniform took his place."

"This really isn't the time for your specialty brand of snark." There was a hitch in her voice, and I knew from experience tears were on the horizon. "You and I have had our share of issues, but..."

I leaned back into the chair and closed my eyes. It wasn't like Daveigh to get worked up on the phone. Evening my tone, I brought my voice down an octave. "What's going on?"

Her words were a mix of garbled sobs, but I could still understand her without a doubt. "It's Daddy. He's dead."

three

I spoke a string of words with my mouth gaping open and the wind knocked out of my lungs. Well, at least I thought I said something intelligent. My brain refused to reply again and again—like a stalled car. The engine wouldn't turn over. Outside of the cheap wall clock's tick, it was quiet. Even it didn't function with a broken second hand that constantly quivered at 39 seconds, never quite able to make it to 40. I often wondered if it were purposely placed in my office by Price as a joke. It was The Little Engine That Couldn't.

"Are you still there?" Daveigh asked.

"I...I think so." Fortunately, I was seated. Numbness coursed through my arms and legs.

A flurry of emotions swilled and sloshed through my stomach like the morning after too many frozen margaritas at a sorority party. Nausea. Sadness. Regret. Pain. Confusion. All of those feelings should've been present, but they faded within seconds of crossing my mind. They were the reasonable and expected reactions to have when someone died. One sentiment took hold within me above all others though. As much as I didn't want to admit it aloud because it'd make me sound like a cruel bitch, I was mostly relieved.

Silence.

"Say something," Daveigh said. "He had a massive stroke, and Mommy found him in the garage by the deep freezer, next to that nudie poster on the wall."

"Give me a second here to process. You dropped a bomb on me."

"There isn't time to assess your feelings. You have to come here and—"

"Whoa! Back your fantasy train up for a sec, 'Veigh. I'm not coming to Steele Falls," I said. "Huh uh. No way."

"But there'll be a funeral. You'll be the only sibling who won't—"

"And there'll still be a funeral without me. Look, I've spent too long moving on from everything that happened there, and I'm not about to relive all of it by coming back to attend that man's burial."

"*That man* was your dad, Blue. You have to come," Daveigh said. "It's all written into the will. If you aren't here when the lawyer meets with Mommy on Wednesday, you won't get anything."

"Step."

"What?" she over-enunciated the 't'.

"Step-father. He wasn't my dad, and I'll never refer to him as that."

"Whatever. He raised you since you were a toddler."

"*Raised* is a stretch. If you call teaching me how to cheat at blackjack or how to cure a hangover after a Friday night bender or how to swing punches 'raised', sure. He raised me. I don't want anything of his," I said matter-of-factly, leaning back in the chair with my arms folded. "Not a damn thing."

"You don't get it. Quit sitting there with your arms crossed, being stubborn. No one will get anything if one of us isn't there. Not Mommy. Not me. Not Finn. No one. This thing's wrapped with enough shiny, red tape to make Santa jealous."

I pursed my lips and unfolded my arms, annoyed Daveigh could peg how I was positioned from miles away. "This 'thing'? What are you talking about? Washington's a community property state. Mom gets everything. Game over."

More silence. It was becoming an unwanted theme.

I felt my tone souring further. "Hello?"

"Look. I really didn't want to tell you this over the phone, but I don't think you'll believe me or come home unless I tell you the truth."

"What truth?" I sat up in my chair and fiddled with the

desk calendar, my heart racing in my chest. *Could she possibly know?* "What on earth could make me drop everything to come back?"

"Mommy and Daddy weren't ever married. Daddy kept most of his money separated from her, and—"

"What do you mean they were never married?" I asked, tension releasing from my shoulders. It wasn't the disaster I expected her to uncover. In other news, my sister was delusional with her psychobabble.

"I mean, a wedding didn't happen. Have you ever seen a picture of a white dress? First dance? Smashing cake in each other's faces? Giant after party?"

"Well, no, but the rings..."

"Think about it. Anyone can wear a piece of jewelry on their finger and get their name changed. Hell, I could go buy a cheap hunk of metal, change my name, and preach to the world I'm married to you today. No one would know the truth."

"Please don't. That's weird."

"I'm not going to actually do it, but I'm trying to make a point," she replied.

"Well, it's still community property, and after seven years—"

"Washington isn't common law. The majority of his assets are all out of state. They're in another woman's name, and everything has to go through her. Plus, Mommy's married. There are so many fucking complications with this situation that—"

"Hold on. We've moved from the fantasy train over to the merry-go-round. Stop the carousel. I'm dizzy and need to get off. You said they weren't married. Now, they are?"

"Exactly. '*They*' weren't. But she was married to that other wackadoo when she was eighteen."

"You mean my birth father?" I asked with a monotone voice.

"Yeah, him. And you know how he took off with that bimbo door-to-door makeup saleswoman from Idaho? Well, Mommy never bothered to pursue a divorce."

"Why wouldn't she? She hates Shane as much as I do," I

said.

"Um. You do know Mommy, right? Pretty sure that's not a topic that'd ever come up in any conversation. Like ever."

As crazy as the whole scenario sounded, she was correct about that part. My mother would never admit any wrongdoing to her children. It wasn't her style. Anything shady and questionable was skirted around with explosions of festive glitter and vibrant rainbows shooting out of her ass. All in the name of maintaining her gleaming image.

My mouth went dry as I thought of the arguments with my step-father, temporarily allowing the news from Daveigh to fall by the wayside. The screaming fits. The throwing. The drinking. The gambling. All of it. The numerous times my mom threw herself pity parties when she thought she was alone, saying she'd wanted to leave, but couldn't because she'd lose everything. Lies. When you've got nothing to lose, nothing from nothing is still...nothing. I could finally see through that ridiculous façade of glitter and rainbows. She couldn't handle being alone or risk having her notch on the political ladder get knocked down a peg or two.

Suddenly, I remembered I was still at work when Gloria's laugh tittered down the hall, breaking the silence like a shrieking banshee. The room felt too hot. Too small. Too constricting. "Daveigh, I've got to go."

"Wait. Are you coming? I want to tell Mommy whether—"

"I said I have to go." I ended the call with the press of a button.

Shock took hold of me by the throat with spindly fingers and razor-sharp nails, gripping tighter and tighter with each attempted breath I took. All of it was so unexpected. I'd spent plenty of time forgetting the past and shoving it away, but all it took was a few words from my baby sister to bring everything to the surface again. Part of me was tired, so exhausted from enduring the fight. And at that moment, I'd officially had enough. I cracked. Broken.

With shaky hands, I turned off my computer monitor, picked up my purse, and forced myself to walk down the hall to Cash's office. He was on the tail end of a phone conversation, using his signature, fake laugh as he admired himself in a full-length mirror. His gaze flicked to me in the reflection for a brief moment.

I waited at the doorway and cleared my throat when I saw him wink at himself and alternate flexing his biceps. *Seriously?*

Cash waved me in with a grandiose arm gesture as he set the phone back on its cradle. "Ms. Brennan, what do I owe the pleasure?" He paused as he looked at my wet clothing. "Did you have an accident?"

"No." I sighed. "Don't ask." I partially closed the door behind me, leaving it open three inches so Cash wouldn't get any ideas about a morning quickie. And I mean quickie. "It's just...I need some time off."

"Time off? Everything okay?" Cash furrowed his brow, concern spanning his face.

"Fine. I need to go home for a few days. Maybe a week." Family wasn't a topic I'd discussed with Cash in our arrangement, and he'd never asked because his tongue was too busy burying itself in my throat. The pronunciation of my sister's name was as deep as it'd gone after he'd thought I was involved with a dude named Davy.

"If this is about the apartment crack I made this morning—"

"No, not my apartment 'home'. My hometown. Steele Falls. Back in Washington." Calling it my hometown made me grimace, as if I'd swallowed a dose of bitter medicine. That was how much I despised my roots. Part of me felt badly about lying to Cash. I had zero intention of hopping on a plane and flying to the little Podunk city, but I knew I needed a break. From reality. From work. From Cash and Price Jensen. From everything. Even if it meant hiding out under the covers in my Sacramento apartment for a few days with my two boyfriends, Ben and Jerry, and a case or three of boxed wine. I needed to find a way to reset myself. Being drunk and on a sugar-high for a week sounded like a legit way to medicate.

Cash tried to read me as he stroked his clean-shaven chin.

"It's no big deal. Really. Family matter. I should be back by next Friday. Monday at the latest."

"N...next Friday?" Cash sounded surprised as he stumbled over the words.

"Yeah," I replied. "You know, it's that day of the week that comes after Thursday. Do we need to review a calendar again?"

"Blue, we should talk." He leaned back against his desk and let a deep breath out through his nose as he slid his hands into the pockets of his designer slacks. "It's not a good time because—"

"Look, I've never missed a day, I've bent over backward for this company, and I haven't taken any vacation time since I started working here. There's more than a month of leave racked up in my account. All I'm asking for is a few days and some understanding. Please?"

A pregnant pause loomed. "You've made some valid points." Then, the conversation curved like a fucking boomerang. "But what's Mini Cash going to do without you?" He gestured toward his dick for the second time that day. Well, it was the second instance I'd taken note of. After a while, I'd become immune to a lot of his innuendoes.

"You make it sound like I'm leaving permanently." I narrowed my eyes. "I'm sure you and your right hand are well-acquainted and can make magic happen."

"It doesn't set the same mood when you're not there." He pouted.

"Light some candles. Play some Marvin Gaye. Watch some lesbian porn," I said. "Figure it out."

"Okay. You win." He chuckled and held his hands up, palms out in a gesture of defeat. "Do me a favor though? Make sure you check in with Price on your way. He's got a nine o'clock, but you can still catch him in his office. I'm stepping out for an early lunch."

"It's eight forty-five in the morning." I scrutinized his face. "Did your appetite suddenly move to Florida where it's three hours later?"

"The stomach wants what it wants. Today, it's begging for a pastrami on rye from twenty miles away." Cash smiled. "Now, kiss me goodbye like you mean it."

"Not a wise idea with Price down the hall and the door

open." I reached out to shake his hand.

Cash turned down my request and crossed his arms. I knew it was another instance of him not taking "no" for an answer.

With as much emotion as I could muster, I replied, "Fine. We can go to that dumb sushi restaurant when I get back."

"Atta girl." Cash licked his lips. "Then, we'll hit up my place for some muffin stuffin'."

"Uh huh. Can't wait." Paranoid Gloria was in earshot, I was cautious of my words as I told Cash a rushed and platonic goodbye, making my way down to Price's office.

As usual, the entryway was cold, both in temperature and in mood. Price's office had always been the most sterile in the building, even more so than the surgery suites. White walls. White furniture. White floor. Not a drop of color existed in the room outside of the man himself. Like he wanted to be under the spotlight, the main focal point. I cleared my throat. "Mr. Jensen?"

A man looked up at me from his desk as I knocked on the open door. He looked like Cash, but a lot older and with a lot less hair. Same icy blue eyes. Same suntanned skin. Same muscular physique. But the receding hairline and valleys of wrinkles spreading near his eyes? They were the dead giveaways, swapping his youth for sophistication and power. Cash was only two years younger than Price, but that one extra percent of the company's ownership aged him physically by more than a decade.

"Can I talk to you for a minute?" I asked.

"Oh, great! You're here. I was hoping to talk to you too," Price said as he folded his hands and rested them on top of his desk. "How are you holding up with the news?"

"Um. Fine?" I arched an eyebrow in panic. *How does he know about my step-father?*

"Thank God. Are you sure?" He rubbed his face, his diamond-crusted wedding ring sparkling beneath the fluorescent bank of lights above. "I thought you'd be upset. I mean, I wouldn't be okay..."

I bit my lip and studied his face.

"Wait," he stretched out the word. "Have you talked to Cash yet today?"

I hiked my thumb over my shoulder. "I just came from his office; he's leaving. I told him I need to deal with a family emergency back home."

"Oh, good." His shoulders slumped as he let out a deep breath. "I'm glad he explained everything to you. It couldn't have come at a better time. Right?"

"A better time? Since when is it a good time for someone... What are you talking about?"

"You know. The layoff."

I didn't need a mirror to see my blank expression.

Price's furry eyebrows squished together into one elongated caterpillar as he took a few seconds to put together what happened. It was a domino effect. Next, he ground his teeth and his face reddened, the giant vein in his forehead protruding as an epic finale. "That fucking son of a bitch. Cash didn't tell you, did he? I asked him to do one task today. One task!"

"What's Mini Cash going to do without you?"

It started to make sense. I thought the wording was bizarre considering I'd only be gone a week. Plus, his sudden desire for a heavy, morning sandwich wasn't like him. I'd officially assigned "coward" as one of my latest descriptors for him. Maybe there weren't enough thumbs and pinkies on the planet to have Cash remain on my elite "ten fingers and ten toes" plan. "Pastrami on rye. Yeah, right," I muttered under my breath.

Price cocked his head to the side. "Huh?"

"Nothing." I pursed my lips in a thin, tight line. "No. He didn't say a word about that. So, let me get this straight. You're firing me?"

"Well, technically we're laying you off."

I let out a slow and frustrated breath. "I've been here for more than a year now, nearing two. I have a perfect attendance record, and I've jumped through flaming hoops to make you happy. Literally. Flaming hoops. Don't you remember the company picnic?"

"Blue, don't make this harder on me than it already is."

"Hard on you? I'm the one losing my job here! The practice is thriving. I've seen the numbers. Who else is being canned?" My nostrils flared.

"Today? We only needed to let one person go."

"Wait a damn minute. You're keeping that gorilla at the front desk and firing me?" My eyes bulged. "She hides in the supply closet and stuffs her face with cupcakes and miniature pies while the phone rings off the hook. One of your patients waited at the front desk for thirty minutes last week because Gloria said she had to finish off her two-liter of cola before she'd sign them in."

Price held up his index finger in the air as he corrected me. "Ah, ah, ah. We're laying off here, not firing. And Gloria has issues with low blood sugar. You know that. Plus, we're skirting around the topic."

"Why? What did I do that was so wrong?"

"Your position has been eliminated due to...cutbacks. Gloria answers phones and greets patients. You work on special projects. The two are like comparing bananas," he gestured toward me with an open palm and then pointed in the direction of the reception area, "and watermelons."

"You can say that again," I muttered.

"Look, I'm offering you a severance package that rivals—"

Thinking back, I should've accepted it graciously, but rage roiled through my stomach. Every unreasonable request. Every unattainable project deadline. Every unpaid hour of overtime. It all bubbled up and over at once. "Fuck your severance, Price. This is unbelievable," I said through gritted teeth as I headed toward the door.

"Ms. Brennan!" his voice held an air of authority and demanded obedience.

My shoulders drooped, and I suddenly felt like a puppy who'd peed on the rug when the back door was open and only two feet away. From past conversations I'd overheard, I knew that authoritative tone well. I'd done the forbidden and crossed a clearly-marked boundary.

Why am I letting this man make me feel ashamed?

I spun around, refusing to let him know I cared. "What?"

"Do you want me to be honest with you?"

I awaited his answer.

"There were no cutbacks."

"What does that mean?"

He held a piece of paper out to me. A sticky note was affixed to the top with my first name and my signature scribbled in blue ink next to an x at the bottom. "Here. It's still warm from the copy machine in HR."

"What's this?" I stomped across the room and ripped it out of his hand. My cheeks reddened as I scanned the single page of legal mumbo jumbo, a section circled with yellow highlighter.

"Is this document familiar to you? It should be. You signed it on your hire date," he said. "A few minutes ago, you asked what you did that was so wrong. It wasn't 'what' you did. It was 'who' you did."

Oh, shit. Shit! Shit! Shit! That's why he made me feel mortified. It was warranted! Message received, loud and clear, boss man. My toes curled up in my shoes as I looked at the intricate autograph on the bottom. It was mine. He knew.

"You should've paid more attention to page thirty-three of the handbook, which is now in your possession. I'll help you out a little in layman's terms. Paragraph seven. Sentence two. It's against company policy to fuck your boss, on or off company time. Cash may be too much of a pretty boy to think I'd never act on it, but you, Blue? Come on. You're smarter than this."

His tone felt parental, and I wanted to melt into the floor.

"You're damn lucky I'm not firing you and ruining your reputation for the next company who considers bringing you on. So, it'd be in your best interest to accept my generous severance package. If you play your cards right and leave before I have to call security, my letter of recommendation will arrive in your mailbox next week."

I opened my mouth and then closed it again. There was nothing left to say. No rebuttal. No argument. Backing out of the corner was beyond impossible—I'd fucked up.

"Now, get out." His focus went back to a stack of papers on the desk, and it was like I didn't exist. The silence spoke volumes as an invisible door slammed. In a much different way than Cash, he'd dismissed me without my needing to leave the room. Price's version didn't involve a swift getaway to a diner where a sweaty man with yellow pit stains sold smelly meat sandwiches. Yet, the finality felt the same.

I was on display, figuratively naked as humiliation filled me from head to toe. One fact was certain. Nothing could overshadow the rage consuming me, even if it were aimed at Cash. Price just happened to be my target. I slammed his door shut behind me. A picture fell from the wall, its glass pane shattering when it met the floor. For all I cared, Gloria could clean up the mess. After all, she was still getting a paycheck.

With tunnel vision, I stormed to my office, passing by Justine on my way. She gave me a questioning look, but I didn't bother to slow down. An empty box of rubber gloves on the shelf of a nearby supply closet was spacious enough for my meager number of belongings. If being canned were an Olympic sport, I'd have taken the gold in packing up. It took less than one minute to jam an orange, a small day planner, and my magic 8-ball inside. Done. Giving the room one last glance, I turned off the light. *Sayonara, spreadsheets.* Vindictiveness tapped me on the shoulder and whispered sweetly into my ear. At the last second, I went over to my computer monitor and cleared the contents from the months-long project I'd been working on for Price and hit 'save'. The IT guru could likely retrieve them all with a few simple keystrokes, but the spiteful and childish action made me feel a fraction better. Minutes later, I did my walk of shame through the lobby of Jensen & Jensen, a pathetic number of knickknacks tucked underneath my arm, rolling around inside the near-empty box.

"I heard the great news! It's like Christmas came early! Someone, get me a growler of rum with a splash of eggnog." Gloria grinned as she clapped excitedly. "I'd say I'm gonna miss you and we should exchange numbers to keep in touch, but we both know that's not true."

I sneered at her. "I hope you choke on your next box of

donuts, Gloria."

"Bye, bye." Gloria waved and wiggled her fingers in a dramatic gesture with a sugarcoated grin, flipping me the bird with her other hand. "Don't let the door hit your scrawny ass on the way out." The smile slipped from her face.

I walked out to the parking garage and kicked the tire of my hatchback before I got in. As much as I didn't want to admit it, Daveigh's words about money resonated. Rent was due, my car payment was due, and my utility bills were due. And I had a broken taillight on my growing expenditure list. I needed cash...and not Cash Jensen.

Whether I liked it or not, I was pinned in a tough spot. Until that moment, I had no intention of going back home to Steele Falls, but being laid off changed things. Fired. Laid off. Whatever Price decided my fate should be with my hasty exit. I needed time to think, but I already knew what had to happen. Every avenue, regardless of my excuse, would point me in the same direction on the map. North. There was only one answer to my problems, and I hoped it wasn't going to create a dozen more. A trip to Steele Falls to face the demons of my past was on the table for discussion.

Four

I went home and opened the web browser eleven times with the intent of booking a flight out of the Santa Rosa airport. A last-minute trip to the dinky airfield nearest Steele Falls was outrageously priced, and I could only afford a one-way ticket. Seattle Tacoma International was just as expensive. Plus, it'd include a four-hour drive. Whichever plan I chose would take everything I had left in my checking account and the measly amount available on my credit card. I banked, pun intended, on funds from my share of the will to be my savior in getting me back home to float for a while after the funeral was over. There was no telling how long it'd take to find a new job in Sacramento during the current economy. As much as I wanted nothing from my step-father, I was out of available options.

Fear of facing my past won out once again, and I slammed the laptop shut. Make that twelve times I remained a chicken. I stood up and paced the room, rubbing the back of my neck.

Stop being a sissy, Blue. You can do this. Your history is ancient. Gone. That life can't hurt you. Not again.

Convincing myself to go because the area was a desirable vacation spot wasn't an option either. Sure. It was near the beach, but there were no tropical palm trees or drinks served out of coconuts. The weather was constantly cold and windy, the Pacific frigid. Swimsuit season barely existed. When it did, it wasn't for the faint of heart. Die-hard surfers and swimmers exited the relentless waves with numb fingers and trembling, blue lips.

Steele Falls was a small town in Washington State,

flavorlessly sandwiched in a cranny between Hoquiam and Ocean Shores. It was nothing shy of bland. Some argued you'd miss the city if you blinked. If you asked me, I didn't miss it at all. Not a damn bit.

Children grew up there, dreaming of ways to get out of the sleepy and dilapidated city. Adults longed to retire there. Either way, few stuck around the aged tourist trap for long. Hurry up and get out or hurry up and arrive to die.

I was one of the escapists, the lucky ones. Leaving meant I was finally home.

It was depressing, and leaving was the best decision I'd ever made. Since I could talk, I'd conjured up ways of busting free to somewhere busier and more exciting. Up until hours before I actually left, I had big plans in place. Elaborate plans. But it was a magical fantasy that faded into the sunset. Life didn't turn out how I'd expected when a figurative curveball hit me hard. I succeeded in starting over elsewhere, but it cost me what I'd valued most. Big time.

For the thirteenth time, I opened the computer and hit refresh. The website had timed out once again, likely annoyed with my fickle attempts at purchasing a ticket. Lucky number thirteen didn't live up to its name. My eyes bulged when I saw the change in price. I was positive the airline had enough of my wishy-washy behavior, in the amount of a $500 price hike.

Well, that seals the deal on not flying in a giant, tin can at 35,000 feet.

I flopped back onto the couch and covered my face with a throw pillow. Driving was my other option. It'd take about eleven hours to get there in my unreliable car, which wasn't the end of the world. I had nothing but time and no job to go back to. Money and bills did remain factors though. Besides, my car might not make it without requiring a funeral of its own. There was no doubt I needed a getaway vehicle. I could only hope it wasn't a pointless trip for as much as the visit was about to cost me, both mentally and financially.

"Guess I'd better get to packing." I stomped down the hall to yank my suitcase from the closet. It was buried at the bottom, practically invisible. Secretly, I'd been hoping to stay in Sacramento and not need to use it again. So much for that.

I turned on the television for some background noise, tuning in to the nightly news. A perky blonde newscaster was mid-story, rambling about a drug bust at a local motel. Most of the words usually went in one ear and out the other. But that day, I listened. The problems in the rest of the world were a welcome distraction as I hoped they'd be enough to make me forget about my own. The channel cut to a low-budget commercial with a catchy jingle as a freckled, red-headed man known nationwide as Gonorrhea Guy pretended to fly in front of a fake sky. He wore a goldenrod-colored spandex onesie, which was telling in itself. But the giant STD logo on his chest, accented with a black circle and a backslash around it was an unnecessary touch. A mile-long string of side effects scrolled along the bottom of the screen of the antibiotic advertisement. He spoke one line with a hint of a southern accent and a wink before the bit ended. "Gonorrhea, be gone!"

"Ugh. Gross." I flipped off the television.

As I stuffed a neon pink bag with toiletries, there was a firm knock at the door. "What now?" I muttered.

Then, I remembered Mrs. Sheetz mentioned stopping by to bring me dinner when she saw the expression on my face after work. With a box tucked under my arm and my early arrival at the bank of mailboxes, it was hard to come up with a fitting lie for what happened. I tried to tell her it was a dead pet, but she didn't buy it. She also didn't believe they were new shoes when I tried to mask the latex label. As much as I'd asked her to not go to the trouble, she insisted. The nosy, old coot wanted the details on someone else's life since she didn't have her own to dissect.

Another knock.

"Mrs. Sheetz, I'm kinda busy right now! Not really hungry either!" I yelled from the bedroom.

The rapping on the door had turned to pounding. More dire. More urgent.

"Fine. I'm coming." I tossed a full-sized bottle of shampoo on the bed and headed down the hall, tripping over Catzilla, my fluffy tabby.

The peephole confirmed I didn't want to open the door. I'd have rather taken a dozen visits from Mrs. Sheetz and maybe an encounter or two with Gloria instead of endure who stood in the hallway.

"Go away," I grumped.

"If anything, you know I'm persistent," he said. "Besides, your neighbors will wonder what's going on pretty soon if I have to cause a scene. Don't make me do it."

"You've got to fucking be kidding me." I rested my forehead against the paneling for a few seconds. Taking a breath, I stepped back and ripped the door open, surprised it remained on its hinges. "What are you doing here?"

Cash stood in the hall, holding a dozen red roses tied with an oversized white bow. "What? We have dinner plans." He eyed me up and down. "But I don't think the dress code at the restaurant allows for oversized bathrobes or animal slippers. Why aren't you ready?"

I tightened the sash around my waist and crossed my arms.

"I get it. You showered because you pissed yourself this morning. Don't be embarrassed..."

"I didn't pee my pants! It! Was! Water!"

"Okay. If you say so." He extended the bouquet toward me. "I brought roses."

"Is this punishment?" I asked, taking a single step backward. "What the hell did I do to you?"

"What?" He gave me a blank look.

"Those." I nodded at the flowers. "I'm allergic. Remember? I told you the past four times you've brought me 'I fucked up again' roses."

He snapped his fingers. "Right. Allergic."

Silence. Awkward, painstaking, unbearable silence.

How did he not get it? Why was he still standing there?

"So, can I come in?" he asked, hope spelled out on his face.

Is he really that dense?

I suppressed my belittling laughter and blocked the doorway. Looking into Cash's eyes, my tone was acidic. "First of all, I told you I have to go out of town. And second of all, Jensen & Jensen fucking canned me this morning and you couldn't even tell me yourself! No heads up. No nothing. You let your brother do the dirty work and fire me! Why did you tell him we were sleeping together?"

"Not fired. Laid off," he replied.

"For fuck's sake, you sound like Price. Let's call a spade a spade here. That doesn't make it any better."

"It makes a difference. Severance compensation. Letter of recommendation. Applying for unemployment. Potential turnaround rate for re-hire at another company." He paused as he counted on his fingers. "Stop looking at me like you want to hurt me."

My expression didn't falter as I awaited an answer to my question.

"Look, it slipped during our monthly meeting. And I didn't think it'd be a big deal. He—"

"Didn't think it'd be a big deal? How the hell does that come up in conversation with a room full of plastic surgeons? Was everyone comparing sex stories about their employees? Were there pie charts? Graphs? A PowerPoint presentation on what their preferred position was?"

"Blue, I'll find a way to make this up to you."

I rubbed my temples. "We'd both been so careful keeping this whole...thing we had going quiet. I don't get it."

"Baby, please..."

"It's too late." I tried to control the tone of my voice as I spoke through gritted teeth. "He quoted the damn handbook to me verbatim. Page, paragraph, and sentence. Do you have any idea how humiliating that was? There was highlighter involved. It was yellow, and there was a lot of it."

"We'll get you wasted tonight, so you can let loose and forget all about—"

I was floored. "Alcohol isn't going to bandage this wound. I lost my job. Don't you understand? You could've warned me this was coming, but you didn't. You sent me in to be blindly executed by your brother."

"C'mon. I didn't want to ruin the mood and tell you this

morning. We'd had amazing sex and—"

My eyes bulged. *"You'd* had amazing sex. The mood was ruined before it even started because I knew I had to fake it... again."

It was clear he still didn't get it. Cash blinked as he spoke slowly. "So...are you saying you don't want to go to dinner?"

For being six-foot two, a lot of information sailed right over Cash's pretty head. On that particular night, I doubted a butterfly net the size of Los Angeles could've helped. Looking into his icy blue eyes wasn't poetic at all either. They weren't the windows to his soul. He was far simpler than that. They were the eyes of someone who invested heavy thought into wondering why croutons came in airtight packages and contemplated why sheep didn't shrink after being in the rain. How that man ever had the smarts to become a plastic surgeon with an award-winning practice perplexed me on a daily basis.

"No! I don't want to go to dinner! I'm done!" I picked up a throw pillow from an oversized chair near the door and dug my fingers into it. "Now, I see why you were okay with us taking our relationship out of the closet to make it public. There was no reason to hide anymore with Price in the loop on who you were screwing. How far in advance did you know about this?"

"Baby, don't overreact here."

"Don't overreact? For the love of...maybe I do need a drink," I mumbled under my breath as I hurled the pillow at him. "Are we really having this conversation right now?"

Cash blocked the shot and flashed two rectangular tickets in his jacket pocket. Oblivious to my annoyed tone, he pushed his way into my apartment. "I have reservations to that sensual art show I mentioned."

I stared at him from the doorway. "I already told you, I don't like art. Haven't for a long time."

"Pfffft. Quit playing hard to get." He grabbed an apple from the oversized bowl on the counter and sank his teeth into it. A drop of juice dribbled down his chin while he mumbled with a mouthful, "What girl doesn't like art?"

I ripped the fruit from his hand and threw it in the swing-top garbage can, the lid spinning around repeatedly from the force. "I don't like glory hole or skin flute art."

He reached out to touch my arm. "Come on. Don't do this."

"Go," I said.

Again, he paid no attention to my requests as his eyes fixated on the laptop across the room. "What've you got there?" He nodded toward the screen.

"It's nothing," I replied, reaching to close it. "Another roadblock."

He grabbed my wrist to stop me and let out a low whistle, pausing long enough to study the obnoxiously bright orange-and-red blocks on the screen. It was about to time out again. "That's one expensive plane ticket. Do customers get a complimentary blow job with it?"

I ignored his sarcasm. "Not that it's any of your business, but I'm driving there."

"In your POS car? That's ridiculous. Let me pay for the airfare. I mean, after everything that happened at the office today."

"I'm not *letting* you do that." Being indebted to the fuckstick who couldn't even lay me off properly, let alone get me off properly, didn't sound appealing.

"Don't be silly." His smile oozed with innocence. "You'd be paying me back in full, every penny. I'll let you."

'Let' me? There was that L-word again. How noble. I tried to mask my disgust, but it became harder with every day spent with him. "You used to sign my pathetic paychecks, meaning you know what my income situation was like. Now, it's non-existent thanks to Jensen & Jensen. I'll pass."

"I have minimal interest." His voice was gentle as he brushed a lock of hair out of my face. The look behind his eyes was so sweet and sincere, and I wondered how he could even swallow his own lines of steaming bullshit without gagging.

I squinted, and the conversation had plunged to a new low. "We've been sleeping together for nearly a year. Suddenly, you have 'minimal interest'? That's classy."

"No." He laughed. "There'd be minimal interest you owe me. On the credit card. I mean, I might require one or two of those blow jobs I mentioned. You know, as a finder's fee for helping you out. Maybe you could even toss in a few one-handed massages."

It was the final straw. "Get out!"

"I'm starting to wonder if you want me to leave." He scratched his head.

"You think?"

"I get it. You're stressed out. Probably PMS'ing or something. You did look pretty bloated this morning."

"Cash!" I growled.

"I'm sayin', a trip or two to the gym might not hurt." He hiked his thumb over his shoulder. "Speaking of calorie burn, are you sure you don't want to blow off some steam in the bedroom with the no pants dance before you take off?"

"Out!" I pointed toward the doorway and stomped my left foot.

"Okay. We'll talk more when you get back from Steele Town. Do me a favor."

I glared and didn't move. Correcting him on the name of the city was pointless.

He reached into his pocket and pulled a silver credit card from his wallet. "Use it. Buy the airline ticket. Hotel stay. Whatever you need. While you're at it, get some slutty lingerie for when you get back. Crotch-less panties. Flavored whipped cream. Oh! And how about a pair of fuzzy handcuffs! Black ones are preferred. Do you want me to text you a list?"

"I already told you I don't want your money." I pushed his hand away. "It's a slap in the face."

"Don't be ashamed of taking my handout, even if it's a short-term loan." He grabbed my hand and closed my fingers around it, shushing me.

"Look, we're done." I let the tension out of my shoulders. "For good."

"Sure we are." He nodded and gave me a look that expressed he didn't believe me.

"If this card gets used over the next few days," I raised it up to eye level, "it means I've been kidnapped by an unfriendly motorcycle gang of garden gnomes and you should send help, flamethrowers, and Belgian chocolate. That should tell you how serious I am right now."

"Gotcha. Mini Cash and I *will* see you as soon as you get back then." He smirked and turned to walk down the hallway toward the stairs. "Mattress mambo! Don't forget to buy some of that spicy massage oil I like!" he yelled over his shoulder while doing a fancy dance step.

I slammed the door and wondered if I were finally rid of Cash Jensen. Doubtful. The illusion of a relationship wasn't worth it. Not anymore. Looking down at the card in my hand, I frowned. It was his attempt at keeping his claws dug in while I was gone. Unsure of what to do with it, I put it in my wallet, tucked behind my debit card. That way, it wouldn't get lost. Why was I so considerate when he was the least of my concerns? I hated my conscience. When I got back, I vowed to mail it back to him, cut it up and bake it into a cake, or send it by courier in a flaming bag of dog crap—on Jensen & Jensen's dime, of course. After all, I knew the account number by heart. Enduring another conversation in the near future with him sounded as pleasant as getting my lady bits waxed twice in a row without a shot of tequila beforehand.

For the next hour, I mashed clothing and bathroom items into my suitcase, taking my aggression out on Cash. I was pissed. Pissed I didn't have a job. Pissed my rent was due. Pissed I'd let the situation with Cash excel to where it did.

"Where did I go wrong, huh?" I asked Catzilla as I flopped down on the bed. "Why can't I have an ordinary life?"

And then I remembered why I couldn't be normal. Ever. I turned on the TV to an old rerun of my favorite sitcom. Anything to sidetrack me in that moment was welcome. Gonorrhea Guy being absent was an added bonus. For the first time that day, I started to relax.

As my eyes started to cross from exhaustion, the memories tried to come flooding back, seeping into my mind. Swells of debilitating anxiety were on the horizon, and fighting back was a chore. But I succeeded. My walls were immediately slammed a mile high to block the waves of my past from crashing into me. I mopped the fragments away and shut the door on the janitorial closet of my head. Squeaky clean again. History was best kept hidden. For good.

Five

The next day, I woke up ten minutes before my alarm screamed for me to get my ass out of bed. I didn't sleep well. The dark bags complementing my bloodshot eyes were proof exhaustion ruled me. No amount of makeup, even costume, could fix it. I'd spend the rest of the day looking like a second-rate TV zombie.

The nightmares all revolved around Cash dancing in a turquoise, sequined G-string, complete with dramatic pelvic thrusts. His stage was a room full of multi-colored vaginas swinging from the ceiling. From two over-sized loudspeakers, *Mambo Number 5* played on repeat in the background. Even in sleep, that man found ways to irritate me. The dream was relentless every time I dozed, so forcing myself to stay awake was the lesser of two evils. All I could do was watch the minutes tick by on the digital clock. Looking back, I'm not sure what I waited for. An apocalypse? Grass to grow? Spontaneous combustion? The world didn't end. I checked. A lump sat in my stomach like a brick, and it became heavier as the hours crept by. What felt like a death sentence loomed because the place I was headed? It was the equivalent of prison.

My cell began to play the chorus to *I'm Too Sexy*. Thanks to Cash, it was his signature text message tone. I wasn't sure whether I was impressed he operated the phone all by himself or annoyed with his song choice. And don't get me started on how he'd stored his name in my contacts. His argument was if my phone fell into the wrong hands, no one would know it was him if they skimmed our conversations. Personally, I think he thought he was clever. I reached over to the nightstand and unplugged it from the charger. With one eye open, I knew I wasn't in the mood for whatever he had to say.

CREAM

You awake, baby?

No.

I thought of something else for you to pick up at the sex shop.

Still not awake.

Three little dots appeared, letting me know he was forming a reply. They disappeared, showed up again, and vanished once more. Then, nothing. I'm not sure what I expected from someone who called himself CREAM to maintain anonymity. It stood for Cash Rules Everything Around Me. I never vocalized it, but I'd assumed his self-proclaimed name had to do with jizz until he'd explained it. Either way was less than heartfelt.

It was dark outside. Even the sky wasn't willing to cooperate yet. No rising and definitely no shining. At four-thirty, I finally stood up and went through the motions of getting ready. My concentration level was at a big, fat zero. I made tea without remembering to heat the water, and I poured milk directly in the box of cereal instead of into a bowl. Oops. I tried to brush my teeth with hair gel, a combination I don't recommend. Of course, it was after I emptied the dishwasher by loading plates and bowls into the oven. Don't worry. It wasn't on. But for the record, don't try it. Whether I wanted to admit it or not, Steele Falls had a vice-like hold on me, even from nearly a thousand miles away. I hoped it wasn't setting a precedence for the days to come.

Pacing my apartment and biting my nails didn't make me feel any better either. All it did was prolong the inevitable and leave me in desperate need of a manicure. The jury hadn't come to a decision on whether I tried to talk myself into going or bagging the entire trip. Hiding from reality sounded as good as a vacation to Maui right about then. Deep down, I knew drinking a Mai Tai with a cute little umbrella wasn't in the cards for me. Nope! There was only one solution to my problems. Step one: Putting on my big girl pants. Step two: Pushing the pedal to the metal.

There was nothing left for me to do except feed Catzilla and leave. Trying to execute that action was worse than anticipating a root canal. The single brick in my gut had morphed into what felt like The Great Wall of China. I filled up Catzilla's feeder to the brim while she watched, ensuring I did it correctly. I'm guessing I passed her test. She cocked her head to the right and looked up at me with inquisitive gray eyes, meowing before she wove her way through my legs in a figure-eight pattern.

Most of the time she was a good listener. And she served as a great obstacle to trip over when she wanted attention at an inopportune moment. That morning, she was too busy to sprain my ankle or break my foot, much to my disappointment. With a robust purr, she flopped onto her side, pointed one foot straight up at the ceiling, and began gnawing her asshole.

"Tell me how you really feel about me leaving." I sighed. "Trust me, I have the same sentiments."

With as much bravery as I could muster, I grabbed both my jacket and tote bag, pushing my squeaky-wheeled suitcase to the doorway. I gave the room one last glance over before I slid the spare key under the mat, in case I needed Justine to stop by and check on the feline butt muncher. "See you in a few days, Catzilla."

* * *

The side streets were open, and every damn light was green, all in my favor on the way to the freeway. It was evident the travel gods hated me. Every other person I knew would be annoyed to be stuck in gridlock, but not this girl. I was the exception to the rule. Blue was my name, and procrastination was my game.

I sucked at it.

A depressing song crept through the speakers about regret and mistakes. The sorrowful lyrics were too much, and I hurried to find a local morning show. Whiny co-hosts spewed news about a recent earthquake across the country, the stock market rising, and Charles, a two-headed bull born in Spain. All of it was far more welcome than getting sucked down the rabbit hole of music.

It took over eleven hours of cruising through foreign highways, which included three breaks at dingy rest stops, two wrong turns, and a partridge in a pear tree...I mean a heartburn-inducing gut bomb of a cheeseburger from a place called The Triple B—Boberto's Burger Bungalow. There was entirely too much time to think as I choked down soggy fries while I drove. I had been so good at using work to focus my attention elsewhere. Without it, I was lost. The monotone GPS wasn't the greatest conversationalist either. It sunk in—I was all alone. Even an occasional glance toward the ocean didn't give me a sense of peace.

The sun was setting by the time I'd reached the outskirts of Grays Harbor County, a rare sight that late in the year. It was five-thirty in the evening, and dread puddled in my stomach, surrounding the brick and burger like a moat. A U-turn sounded as tempting as a sip of water to a dying man in the desert. Yet, I was strong and didn't give in to temptation.

I maneuvered through the familiar ess-curves in the valley, my hands easily predicting each turn while my eyes scoped out various landmarks—all of them still present and all of them still exactly the same. None of it mattered though; I still felt like a stranger as I headed toward the sleepy town half an hour later. I'd outgrown the space since I'd been gone. Everything felt so small, so limiting. Wide-open cow pasture after vegetable farm after abandoned field cemented it in my head. I had zero regrets.

I was only a quarter mile away from the edge of Steele Falls and a few miles off the 101 when I heard a distinct sputter. It quickly morphed into a repetitive clunking sound as my car slowed to a stop on the side of the road. As a finishing act, a plume of steam poured from under the hood with a hiss. I prayed there wouldn't be an encore.

There were no other cars in sight when I looked in the rearview mirror. It was nothing but endless fields, cow pies, and me. A shitty situation. Literally. All I could do was sit there and watch in disbelief before I rested my head on the faux leather of the steering wheel. "No." I groaned, which quickly turned into a whine that could rival one of a six-year old having their favorite toy taken away. My worst nightmare had come true—a common theme in the past twenty-four hours. Steele Falls had taken me prisoner once again. *Hello, invisible shackles and orange jumper. Oh, how I've missed you.*

I got out of the car and leaned against the door, taking in a breath of fresh sea air. The soothing breeze blowing in from the ocean used to help me calm down. That day, it wasn't consoling a damn bit. "You won, Steele Falls. I'm here," I muttered under my breath and slapped my hands against my outer thighs. Then, I remembered I had AAA. The figurative life preserver would save me! Dialing the 1-800 number on my cell phone revealed another disappointment as I held it high over my head, searching. Failing. A bold red X blinked in the corner and taunted me. I'd forgotten there were few cell towers around before crossing into the sad excuse for city limits. It was my shithouse luck.

I shielded my eyes from the setting sun as it dipped below the horizon, sending a shimmer of rainbow-colored light across the calm ocean surface toward the beach. The picturesque setting belonged on a sappy greeting card and was lost on me. My heart was cold, and all of my sentimental emotions were under lock and key where they belonged.

A familiar sign up the road read Fast Eddie's in worn red paint on a splintered board. It swayed in the wind, rusty hinges creaking. Tufts of tall grass had taken charge around the tires of a weathered tractor sitting near the gravel drive. If I had to guess, it hadn't run in over a year and was being used as a glorified planter box or a poor attempt at a business card.

"Hello?" I asked as I walked toward the property with my suitcase in tow.

From what I remembered of the rumors, Fast Eddie was in his late thirties and a workaholic. I'd never met him, but I was once told he had a horrible laugh punctuated with a piggish snort. His sense of humor was known to be even worse, but the man knew his way around a vehicle. Fortunately, I didn't need a stand-up comedian.

The metal gate at the entrance was partially open, propped in place with a rock. Knee-high blades of grass and a few cattails had grown around that too. Unless it was a kid's toy, the smallest car wouldn't fit through the gap. I had a bad feeling about Fast Eddie's in the current day and age. My hunch was soon confirmed.

"Hello there!" a croaky voice shouted from the porch. The figure waved at me in an overhead gesture.

It was clear I'd entered a time machine. The guy wasn't in his thirties; he was ancient. A two hundred-year-old man hobbled down a rickety ramp with a homemade cane whittled from warped driftwood. Each of his movements was shaky and calculated as he jabbed at the ground twice with his walking stick before moving each foot a few inches in front of the other. It was painful watching him repeat the same actions over and over again, making his way down the gravel driveway. My fingers were crossed he didn't fall and bust a hip.

"Is your son or grandson around? I need a mechanic." I hiked my thumb over my shoulder as I walked toward him. If I didn't, I was afraid it'd take him nearly a month to get to where I stood. "My car broke down back that way about a quarter mile."

The wrinkles on his face deepened as he looked bewildered. "My kid?"

"Yeah. Fast Eddie. He owned this place not too long ago." I glanced up at the sign. "This is still a mechanic shop, right?"

"Oh, well if you're lookin' for Fast Eddie, you're starin' right at him, ma'am." He jutted his thumbs under the straps of his faded overalls and gave them a firm tug. "Edward Miller. Steele Falls' finest mechanic."

I had a feeling he was Steele Falls' *only* mechanic.

"You're," I visually assessed him from head to toe, trying

to hide my distaste, "Fast Eddie?"

"Darn tootin'!" He smiled, revealing few teeth in his mouth. "Well, the previous owner was my son. He's Eddie Jr., but he took off to discover himself in Bermuda. Said the pace of this town was too slow for him. So, I took over."

I held back my eye roll. Passing the torch to the elder was a bass ackward concept to me. Then again, I was back in Steele Falls, the last place I thought I'd ever step foot.

He pulled a handkerchief from his pocket with quaking hands to blow his nose, which sounded like a dying goose. It was clear nothing about Eddie was swift. My cell service was still non-existent when I glanced from the corner of my eye, so AAA was out of the question. Hell, trying to contact Cash wasn't an option either, not that I wanted to anything to do with that douche canoe. Desperation set in though. I was stuck with prehistoric Eddie, and I could do nothing but hope he didn't keel over while we talked.

"What about Dave Bower? He owns the little auto body shop on the corner of Main and Olive."

"Own*ed*. Past tense. Closed up," he looked thoughtful as he rubbed the white stubble on his chin, "about six months ago when he had the second heart attack. Right about the time I moved here."

Theory confirmed: moved here to die.

"And I'm guessing you're the only outfit in town now?"

Eddie's head bobbed comically with a silly grin on his face. Part of me wondered if he had all of his marbles and whether he should be trusted to operate any vehicle.

I sighed at the inconvenience. "Is the nearest dealership still over in Ocean Shores?"

"That's right." He nodded. "But they're closed this late on Saturdays."

"Of course, they are." I rubbed the back of my neck and mumbled, "This isn't happening."

"You in town for the annual pancake breakfast next Thursday?"

"Um. Not exactly." I left out the fact I remembered the event well. If the biggest celebration a town was known for included flattened carbohydrates and tapped tree sap, peace out, homey.

"Too bad. They're somethin' else. Suckers stick to your ribs like glue for a week." He smacked his lips. "Where you headed? Maybe I can help you out."

"1468 Poplar," I replied, glancing at my watch. It was already six-fifteen.

"The Meyers property?"

"Meyers. Mayor. Whatever." I shrugged. "That's the one."

"I heard about what happened to Tom. A shame to lose such a great man."

"Yeah, well..."

"Tell you what. My assistant mechanic is working down in the shop right now." Eddie looked at the numbers on his ridiculously large watch. "He should still be here. I'll have him give you a ride, and I'll look over your car tonight. Give you an estimate tomorrow."

"Tomorrow?" I blurted. The thought of being stranded in Steele Falls at any point without an immediate escape plan left me weirdly claustrophobic. Unfortunately, I was out of options. Eddie was my dusty, old, crotchety knight in rusty armor whether I liked it or not.

Reluctantly, I removed the key from my ring and placed the single piece of metal in the palm of his liver-spotted hand. Convincing myself to let go took multiple tries. It felt as if the door to the prison creaked closed, about to slam in my face.

Eddie whistled loudly and then cupped his hands around his mouth. "Hey! Wesley!"

Two awkward minutes ticked by, and I wondered if the assistant mechanic was as slow, and as old, as Fast Eddie. If things continued at such breakneck speed, I was starting to question if I'd gone there to die too. A figure finally emerged in the distance. I couldn't see much from afar though. The sun had dipped well-below the horizon, shadows cast over the person approaching. As they got closer, I could make out jeans with smears of grease stains, work boots, a faded graphic tee shirt, and a baseball cap. It didn't appear he was antique like Eddie.

The mechanic walked up to us, the jingle of keys in his

pocket rhythmically slowing while gravel crunched beneath his feet. The man's hat shielded his face from the angle where I stood. "What's up, Eddie?"

"This fine, young lady here needs a ride to 1468 Poplar." Eddie's attention turned to me. "I'm sorry, I didn't catch your name."

"Blue," I replied.

Wesley adjusted his hat, looked up at me, and his eyes widened. "Holy shit. Blue Brennan?"

It was a distinct voice I recognized from my past. The tone was one I'd know anywhere. Smooth with a hint of southern accent. Seeing his face confirmed his identity, and I wanted to run in the other direction. "Beanbag?"

"It's Wesley now," he replied, his cheeks reddening as he hooked his thumbs into his belt loops.

"Say, you two know each other?" Eddie asked.

I let out a slow, deep breath and stilled. "You could say that."

Eddie fished around in his pocket and pulled out a one dollar bill, reaching out to Beanbag with a quaking hand. "Why don't you take off early for the night? Grab somethin' to eat."

"That's not necessary. And not on your dime, Eddie." Beanbag's eyes flicked over to me. "Not worth it. Trust me."

"Oh, come on! It's less than an hour before your shift ends, and it's on your way home. You two can grab a cup of sludge over at The Lean, Mean, Coffee Bean and catch up. My treat." The dollar remained extended in Eddie's trembling grip. "Besides, you've been working that hunk of rust on the lift through your lunch breaks for the past two weeks. I owe you."

Although the gesture was oddly sweet, it was clear Fast Eddie had no idea how much a cup of coffee cost, let alone overtime, in the current decade.

I shook my head left and right, formulating a lie. "I can't. They're expecting me at the house and—"

"See? She can't, Eddie. No big deal," Beanbag cut me off. "It's cool. I'll drop her off and head home for the night."

Declining the ride from Beanbag at that moment would've resulted in Fast Eddie wanting an explanation and me dragging luggage across town by foot. Neither a long walk nor story time sounded appealing. I was stuck being gracious and accepting while I strained a smile.

"Well, you two have fun catching up," Eddie said with a grin as he turned to start the painstaking walk back up to the house. "Wheel of Fortune starts in half an hour. Can't miss it."

"What about my car?" I asked.

It was clear he didn't hear me, a momentary distraction before noticing Beanbag about twenty feet away already.

"Hey! Wait up!" I shifted the suitcase to my other hand and hurried to catch up with my unenthusiastic chauffeur.

He motioned over his shoulder for me to follow him without looking back. "C'mon. I don't have all night."

"But I thought you didn't get off work for another hour?"

If looks could kill, I'd have been dead on the spot.

The wheels on my luggage didn't cooperate against the tiny rocks when I yanked harder on the handle. Picking it up left me off balance, so I resigned to tugging it along in an off-road manner once again.

Beanbag didn't offer to help. I didn't blame him. He opened the driver's side door to a rusty pickup truck, got in, and slammed it shut. There was no checking in the rearview mirror to see if I was all right. No offer to open the passenger door for me. No asking how my day went. He sat face-forward, waiting. After three tries, I succeeded in lifting my heavy luggage into the bed on my own and climbed in on the passenger side.

Gravel spun out beneath the tires as we immediately took off like a bat out of hell on the lumpy dirt road. The needle on the odometer was broken and didn't waver, so I was left to guess how fast we were going. Forty-five miles per hour. Maybe fifty. There wasn't time for me to affix the latch of the seatbelt into the floppy end of the anchor before we'd hit our first significant pothole. With a solid thunk, my head collided with the ceiling. Stars exploded behind my eyes as I squealed.

"My bad. Guess I didn't see that," Beanbag said.

My body lurched as he took a sharp corner, my shoulder slamming hard into the door. Instinctively, I flailed for the 'Oh, shit!' bar above the passenger window. It must've been hanging

SARAH JAYNE CARR

on by a single screw because the whole thing came off in my hand when I grabbed on tight. My elbow smashed into the lock nub on the door, a burst of numbness and tingling coursing through my funny bone. I rubbed my upper arm, certain a black-and-blue bruise was in my future. "Who taught you how to drive?"

"Whoops," Beanbag said under his breath, his focus remaining on the road in front of him.

Once we'd hit the main roads, his race-style driving skills mellowed out. Cops were known to ticket drivers in the area for going one mile over the speed limit. Regardless, I was thankful. It gave my heart a chance to crawl down my throat and back into my chest.

The rest of the ride to my mother's house was quiet except for twangy music playing in the background. Country tunes made my teeth itch, but it was evident Beanbag and I weren't close enough to where I could ask to flip the dial. He nervously tapped the faded steering wheel and hummed as we sailed through the sleepy town, slowing to a whopping maximum of twenty-five miles per hour. It was no surprise that we drove past The Lean, Mean, Coffee Bean without his foot making way for the brake.

"Sorry to hear about what happened to your dad." His forced attempt at small talk made the experience worse. "You know, his dying and all."

"Dead as a doornail. And he was my *step*-father." The temperature had spiked inside the cab of the truck with the topic. I rolled down the window and looked out at the ocean.

"Right. I forgot." He paused. "So, you're just in town for the funeral? Then, you're takin' off again?"

I flinched and shut my eyes. "Something like that." The frayed edge of the seatbelt gave me something to concentrate on before I gathered enough courage to glance at him.

Not much had changed, like everything else in town. He'd grown up a little over the past two years, his reddish, bushy facial hair filling in. Less lanky. More muscular. More freckles. He looked more like a man and less like a boy. But he was still Beanbag. His face was tan from the summer sun, but his eyes didn't hide he was more than tired, almost exhausted. His sunglasses did little to mask that. Part of me wanted to ask him how he was doing, but a bigger part of me knew I didn't have the right. That bridge burned to the ground long ago.

After another few minutes of painstaking silence, we pulled up alongside the house where I grew up. The windshield was cracked on the right, but the kaleidoscope of colors and shapes didn't alter reality. It still terrified me. A shiver crept up my spine, sending a flurry of goosebumps down my arms. On the left, I saw the rickety porch stairs. The third one up always groaned and bowed when someone stepped on it. I remembered falling down and scraping my knees there. A lot. On the right, a faded rope swing dangled under the willow tree. That was where I spent countless hours pushing both Daveigh and Finn. I could almost hear our laughter if I tried hard enough. Farther on the right was the flat-roofed garage. It was where I'd sneak out of my window late at night. Well, that was until I put my foot down and moved into the mother-in-law cottage out back.

Nothing changes if nothing changes. It was the same manicured hedge. It was the same worn, picket fence. It was the same blue house. It was the same uninviting front door. All of it was the same, except for me.

For a minute, I'd forgotten I wasn't alone.

Beanbag jammed the gear shift into park, adjusted himself in the seat, and turned toward me. He looked uncomfortable as he opened his mouth three times, closing it again like a fish. Nothing happened. Closing his eyes, he inhaled sharply and thought before speaking, his voice soft. "We need to talk about what happened before you left. If you want—"

Boom. That was my hard limit. "There's nothing to discuss," I said quickly as I unbuckled my seatbelt and exited the truck, slamming the door.

"Blue, wait...." he said through the open passenger window. "Don't do this. Please?"

"Thanks for the ride, Beanbag."

"Wesley," he replied. "It's Wesley."

"Right." I brushed him off. "Tell Eddie thanks too." I hopped up into the bed of the truck and grabbed my suitcase, rolling it over the side and letting it fall onto the lawn. The jury was out on which was worse—hanging out with Beanbag in those few seconds or heading up the porch.

"You really don't want to hear what I've got to say?" He pulled his sunglasses down and looked over the rims. "Are you being serious right now?"

The hot tears were nearly impossible to hold back as I shook my head no. Crying hadn't occurred in months, and I wasn't about to start then. The emotions I'd tried to avoid fought me tooth and nail. I couldn't let them win. Instead, I decided to repress it all for the millionth time. "I have to go."

Part of me regretted my decision to come back more than ever, and I'd only been around for less than an hour. It was another moment where I'd have taken Mrs. Sheetz with her casseroles full of mystery meat and stray cat hair. It all sounded a million times better than what I'd already endured.

As I stared at the porch, that prison door had officially slammed shut with a harsh echo. There was no key and no way out.

Six

"**F**ine. Have it your way." Beanbag gritted his teeth and locked eyes with mine before shifting the truck back into drive. "You can let me know when or if you're ever ready to talk. Since I can see this visit is all about Blue." His tone was edgy and curt, filling the air quickly with tension. Beanbag was one of the most laidback and even-keeled people I knew. To see that side of him made me realize he still hadn't forgiven me. I doubted he ever would.

I didn't warrant his words with a response. Nothing felt adequate.

"Heartless bitch," he muttered under his breath.

I stood still and accepted every syllable of that two-word blow, letting the sound of each consonant and vowel resonate in my head. Part of me felt badly and wanted to tell him to stop when he gunned the engine. That was the part filled with guilt about the past. It was the part that knew Beanbag was due an explanation. But a bigger part of me, a more self-serving part, wasn't ready to hear what he needed to say. To be honest, I didn't know if I'd ever be prepared to have "that" conversation with him. All I could do was stand there with downcast eyes, living up to the shameful name he'd called me.

I lingered at the edge of the property until he was out of sight, and I was alone with my thoughts. Those days, it was a scary place if I couldn't focus elsewhere. It was quiet. Too quiet. My ears tried to pick up on the most minute noises, but the wind was suddenly absent and the sound of booming waves in the distance was non-existent. There was nothing. Steele

Falls was as shocked as I was with my arrival. The town hushed in anticipation of my next move.

So much time had gone by since I'd walked up the narrow porch of my childhood. Past moments tried to suffocate me as I fought to tread water, their invisible weight crashing against my chest like massive waves, pushing and pulling. It all culminated so fast in that moment. I felt myself sinking, drowning.

A seagull flew overhead and screeched out its signature high-pitched sound. For some unknown reason, that one stupid cry was enough to push me over the edge. It was all too much. Fast Eddie. Beanbag. The house. A fucking bird. I spun around and headed toward the sidewalk, ready to never look back. Ever. Coming to Steele Falls was a dumb decision. Going back home to Sacramento was the safer option, even if I had to figure out how to get to California without any money. Hitchhiking was a more harmless bet than sticking around. I couldn't be convinced otherwise...until three seconds later.

The front door creaked, causing the hinges to squeal. I'd always thought it sounded like a tinny version of "Shave and a Haircut". Two years had gone by, and no one had sprayed the damn thing with WD40 still. The flimsy metal screen door flew open and then slapped shut. I froze in my tracks, turning around slowly. But I was too late. There was no running away.

"Mommy, I think I heard your mailman! This is the latest he's been yet," a female voice said. "It's nearly seven o'clock. Maybe he's afraid of the neighbor. I mean, I know he said he improved the post both of your guys' mailboxes are on, but he assured me he didn't booby trap it again. I'm not sure if I was relieved or concerned when he told me."

My grip tightened on the suitcase handle. I didn't have to look to know my knuckles were white. It had been so long since I'd seen my sister. There it was, all coming to a head and outside of my control, speeding toward me like a freight train. I stood on the proverbial tracks and could do nothing but stare at the bright, oncoming light.

A young woman appeared on the porch. She was barely into her early twenties. Daveigh was thinner than I remembered, almost skeletal. Her wealth of dark hair hung down to the middle of her back and was styled in a sloppy braid. I couldn't remember a time when I'd seen it that long. Loose waves framed her dainty face, wisps dancing in the breeze. She wore faded blue jeans with frayed holes in the knees and an oversized sweatshirt that said, "Fries Before Guys" on it. The soles of her flip flops smacked against her feet as she walked down the top few stairs before pausing to look out at the ocean.

I watched in silence. She wasn't the sister I was used to seeing in form-fitting tops, mini-skirts, and expensive high heels. The fashionista and trendy sister had been replaced by someone far more subdued. After being gone, I guess I expected her to not change either, similar to the scenery around me. Like I assumed time had stopped when I left.

"Hey, 'Veigh," I said quietly, announcing my presence.

She froze. Her puffy-eyed gaze panned over to me slowly and her jaw fell. A wad of tissue was balled in her left hand. It fell to the ground, quickly forgotten. "Shit. Blue? You...you came?" She continued down the steps and fumbled for the railing while not taking her eyes off me. The little bit of color in her cheeks drained, making her complexion whiten further.

I remained still, afraid to move, unsure of how my visit would be received by anyone. Would they hate me? Would they welcome me? Would they even recognize me?

She stopped a couple of feet away from where I stood. "I'm afraid to blink. What if you disappear?"

Her point was valid, but I tried to soften the blow with humor. "Pretty sure I don't know a magic trick for that." Although I secretly wished I did.

She reached out with her right hand and pulled back, her chest hitching. A combination of fear and tears filled her eyes. With a deep breath, she touched my face, the pads of her fingers tracing my cheek down to my chin. "God, it sounds like you, looks like you, and feels like you." A faint smile crept across her face as the childish giggle I remembered so well escaped her. "It's really true." With brute force, she leapt forward and hugged me.

"It's me," I croaked as she crushed me against her.

"I can't believe it. You're really here."

I nodded, which was all I could muster with my internal organs and ribs being smashed into the same space.

She pulled back and her tone morphed from loving to reprimanding. "Where the hell have you been?" She flicked me on the ear. Hard.

"Ouch!" I instinctively moved my hand to protect myself. "Jeez, 'Veigh. We're not eleven anymore."

"Yeah, well you sure know how to piss me off."

"Noted." I glared at her.

"I don't know whether I should be happy you're here or if I should yell at you for what you did to me, to us."

"I—"

She crossed her arms. "Where are you staying? Why is your car not in the driveway? Did you get a cab? I've asked for your address. Why don't I ever get a response? You've changed your phone number, but it's like an act of Congress getting a hold of you. Why? Give me some answers to work with here."

I closed my eyes. "Can we not do this right now?"

"Sure. I mean, it's only been two years. What's another hour or three?"

A welcome distraction caught my ear. The spotlight was taken off me for a moment, and I could breathe again. Classical music intensified that I hadn't noticed moments ago. The robust song was punctuated with repeated crashing of cymbals. I looked around to determine where it came from. No people and no orchestra were in sight. "What's that?"

"That?" She nodded toward the neighbor's house. "It's just Ralph." Daveigh shook her head.

"Ralph is still alive?" My eyes widened as my jaw went slack. "Isn't he like ninety now?"

"I think he's in his seventies, Blue. I know some time has passed since you've been gone, but let's not get carried away."

"And he's still the same? Like wandering-down-the-street-in-his-brown-bathrobe-type same?"

"Same old. Same old."

Old was right.

I looked across the street. Ralph's home was heavily distressed from the sea air, and it hadn't gotten any better since

I'd left. To put it politely, he wasn't Mr. DIY. At all. Once lemony yellow, the paint had turned to a deep shade of Dijon with a hint of mossy green around the edges. A solid layer of the same avocado hue coated the roof. The once-white trim had died off to a sickly gray. The patchy grass tainted to a pale tan. It was similar to a box of sad crayons that needed anti-depressants. The color-challenged setting was masked with thorny bushes that'd taken over his front porch, half-covering his front door from view. I'd once joked it was the old man's security system.

There was one detail I remembered about Ralph that stood out above all others. He was some kind of weird animal whisperer. Well, there was that and the black layer of dirt residing inside his ears. I never did figure out how it got there or why it didn't disappear when he showered. More so, the animal thing though. Personally, I'd thought he'd found a way to channel Snow White. Ralph was well-known for letting small creatures into his garage, or house, to snack on bags of birdseed or peanuts. It backfired more often than not by inviting unwanted wildlife into the entire neighborhood. Deer. Frogs. Skunks Mice. Rats. Squirrels. Even a rogue coyote showed up once. There was a series of gunshots that day. I didn't ask what happened, and he didn't tell.

The trees at the edge of his property were overgrown, weighted branches looming like massive jungle vines over the drive. It was his own private fortress though, and he was good at keeping to himself most of the time. Through the ropy veil of creepers, you could still make out what happened in the background. On the left, a faded tarp half-covered a few hundred birdhouses he'd spend his days building throughout the year. That whole idle hands, idle mind thing. On that particular day, the doors of his little, blue sports car and the trunk were open wide. Another classical tune commenced from a small boom box on a sawhorse.

"What's he doing this time?" I whispered.

She took a step toward me and quieted. "Rumor was going around town there'd been a string of robberies between here and Ocean Shores. All residential. Ralph is convinced he can catch the guy. Everyone's already explained to him they arrested the dude three days ago. But Ralph thinks it's some kind of conspiracy theory and doesn't believe it."

"Sooo...he set a trap? He's luring said non-existent burglar to burgle him?" It took me a minute to replay the words in my head to determine if what I said made sense. "Does he remember he's not a cop? Someone's going to get hurt."

She shrugged and glanced up at a nearby tree where leaves rustled. The heel of a brown loafer and an argyle sock was in view as Ralph lost footing on the branch and then regained it quickly on a nub of the trunk. "Some things never change."

"How long's he been up there?" I looked upward.

"Since around lunchtime. So, six hours? Maybe seven."

I sighed. "And let me guess, he's got his .45, waiting for the chance to shoot?"

"It's like you never left," she said sarcastically. "Last week, I caught him in the backyard eating those weird winter berries off the bushes while wearing that yellow rain suit of his."

"The one that makes him look like the guy on the fish stick box?"

"That's the one," she replied. "And he ate all of them. He must've had the shits for days."

"Did anyone say anything to him?" I asked.

"Come on. It's Ralph. You know damn well no one's gonna stop him." She rolled her eyes. "I watched through the window and ducked when I thought he saw me."

Ralph had been our neighbor for as long as I could remember and then longer. He was one of few who'd made a permanent fixture of himself in Steele Falls. If I had to describe him, I'd say he was full of piss and vinegar. Oh! And bison grass vodka. I should know. He brought me a bottle as a gift when I was fourteen. A couple of shots had been consumed, but he'd taken careful measure to use a piece of electrical tape, affixing the lid shut again before gifting it to me. Totally thoughtful, considering he'd given alcohol to a minor. He meant well; he truly did. When I sprained my ankle? He brought his old spider web-infested walking boot from the bowels of his garage that would've gone up to my hip. When the basement flooded while my parents were out of town? He showed up with sandbags to help clean up the mess. It was just so difficult defending most of his actions to anyone else while sounding sane.

"I'm not sure I want to see how this one ends," I said. "Where's the momster?"

"I really wish you wouldn't call her that anymore."

"Old habits die hard. 'Mom' and 'monster' is a perfect combination for her." I adjusted my tote bag up higher on my shoulder. "You know it's true, 'Veigh."

"I'm not getting in the middle of your squabbles."

"We're talking about the woman who threw me a birthday party when I was four."

"That bitch!" Daveigh's tone was laced with mockery.

"You were too young to remember, but I had strep throat. Rather than disappoint all the other kids, she let her own spawn down and had the party. But she confined me to my room like a prisoner. Momster assured me she'd at least save me a cupcake." I paused. "Later that night, I snuck downstairs and caught her and Tom eating the last two. The next day, she told me some cookie monster broke in and ate them. So, momster was born."

"We'll find you a good therapist while you're here." She sighed. "Mommy's in the house. Let's go. I can't guarantee how warm your welcome will be though. I mean, you've been gone almost two years. A phone call, postcard, or a holiday fruitcake would've been nice. Something. Anything."

I didn't respond to her chastising words. Being a diary and spilling the details about everything that'd happened wasn't up for discussion. Talking about the time I'd been gone would have to wait, maybe for eternity. I'd been standing on the driveway for five minutes, and my baby sister had already served me with a round of twenty questions. In return, I'd lobbed back zero answers. It made me wonder if she'd held any topics back for later.

I walked up the porch with my luggage in tow, the wheels of my suitcase methodically clunking against the edge of each concrete step as I ascended. Flakes of paint from the railing broke free under my touch. The welcome mat was as uninviting as ever, not making me feel any more at home. Shit was about to get real. I grabbed the handle of the screen door with clammy hands, hesitating.

"Go on," Daveigh said quietly. "She's not gonna bite."

"Says you. You're the golden child who can do no wrong," I muttered.

"Yeah, well I'm not the one who went MIA. Remember?"

"Trust me. I recall more than I'd like."

She sat down on the porch swing and kicked off her flip flops, crossing her ankles.

I did a double take. "Wait. Aren't you coming inside?"

"I think I'll wait out here for a few minutes to see how everything goes first."

"Chicken."

Like ripping off a bandage, I gave the door a swift tug and walked through the doorway. It amazed me how much I'd forgotten, and how quickly it came rushing back. The smell was first to sock me in the stomach, sending a wave of nostalgia through my gut to contend with the brick wall from earlier in the day. It was a spicy combination of cinnamon and cloves that burned your sinuses if you weren't accustomed to it. Anyone who visited, a rarity, joked it was year 'round autumn at the Meyer's house.

I made my way through the darkened living room. Nothing had moved. The same hideous afghan was laid out over the back of the couch. It was a horrible mess of olive green and beige displayed atop the protective slip cover. A wooden cuckoo clock I hated, complete with pine cone pendulum, still swung from side-to-side. Pictures adorned the mantle and end tables, mostly of my mother at various ribbon-cutting ceremonies and political rallies. A few of the smaller frames displayed images of Daveigh and my brother, Finn. As I scanned the room, I didn't see a single picture of me. Anywhere.

A voice from the kitchen stopped me from taking additional inventory of the living room. It was stern, forceful, and full of authority. But it was clear the words weren't directed at me. With wobbly steps, I made my way to the rounded entryway and stopped.

Across the room, I saw my mother. She stood, facing a wall calendar with a pen in one hand, the other gesturing wildly while she spoke on a corded phone pinned between her neck and shoulder. The few strands of gray hair I'd remembered her pulling had turned to prominent streaks. I recalled how she'd vowed to never become a "silver vixen" as she'd deemed it. Times had changed. She paced a few feet, back and forth. The red cord circled her body with her movements as she fought to constantly unwind it.

"I don't care what it costs or if the other one is discounted. Besides, it's the coffin we both decided on. Stop trying to talk me out of it, Harold. I'm not going to budge."

A pause.

"Yes, I understand it's for a dead body."

A second pause.

"Yes, I also understand he won't know the difference, but I will."

A third pause.

"There's no alternative on the table for discussion. Zero. Got it?"

The voice on the other end of the phone sounded frazzled as he stuttered, and I could sense his nervousness even from where I stood across the room.

"No, we decided on calla lilies for Wednesday. It's a funeral staple and symbolic."

This time, I was unable to hear his reply.

"I don't know why it's symbolic. It just is. Some crap about the soul departing and innocence being restored. Go Google it."

A fourth pause.

"I don't care how much it'll cost to get the death flowers to Steele Falls mid-October. Make it happen!"

Harold's garbled response was meek.

"Do you not listen to a word I say? Clean out your ears. Look, I don't have time for—" She spun around and saw me.

Terror set in.

The phone fell a few inches away from her ear as she assessed my face. "I've got to go." She ended the call without looking down at the receiver, fumbling to place it back on the wall cradle.

We stared at one another for what felt like minutes.

"Hi, Mom," I finally said.

The ticking of that horrid cuckoo clock and my breathing were the only sounds in the room, both resounding.

"Blue." She pursed her lips in a thin, straight line as she let a deep breath out through her nose. There was no emotion in her voice. There was no softening behind her eyes when she saw me, her own daughter. There was no adjustment in her posture. Utter stillness. She'd dealt me her signature poker face, and it was the game she'd taught me to play so damn well.

I really wasn't sure what I'd expected. In my head, the scenario played out a thousand different ways. My exit stunt sealed the deal that a warm welcome wasn't in the cards for me. There was no one to blame but myself. The day that woman gave me a warm hug, offered me a cup of hot chocolate while we talked in front of the fire, or even a two-second smile would be the same day hell froze over.

"Well, I see you two have reconnected." Daveigh walked into the room with a bounce in her step. Her upbeat mood quickly skidded to a halt as she took a moment to watch both of us in our stoic splendor. "Damn, it's cold in here," she muttered.

Much like a game of chess, both of us were waiting for the other to make the next move. It had become a test of wills, and a checkmate was impossible.

"Someone, say something," Daveigh said. "Both of you are making this place as uncomfortable as a whore sitting in church."

My mother's stare suddenly broke free from me, and she turned toward my sister. "I'm glad you're here, Daveigh. I know you only live ten minutes away, but the gesture is appreciated." The words were intended to hurt while they excluded me from the equation. My defenses were already up, and I paid little attention to her attempt at paining me.

My mom's focus shifted, turning toward the kitchen table.

Memories of a million family dinners infiltrated my head. Most of those held me as the parental role since I was the oldest. Tom and Elana Meyers were too busy to break bread with their own kids. Even from childhood, I was forced to grow up early on to take care of Finn and 'Veigh.

A pile of mail was neatly stacked at the place setting where my step-father rarely sat. The gingham cushion on the seat was still plush, a pristine white and red. The thing was as new as the day it was purchased many years ago. Three others were worn with age, flattened, slightly discolored. She walked across the room briskly and grabbed two tablets of paper from the top of the pile, each with a pen hooked to the top.

She handed one set to my sister and tossed the second to me. "Here."

"What's this?" I asked with a frown.

She only spoke to Daveigh. Maybe it was easier for her that way. "I'd like for you to each prepare something to say at the funeral. Make it heartfelt, but not too sappy. The election could be affected if this gets screwed up. There's no doubt a reporter from the Steele Falls Chronicle will be at the service. Everything has to be perfect."

The fucking election. How quickly I'd forgotten about that time of year. Elana Meyers had a sick fascination, nearly an obsession, with being mayor for the small city. I'd secretly joked her dick was bigger than half of the men in Steele Falls. Massive hours, not to mention dollars, were poured into her campaigns to ensure landslide victories. And she'd prevailed. Every time. Without a limit on how many terms an individual could serve, she'd made it her lifelong mission to keep everyone else out of the position so she could maintain her throne.

"Whoa," I said, putting my hands up to stop her from continuing. "I'm not speaking a damn word at the—"

"Watch. Your. Mouth." A thin layer of bitter rage bubbled beneath her words, setting off a domino effect. Next, her nostrils flared and finally her lower lip trembled. "You *will* speak at your father's funeral, and you *will* be sincere about it. You *will* dress appropriately for the occasion, and you *will* converse with anyone who wishes to express their condolences to you. Do you understand?"

"Step," I muttered.

"And if you don't..." She paused. "Do not *step* me; he was your father, Blue Ann Brennan. And if you don't follow my directions, there will be consequences. Outside of writing, I want you out of my sight for the next few days. Is that clear?" Her voice lowered to a hiss, "Don't you forget about what I did for you."

My shoulders wilted from the string of words she used against me. I'd chosen the wrong moment to stand up for myself.

"Public speaking freaks me out," Daveigh said meekly. "Don't you remember when I passed out in high school during the homecoming ceremony? I dropped like a leaf at the football game, halfway bent over the float when they called the paramedics. And don't get me started about when the goat mounted me from behind and tried to hump my ass. Some queen I turned out to be. I don't think I can..."

"You'll do fine. And your school mascot won't be at the cemetery." Elana's voice and expression were both tender as she brushed Daveigh's hair out of her face before cupping her daughter's chin in the palm of her hand. "I have faith you'll string a beautiful speech together and execute it without a hitch."

"Of course." Daveigh nodded once before averting her eyes. "Whatever you want, Mommy."

I'd been in the house for less than fifteen minutes, and I was already being ordered around and shunned. Just like old times. It helped remind me why I left in the first place, amongst other weighty reasons.

Elana strode across the room and grabbed a bright, blue blazer from the back of a kitchen chair. "There's a council meeting tonight, so I won't be home until late. I assume you two can handle finding dinner?"

"I'm twenty-three and I live on my own, Mom. Pretty sure I've succeeded in keeping myself alive without anyone's help." I knew my tone was rude and it warranted the glare she gave me. In my defense, she'd started it.

"We'll be fine, Mommy," Daveigh reassured her.

Without another word, she grabbed her Gucci purse from the counter, and her Louboutin's clacked across the floor as she left without a goodbye. Even with zero words, Elana Meyers was able to make her presence loudly known.

Daveigh blew her hair out of her face. "Well, that could've went worse."

"And it could've went a lot better." I let the tension out of my shoulders.

"At least the house didn't implode."

"Thank goodness for small wins." I rubbed my face. "I need a drink."

"C'mon," Daveigh said, grabbing her keys and purse from the counter.

"Where are we going?" I asked.

"Fill & Spill. You said you needed a drink."

"Is going to the town bar appropriate considering what—"

"If Mommy can go to a political meeting in light of recent events, I think we can go grab a burger and a beer without being judged. Plus, I could use the break from reality and from crying."

For the first time since I'd arrived, I looked at my sister and tried to empathize with her feelings about losing a parent. It was an unsuccessful attempt. That part of my heart was ice cold and shielded by a suit of armor. While I was able to comprehend that Tom's death hit Daveigh much harder than it hit me, by about a thousand percent, I was immune to being emotional about it. Then again, he was her blood relative. He wasn't mine. My own birth father was a pathetic excuse for a douche-bucket who I hadn't seen since I was an infant. I rarely thought about him and spoke about him even less. There were no emotional ties to the man who I equated as a sperm donor. Yet, I still never considered my step-dad an actual parent either, even though he'd been a fixture in my life since I was a toddler.

I opened my mouth and closed it, wondering why I bothered to defend my mother after the way she'd treated me.

"You know I'm right," Daveigh sang confidently. "Admit it."

"Fine. You win. I'll be right back."

Daveigh rolled her eyes. "Sure you will."

"Stop it. I want to take my luggage out back so I don't have to do it later."

"Right." She elongated the single syllable into a much longer word.

I ignored her snarky retort and quickly wheeled my suitcase out through the kitchen door, across the covered patio, and down the cobblestone path to the mother-in-law cottage on the edge of the property. A thick layer of trees surrounded the area, which was once my personal sanctuary. As always, it was unlocked. I opened the door and flipped on the light. Nothing had changed or been moved from the last time I'd been inside. At that moment, I doubted anyone had even stepped foot in there.

I left the suitcase near the entryway of the one-bedroom space and shut the door behind me.

My old clothes I'd left behind still hung in the open closet. Flannel button-ups and spaghetti strap tank tops on the left. Flowy ankle-length skirts and jeans on the right. A row of shoes neatly spanned the floor. My favorite picnic blanket was draped over the foot of the bed, my worn, one-eyed teddy bear perched on the pillows. With the way the rest of the day had gone, I wouldn't have been surprised if the momster avoided the mother-in-law all together. Out of sight, out of mind. Everything had been preserved, or forgotten, hermetically sealed in a time capsule. The living room space caught my eye. Leather couch with matching chairs. The memories of being in that room attacked me quickly. I bolted for the exit, threading the key into the lock with trembling hands, wondering whether I'd be able to sleep inside without having nightmares.

I leaned back against the door and closed my eyes, fighting to catch my breath. It was important I regain my composure before I went back inside to Daveigh. After all, there were parts of my history she didn't need to know about.

The time had come to put on my own poker face.

Seven

I was out of practice.

"Okay. I'm ready." I walked back inside the kitchen with a phony smile plastered on my face. It was one of those moments where you weren't sure how to let go of the facial expression naturally because it was so forced it left a bitter taste in your mouth.

"Are you okay?" Daveigh asked.

"Yeah. Why?"

"You look guilty or pained. Constipated maybe? I don't know how to explain it."

"Well, I did drive eleven hours through three states. It's nothing. Just a long day." I sighed and was content with the lie I'd scrambled to feed her. Even after two years had gone by, Daveigh still knew when something was wrong. It pissed me off. For being the younger sister, she'd always been the one to be more in tune with Finn's and my emotions. I felt like that should've been my job as their protector.

"So, if you drove, then where's your car?" she asked as she closed the front door behind her.

"It's across town at Fast Eddie's," I replied.

She turned away from me and shrugged into her jacket. "Oh?"

"Broke down right down the street from his shop. Beanbag gave me a ride on his way home. Did you know he worked there? Surprised the hell out of me. Figured he'd pursue his acting career or something."

"So...Fast. Eddie's?" She rifled through the set of keys on

repeat at breakneck speed before she located the one for the house. It shouldn't have been rocket science since the ring only occupied four keys.

"Maybe it's my turn to ask. Is everything okay with you?" I studied her, our own game of chess growing more complicated as the evening went on.

"Yeah." She focused on locking the front door. "It's just lucky you were so close and weren't stranded in the middle of nowhere. That's all."

I didn't believe her explanation, and I knew luck had nothing to do with my life. Karma had a funny way of biting me in the ass. Sarcasm laced my words like a tight corset, but I wasn't sure whether she noticed. "My days are chock full of horseshoes and four-leaf clovers these days. Better buy a lottery ticket. Quick."

"Either way, I'm glad you're here." She gave me a slap on the ass as we headed down the porch, the third step from the bottom living up to its reputation with a significant groan. It was clear both of us were making some kind of effort at bridging the gap in our screwed-up relationship.

We got into Daveigh's Ford Thunderbird, a gift from Rent-A-Cop Gene, and headed toward The Fill & Spill, less than a mile from the house. She flipped on the radio to a local station that played budding indie artists—my favorite. Anything was better than Beanbag's lame sauce country tunes. Plus, the break from talking was welcome.

As we waited at the stoplight across the street from the standalone bar, I looked at the brick building. The substantial crack from a previous earthquake was still as obvious as ever on the lower corner near the entrance. A few bricks near the roofline were still missing too. The blinking neon sign spun slowly high on a pole near the street. Just like the old days. Giant letters displayed a burned-out F, leaving it to read "Ill and Spill" in curvy red font. That? That was new. Knowing some of the terrible bar food they served, the updated name, although unintentional, fit. Someone should've really jumped on fixing that. Nothing could beat Boberto's Burger Bungalow for heartburn though. Hours later, I still paid the price for that decision.

The small gravel parking lot was nearly full, which was what I'd expect for a Saturday night. There were two activities on the weekends in Steele Falls: drown in the ocean or drown your sorrows. Most people chose the latter. Either way, it was an escape. Few people stood outside in small clusters, smoking cigarettes, gesturing, and laughing. A young couple made out heavily in the corner under the shadows cast by a nearby streetlight. The dumpster overflowing with black trash bags in the background was a nice touch to their romantic moment. Scanning the crowd, I didn't recognize a single soul. That was enough to make me relax a little.

We pulled into the lot and parked in one of two remaining spaces. For as many times as I'd been to the dive bar, I felt remarkably like a stranger in my own home town.

"Hungry?" Daveigh asked.

"Not really," I replied. Thinking back to the pile of grease-soaked fries swimming in their respective cardboard boat from earlier in the day left me feeling green when it came to food. "I'll probably drink my dinner tonight."

She glanced at her phone before jamming it into her purse with a scowl. "Me too. My appetite is suddenly gone."

I studied my sister from the corner of my eye when she got out of the car and slammed the door. Hard. Staring didn't give me any answers like I'd hoped. I trailed after Daveigh toward the entrance and bit my lip. Knowing her, if I pushed for information on her mood, I was likely to get even fewer answers. It wasn't surprising. She was difficult to read, much like me. It was a trait inherited from Mother Elana herself.

"So, when's Finn flying in from London?" I asked.

"Finn?"

"Finn. Our brother? You said everyone had to be here for the funeral. Remember?"

"Oh yeah. That." She adjusted the shoulder strap on her purse. "Can we not talk about the funeral tonight? I'm sure Mommy will give you his flight information tomorrow."

More memories came tumbling back as I looked through the frosty window from the outside. The mechanical bull.

Goldfish races. Beer pong. The Fill & Spill was where I spent my twenty-first birthday. It was where I first—

"Hey. You coming or not?" Daveigh snapped her fingers in front of my face as she'd held the door for me.

"Huh? Yeah." I blinked quickly.

"Sometimes, you're like talking to a freaking doorknob," she muttered. "And that's insulting the doorknob."

Music funneled through the loudspeakers and was still as loud as I remembered, the hot pink and green-colored wallpaper with gold accents even louder. I grimaced in its ugly glory. Whiffs of stale beer and fried food floated through the air, and it made my stomach flip-flop. I'd forgotten I'd always showered after leaving the bar because everything was tainted with the scent of Marlboro's and over-cooked chicken tenders.

I followed in Daveigh's wake across the room to an open seating area. Barstools with worn wooden tops, their glossy luster faded, were lined around rectangular tables. The top of each one was adorned with half-filled salt and pepper shakers and a messy stack of paper coasters. An olive-colored couch with etched woodwork on the base was perched in the corner with a matching chair cattycorner to it. Both were stained from one too many spilled drinks, and both were the most uncomfortable pieces of furniture I'd ever put my ass on. I was surprised they were still around.

At the far wall, a woman was seated on one of the stools at a table for six, talking on speaker with her cell phone in one hand and a glass of blush wine perched in the other. She wore a sheer cold-shouldered top with a camisole underneath and black leather pants. It didn't seem to bother her that she was the only one in the bar who sat alone. Her long red fingernails sparkled under the smoky hue of the pendant light overhead while she examined her manicure against the glass of her drink.

"Hang on a sec!" Daveigh yelled in my ear.

I nodded, mindlessly swaying to the beat of the music.

"Lucy!" Daveigh hollered at the woman to compete with the bass. My sister yelled again and waved enthusiastically. "Over here!"

The woman spotted my sister a few seconds later and

immediately ended her call with a quick goodbye. She stood up and squealed loudly before hugging Daveigh, both of them gushing and tittering at each other. Once again, I felt like I didn't belong.

Daveigh must have sensed my feeling of displacement. "Oh! I forgot! You two haven't met yet. Lucy, this is my older sister, Blue." She nudged me with her elbow. "Blue, Lucy."

"Nice to meet you." I extended my hand.

"I've heard a lot about you." She had a strong handshake and a sultry voice. "So sorry to hear about your dad," she said with a pained look on her face. It reminded me of the consoling look I received when someone heard one of my Cash stories. Any semblance of pity being present tainted genuine concern.

I almost corrected her and said, "step", but I didn't see the point. Lucy didn't care if Tom was my step-father. I'd likely never see her again, let alone carry on meaningful conversation. The simplest response seemed the most appropriate.

"Thank you," I replied.

"I didn't know you were back from The Bahamas already." Daveigh sat on the barstool next to her. "When did you get into town?"

"It was only a five-day. Got back this morning. Jet lag is a real bitch. Boat lag. Whatevs."

"Well, your tan is incredible," Daveigh replied. "I swear, you always look like you jumped out of a magazine."

"Thanks!" Lucy beamed. "My bikini lines are almost non-existent now after I spent time on that nude beach I told you about."

Daveigh explained, "Lucy has *the* best job in the world. She works on a cruise ship."

"Nice. What cruise?" I asked.

"Oh, thanks! I got it at Macy's." She glanced down at her top and adjusted it to showcase more of her ample cleavage.

It was clear she didn't have a clue what I'd said as the music pumped louder, deafening anyone within a five-foot radius. Again, I was left to let the unnatural look slide from my face with her response. The wooden planks beneath my feet vibrated with the level of bass the speakers produced. Lyrics weren't even comprehensible anymore, and a massive dose of ibuprofen would be in my near future. I was getting too old for the bar scene.

"How do you two know each other?" I changed the subject, competing against the booming song lyrics.

"We went to high school together," Daveigh said. "Well, she moved here during the second half of my senior year. Didn't start really hanging out until a while after graduation..."

"So, what are you doing here then?" I stopped her from having to finish the sentence, and then I wondered if my bluntness had come across as rude. No one in their right mind would stick around Steele Falls if they had a job on a cruise ship lined up. Seeing the world or waiting around to rot and die? The choice seemed pretty obvious to me.

"I've got a cousin who lives across town. He rents me a room for a screaming deal. That way, I don't have to buy an entire house or worry about an apartment. Seems pointless until I'm ready to settle down, which still sounds like the most horrible thing in the world. Monogamy. No, thank you." She shuddered. "Plus, it saves me a shit ton of money for other stuff."

"Like giant boobs," Daveigh replied.

"They are fantastic, aren't they?" Lucy grinned and puffed her chest out with a little shimmy.

"In all of their legiti-titty double-E splendor," Daveigh said.

I was sure both of them needed to learn the true definition of "legiti-titty" because there was nothing natural about Lucy's massive rack. She reminded me of a children's doll, the kind where the waist was unreasonably disproportionate to the boobs. Lucy was top-heavy, and I wondered when she'd topple over.

"Wanna feel 'em?" she asked me, jutting her chest out. "The swelling's almost completely gone now."

"I'll pass," I replied, jamming my hands into my pockets and out of sight.

"Suit yourself." She shrugged. "The doctor in Tijuana did an amazing job though. Dirt cheap too."

Doctor. Plastic surgery. Suddenly, I was reminded of Cash and his extensive schedule for fixing botched titty tucks and overinflated trout pouts.

"How long are you in town for?" Daveigh shouted.

"About a week," Lucy replied. "Then, it's on to Mexico. We should totally do dinner before I take off."

"Yes, please!" Daveigh replied. "I could use the escape."

I looked over at Lucy. Most girls would be envious. She was like Goldilocks. The stereotypical "just right", well, outside of her oversized headlights. Flawless creamy caramel-colored skin was a perfect contrast against her emerald green eyes. Her hair was worn down and hung to the middle of her back, a few loose locks draping over the front of her shoulder. Like a damn shampoo commercial, not a strand was out of place. It was a gorgeous sea of tightly-woven blonde and coffee-brown spirals.

I was caught off guard when a male voice sounded.

"Ladies, what'll it be?" A waiter approached the table with a thick accent in tow, pad of paper in-hand, and a pen perched behind his ear. He appeared to be roughly my age, but I definitely didn't remember ever seeing him around Steele Falls before. A metallic nametag read "Santi" on a gray button-up that was tucked into a tight pair of blue jeans. *And I mean tight.* You could see everything God gave that man. His sleeves had been rolled up to his elbows, accentuating each individual muscle on his tanned forearms. I continued to take in his bold features. Strong jaw. Convex nose. Jet black hair was slicked across his scalp and barely greeted his shoulders. I wondered what part of Italy he'd moved from, and why on earth he'd ever want to come to Steele Falls. Deep dimples appeared when he smiled. Just like Lucy, I was certain he was the envy of many.

"Hello there, sailor. I didn't know you were working tonight." Lucy batted her eyes, adjusting the way she was seated so she could make a production out of crossing her legs. "It's been a while."

He smirked at her, the look saying more than words could convey. "Jackie just left. I'm only working for a few hours to cover for her, but with you here, I'm definitely standing at attention now."

Oh, the innuendo.

"I'll have a beer," I replied, ignoring the obnoxious level of flirting that occurred next to me. "I don't care what kind. Make it a surprise."

"Another glass of rosé," Lucy held up her near-empty glass, "and you if you're available later tonight."

"How about eleven o'clock?" Santi asked, his voice barely elevating above a throaty purr. "That's when my shift ends. Maybe you could meet me up at the bar. You know, whet our whistles before we take off?"

"As if you even need to ask when it comes to your whistle," Lucy replied with a devious grin.

She turned toward my sister as Santi walked around to the other side of the table to hear Daveigh's order better. "He's got the biggest...feet," Lucy mouthed with a giggle. "Like gigan*dick*."

"I'm not sure what I want yet." Daveigh fished her gold-toned cell out of her pocket, a series of lights blinking around the perimeter in a rainbow of colors. Even though her level of fashion had waned a few levels over the past two years, her phone was as attention-grabbing as ever. Studying the illuminated screen resulted in her shoulders slumping. "I'll be right back. Gotta take this."

My little sister stormed through the doors toward the parking lot, and I wondered what could've stolen her attention so quickly from a friend back in town and a sister who'd reappeared after two years. Then, I remembered I was alone with Lucy. Lucky me.

It was quiet in the bar between songs, leaving me to feel thirteen levels below uncomfortable.

"You lucked out. Karaoke ended a little while ago. It was especially abysmal tonight. The last act, the drunk chick wearing the corset in the corner," she nodded across the room, "thought she was an opera singer. The next artist is amazing though. She's the main reason why I come here on Saturday nights when I'm in town." Lucy's voice was loud as she competed with the group of people sitting next to us. "Well, that and for Santi. Sometimes, you get a craving for...bar food."

She winked at me and scoped him out across the room again.

The local radio station continued playing another round of 90's rock, and I slumped back in my chair, trying to digest the day. My momentary reflection was short-lived when Lucy wanted to strike up conversation again.

"So," Lucy uncrossed her legs and adjusted the scoop of her top to showcase even more of her cleavage when she saw Santi walking back with our drinks, "how are you doing with the news? You know, about your dad."

I didn't know what to say, so I merely shrugged my shoulders. My desire to discuss the topic hovered on empty. Plus, it felt uncomfortable to be chatting about family with a complete stranger. Who was I kidding? It felt weird to talk about family with family under the circumstances. The line between being polite and an asshole to Lucy was paper thin, so I did my best to not offend my sister's friend.

"I know Daveigh's been a hot mess," she continued. "Her moods have been swinging from one extreme to the next. It hit her pretty damn hard."

"Well, I've never been an emotional or social butterfly." I lifted my beer to my mouth and took a drink from the plastic cup. "I tend to hold it in and hide out in my cocoon."

"As she's mentioned on more than one occasion."

I frowned. It bothered me not knowing what else Lucy might or might not have known about me. After all, we'd just met, and I didn't know a damn thing about her outside of her flavor preference for whetting Santi's whistle.

A few minutes later, Daveigh walked back up with a beer in her hand from the bar. "Sorry. It was an important call." She glanced at her watch. "And now I've got to tinkle. I'll be right back. Promise!" I watched my sister weave her way toward the bathroom and I was abruptly left with Lucy once more. Who knows? Maybe she'd end up being my new best friend. *Nah. Hello, round three of difficult conversation.*

"So, tell me about Steele Falls. What's it like these days?" I asked.

"Ehh...I leave for a cruise one week and come back five or ten days later. Not much ever changes during the time I'm gone. You know how things go around here; you've lived it."

I decided to curve the topic away from family and town as a list of subjects flitted through my head. "So, what's your position on the ship? Like an activities director?"

She snorted, nearly spilling her glass of rosé on the table. "I guess you could call it that. In fact, I think that's the most politically correct description I've heard for what I do."

"My other guess was going to be bartender." I took a drink of beer. "You've got that look. Like people open up to you and you've heard a lot of sob stories about their lives."

"You're good." She pointed at me with her index finger. "Also fitting, but I...do a different kind of mixing." She smirked as she took a sip of her wine.

I raised an eyebrow to inquire as I played with the condensation ring on the worn tabletop. "Well, you've piqued my curiosity."

"I'm a sex therapist. A couple's expert," she replied.

I instantly spit my mouthful of beer in a fine mist across the table and choked.

"Oh, my gosh. Are you okay?" She whacked me on the back and handed me a napkin.

"Fine," I croaked. "Just swallowed wrong."

"Looks like you're a spitter to me," she said, looking at the droplets on the table.

"You're so young. Didn't you have to go to school for years to do that?"

"It was nothing short of a miracle with how much I had to work my ass off. I did Running Start in high school. After I graduated, I pulled a double major in college. Living on nothing but energy drinks and coffee for a few years probably aged me more than I'm willing to admit, but I've known this was what I wanted to do since I was sixteen."

Good night! When I was sixteen, I was more concerned about finding ways to sneak out late at night and what new CDs were going to drop that week. Not one fiber of my being knew what I wanted to be when I grew up. Thinking about it, I had no clue while I sat with Lucy at The Fill & Spill that night.

"So, which cruise line do you work for?" I asked hoarsely.

"DeLuge. Well, technically, I'm still job shadowing for a couple of more months. But when the new ship sets sail to Alaska next year, I'll be considered permanent staff."

"Isn't the DeLuge Cruise like a giant orgy?" I asked, my eyes still watering from the beer I'd somehow inhaled into my lungs. Everything stunk like hops.

"Come on. That makes it sound so grimy." She paused. "I'd describe it as a multi-day wild party with unrestricted, sexual activity. Nothing wrong with exploring your options. Gotta know what floats your boat." She winked.

"I see what you did there. Cruise. Boat."

"I like you." She laughed. "If you're interested, I can give you my employee discount. You know, if you need a break after all this funeral stuff is over. Half off."

"I don't think a sex cruise is really my style," I said.

"Suit yourself," she replied. "But they have an amazing gift shop. There's a four-star buffet. The chef makes the best crème brûlée. It's out of this world! Oh! And there's shuffleboard. See? It's not all sex, all the time."

"Well, with a slogan like, "If you build it, they will *come*", that accompanies softcore porn music on the TV commercials, it doesn't lead the mind to believe much else goes on," I said.

"And come, they sure do." Lucy got a dreamy look on her face and raised her glass in an imaginary toast. "Over and over again."

Three years ago, Jonathan DeLuge discovered there was a niche in the dating industry, a demand for a sexually driven cruise line. A place where men and women, regardless of sexual orientation, married or not, could explore their fantasies without risk of STDs, an extramarital affair, or non-consensual sex. It was all-inclusive, which included limitless room-hopping. Money wasn't allowed while the ship was at sea to deter any whisper of prostitution. I'd heard the application process was extensive. Blood tests and full-body physicals were required to rule out any diseases. Spouses were required to sign off via notary if both weren't embarking on the trip. For a shady-sounding setup, a lot of thought had been put into it. And the business model brought in a ton of money. A ton. Numbers on the stock market soared. That specific cruise line had been under scrutiny on the news since it'd opened, but it still operated without less than a stellar rating on the Better Business Bureau. And it was more often referred to in the everyday world as the "Spooge Cruise". I wouldn't want to be a housekeeper on that boat. The thought of what those stiff bedsheets endured was enough to make me cringe.

"What do you do for work?" she asked, not taking her eyes off Santi as she shot him a wink and a flirtatious wave.

"Nothing fancy or exciting like you. I worked...work for a plastic surgeon. A company called Jensen & Jensen." I wasn't ready to reveal my unemployed status, especially to a sex therapist who represented a smutty cruise line.

"Oh, wow. That must be rewarding, right? Helping people feel better about themselves."

I thought back to Cash and our one-sided arrangement. One-sided dates. One-sided dinners. One-sided sex. One-sided decisions. There was no reward on my end. I was the giver, and he was the taker. I still wasn't ready to admit what we'd had was ever classified as a relationship...because it wasn't. None of it mattered though; it was over. "Yeah. Super satisfying. Can't wait to get back."

Just then, the 90s music faded away as a solo performer walked up onto the stage. Most of the crowd hushed, with the exception of a group of men wolf-whistling at her. Her level of confidence was unrivaled; she didn't flinch. The woman looked young, but something behind her eyes told me she had experience. If I had to guess, she was probably in her mid to late twenties. The A-frame sign propped up on the corner of the stage spelled out "Wonder" in curly chalk letters on a black backdrop. She wore thick-knit fishnets and a strapless black dress that accentuated the many tattoos spanning her arms. Heavy eyeliner made her appearance look fierce, yet it remained feminine. Her hair was an impressive masterpiece though. With her head shaved on one side, the other side hung down to her shoulder in a reverse bob, a sea of bright pink and blue.

A man with kinky white hair spoke into a microphone

near the edge of the stage behind a folding table that overflowed with DJ equipment. "Karaoke is over for tonight, and you all did an amazing job. Now, let's give a warm welcome to Wonder!"

The audience applauded and chanted her name.

I steered the conversation once again, not wanting any chance of the spotlight remaining on me. "I didn't know Wonder played here. I adore her music," I said.

"Me too! Fucking love her! Hey, she's going to be playing up in Leavenworth next month when I'm not working. We should totally go and make it into a girl's trip with 'Veigh. Plus, all the Christmas stuff should be up soon."

"I'm only in town for the funeral," I replied, trying to weave disappointment into my words. "Leavenworth's a little far from where I'm living now."

"Too bad." She stuck out her lower lip. "I haven't met too many others who knew of her right off the bat. I'm still not sure how this chick hasn't landed a huge record deal yet."

Where is Daveigh? I craned my neck, trying to look over the crowd.

"Are you sure you're okay? You're wound up tighter than a two-dollar watch," Lucy said.

"I'm fine." I wrung a bar napkin in my hands while my knee bounced nervously.

"Right." She studied me. "Is that why you're killing that poor thing?"

I looked down at the coiled-up piece of paper. "Rough day. Week. Month. Whatever you want to call it." I set it down and drank the remaining two thirds of my beer without coming up for air.

"Blue, when was the last time you were laid?" she asked me with a straight face.

I spit my drink across the table for a second time that night, the spray hitting the sleeve of her shirt. "Excuse me?"

"You're two for two. Goes to show spitters aren't quitters." She blotted her arm with a napkin I hadn't destroyed yet.

I felt my cheeks redden. "Sorry."

"Well?"

"Well what?" I asked.

"You know. When did you last sink the sausage? Cuddle aggressively? Participate in performing the disappearing cane trick?"

My jaw fell slightly and I was at a loss for words. Being that brazen about sex with a stranger wasn't a normal Saturday night activity for me.

She reached across the table and rested the pad of her index finger below my chin and lifted slightly to close the gap between my lips. "This is Steele Falls, honey. There are no secrets here. We're all friends. So, when was the last time someone dipped their wick in your honey pot?"

"Look, I just got out of a relation...arrangement, and he—"

"The sex was that bad, huh?" There was that disapproving head bob, wince, and a consoling pat on the shoulder again. The SHAT combo wasn't contained to Sacramento. That nugget of goodness stretched all the way to Steele Falls.

Once again, I was floored.

"Your face says it all. It's okay. We'll find you someone to have gland-to-gland combat with."

"So, how many euphemisms for sex do you know? Is that a requirement for your job?"

She smiled wide. "Trust me, I could go on for days. Look. If my crystal ball is right, you could use some kind of release, even if you have to ménage a moi yourself."

I tried to focus on a drunk woman who crawled up on the stage, trying to sing backup for Wonder. She wore a tight corset, her chest spilling over the top. The artist took it like a champ and embraced performing the duet, no matter how much the stranger destroyed the song. Corset Lady staggered and almost fell three times within the first two lines of the chorus. It was like seeing a train wreck. I couldn't look away.

"Here. Take this with you," Lucy said.

"What is it?" I asked, watching the drama unfold as a bouncer pulled the woman off the stage with a swift yank. Punches were thrown, and the woman succeeded in hitting herself in the jaw. The crowd cheered as she crashed to the floor with a giant thud.

"Reading material. You can thank me later. I've got it all

bookmarked for you."

By ignoring Lucy, she should've taken the hint and stopped talking. At least that's what a normal person would do. I'd assumed she baited me with information about the cruise she pushed. I also assumed she was paid on commission and got some kind of kickback for recruiting customers. Those kind of marketing schemes pissed me off. If I wanted to go on a naked cruise, I'd say I wanted to go on a naked cruise.

I vaguely recall her slipping something into my tote bag. In my stupidity, I was trying to not focus on what she said. A security guard escorted the drunk karaoke artist toward the exit with her arms pinned behind her back. All I registered were the words: "borrow", "80%", and "enjoy".

Lucy continued talking, but I still wasn't listening. By that time, tuning her out was easy as corset woman wriggled free. She made another mad dash for the stage, swinging and punching as she tripped over the laces on her combat boots, smashing her face on the edge of a table. There was blood.

Where the hell is Daveigh?

"Got all of that?" Lucy asked.

"Huh? Yeah. No problem," I replied with a smile even though I didn't have a damn clue what she'd said in the past two minutes.

As the first song came to an end, the DJ tapped on his microphone twice and announced a brief five-minute intermission until the commotion subsided.

As silence took hold, a small grouping of people up at the bar caught my eye. One of them appeared to be the main focus, telling a story with enthusiastic arm gestures. The few who'd gathered around him hung on his every word.

"Who's everyone captivated by over there?" I pointed toward the crowd.

Lucy looked up. "Huh? Oh! The specimen on the end?"

I nodded.

"That," Lucy took a swig of her near-empty wine, "is Zachary Main, most eligible bachelor of Steele Falls. He moved here last June. July maybe? I'd ask, but it doesn't matter. No need for him to talk with what I get out of our arrangement.

I've done Zack half a dozen times. He's a decent fuck, but sometimes I wonder whether he's worth the town hype, you know? He handles his business like his relationships. A real wham, bam, thank you, ma'am-type."

Thinking of Cash, I more than knew what she meant.

"He looks like he enjoys being the center of attention," I said, watching the man clap one of his friends on the shoulder once, offering a punchline to a joke. As if on command, they all laughed loudly at the exact same moment.

"He comes from money. Some fancy real estate investor who has more than he knows what to do with. Started buying houses and flipping them fresh out of high school. And his empire exploded. His next conquest is taking down Steele Falls, home by home, remodeling to help boost the economy out of its perma-slump. Sheer brilliance, if you ask me, considering this shit hole."

I popped a stale pretzel from a bowl on the center of the table into my mouth and rolled the rough texture around against my tongue, the bits of salt making me salivate. Silently, I screamed for Daveigh to return from the bathroom for the hundredth time. I'd learned way more than I'd ever wanted to know about Lucy and her sex life.

Zack took a step back to study a leggy blonde honing in on the group of men like a heat-seeking missile. She wore a hot pink low-cut top with a matching mini-skirt showcasing her midriff. Blonde hair cascaded down her back, nearly touching her ass. When he leaned in to kiss Ms. Endless Legs on the cheek and whisper in her ear, it revealed another man standing next to him. A frowning man. Mr. Scowl leaned against the bar as he typed furiously on his phone, not paying any attention to Zack or his stories.

"And that's Zack's friend, Adam Rockwell." Lucy nodded across the room. "Polar opposites, if you ask me. I've been trying to screw that one for months now. Done everything but spread my legs and crawl on his face to show him I'm interested. Seriously. I've been throwing myself in front of him for so long I'm starting to wonder if he bats for the other team."

Santi slowed down long enough to hand Lucy another

glass of wine and give her shoulder a gentle squeeze before he continued onward to the next table.

"Thank you, love." She smiled at him and then turned her focus back to me. "I mean, how do you think that makes me look if I can't bag someone like Adam Rockwell? I'm the fucking relationship professional around here," she continued.

The rest of Lucy's words were lost on me as I studied the man across the way. Even in a crowd, his presence was compelling. Goosebumps crawled up my arms and down my back as I drank Adam in from head to toe. His dark hair was long enough to run my fingers through. From afar, I could still see the vibrant color of his irises. I envisioned up close his eyes were the color of warm caramel ribbons. It reminded me of that brilliant gold when you drizzle the rich confection over vanilla ice cream as a pristine backdrop. His mouth—

"Hey." Lucy snapped her fingers in front of my face, a knowing smile curling at the corners of her garnet-colored lips. "Did you hear what I said about Zack? Last I heard, he's still single and a mediocre fuck if you need...." Her line of vision traveled to where I looked, and she cocked her head to the side while her expression turned from coy to pity. "Oh, honey. Don't waste your time. It's not gonna happen. Your vagina will curl up and die before you get that one horizontal and naked. Trust me."

I shook my head. "I wasn't...I..."

Lucy lowered her voice to a throaty whisper, "Rumor has it Adam's last girlfriend broke him in every way imaginable. Fuck." She downed her last mouthful of wine. "I'd like to break him, if you know what I mean. Lucky bitch."

I tried to tear my stare away from Adam's physique, but found it difficult to stop looking. He wore a simple white t-shirt with a black and gray flannel over it, unbuttoned. It was casual. Questions filtered through my head. Who was he talking to? Why was he frowning? Was he wearing aftershave? Even his faded blue jeans were enough to mesmerize me while the sounds of clinking glasses, laughter, and Lucy faded away to a dull echo.

Lucy grabbed my arm and brought me back to reality,

hopping down from the barstool. "I've got a great idea." She staggered in her stilettos, reminding me of a baby deer fresh from the womb.

"What are you doing?" I hissed, yanking my hand from her grip, nearly losing my beer in the other.

"C'mon. I'll introduce you to Zack. You look like you could use a little squeeze and a squirt in your life after everything that happened at home with...well, you know...death and all."

My eyes widened. "Oh! No, no really. That's okay. I'm only in town for a few days, and I need to go. There isn't time for—"

"Please. Everyone has some time for Zachary Main in their life and in-between their legs."

Again, Lucy got grabby, and gripped my wrist in one hand and her purse in the other, weaving us through the crowd toward the grouping of men. "This'll be fun."

It was clear Lucy's idea of "fun" was far different than mine. Give me a cup of tea, the latest Aurelia Fray book, and Catzilla on a Saturday night to color me happy. Isolation was where I belonged, not in a crowded bar. I wondered whether I'd have rather endured sushi and "dangling cock sockets" as Cash had so romantically put it. I'd officially sunk to a new low. Weighing my options between perusing artistic vaginas and hooking up with a stranger—neither seemed tempting. At all. *When did my life become so odd?*

"This really isn't necessary." I tried to wrench my hand free from her grip. By the time I turned around, Adam was out of sight. We were making a beeline directly for Zachary Main.

"Pish posh. You can thank me later, post-bed head." Lucy gave me a swift shove from behind until I collided with Zack's chest, my left palm greeting warm, firm pectorals through a silky shirt.

Slowly, I looked up into inquisitive gray eyes, my hand still pressed up against him. His aftershave took me by surprise. It held a pleasant blend of bold spice with hints of grapefruit and tangerine. "Uhhh..."

"Well, hi there." Zack paused, the bitter scent of vodka lingering on his breath as he looked down at me. Heat radiated through his shirt with his slow, deep breaths and I froze.

"S...sorry." My body tensed and I shot Lucy a glare. "I must've slipped or something."

"No need to apologize with blue eyes like those," he said. "I'm Zachary Main."

"I know...I mean, I've heard." A bead of sweat trickled down my back, and I was thankful the lighting was subdued to detract from the pink tingling my cheeks. "Lucy had nothing but great things to say about you."

"Lucy?" Zack glanced up and furrowed his brow to match a name with a face. "Lucy!" he exclaimed as he rubbed the back of his neck in embarrassment. "It's been a while."

"Too long if you ask me." Lucy smirked. "Enough about me though. I'd like you to meet Blue. Blue Brennan."

"Brennan...why does that name sound familiar?" Zack set down his glass next to a grouping of others. From the empties, it appeared he was on his fifth drink already.

"Her little sister is Daveigh Meyers, her mom's the mayor, and her uncle owns Brennan Construction."

Zack snapped his fingers. "That's right! Of course! Sorry. The alcohol's talking tonight. One too many vodka tonics. Ty Brennan was one of the masterminds behind my house and inspiration for some of my current work."

At that precise moment Zack mentioned my uncle's name, an idea struck, a brilliant lightbulb going off over my head. It was late though, and it would have to wait until the next day to put into motion. I filed the mental bookmark for later.

Zack continued, "Couldn't have asked for more gorgeous craftsmanship."

"I'll be sure to pay him the compliment if I see him while I'm in town."

"Please do." Zack smiled. "Also, be sure to tell him his niece was beautifully-crafted."

I averted my eyes and blushed.

"And I'm sorry. I heard the news about your dad. Never met him face-to-face, but I heard he was an upstanding pillar in the community. A real go-getter."

We'd made a pit stop on the topic of family, and that was my cue to leave. I hesitated before words found my mouth. "Well, it was nice to meet you, Zachary," I said, scoping out the nearest exit.

Zack's gaze sought out mine while he slipped his business card into my hand, the palm of his other sliding across my knuckles. The tips of his fingers slowly trailed small circles around each one before moving onward to the next.

I gulped.

His hand greeted my wrist and squeezed lightly. I wondered if he could feel my pulse racing beneath the skin. "My friends call me, Zack," he murmured into my ear, "but you can call me anytime. This is my personal number."

I shivered, and not because I was impressed. Zack's eyes were intense, as if I were the only one in the room. The way he looked at me felt more like a warning signal, but oddly familiar. And then it hit home. The line sounded like one Cash would've used on me back when he tried to win me over in the beginning.

"Damn, I could drown in those baby blues." He paused. "Can I buy you a drink before you—"

"I...can't." It was all too much, too recognizable. I needed to escape. Fast.

Spinning around, I sped toward the door with Lucy hot on my heels, but I only got as far as the end of the bar counter before she grabbed me by the wrist again, jerking me to a halt.

I glanced over my shoulder at Zack for a brief moment while she braced me in place.

He looked confused, shouting after me, "Did I say something wrong?"

I tried to pull away again, but her grip maintained its firmness.

"Wait!" Lucy hissed. "Zack was about three seconds away from taking you home for the night. Where are you going?"

I felt tears pricking at the back of my eyes. "I don't know what I'm doing. Here. In Steele Falls. At this bar. Any of it. I shouldn't have come back."

Lucy was at a loss as she looked around, grasping at straws to keep me from leaving. "What about Daveigh? Don't you want to wait for—"

"Tell her...tell her I had to go." I scrunched my eyes shut. "Tell her...I walked home. Tell her I went home with Zack. Whatever you want."

I turned toward the door with determination fueling my steps when I collided with someone else. Hard. It was the scent of aftershave that made me stagger and lose my balance, but it was far different from Zack's. The smell of fresh pine trees and rain filled my nose. It was accompanied by a hearty slosh of beer as the full cup I held spilled, emptied, and crushed between myself and the person in front of me.

Strong hands grabbed my upper arms to keep me from falling. "Damn it," a husky voice sounded while the crunched piece of plastic fell to the ground.

My eyes traveled up slowly, finding myself staring into the eyes of an angry Adam Rockwell.

Eight

His stare was menacing as he looked down at me, nostrils flared, jaw clenched.

"I...I'm sorry," I stammered. "I didn't mean..."

Lucy grabbed a white bar towel from the end of the counter and patted at the mess soaking through both of Adam's shirts. "Let me—"

"It's fine. Really." He swiped the cloth from her and blotted at his flannel. "Here's to hopin' I don't get pulled over on the way home tonight. Last thing I need is a cop trying to nail me for another fucking DUI."

Lucy let out a frustrated sigh with Adam's refusal of help. She elbowed me in the ribs and hummed the tune to the death march before whispering, "See? Vaginal funeral."

"Let me pay you for the beer. For your shirt." I reached into my tote bag and gripped a crumpled twenty-dollar bill and a ten, holding them out to Adam. It was the only cash I had on me. My hands quaked and I couldn't stop them.

"Thirty bucks?" Adam raised an eyebrow. "Are you kidding me right now?"

"Blue Brennan, meet Adam Rockwell," Lucy said quietly.

"I'm just trying to help," my voice was meek as I ignored Lucy's introduction. "It was an accident."

"Believe me, you've caused enough damage. Thanks," Adam's words were as cool and clear as ice water.

My skin prickled.

He shook his head and frowned at me for a few seconds longer than what felt comfortable. Additional words weren't necessary. His actions said it all. They spoke volumes as he turned around and blasted through the double doors. The wood paneling banged against the brickwork of the building hard enough to shatter the mosaic of stained glass, sending a mess of sparkling shards to the ground.

The bar fell silent.

My shoulders sagged as I stood there, stunned. The balled-up wad of money was still clasped tight in my hand. "I... didn't mean to..."

Lucy wrapped an arm around my shoulders and led me out of the bar, taking a dramatic step over the mess on the ground. "Fucking asshole. What a shitty way to react. It was an accident."

I sighed. "Thanks, but—"

"I used to think he was hot as fuck, but after that dick move he pulled? Don't you worry. I've got your back, girlfriend." Lucy gave my shoulder a pat.

"You've got my back? Oh, please," I said. "You don't know me from...well...Adam, as the saying goes." Suddenly, I hated that phrase.

"Honey, chicks before dicks. He's just another douche waffle, and he's never gettin' near this squeeze box." She made a gesture near her waist with both hands. "Trust me, you'd be way better off spending the night with Zack. He's still inside. It's not too late." Lucy nodded toward the doorway of The Fill & Spill.

"Why are you so interested in who I go home with?" I placed my hands on my hips. "Do you get your kicks from playing matchmaker off the clock or something? Does Zack pay you to find him women to screw?"

"Oh, honey, it doesn't matter to me who or what you fuck in your spare time. It could be a cucumber for all I care. I know Zack's an average lay, and you look like you haven't gotten any in a few months. You're all worked up. It's not healthy. You might explode."

"I want to leave," I said.

"Okay. Chill for a sec." She raised a hand to halt me. "No one's holding you hostage. Check out the e-reader when you have a chance. Trust me. Daveigh can get it back to me later."

"Look, the last thing I need is for you to ram a cruise down my throat like a giant dick. A cruise where one of the tag lines is probably "don't come a knockin' if the boat's a rockin'"."

"What are you talking about?" she asked. "I didn't try to shove anything—"

"Just please tell Daveigh I'm sorry. All of this was a bad idea." I walked away, tightening my jacket around me, before Lucy had a chance to reply.

* * *

I replayed the evening on the walk home, constantly rewinding and hitting the play button over and over in my mind. Things could've gone so differently, but I was still unsure of the exact catalyst that propelled the night into a downward spiral. The temperature had dipped dramatically and the wind kicked up when I turned onto Poplar. Miniature droplets of icy water fell from the sky, pelting my face. It felt like the world was against me. Every damn component. Even the weather tried to run me out of town. I tucked my hands up inside the cuffs of my jacket sleeves to stop the numbness from taking over my fingertips.

Lucy's babbling. Zack's steely gaze. Daveigh's weird behavior. My mother's bitchiness. All of them were minor because nothing sounded more loudly than the silent hatred that blazed behind Adam Rockwell's eyes. A whiff of beer caught me off guard, a pungent reminder of the evening, bringing everything round robin once again.

I approached the gravel driveway when a series of gunshots blasted in the distance. My heart pounded as adrenaline filled me, the cold quickly forgotten. It took a moment for me to gain my bearings and slow to a stop. Like clockwork, I remembered I was in Steele Falls and not Sacramento as I began to calm down. It was second nature as I turned in the direction it was coming from. "Just like old times." I wondered what the hell Ralph shot this time.

When I walked around back, the honeyed light of the standing lamp still shone through the window. I pulled the key from under the mat and slipped it into the lock, jiggling it twice to the left and then three times to the right. It was like having a security system and key in one.

For as safe as I should've felt, I didn't. Vulnerability took hold. Standing in the open doorway, I was terrified of what waited within. It wasn't anything tangible I feared. People. Objects. Animals. That all would've made too much sense. What I was scared of could only hurt me if I let it. The worst part was not knowing if I had enough strength to keep myself from breaking down until I was back in California.

I jumped when I heard a second round of gunfire from Ralph's direction. Nope. Still didn't feel fully at ease. An old man hanging out in the trees with his trusty .45 didn't seal the deal on refuge for me. "Jeez. How long before someone calls the cops?" Maybe they'd become immune to Ralph and didn't bat an eye, much like how no one paid attention to the slow pace of the run-down city.

Naked, swaying tree branches cast murky shadows through the darkened kitchen window from the moonlight, giving the surroundings an eerie, yellow glow. I tried to pay little attention to the imaginary monsters lurking in the corners and in my mind, but it was difficult to reign in my irrational thoughts. The ambience. The lighting. The smells. It all took me back to another time. "Focus," I whispered. "It's been two fucking years since you left. Get over it, Blue."

I was convinced a shower was the best dose of medicine to warm me up, rinse the beer off, and to also wash away the events of the evening. The last one was a longshot; I had a feeling it'd still linger if I bathed in battery acid.

Before I resigned to allow myself a moment of attempted peace, I stood in each area of the house. Like it was some form of penance. And trust me, I didn't want to do it. Being only a 535-square foot space, it shouldn't have taken long. Yet, the task at hand felt insurmountable. I tiptoed through each room and held my breath for as long as possible, fingering over the surfaces of countertops, cushions, and tables. Even the texturing on the walls didn't go unscathed. For the millionth time, I wondered if I should turn around and leave. Every bit of the Meyer's property felt more like a bully than any school-aged child ever could.

Another gust of wind howled outside. The windows rattled and the lights flickered, temporarily leaving me blind for a few seconds before the room came into view again. Knowing the layout like the back of my hand wasn't enough to help console me either. When the power threatened to go out for a second time, I panicked. The thought of being in the dark got more of a reaction out of me than Ralph's target practice. It was also enough to stop me from reminiscing.

Hurriedly, I went through the motions of unpacking my suitcase with shaking hands. It was a race—me against myself. The longer I was awake, the more time I had to think. The more time I had to think, the longer I was awake. It was a vicious cycle. I grabbed my bag of toiletries and headed for the bathroom, turning the shower handle as hot as I could tolerate. Plumes of steam filled the room as I peeled off my beer-soaked clothes. The stream of water poured over me until it ran cold, and I'd unrealistically hoped it'd give me a brief escape from reality. I was left disappointed.

After I brushed my teeth and towel-dried my hair, I climbed into the full-sized bed, the abrasive sheets cold against my shivering body. Not a damn thing in Steele Falls had given me peace since I'd arrived. Maybe I'd hoped for too much. I scrunched my eyes shut, hoping to fall asleep quickly, but I had a feeling it'd be another long night of tossing and turning mixed with bad dreams. Counting flock after flock of sheep even proved to be useless. Visions of Adam Rockwell trumped everything else in my mind. His glare was heightened by an unspoken pain unlike any other I'd ever encountered, and it was etched into my memory as much as I fought to shove it away.

* * *

The next day, I woke up to the sound of a pair of Canadian Geese honking near the tree outside my window. Those damn birds were useless, nothing more than a nuisance. They shit everywhere and rushed off other birds. Every winter, I'd hoped they'd fly south, but the temperature was never frigid long enough for them to leave. One of those assholes even chased me down the beach when I was a kid. I peeked through the blinds and saw a male with outstretched wings, flapping in the middle of the grass.

"Seriously?" I looked at the clock on the nightstand. At least it was the seven o'clock hour instead of an ungodly four-thirty. "I can't wake up on time for work, but as soon as I'm jobless, bitch geese act as my new alarm."

I couldn't figure out why I felt sick to my stomach, and then everything replayed in my head from the night before. Dreams. Cold sweats. Racing heart. It felt as if I'd done nothing but run in my sleep. This time, Cash Jensen was absent. A new lead had taken his place—Adam Rockwell.

"What do I have to do to get some rest?" I smashed the pillow over my face and groaned while kicking my feet into the lumpy mattress. Staring upward at the gap between the windowsill and the half-open blinds, the sky was a deep shade of dreary ashen gray, and heavy rain relentlessly pounded against the panes. Droplets fell down the glass like falling tears. It was typical Washington weather. Depressing.

Eventually, I coaxed myself out of the warm bed and made myself a cup of tea in the small kitchen nook. Examining the box with a sniff, the expiration date was flagged for eight months prior. It still smelled fine. I zoned out and dunked the bag far longer than I was willing to admit. There was no doubt in my mind I procrastinated. Standing still with my hands wrapped around a warm mug only dragged the time out until I had to face my mother again. She was an early riser, always awake before the sun came up. I remembered joking she was a vampire and never slept. If I believed in pretend creatures, I'd have taken more stock in the idea. Plus, it'd have made perfect sense with her cold heart.

I took a sip and scrunched my nose at the flavorless drink. "That's gross. I guess tea leaves do go bad." I dumped the full cup of liquid down the drain and rinsed out the mug, no longer in the mood for what soothing elements expired chamomile had to offer. "Might as well get this over with."

The little lightbulb flickered over my head again from the night before. I froze in front of the sink. There was still one task to handle before I faced Elana. I pulled my half-charged phone from my tote bag and found a phone number in my contacts list. My thumb hovered over the send button while a little nagging voice in the back of my head told me the answer would be a resounding "no". Out of fear, I cleared the digits from the screen three times before I got ballsy enough to hit the send key.

One ring.

Two rings.

Three rings.

"Brennan Construction," a deep voice said. "This is Tyler."

"Hey. I mean hi." I paused. "Uncle Ty, it's Blue."

The silence was lengthy before he replied, his voice softening around the edges. "Blue? Is that really you?"

"Last time I checked." I fiddled with a small sliver of wood that broke free from the door frame.

"How are you doing?" he asked.

Even though he was my birth father's brother, Ty Brennan cared about me. Or he was a great actor. We both knew I was doled out a shit-head for a dad in Shane Brennan. That was beyond my control. And Tyler was the polar opposite of Shane. The best thing was Ty never forced me to talk about any of the past. The even greater thing about my uncle was I wouldn't be reprimanded for leaving, there'd be no massive number of questions on what happened two years ago, I wouldn't be shot any disapproving looks for what I'd done, and there'd be no string of phone calls wondering where the hell I'd been. It was a simple question about how I was doing in that particular moment—present tense. No mention of Tom. No mention of Elana. No mention of Shane. No mention of where the hell I'd hid.

"I'm...good. I mean, okay, considering the circumstances, trying to remain semi-respectful of the fact I was in Steele Falls for my step-father's funeral," I said. "Listen, I don't want to occupy much of your time, but I wanted to know if I could set up a meeting with you while I'm in town."

"Hang on. Let me grab my planner and check my schedule. Business or personal reasons?" he asked. The sound of papers rifling and crinkling was audible through the speaker.

"Business," I replied. "Definitely business." Talking about anything personal sounded about as great as walking across hot coals. Barefoot. Slowly. With an elephant on my shoulders.

I heard a long, slow breath on the phone. "My schedule is pretty full today. Nuts for a Sunday, I know."

The resounding "no" I'd anticipated was mere seconds away. I deflated and opened my mouth to thank him for his time anyway, but he'd beat me to speaking.

"Wait. I have one opening tomorrow morning. A contractor canceled late last night. Does nine work for you? My office?"

"Nine is perfect," I replied.

"Great. Tell the receptionist who you are. I'll let her know you're coming." He paused. "Oh, and Blue?"

"Yeah?" I forced my feet into my Chucks without bothering to untie the laces first.

"I hope you're really doing okay. With everything."

"Thanks," I replied quickly. "See you tomorrow."

I ended the call before either of us had a chance to elongate the conversation any further. A smile curled at my lips at my success. It was the first one in a while. Proud of myself for following through, I put my cell phone away.

Standing near the screen door, I stared out at the yard. It was then or never. As much as I wanted to opt for never, it wasn't realistic. Time to rip off the bandage. I put on my jacket and flipped up the hood, dodging massive puddles that lined the walkway between the mother-in-law house and the kitchen of the main house.

I paused on the middle of the walkway, the pitter-patter of raindrops pelting the synthetic layer of my jacket. From the corner of my eye, I saw Daveigh through the window. She crossed from the living room into the kitchen with purpose. The pane of glass didn't detract from her level of anger. Her mouth was turned downward as she stomped by, slamming every overhead cupboard in the kitchen as she rifled through dishes, pots, and pans.

Our relationship was already rocky, but I had a feeling I'd damaged it tenfold by ditching her at the bar last night. A simple apology wasn't going to cut it.

More than ever, I didn't want to go inside. Both Elana and Daveigh Meyers were on the warpath. That was a force to be reckoned with. Reluctantly, I put on my big girl pants once again and placed one foot in front of the other. By the time I got inside, I found Daveigh drinking coffee at the dining room table. Both of her hands were tightly wrapped around the mug. Either she didn't notice my presence or she didn't care. The oversized coffee cup remained perched at eye level as she peered over the top of it, staring directly at the blank wall. Wisps of steam floated upward, but it didn't faze her.

"Hey," I said.

Daveigh was silent and didn't look at me.

I walked over to where she sat. "Sorry 'bout last night."

"Whatever, Blue." She stood up and took her half-full cup to the sink, rinsing it out before putting it in the dishwasher. "By the way, you owe me for the beer."

"Did you 'whatever' me? What's that supposed to mean?" I asked.

She smirked. "History has a funny way of repeating itself, don't you think?"

"I'll say it again." My blood pressure rose. "What's that supposed to mean?"

"You ghosted me." She pointed toward the front door. "Ran out just like you did two years ago. Without a trace. I figured you'd be gone to wherever the hell you've been for the past two years by the time I got home last night. Shocked to see you this morning, to be honest."

"What happened at the bar had nothing to do with—"

"Bullshit." Daveigh gritted her teeth. "Daddy's gone. Try thinking about someone else than yourself for a change. Huh?" She walked toward the front door and slammed it on her way out, repeating the same hostile action with the screen door.

I'm not sure what triggered it. Events at the bar? Events with Cash? Events that brought me back to Steele Falls? Whatever it was, it was the wrong moment to screw with me.

I followed her outside to the porch, stomping my feet like a petulant child. "Look, I've had enough going on in my life right now."

"You've had enough going on, Blue? You have no idea." Tears spilled down her face. "No damn idea at all."

I began counting on my fingers. "Let's see. I got fired yesterday from Jensen & Jensen. Me. Fired. Wanna know why?"

My sister crossed her arms and looked out at the ocean.

"Because I'd been fucking my boss. That's why. My condescending, narcissistic, asshole of a boss. To boot, it was against company policy. Price Jensen himself, president extraordinaire, about shoved the company handbook up my ass when he showed me the door. Wanna know why?"

She looked at me with a blank expression. "Why he shoved the handbook up your ass?"

"No. Why I was sleeping with Cash." My shoulders slumped at her inability to keep up with the conversation. "The longer I'm away from California, the more I don't even know why I did it. Him. The sex sucked. The conversation was terrible. I couldn't stand being around him, but there I was, like a dog being thrown a stick, running back to it over and over again.

"Then, I come here because my step-father dies. My sister asks me a million questions before I even have a chance to take my coat off, my mother couldn't give any less of a shit about me, and then you and I go out for a drink. Sounds good, right? But then I meet your sex therapist friend, Lucy, who tries to be my BFF when my sister vanishes. Wanna know why? Oh, wait! It's me who wants to know why *you* kept disappearing.

"And did I mention Lucy tried to ram her giant dick of a cruise line down my throat too? After that, I turn down her attempt to hook me up with Zachary "Eligible Bachelor" Main, I spill beer on Adam "Douche-Canoe" Rockwell. I tried to apologize, and—"

"Wait," Daveigh held up her hands. "Stop right there. You

spilled beer on Adam Rockwell?"

"Yeah. So?"

"Okay, Blue. I know I'm pissed as hell at you right now about more reasons than I can count, but I want you to steer clear of that guy. You hear me?"

"I'm pretty sure he hates me. You don't have to worry about him coming anywhere near your big sister."

"I'm serious. A while back, I was down at The Fill & Spill late one night, celebrating one of my breakups with Gene. I was supposed to meet Lucy, but I was running late and told her I'd just meet her there."

I opened my mouth to cut her off, but she shot me a glare.

"No Gene jokes. It's my turn to talk. Later that night, I was outside having a smoke and I saw that Adam guy hit Daddy."

"Like with his car?"

"No, with his fists." She held up both of her hands and balled them up.

I furrowed my brow. "I don't understand."

"No clue why he started wailing on him. I saw it happen from across the parking lot. Adam pulled in, got out, and slammed his truck door. He looked pissed off about something, but when doesn't that dude look hostile? When he headed inside, Daddy bumped into him on the way out, and Adam went ape shit crazy. It was nuts. Arms were swinging. Legs were kicking. They slammed into Daddy's truck so hard. The glass busted out of the passenger side window when Daddy's head smashed into it. And the blood. Jeez, there was so much of it. Adam got this wild look behind his eyes, I'm not sure if it was rage or pain or what, but I could still see it from far away. He punched Daddy square in the nose three times, shaking him by the lapels on his jacket. Limp like a fucking rag doll. I'd be surprised if Adam didn't bust the bones in his hand."

"What did you do?" I asked quietly.

"I was kinda paralyzed. Really wasn't sure what I should do. I'd snuck out and was using a fake ID. You know, the ones William made up for us a long time ago? At that point, I was lucky he didn't see me. I mean, I didn't want Daddy to die either though. And that was when Harold rushed over to help him. He'd seen the whole thing happen from inside the bar."

I remained still.

"It was the weirdest thing. I heard every word clear as day. There was no mistaking it. Daddy told Harold it was all a misunderstanding and he didn't want to press charges against Adam. I don't get it. Someone beats the shit out of me, I'm sure as hell gonna make them pay. That guy rubs me the wrong way, Blue."

"I've got to go," I said, zipping up my jacket.

"Where are you going?" she asked.

"I think I need something stronger than coffee and weaker than a narcotic."

"So, that's it? You're going to walk away from me again?"

"For now." I hurried down the porch steps. "And I'm still sorry about last night."

"Blue!" she shouted after me.

I headed down the sidewalk and didn't look back. If I saw the look on Daveigh's face, I wasn't sure I could simply walk away. But I needed to. A drink was required to clear my head. Options were limited since it was only nine in the morning. I'd have to settle for something from the local coffee shop. The last thing I needed was to be deemed the town lush.

About ten minutes later, I opened the door of The Lean, Mean, Coffee Bean and let the smell of robust beans and sweet toffee fill my lungs while a whimsical bell chimed to announce my presence. Not much had changed there either. The tan and chocolate-colored wooden planks on the floor still mimicked the pillars between the windows. Oversized singular lightbulbs hung from the ceiling over each table. They, too, were the same as I remembered. Couples occupied most of the quaint tables for two, and a bar along the window was filled with customers busily working on laptops or surfing their cell phones. It was one of the more popular businesses in Steele Falls.

I stood in line and stared at the green chalkboard of fancy drinks written in swirly, pastel writing, not really focusing on any of the words. Daveigh's voice calling out my name echoed in my head. When it was my turn, I placed my order with a gothic cashier named Mary as I fished for a handful of quarters in my pocket.

"Name for the order?" Mary asked as she clicked her tongue ring against her teeth and drummed her tattoo-covered fingers against the concrete countertop.

"Blue," I replied absentmindedly.

"I'll pay for hers," a velvet-edged voice said from a table near the doorway.

Mary was forgotten. Daveigh was forgotten. Steele Falls was forgotten.

I looked over and saw a familiar face approaching me with an air of confidence and a hint of arrogance in his step. He wore dark jeans and a checkered button-up shirt, the shade of gray accentuating his eyes. Zachary Main held a twenty out to the cashier, but his gaze remained locked on my face.

"You don't have to do that," I replied, pushing the crisp bill back toward him with one hand. "I can buy my own—"

"Come on." A faint light twinkled behind his eyes. "I've been thinking about you a *latté*."

I raised a brow. "Does that line work?"

"I don't know. Did it?" He grinned and gestured between our bodies with his index finger. "You may not yet, but I can feel something *brewing* between us, Blue Brennan."

I felt color creep into my cheeks as I released the handful of coins back into the pocket of my jeans.

"I'm glad I ran into you because," he took a sip from his paper cup, "I'm having a party at my place on Tuesday, and I wanted to know if you'd come as my date."

"A party?" I scrunched my nose. "That sounds awfully high school."

"Call it a gathering. Call it a BBQ." He took a deep breath, a lock of wavy hair casually falling over his forehead. "Call it a social function where there'll be food, alcohol, and I'm hoping a beautiful, blue-eyed girl."

Words to decline failed me, so I shook my head left and right slowly.

"I had an end of summer bash last year and called it a housewarming when I moved to town. Everyone had a good time, so I decided to make it a tradition. Plus, it'd be a great excuse to get to know you better."

"End of summer? It's October."

"Then, we'll call it a better-late-than-never-gathering-BBQ-social-function-where-there'll-be-food-alcohol-and-I'm-hoping-a-beautiful-blue-eyed-girl. Is that better? Not sure it'll fit on a formal invite though, so please don't make me write it out."

"Are you always this clever with the comebacks?" I asked.

His smile was smug. "Only on days that end in Y."

I withdrew from his attempt to lure me in. "I...I shouldn't. There's a funeral to plan and—"

"In all seriousness, maybe it'd help if you took your mind off things. Even if just for a few hours." There was a hint of pleading on his face to mimic the tone behind his words. "C'mon. Please?"

"I can't. Really," I replied, although any excuse to avoid my mother was tempting.

"Drink for...Lou!" the barista shouted as she scrutinized the sloppy handwriting on the cup.

The intense moment was interrupted as I looked around. I was the only one waiting at the counter. "Guess I'm Lou today."

"See? The staff here already forgot who you are, but I didn't. That has to count for something."

"In all fairness, 'Blue' isn't the most common name," I said.

"Come on. Give me a *shot*. Plus, who can turn down all of these witty coffee quips I'm throwing your way?"

"A girl who prefers her caffeine injection with tea." I picked up the cup from the counter and tugged gently at the tag on the end of the string. "Black peppermint."

"Noted for any future coffee shop dates," he said. "Words can't *espresso* how much it'd mean if you came."

I groaned and laughed. "Stop with the horrible pickup lines. Who does that?"

"Guess you'll have to stick around Steele Falls to find out." His next words were both firm and final. "I'll pick you up on Tuesday afternoon."

Reluctantly, I found myself accepting the invitation.

He nodded toward the door. "Come on. I'll walk you out."

I adjusted my tote bag when the unthinkable happened. A woman's breathy voice sounded, as if from right behind me. She had an accent and enunciated every syllable clearly. Too damn clearly. And too damn loud.

I froze.

I yelped as his impressive length filled me again. "Don't stop," I said. "Please don't fucking stop now."

"What the hell?" I spun in a circle. Once to the left. Twice to the right. I looked like an animal chasing its tail. Where a dog would typically lose interest and stop, my embarrassing situation continued.

The line between enjoyment and pain was almost non-existent.

The corners of Zack's mouth curled upward as he fought off a laugh. "I think the hot and heavy's coming from your bag."

"Zeke." I panted as he stroked me, the sensation of nerves firing. My body thrummed and threatened to erupt.

"No. It can't be!" I shrieked, the heads of half a dozen customers turning around to see what the skin flick commotion was all about.

Zeke locked eyes with mine as he moved behind me, guiding his thick—"

"Whoa-kay!" I found an e-reader in my tote bag operating at full-volume. Thoughts of Lucy from the night before slapped me in the face while I fumbled for the off switch. Hell, at that moment I'd have welcomed an eject button, an explosion, anything to make the freight train of porn stop. Success was found when I toggled the microscopic mute button. Unfortunately, an additional slew of dirty slang for anatomy peppered the air in those extra few seconds. I looked at the screen of the device. The cover in the upper left corner displayed black and white image. A blonde woman with dreadlocks was being cradled by a man. Local erotica author Trixie Taylor's name was emblazoned at the bottom along with the title and a miniature 80% sign.

Serves me right for not paying attention to what Lucy was doing. Her words echoed in my ears. Borrow, 80%, and enjoy, my ass! It all made sense.

"Been doing some heavy reading?" Zack arched an eyebrow.

I shoved the ereader to the bottom of my tote bag. "Lucy."

"Hey, don't be ashamed. There's nothing wrong with a little bedroom material for your spank bank. I didn't take you for the Trixie Taylor type. That's all."

"No, really. It's Lucy's." I shook my head, and I was certain my face was the color of a beet. "I don't...it's not...I..."

"Tuesday!" Zack walked away with a twisted smile on his face.

I watched as he disappeared down the street. There was no room to change my answer to "no", and it was an invisible blow to the gut when I realized what happened. I'd agreed to go on a date with a man who was the equivalent of Cash Jensen and who thought I was into kinky reading material. All of it was sex therapist Lucy's fault.

Nine

The rain had stopped, and the sun fought to shine, the temperature still deceivingly cold. An upgrade in weather was a small win in my day, but it seemed like it was the only one. I walked back toward Poplar and vowed to myself I'd never go out in public again. It was probably a little dramatic, but I sure as hell wouldn't be caught at The Lean, Mean, Coffee Bean anytime soon.

"Blue!" a thick accent called out to me as I approached the driveway at home.

Ralph was outside in his brown bathrobe, clumps of white hair atop his tanned scalp in disarray. What he wore was the norm for him, but it could've been ten times worse. I'd been the lucky recipient of seeing him work on his Volkswagen bus in nothing but neon green short shorts once. Said short shorts did little to conceal his weapon, and I'm not talking about his .45. Catching an eyeful of his twig and shriveled prunes, because calling them berries doesn't supply an adequate enough visual, is something I'll never be able to un-see.

He stood near the mailboxes with a box tucked underneath his arm, waving at me overhead with his other hand. "Ahoy!"

"Ralph, not today," I pleaded under my breath.

"Ahh!" He shuffled across the street. "Welcome back to Steele Falls! I have a gift for you."

I closed my eyes and tried to not lose my shit. "That's really not necessary..."

He lifted one of his liver spot-covered hands once again, raising his crooked pointer finger into the air. "Here." He extended the box toward me with a smile. "Take it."

Internally, I turned around and walked away. Externally, I humored the old man and lifted the lid on the shoe box. The bottom left corner was soaked in a thick layer of grease, and it reminded me of the French fry aftermath from Boberto's Burger Bungalow. The smell was the worst part, like rancid meat.

Beaming with pride like a baby who'd shit their pants, he explained, "A grapefruit I picked in Yuma four days ago and a pound of dates from my trip to Louisiana. For your family. Wanted to get them to you before I take off on my motorcycle trip."

"Thank you?" I answered. By far, it wasn't the strangest gift I'd received from Ralph, especially considering he'd come over to the property with a live lobster in a wheelbarrow once before. That same day, he also handed me the phone number of a woman who worked at the local credit union on a sticky note. The top said, "Sharon" on it. His secretive expression when he'd given it to me told me I should've known why, like he spoke in code. I didn't have a flipping clue. But I'd learned over the years not to invest much thought in why Ralph did the things he did.

He peered down into the box and pointed to the darkened corner. "There was alligator meat from Baton Rouge in there too. But, man, you wouldn't believe how much that stuff changes up your stool. I saved you from suffering through the carnage."

Yep. That explained the odor. I wrinkled my nose and grimaced, not spared from the vivid poop picture he'd painted for me.

He looked at his watch. "Ahh! I've got to shower and get dressed. Church starts in an hour. I finally convinced Clarabelle to go with me." He waggled his bushy eyebrows. "See you later."

Clarabelle was our neighbor three doors down. Much like Ralph, she was ancient, but she was much quieter and kept to herself. It'd been four years since her husband, Peter, passed away. Rumor had it, he died of a heart attack in the middle of a bedroom romp. When he came, he took it a little too far and...

went. I guess if you're gonna go, that was the way to do it. She spent most of her time staring out the window at the hired yard help and making a ridiculous number of apple pies. Ralph had been jumping at the opportunity to get her into bed for years. Gotta give his old man libido credit.

I welcomed his abrupt departure and headed up the steps to wipe my feet on the unwelcome mat. The bottom of the box sagged against the grease, the grapefruit threatening to break through as it rolled from one side to the other. After I was certain Ralph was out of view, I set it down on the porch, resigning to throw it in the trash later.

I opened the front door and walked inside, slipping my shoes off and onto the area rug near the door. "'Veigh?" I asked. "You home?"

"Daveigh isn't here," a cold voice sounded.

I closed my eyes and regretted opening the front door. Maybe my day wasn't looking up after all.

"Hi, Mom," I replied and leaned against the doorway of the kitchen with my arms crossed.

She still didn't acknowledge my presence. The room was silent as she downed a handful of pills from a yellow bottle on the counter. No glass of water was in sight as a chaser. Hardcore. The woman had achieved professional status.

"So..." I said.

The following words didn't come as easily as I'd hoped. What do you say to someone you haven't spoken to in two years? Someone who you were so busy holding a grudge against where you didn't know them anymore? At all. How do you open up the lines of communication to that? Do you ask them how they are or dole out a high five? A hug was out of the question.

She turned around and leaned back against the counter, bracing the edge of it with her hands, the bottle still in her grip. "Have you thought about it?"

"Thought about what?" I took off my jacket and hung it on the coatrack.

"What you're going to say at the funeral on Wednesday. What else?"

The topic of speaking at Tom's funeral hadn't crossed my mind since I'd arrived, even with my mother grabbing my head and ramming her non-existent dick down my throat by way of demanding I piece some non-existent bullshit together. "Not yet."

"Well, you'd better work on it. I don't want you slapping some crappy speech together at the last minute. This is a big deal, you know."

Yep. A big deal for someone who needs to tug on the heartstrings of Steele Falls' citizens, so she can ensure she wins over their votes come election time. This time, I was smart enough to not say what I thought aloud.

She motioned to the empty pad of paper I'd left on the counter the day before. Of course, she'd known I hadn't worked on it, but by asking about it, she put her own special, condescending Elana-type twist on it. Like usual.

I changed the subject. "So, when is Finn flying in?"

"What on earth are you talking about now?" Her eye roll was distinct.

"Finn. Daveigh said he was flying in when I talked to her on the phone Friday, but she didn't have his flight info when I asked her last night. Said I had to ask you for it."

"Of course, she did." Elana shook her head and laughed through her nose.

The muscles in my shoulders tensed. "What's that look on your face for?"

"You're being absurd. Finn's not coming home for this. He has finals to study for, and with what I have to pay for his tuition? Just no."

"But Daveigh said everyone had to come—"

"Naïve, naïve Blue." She set the pill bottle back down on the counter. "Did you ever think she might've told you that so you'd come back to Steele Falls?"

I sank onto one of the dining room chairs, the flat cushion doing little to soften the blow. My expression must've said it all. So much for my poker face.

"Think about it. She's as manipulative as I am. It's in our blood, and it's what we do."

I remained deceptively calm. "Maybe it's what *you* do."

"Look at the outcome. She won and got what she wanted, even if it wasn't what I—"

There was a knock on the front door.

She huffed. "You get it before I say something to you I'll likely not regret. I have to go down to the funeral home this morning, and I don't have time for any solicitor's shenanigans."

"Yes, your majesty," I ground out between my teeth, knowing it wasn't loud enough for her to hear.

Just like the night prior, Elana went through the same motions of grabbing a suit jacket off the back of the chair. It was the same style, but this version was a deep burgundy. The woman owned one in every color and pattern. If anything, my mother was predictable with her wardrobe. She shrugged her way into it, grabbed her purse, and walked out the kitchen door.

The doorbell sounded twice, one chime immediately following the other to deliver its urgency.

"For the love of..." I stomped my way over to the entryway.

Three more rings.

"Hang on, would you?" I looked through the peephole, but years of sea salt had clouded the circular bubble of glass, and I couldn't see much outside of a distorted figure. "Who is it?" I asked.

"Open the door, Blue."

I turned the knob and pulled. "Beanbag?"

He closed his eyes halfway. "It's still Wesley. All day long. Twenty-four seven. Wesley."

He stood in the doorway, wearing a brown Carhartt jacket and matching work pants. His black boots were scuffed with wear, and his baseball cap was worn backward on his head. Disheveled reddish blond locks poked out beneath it. Everything about him screamed "mechanic", which was a one-eighty from the past.

"Are you here with the estimate for my car?" I asked.

"Nope," he replied. "That's Eddie's deal."

I lowered my voice, almost forgetting I was home alone. "I already told you I wasn't interested in talking to you."

"Well, this might come as a surprise, but I'm not here

for you. Believe it or not, carrying on this conversation hasn't made the top five on my bucket list."

"You're not here to try and talk to me again?"

"You've already made it crystal clear you don't want to hear what I've got to say, whether it benefits you or not. And I'm not about to chase you all over town like a mutt begging for attention."

"Then what else could you possibly be here for?"

"Don't flatter yourself." He craned his neck, trying to look over my shoulder. "Is Daveigh here?"

"What do you want with..." I looked up at the ceiling, my lungs deflating. "Good night. Please tell me you aren't interested in my little sister."

"Not that it's any of your business or that you have any say in it, but we've been together for about seven months now." He crossed his arms. "Maybe if you'd call once in a while, you'd know that. But you don't. So..."

"Enough reprimands about my past are doled out around here. I don't need any from you. Thanks."

He adjusted his hat. "Look, I don't want to fight right now. I really don't."

"Then leave. 'Veigh isn't here. Did you try calling her cell phone?"

"Sure did, genius. She didn't answer, so I figured I'd stop by."

"Maybe she's at work," I said.

"She hasn't worked since...You know what? Never mind. I've got to go."

"Since what?" I asked.

"Forget it. Been real nice catching up with you." His sarcastic tone didn't go unnoticed as he turned around and stomped down the stairs, skipping the third from the bottom to avoid the creaky groan. I froze. It was then I knew he was serious about what he'd said about dating 'Veigh. He'd been to the house often enough to know to avoid that step.

I closed the door and leaned against it. The smells of cinnamon and cloves were too much, and I needed fresh air. I walked into the kitchen to grab my jacket when I saw the tablet of paper on the table. Still pristine white. Still no heartfelt words. With a scowl, I picked it up, shoved it into my bag before heading out the door.

One of the few fortunate aspects about Steele Falls was it being so small. It left the gossip mill with the ability to spread like wildfire. On the other hand? Most of the places I used to frequent were within walking distance. My feet were on auto-pilot, leading me to the place where I did my best thinking—the beach.

Twenty-five minutes later, I trudged across the hilly dunes of soft sand until the hard-packed layer of grit met my feet. I took my shoes and socks off, letting the numbing grains mold against my soles and squish between my toes as I walked. The fact it was October and cold didn't matter to me. With the beach, it never did.

The massive piece of driftwood I remembered was still there. Most of it had been bleached to a dirty, pale gray by years of wind and the sun beating on it. Nubs and branches stuck up in various places, making it look like a mess of deer antlers exploded from within. I sat down crisscross applesauce with my back pressed up against a flat spot. Using my jacket as a blanket across my lap, I snuggled against myself for warmth while gusts of wind fought to steal my body heat.

Glancing to the left, an unexpected memory took hold. It amazed me how many little fragments of my past I'd let go. Graffiti had been carved into the wood with a pocketknife. Tracing the indentations with my fingertips resulted in a lump forming in my throat. I reached into my bag and pulled out a switchblade, fingering over the iridescent strip of color on the handle. I quickly shoved it to the bottom of the bag, burying it deep before I scooted over to cover up the initials with my back. Out of sight, out of mind.

A house in the distance caught my attention, but I forced myself to look away quickly. Relentless waves smashed against the coastline, trumping the rest of the scenery, the home quickly forgotten. I fingered over the tablet of paper, but didn't even know where to begin. Procrastination was about to be my crutch once again. Plus, I needed advice.

Pulling out my phone, I scrolled through my contacts to another number I hadn't used in years. It was time. Pushing send, I drew my feet up to my chest and waited.

One ring.

Two rings.

"Hello?" a male voice answered. Loud music played, intertwining with multiple voices talking and laughter in the background.

"Hey, Finn," I replied.

"Guys, turn it down, would you?"

The level of background noise remained at a sustained decibel.

"Hang on a minute! Maybe two! It's loud in here!" he shouted.

I looked out at the giant waves as they crashed on the shore while tears filled my eyes. The paper in front of me was blank, an empty canvas. I had no idea what words I could possibly bring myself to string together. There was no way to paint Tom in a positive light without casting shadowy lies. Daveigh had a better relationship with everyone in the family. I was the blackest of the sheep.

It wasn't fair of Elana to ask me to speak at the funeral. I hadn't talked to either of my parents in two years. Two fucking years. Christmas's were missed. Birthdays were forgotten. Thanksgiving was non-existent. I made sure to remember little of the man who'd "raised" me. Over time, I'd taken those memories and boxed them up securely, packing them away for good.

If Daveigh was right about what the will said, I had to attend the funeral. If I didn't meet with the lawyer, no one would get what was coming to them. Why was I always left to be the responsible one?

The background became quieter. "Okay, I'm outside. Much better."

"How are you?" I asked, letting a handful of fine sand grains sift through the gaps between my fingers.

"Fine?" he replied. "Who is this?"

I sat up straighter, adjusting the pen and paper on my lap.

"It's Blue."

"Holy fucking shit. Blue?"

"I've gotten that response a lot lately. You're developing a hint of British accent, baby brother."

"Yeah, well a few years across The Pond will do that to you. How the hell are you?"

"I'm...good," I lied.

"No, you're not. You hesitated. What's wrong?"

"I...I don't even know where to start." I sniffled and wiped at my nose with the back of my hand.

"Start with what? Where are you?" The level of concern in his voice elevated and was almost demanding.

Even though he was my little brother, the youngest sibling in the family, Finn had always tried to act as my defender.

"Steele Falls," I replied, tossing the pen and tablet in the sand out of frustration. "On the beach. Writing. Trying to write. Failing at writing."

"Hold up. You went home? I didn't think you'd ever go back."

"Me neither, honestly. Daveigh said you'd be here too, but I guess I was wrong. I figured there'd be safety in numbers. You know?"

"Safety for what?" he asked with a laugh. "Against a burger from The Fill & Spill?"

"Against Mom." I smirked.

"Well, I don't know if there's any protection for that. Plus, she and I haven't spoken in months. That woman's avoided my calls like the plague. You can only reach out for so long before the rejection becomes one too many slaps in the face. You know?"

"Wait." I chewed my lip. "You haven't spoken to her in months. But you've talked to her in the past week, right?"

"No. Why?"

I was silent.

"Blue? Are you still there?"

It felt like my stomach dropped ten feet below the sand and churned into a sea of knots while my mouth went dry. *Shit.* My manipulative bitch of a mother hadn't told Finn that his father died, and there I was, left to handle it all myself. Hello, parental role. We meet again. Oh, how I haven't missed you either.

I fought to focus. "Yeah. I'm still here."

"What's going on?" The fear behind his voice intensified again, knocking his voice up an octave.

"I really don't want to be the one to tell you this."

"Tell me what? You're scaring me. Why are you in Steele Falls?"

"It's Tom." I rubbed my face with my free hand. "How do I say this? Finn," Taking a deep breath, I spewed the last two words quickly. "He died."

The other end of the line went silent. I couldn't even hear the sound of his breathing.

"Did we get disconnected?" My eyes brimmed and the world blurred. The emotion wasn't out of sadness for Tom. A single tear wasn't shed on his behalf. My grief was in knowing Finn was halfway around the world, and I couldn't console him. I couldn't see the look on his face to know whether he was okay or not. Was he crying? Was he shaking? Was he in the fetal position on some British sidewalk?

"I'm here." He let out a deep breath through his nose. "When's the funeral?"

"Finn..."

"When. Is the damn funeral, Blue?"

"Wednesday. It's on Wednesday," I replied.

"I have to go," he swallowed hard enough for me to hear through the phone, "deal with a few things."

"Wait...I didn't mean to upset you."

His tone softened. "Don't worry about me. We'll talk soon. I promise. Love you."

"Love you too."

And then, the call ended.

I covered my face with my hands and slammed my cell on top of my tote bag. "Why is my family so fucked up?"

I shouldn't have been the one to tell Finn about Tom, and spilling the beans wasn't my intent. It was my mom's responsibility, but she'd flung that stinky turd right over to me, where it didn't belong. That was par for the course. Elana Meyer's was devious, and it was in her nature.

I sat and stared at the endless ocean, feeling as if I were comatose. *Did I do the right thing?* My limbs were like lead, and I'm not sure whether I blinked or breathed. Even though you couldn't see it from the outside, my mind raced, dissecting the conversations I'd had since arriving in Steele Falls. Minutes ticked, but I didn't know how many. Two hours? Maybe three? When the sun began to set behind a gauzy layer of clouds and the temperature began to wane, I knew it was time to leave. Looking down at my lap, the pad of paper was still as blank as it was when I'd arrived. The afternoon had been a failure—in so many ways.

I walked back toward the house feeling defeated below a darkening sky. As I passed by The Fill & Spill, I stopped and did a double take. Daveigh's Thunderbird was parked along the sidewalk, the hood cold.

It was a rash decision. The chill had worn off me, and a fire ignited in the pit of my stomach. Confronting my sister consumed my thoughts. I was afraid if I didn't take charge at that moment, I'd have let it all fester inside me for the rest of my life.

I changed my direction away from heading toward Poplar, bee lining toward the front doors of the bar. The stained-glass window was still absent, thick packing tape and a layer of plastic combined with newsprint taking its place. That night, the music was more subdued but twangy, and I'd forgotten Sunday evenings were deemed country night at the bar. I looked around the hazy room and honed in on a large round table in the corner. Lucy and Beanbag were drinking beer, deep in conversation. The remaining chairs surrounding the table were empty—including one between them.

I marched over to the table with my fists balled and my teeth clenched. "Where is she?"

"Hey!" Lucy smiled.

Beanbag crossed his arms and leaned back in his chair. "Blue."

I opened my tote bag and pulled out the e-reader, letting

it fall to the table from a few inches too high. The device made a harsh clunking sound. "I think this is yours."

She glanced at the screen. "Did you like it? It's way hot, right?"

"Where is she?" I asked again.

"Who? 'Veigh? She's in the little girl's room," Lucy replied. "Is everything okay?"

I turned on my heel and headed toward the bathroom, shoving my way past the swinging door. A frizzy-haired, redheaded woman washed her hands as she spied me in the mirror. Her eyes widened. The faucet handle squeaked as she spun it to the right, her hands covered in bubbles. She didn't bother to rinse or dry them before she scurried through the doorway.

"Daveigh!" I shouted as I walked through the bathroom, beating on the door of the only closed stall with my open palm. "I know you're in there."

"Can't a girl pee in peace?"

"We need to talk," I said.

"Right now? When I'm in the pisser? About what?"

"First of all, tell me you aren't banging Beanbag Peters."

The toilet flushed. "He goes by Wesley now."

"As I've heard." I grabbed her upper arm as she exited the stall. "Look at me. Do you think that if he changes his name, it automatically cleans up his reputation?"

She shook free from my grip. "Since when do you get a say in who I'm seeing? From what I remember you haven't been around for the past two years."

"Daveigh. He was the poster child for the clap."

"That was a long time ago, Blue. People can change. You, of all people, should know that."

I pursed my lips and placed my hands on my hips.

"Quit standing there like Mom, like I've failed you or something." She focused on washing her hands. "I'm not even looking at you and I know the expression on your face without even seeing it. And for the record, Wesley's not the spokesperson for the clap."

I let my arms fall to my sides dramatically and cocked my

head to the side.

"What? It's not like he actually had gonorrhea," she said, reaching for a paper towel.

"It doesn't matter. He's got a billboard reputation."

"He does not."

"He does. They still play his commercial on channel seven late at night. I've seen it. He's known all over the place as Gonorrhea Guy, like it's some gross superhero name. And I don't even want to think about what his powers would be."

"That whole thing was more than a year ago, and he hated every second of participating in that commercial. His cousin is some big time TV guy in LA, and Bean...Wesley needed the money. It was no big deal, and he learned acting wasn't his thing. Being a mechanic at Fast Eddie's is a completely respectable job. It suits him."

I curled my lip and let out a sigh. "Well, Mr. STD came to the door looking for you earlier today at the momster's."

"He doesn't have a...he did?" Her face blanched. "I mean okay."

"Second of all, and this one's a doozy. Did you ask me to come back to Steele Falls because you wanted me here or because I had to come?"

Guilt flooded her face, and I already had my answer. "The..."

I pinched the bridge of my nose. "Do you know how much a plane ticket would've cost me at the last minute? I could've jeopardized my job."

"You don't have a job. Remember?"

"At that point, I did. So that's irrelevant," I replied.

She looked at the floor. "You wouldn't have come otherwise."

"There are other ways you could've gotten me here, you know. If you'd have just asked me—"

Daveigh's jaw fell. "Asked? So you could've come up with some petty excuse? There was no other way. I'm pretty sure using a horse tranquilizer on a person and putting a burlap sack over their head is considered kidnapping, which is still illegal in the US unless things have recently changed."

"And onto topic number three. I found out Mom didn't tell Finn about Tom. Were you in on that clusterfuck too, or did she drive the crazy train all by herself?"

She blinked rapidly. "What do you mean? Mommy said..."

"Yeah, well *Mommy* says a lot of things you can't cash in at the bank. All I know is he had no idea until I ambushed him on the phone." I paused. "But he sure as hell knows now."

"You had to be the one to tell him? Shit." Daveigh looked as if she'd had the wind knocked out of her as she leaned back against the tiled wall. "I had no idea. How did he take the—"

"How do you think he reacted? Not good. Think about this for a sec, 'Veigh. If you hadn't called me to tell me about what happened, do you think I'd be standing in a smelly bar bathroom having this conversation with you right now? Probably not. You'd be the only sibling attending the funeral."

"I can't believe she didn't tell him. Finn's his kid too." The little remaining color drained from her face and she covered her mouth, lunging for the bathroom stall, locking it behind her. "I think I'm going to be sick."

"Yeah, well it was a shock to me and made me nauseated as fuck too." I looked at my reflection and gathered my hair up into a messy bun, affixing it with the pen from my bag.

A hearty splash of vomit hit the toilet water, accompanied by a round of dry heaves.

I frowned. "I don't know whether I should confront her. Whether we should..."

"I think I need to be alone for a few minutes. To process."

I stared at the stall door, feeling alone and defeated. So much for being a team. "You don't want to talk about this? Mom's a raving lunatic who—"

"Go, Blue," she said. "I can't deal right now. Everything around here's been too much lately."

Too much? Was she serious? As much as I didn't want to admit it, Daveigh's fucked up relationship with Gonorrhea Guy...I mean Beanbag...I mean Wesley was more normal than the one I'd been in with Cash. If she only knew what I'd endured, she'd realize her problems were trivial in comparison.

She didn't even let me get to bullet point number four

and ask why she wasn't working as a barista at the coffee stand anymore. However, I knew better than to continue onward with bombarding her. It wouldn't help matters. I just hoped her hang-up didn't have anything to do with Rent-A-Cop Gene.

With slumped shoulders, I walked back out of the bar bathroom and let the door swing shut behind me without saying goodbye. It seemed like whichever way I turned, there was a road block to deter me. Every fucking family member was clammed up or screwed up. There was no in-between. Like a hamster in a habit trail, I continued hitting dead end after dead end.

Tired of thinking, I needed a break. Steele Falls was some weird parallel universe and things didn't make sense anymore. There was no new normal to achieve. Fuck. There was no old normal. In that moment, all I wanted to do was forget. Everything. Even if it were only temporary. And I was in the place to do it. I didn't need Daveigh. I didn't need Beanbag. I didn't need Cash. I didn't need Lucy. I could hang out with my good friend Jim Beam by myself. I didn't have a car to worry about. I could drive myself home by way of my own two feet. The answer was loud and clear as I looked to the left and saw my savior, Santi. Bring on the alcohol.

ten

I headed up to the bar with mixture of determination and anger fueling my pace. Lucy spotted me from the corner of her eye, but she continued talking to Beanbag in hushed tones. Every so often, she'd glance at me and then look away. Not at all subtle. I tried to read her lips, but couldn't make out what she said with her glass of wine nearly glued to her mouth like she was practicing for Santi's whistle. Giving myself a onceover, I made sure my ass wasn't hanging out of my pants and my boobs weren't on display. It was incredible. I'd known Lucy for less than twenty-four hours, and she was able to make me feel insecure about myself.

Santi was behind the counter, tightening the lid on a bottle of cheap vodka. He looked up at me with the same coy grin I recalled. "I remember you. You were the one here with Lucy last night. How are—"

"Yeah. Yeah. Yeah. Enough small talk," I replied. "I'll take a shot of Jim Beam."

He wiped the oak bar top in a circular motion with a white towel. "We're all out."

"Of course, you are." I smirked. *Could this day get any better?* "How the hell does a bar run out of JB?"

"The party in the banquet room has sucked us dry tonight. They're like fish back there. Another shipment doesn't arrive until tomorrow," he said.

"Cloud Nine then," I replied.

"Sorry, beautiful. All out of that too. I've got Bulls Eye, French Kiss, and," he glanced at the shelves behind him,

"Alejandro's."

I scrunched my nose. "No, thanks. I'm picky. How about an Orgasm instead, please?"

"Just one?" a nearby voice startled me. "I'm willing to bet I can bring you to a double or a triple, no problem."

I turned around and saw Zack sitting next to me, serious gray eyes observing my face, softened only by the curve of his flirtatious smile. A deep dimple appeared on each of his cheeks. That night, he wore a white linen button-up shirt and khaki pants.

I did nothing more than sigh to convey my mood.

"So, what's new, Trixie? I mean Blue." He took careful measure in squeezing the oversized lime slice into his gin and tonic while shielding me from being squirted.

"Not tonight." I downed my drink, not bothering to taste it before I turned my attention back toward the bartender. "Another please, Santi."

"Bad day?" Zack asked. "I mean, I already know how your morning went. Hopefully, you were able to get some relaxation downtown before coming to The Fill & Spill tonight."

I pursed my lips before I downed the second shooter with a grimace and full-body shudder.

"Slow down there, sunshine." He laughed as he grabbed for my miniature glass. "I'm all for feeling good, but we don't want you passed out on your face in a matter of minutes. Let the last one take hold before you dive into the next. When was the last time you ate?"

"Yesterday, I think," I replied. "I can't remember."

"Santi, order up this girl a grilled cheese and fries." Zack's attention turned back toward me again. "You'll thank me later. I can feel it."

"Yeah, well I have mixed drinks about feelings." I sighed. "Let's just say I'm ready to leave and go back to Sacramento. Tonight."

"That must've been one hell of a day. Do you want to talk about it? I'll keep you company."

Warning sirens went off in my head loudly. I fumbled for an excuse, my mind already reeling from the alcohol. Zack being in the same room screamed danger to me, and him being on the next barstool over made it even worse. Don't get me wrong. He was good looking. Scratch that. Most women wouldn't have turned down his advances to clink glasses and shake asses. But I knew his type, and I had zero interest in a hump and dump. Cash was a big enough mistake, and I wasn't looking for history to repeat itself.

"I...I can't. My friends are over there." I pointed in the direction of Daveigh's table. Calling them "friends" seemed like a long shot, and I didn't know if I'd be accepted if I walked back to where they sat. I'd shunned Beanbag, yelled at Lucy, and nearly stalked my sister in the bathroom. That whole "do unto others" thing was out the window. But they were the only viable escape I could conjure with two shots medicating my body on an empty belly.

"Tell you what. I'll join you over there for a few minutes," he nodded across the room, "but you should know I'm waiting for someone."

Someone! I felt a sense of relief. *Yes!* At least Zack had a date, so it'd keep him from trying to crawl into my pants. That alone made me feel a little bit better about having him around. I was reminded of the leggy blonde from Saturday night and assumed she'd walk through the door at any moment for her own turn at the bedroom rodeo with him. All that mattered was I wouldn't be drinking alone to become the latest Steele Falls gossip story.

Santi handed me my third shot and I stood up too fast, swaying as if I were on a boat in rocky waters. I took a moment to right my equilibrium with one hand braced on the edge of the bar. It wasn't enough to deter me though. I was on a mission. "Keep 'em coming, bartender."

I walked across the room with the glass in my hand, knowing I'd zigzagged horribly through the impossibly close tables. Trying to fake my sobriety was a fail. My feet somehow crossed and I stumbled, Zack catching me by the arm.

He reached for the shot in my hand that I'd barely salvaged, intense eyes surveying me. "You sure you want to keep up that pace?"

The temperature in the room skyrocketed as my pulse raced. "I know what I'm doing," I said, wrenching my arm away from him. "See? I didn't spill a drop. Call it drinking responsibly."

Zack opened his mouth to say something and then stopped himself.

Maybe it was the look on my face. Maybe it was the fact he didn't know how far he could push me. Maybe it was because we barely knew each other. Whatever the reason, he knew it was a line he shouldn't cross.

Drinking anyone else under the table wasn't my specialty, and it wasn't my intended goal that night. I was the classic definition of a lightweight. Alcohol always hit me hard and fast, especially shots. The perfect cheap date as Cash used to call me. You'd think I'd have been smarter considering I was still pissed off, but that night emotion trumped intelligence. And that meant drinking more of the big-O's was the clear winner. I stared at the seating arrangement. Daveigh was back. Zack was in tow. The group dynamic had altered drastically.

"Well, well, well," Lucy said with a sly grin as she arched an eyebrow. "Who do we have here?"

Zack set his drink down on the table. "Hey, Lucy. Care if we join you?"

"Not at all, Mr. Main." She winked. "What are you two up to tonight?"

I forced a smile and a nervous chuckle. Maybe the group setting wasn't such a good idea after all. "You know, stopped by for a drink before I go home...alone."

"Uh huh," Lucy replied with a knowing look as her eyes flicked toward Zack. "The best way is by whetting your whistle first, right?"

I didn't bother acknowledging her response verbally. The glower on my face should've been enough for her.

Zack pulled a chair out for me to sit down and followed suit as he straddled the seat next to me. My posture went rigid when I felt his left hand at the small of my back, warm fingertips stroking the two-inch gap of exposed skin between my shirt and the waist of my jeans.

"Wesley," Beanbag said, extending his hand to shake Zack's. "I've seen pictures of the houses you've redone across town. Some pretty epic shit."

"Thanks. With the risk of sounding like a conceited asshole, I think it's some pretty epic shit myself." Zack laughed.

"We've already met," Daveigh said. "At your Halloween party, last year."

"That's right!" He snapped his fingers and pointed at her. "You wore that provocative little she-devil number. And, if I remember, that guy you brought was dressed up like a ridiculous mall cop. Man, that getup he had on was over the top. If I'd have held a costume contest, he'd have won. No doubt."

"His wasn't a costume." Her face reddened as she fiddled with a lock of hair and looked down at the floor. "Gene came to the party straight from work."

The table tanked to silence.

"Okay then." Zack picked up on the discomfort and puffed out his cheeks. "My bad. Regardless, my condolences about your father."

"Thanks." She nursed her beer as Beanbag gave her a compassionate glance.

Santi swung by with a fresh round of drinks as he did a lap around our table. I'd finished my third shot and was ready to take on the fourth when the door to the bar opened. A couple stumbled inside, completely engrossed in their own laughter and hand-holding. They headed toward a pool table where three more people were motioning them over. A third person caught the door before it clicked shut and slipped inside. Suddenly, I felt like I needed a fifth and sixth shot. Maybe even a dozen after that.

The rest of the world went silent as I focused on the man who'd entered The Fill & Spill. He took off his rain-covered leather jacket and gave it a shake, droplets of water falling to the mat at the door. Zack whispered something to me, his lips tickling my earlobe. None of it registered with my brain though. Not a damn word. My heart was too busy cowering behind my spine while I watched Adam Rockwell.

He looked around the room and saw Zack, offering him a

single nod. Then his expression darkened when he saw me—a day and night difference. At that moment, I realized the person Zack waited for wasn't Ms. Endless Legs, after all. It was his buddy. How could I have not put that together as a possible scenario? *Stupid, Blue!*

Adam scanned the rest of the customers in the room and headed toward Santi up at the bar, a beer already waiting on the counter for him as he gave the bartender his order. It was a no brainer. He was trying to avoid me.

Zack stood up and gestured toward his friend. "Hey, Rockwell! Over here!"

Adam cringed as he glanced our way before looking around for a quick getaway. Reluctantly, he headed our direction with a drink in his hand. His gaze stumbled, lingering on me longer than anyone else's. "Hey, Zack. I came to...tell you I can't stay."

He frowned. "What are you talking about? You just got here, and you're holding a beer. We agreed to meet when you got off work."

"Yeah, well plans change," Adam replied. "I'm downing this before she," his eyes flicked toward where I sat, "has a chance to commit a second round of alcohol abuse against me, and then I'm heading home."

Zack lowered his voice. "You specifically said you needed a drink when you called me this afternoon. Figured something major went down at work today. Is everything all right?"

"It's...great. Couldn't be better." His voice cracked. "Had some unexpected news fall onto my lap. That's all."

"If it's your boss who's being a tool, fuck him. I told you I've got a position open when you're ready to make the move over to Main Enterprises," Zack said.

Adam let out a slow breath. "Look, I really don't need to bore anyone else with this. I'll figure it out on my own."

"The offer stands. I'll make it work," Zack pressed. "If it's the money, I'm positive I can meet or beat—"

"I know and thanks." He looked at his watch. "I should head out."

"See? He has to leave." Daveigh's tone was laced with

fake sadness. "Too bad. Maybe he can join us another time." She blinked rapidly and flashed him a forced smile.

Santi came by and growled seductively at Lucy before he fixated on me. "Do you want another Orgasm?"

Zack narrowed his eyes at the bartender. "Back off."

"Better make the next one a double," I replied quietly as I slunk down in my chair, wanting the unwanted level of testosterone in the room to nosedive. "Maybe a triple."

"You got it. I'll be remembered for giving you the biggest Orgasm you've ever had. Trust me, you won't know what hit you," Santi replied as he wove his way through the tables and back up to the bar.

Zack's hand worked its way around my back a few inches and I squirmed. When his fingertips greeted my ribcage, I jumped up and practically knocked my chair over. "I've got to pee," I squeaked. "Right now. I'll be back."

The bathroom was empty when I hurried inside. The music dwindled to a hushed whisper as the door shut behind me. Beautiful, pristine silence. I braced either side of the sink, my palms greeting the chipped porcelain. My reflection displayed an exhausted girl when I looked up. Dark waves of hair hung down to my shoulders, the tangled mess in disarray. Faded eyeliner had started to smear under my eyes, and I knew I'd look like a raccoon if I stuck around much longer. I, Blue Brennan, was a hot mess. It left me questioning why Zack's flirting was so over the top while I ran a paper towel under cold water and pressed it to the back of my neck. The alcohol and the uncomfortable situation were both competing for my attention. I was no longer sure which was in the lead.

A few minutes later, I staggered back to the table and plopped down. It was a weird combination of personalities between Daveigh, Beanbag, Lucy, Zack, and myself. But with Adam unexpectedly added to the mix? I didn't know what to think. Like a magnet, Zack's hand was affixed to my body again. Everything was too much, all at once.

"I need to leave," Adam and I spoke in unison as we both put our hands on the table and went to stand up. We locked eyes and froze. Thinking back, I'm not sure whether either of us were breathing anymore.

Zack grabbed my hand and squeezed. "Don't go." His attention turned to Adam and his tone firmed. "Sit down. We all know you have nothing better to do tonight but sulk about whatever bullshit happened at work. Have a few more drinks and forget about it." Zack clamped his palm down on Adam's shoulder until he sunk back onto the seat of his chair. "I'm sure your problem isn't going anywhere."

"You can say that again," Adam mumbled as he leaned back into his seat. "I guess I'm having another beer, Santi."

"See? You can deal with it tomorrow." Zack scooted his chair closer to me. "Now, chill. Maybe eat something. The special tonight is spaghetti."

Adam grimaced. "No, thanks. I can't stand Italian food."

"Hold on." I looked up at a flat screen television screen over the bar. The volume was off with only a series of subtitles to describe what was being said. But I didn't need sound to explain what I saw. Ornate marble pillars. Offensive lighting. Gorilla Gloria pretending to be studious behind the front desk. A news story panned the exterior of Jensen & Jensen and then the shot flipped to a side-by-side interview with Cash and Price. "Fuck me sideways," I muttered. *Where was Santi with the promise of an earthshattering Orgasm when I needed it?*

Lucy kicked me in the shin under the table. "Blue, isn't that where you work?"

"Worked." I grabbed Zack's drink and downed what was left in two massive gulps. "Past tense." I grimaced. "Ugh. How can you drink that shit? It tastes like I licked a Christmas tree."

The scrolling words on the screen conveyed they were being presented by one of the TV channels with an award for best plastic surgery suite in Sacramento. Price did most of the talking while Cash sat there, mostly smiling and nodding as he rode on Price's coattails.

"You didn't mention you don't work there anymore when we were talking last night," Lucy replied. "What happened?"

"It's a long story." I knew if I didn't rein it in, the alcohol would start talking on my behalf. And drunk Blue didn't know when to shut up. Remaining vague was key. Play it cool. "It didn't pan out. There were conflicts of interest with my boss."

"Who is he?" she asked. "One of those two?"

"Both. My direct was the one on the left." I nodded toward the screen as Santi slid another drink in front of me along with a grease-soaked sandwich and a large pile of overcooked French fries. The glass he'd presented me was far bigger than a shot glass. It was a snifter. "Cash Montgomery Jensen."

"That hottie was your boss? Aww, honey. I'd let him nip and tuck me anytime," Lucy moaned a sigh of approval. "Are you two on good terms? Maybe you can slip him my digits?"

"Have at it. He's nothing to write home about in the romance department. Believe me," I said under my breath, my speech starting to slur. I was too drunk to realize I'd taken it one step too far. "Damn. Where's Santi? I need another orgamasm...orgasmasm...another drink." *Why is that one word so difficult to say?*

"Sweetie, Santi already brought you one." Lucy slid the massive glass toward me a few inches. "Did you say you dated that guy?" She pointed to the screen. "Spill! Details!"

"He was my boss, Lucy. It's complicated." I closed one eye deep in thought before downing more of the drink than I should have. "Was complicated? That company wasn't good for me anymore."

Lucy flapped her hands frantically like a bird who was about to be fed a big, juicy worm. "Oh! Hold! Up! Is he the one who you know...made you all uptight in the pants and shit?"

"Sleep your way to the top often?" Adam offered his first tidbit toward the conversation, taking a slow drink from his beer. "Seems admirable."

"I don't know. Are you," I pointed at him and garbled, "always this ass of a much-hole? This much of an asshole?"

"Maybe I am. Guess you wouldn't know since you don't live in town," he replied, kicking his feet up on top of the table, crossing them at the ankles.

I carefully spoke. "Well, I'm surprised they even let you in here after you destroyed that window last night. Isn't that considered destruction of property? You could really, really, really use some anger management classes."

"Not that it's any of your business, but I settled up with the owner this morning. We work together. And none of that is interesting to anyone at the table, unlike you sleeping with pretty boy up there on the screen."

I rubbed my face, tired of being under the spotlight. "Okay! Enough about my dating life."

Lucy looked disappointed. "But—"

I cut her off, the snifter halfway to my mouth. "I said enough."

Everyone at the table fell silent.

"Anyone else want to open up about their baggage? Beanbag? Daveigh? Got anything you want to confess?" My sentences were a giant smear. With the way they'd acted in public, it was safe to say their relationship was still a secret.

Both of them were quiet as they looked away.

"Lucy? Zack? Wanna talk about the last time you two had sex together? Lucy, you had some pretty specific opinions about the experience. Care to share?"

"I...I," Lucy stuttered.

"You do, Luc?" Zack asked before his attention turned back toward me. "I mean, what's going on, Blue? Are you okay?"

"I'm fine," I said. "More than fine, actually. Why's everyone got a problem with me being shithammered? Hammerfaced? Whatever." I turned my attention toward Adam and tried to stop the world from swaying. "Why don't you tell us about your girlfriend? I mean, an angsty, brooding guy like you has to be a big catch around here." I balled my fists, my expression cold.

It was a low blow I'd likely regret later, and alcohol remained my liquid courage. But I was desperate to spin the tables and take the focus off myself. Adam happened to be next in the line of fire. Remembering that Lucy said his past was pained, made taking the dig a little easier. Hell, it made it a lot easier.

"I'm not seeing anyone, and I doubt anyone wants to hear about my exes." Adam sat up and placed his feet back on the floor. "My love life's a snore-fest."

"Oh, come on. I'll bet there are great stories in there

somewhere," I egged him on.

As if it were perfectly choreographed, the music lulled, and I swear, he growled at me.

"All right. Since you're so eager to know." He drank the rest of his beer without stopping, his stare menacing. "My last relationship? I fell for my best friend."

I gestured with my hand. "This ought to be good. Go on."

"It was the usual garbage. Fell in love. Planned a future together." He paused, looking as if he were lost in a memory. Suddenly, his tone changed, softening briefly. A flicker of emotion crossed his face, his angry mask threatening to falter. "God, I worshipped her."

"So, what happened? There has to be more to it than that." Lucy was on the edge of her seat, waiting for the perfect opportunity to pounce, like a cat stalking prey.

Wait. Why did I care? That's right. I didn't because Zack's hand had snaked its way to my stomach.

Adam composed himself. "Summed up? Don't get involved with someone you know. Never works out." A nervous chuckle escaped his lips. "Like I already told you guys, there's nothing to tell. Rest in peace," he said as he toasted the ceiling with his newly-refilled glass of beer.

"Oh, shit! She died?" Lucy exclaimed and scooted closer to Adam, rubbing his arm. "You poor, poor baby. That had to be so awful. If there's anything I can do...anything—"

"I didn't say 'she' died," Adam scooted a few inches away from her, "but the 'we' died, which is the same if you ask me."

"How fucking poetic." I rolled my eyes. "Relationships are simple. Black and white. If you ask me, they're about knowing when to hold on and when to let go."

"Well, no one asked you, boozehound." Adam eyed my glass.

"Who broke it off?" Lucy asked. "Was it amicable? Do you two still talk?"

"Doesn't matter. I moved on," he said.

Lucy sipped her wine. "So, the million-dollar question provoked by Alfred Lord Tennyson is, 'Tis it better to have loved and lost than never to have loved at all'?"

"Who knows? You have to learn some lessons the hard way. Real pain comes from clinging to a love that never existed." He shrugged. "All that's left are scars, proof that some wounds never heal. Fortunately, they go numb after a while."

"I'd be happy to nurse those wounds for you," Lucy said her lower lip on the verge of pouting. "I'm serious. Whatever I can do—"

"I'm done chasing ghosts." He deadpanned her. "Can we talk about something else? Some relationships aren't worth resurrecting."

Part of my heart broke as I realized Adam had one of his own. It may have been shriveled and black, but it was in there. Somewhere. In that moment, I could see it in his eyes. His tough, outer exterior had weakened a little. And in that, he'd became human to me. It was clear he hurt, and part of that was my fault. I'd dealt out some of that pain by revisiting his past.

Santi set my tab down on the table and I blinked back into reality. It neared two o'clock in the morning. Closing time. I'd lost count of how many Orgasms I'd had, including the mammoth one he'd last brought me. I feared the final price on the bill. Zack's hand had slid up to my inner thigh from my knee, and I wondered how long it'd been there.

The sobering moment reminded me of how drunk I'd gotten and the control I'd lost. The most recent Orgasm suddenly threatened to resurface and I dry heaved. Too much alcohol was in my system and not enough food. It was about to get messy. Fast. Glancing at the untouched sandwich with globs of congealed cheese, I was pushed over the edge. My hand clamped over my mouth and I stood up, shoving Zack away.

The world was fuzzy when I wove my way around the table. I gulped and managed to pull it together long enough to string a few sentences. "'Veigh, give Santi my debit card to pay. It's in my wallet."

"Sure," she said. "You okay?"

"Fine. Just gonna pull a Daveigh and go release a drink or five into The Fill & Spill bathroom. Standard Sunday night."

A second round of gagging took hold as my mouth salivated. Next stop, vomit-ville. Population: One. My hands began to sweat, and I wasn't sure if I'd make it. I raced for the bathroom, shoving my way through a crowd of people deep in conversation, blasting through the door for a second time that night.

I looked to the left. The first stall was open. Saving grace!

The same frizzy-haired woman with oversized glasses who'd been washing her hands before was back once again, hands covered in suds. She looked at me in the mirror and slumped her shoulders. "Really? Are we on the same pissing schedule or something?" she muttered.

"It's okay," I rushed by her. "You don't have to go this time."

"Gee, thanks."

I slammed the stall door behind me, the lock not taking hold as the door flung back open again. But it didn't matter if I had an audience. There was no time to spare.

Every Orgasm I'd had that night erupted and my stomach muscles cramped as the exorcism took hold. Four massive rounds of that abdominal workout are what it took for my body to calm down as I braced the sides of the toilet with a deadly grip, saliva trailing from my mouth to the toilet bowl. It was one of my finer moments. Slow deep breaths seemed to be working, keeping a repeat of the performance at bay.

A few minutes later, I convinced myself to leave the sanctuary of the stall and rinsed my mouth, taking a few moments to press another cool paper towel to the back of my neck. "Never again." I blew my nose and let out a long sigh with my head inches above the sink.

For the first time, I noticed the redheaded woman stood in the corner, leaning against a twenty-five-cent tampon machine. "You gonna be okay?" she asked.

"Yeah." I inhaled deeply. "Just a rough night."

"I couldn't tell." She glanced toward the bathroom stall and frowned. "They should retire that toilet after what you put it through."

"Well, everyone needs a talent they excel at."

"Can't drown your man troubles in alcohol forever, you know," she said as she fished around in her purse. "Here." She offered me a tin of breath mints. "You look like you could use one of these. In fact, take the whole thing. They'll help settle your stomach. What were you drinkin', anyway?"

"Thanks," I replied. "Orgasms." The bold flavor of spearmint was far better than regurgitated coffee, amaretto, and Irish cream.

She laughed heartily. "Don't you know nothin' about drinkin', honey? You never binge on anything that can curdle and—"

The word "curdle" made my mouth wrench as I thought about the sandwich on the table. "Look, I've got a lot of heavy shit going on right now, but I don't have man troubles."

"Uh huh," she replied. "Right."

Stupid stranger. I bit my lip and thought about Zack's wandering hands, Adam's snarky attitude, and Cash being too much of a cheese dick to fire me.

She shook her index finger at me. "No more Orgasms for you tonight. Otherwise, you're gonna regret it in the mornin'."

Considering Zack's persistent advances, that much was true in more ways than one. "Trust me, not happening. And thanks again for the mints." I nodded toward the tin.

"Get yourself some sleep." She patted me on the shoulder and paused at the exit of the bathroom. "I'd say you'll feel better after some sleep, but the hangover from what you drank probably won't be a pretty picture."

The door swung shut behind her.

A few minutes later, when I was confident I wouldn't encounter her on the way out, I headed back toward the table.

"You okay?" Daveigh asked. "You're all pasty and gross-looking. I think you broke some blood vessels on your face too. I could play connect the dots right up here on your cheeks and make—"

"Stop." I shooed her hand away and picked up my tote bag. "Better after barfing, but still not one hundred percent. Gonna go home and lie down."

"I used the card in your wallet to settle up your tab, and the receipt's in your purse. Forged your signature. By the way, you're a good tipper." Daveigh's voice competed against the latest song. A country line dance began up on the stage. It was Fill & Spill tradition and how they'd always closed down the bar on Sunday nights.

"Thanks." My heart sank at the thought of my dwindling bank account.

"We've got to head out too," Daveigh said. "I promised Lucy a ride home."

I'm not sure what prompted it. Being remorseful. Being drunk. Being a giant asshole by dredging up Adam's past. Maybe it was a recipe including all of those ingredients. Any way you looked at it, I was trying to be the bigger person by waving the white flag. With a deep breath, I walked around to the other side of the table and reached my hand out toward him.

"What are you doing?" He looked up at me, a confused look on his face.

"It's called a handshake. They're commonly used in greeting or to finalize an agreement." I paused. "I thought it could be a fresh start."

He stood up slowly and looked me over from head to toe. I could almost feel the unadulterated animosity he'd harbored for me buzzing in the air. It remained a constant, no matter how many glimpses of him I'd snuck throughout the evening. The sole exception was when he'd taken his stroll down memory lane.

He offered me one word, and he spoke it slowly as he shook his head left and right. "No."

I was left to stand there, feeling like an idiot with my hand outstretched, waiting for a handshake that wasn't going to happen. After a few more uncomfortable seconds, I allowed my hand to drop back down to my side.

It was only one silly syllable, but it wasn't what I expected. Hell, I didn't know what I wanted him to say. Acceptance would've been ideal. Part of me wanted to be absolved of everything that'd transpired. After how I'd acted, I didn't deserve it. At least I could say I tried.

Country music blared in the background as the crowd chanted for one more round of the song, but our table was as silent as a grave. Everyone stared with wide eyes while I wanted to disappear.

"Dude," Zack said quietly, "don't be a dick. She spilled a beer on you. She didn't kill your puppy. I know you had a shit day at work and all, but let it go. Be nice." His voice lowered, "I'm interested in this girl."

"Yeah, well 'this girl' shouldn't have been so reckless." Adam shrugged into his jacket and then his attention turned toward me. "It's been forgotten, but not forgiven. Don't expect that to change," he said. And I knew those words, carefully crafted in their specific order, were intended to hurt.

Eleven

"**C**ome on. I'll take you home," Zack said as we stepped outside and into the misty air.

Beanbag was already gone. I didn't blame him a damn bit. Everyone else from our table had scattered like ashes into the wind, and I'd been left with Zack and his wandering hands.

"I don't think a ride's necessary." I tripped over a crack on the sidewalk, barely catching my balance. "I can walk."

"Um. I think it is necessary. Not sure you'd make it the entire way back home by yourself, wobbles. And we don't need to find one of Steele Falls' finest passed out in a ditch tomorrow."

There was no arguing; he was right. Hesitantly, I followed Zack into the street, my stare lingering on Adam. Zack opened my door and helped me inside before he closed it gingerly. The interior smelled brand new, the leather shiny, and the floor mats pristine. But I barely paid attention to any of it. I was too busy watching Adam's figure shrinking as the distance between us increased while he headed toward the beach.

"I feel like I should apologize for him," Zack said.

I was a space cadet and didn't respond.

"He's not usually like that," Zack continued.

"Huh?" I blinked back to reality. "Who?"

"Adam. He's not a tool. Guy's been through a lot though, and he's not real big on sharing much of his past. But the little bits I've learned? Rough."

I clutched my tote bag tightly and watched him disappear over the hill.

A few minutes later, while listening to Zack ramble on about his latest business acquisitions and his soaring profit margins, he turned onto Poplar and parked alongside the curb. He turned off the headlights and killed the engine, pulling the keys from the ignition before placing them in his pocket. Getting out of the car would take me mere moments—even when blitzed. Shutting down the truck wasn't necessary and told me he was interested in something more. Red flag number one. Actually, it was closer to red flag number one hundred over the past couple of days.

Even though I revisited every drink I had that night, I was still drunk. Yet, I was sober enough to know Zack wouldn't be slithering into my bed. I wasn't sure whether he knew it or not. He got out of the truck and walked around to my side to open the door for me.

"So, chilvary...chivillarry... still isn't dead in Steele Falls?" I asked as I practically fell into his arms. So, maybe I couldn't walk after all.

"Chivalry." He caught me when I slid out of the truck, my knees buckling for a moment.

I looked up at him as he peered down at me, his right arm snaking around my torso once again. His frame was muscular and warm, his body pinning mine tightly against his. The scenario was already being steered in a direction I didn't want. Intoxicated me still didn't fully care. Fortunately, sober me could keep her in check. That bitch knew I needed to escape his embrace and fast.

And then it happened. An absurdly bright light turned on across the street that caught us both off guard.

"Jesus! What the hell?" Zack squinted, moving in front of me to act as a shield.

"Calm down. It's a motion light." And then I saw what he was talking about. A glint of something silver shone under the moonlight in the distance along with a silhouette. I wasn't panicked. Not a bit.

"That is *not* a motion light," Zack said. That's a fucking supernova."

I looked across the street and squinted. "It's just Ralph."

"Just Ralph. Got it."

The momster's neighbor stood at the edge of his driveway, wearing his brown bathrobe while spinning the handle of his hatchet. And that wasn't a euphemism. The man had a giant silver axe he toted around the neighborhood when he was out on walks. It was like carrying a Swiss Army knife on steroids. I guess I was still immune to his craziness, even after being gone for nearly two years.

"You two haven't met?" I asked. "He's lived here forever."

"Uhhh. No," Zack replied. "And I don't think I need to with that blade slung over his shoulder."

"He's harmless. Ralph is ...different," I said, searching for the right word.

"You could say that again," he replied. "Does he always stand outside in his bathrobe at two in the morning to blind people?"

"Pretty much. Nighttime. Daytime. He doesn't discriminate."

"Fucking bizarre," Zack replied.

I kept my voice low, about to release another story sober Blue wouldn't usually reveal. "Could be worse. A few years ago, he brought over a wheelbarrow with a dead animal in it and a giant grin on his face." I paused and thought about my words. "Ralph had the grin, not the animal. Anyway, the gunshot wound had blown half its face off. Said he wanted to show me what a coyote looked like, so I'd know what to look out for in the neighborhood. That was no coyote; it was a domestic dog. Honestly, I think it was Clarabelle's down the street. He skinned that sucker and dried the pelt out on the side of his house. The damn thing was tied down to the oven rack from his kitchen and propped up against the siding for three weeks."

Ralph loudly whistled the theme song to a horror flick while he paced the edge of his driveway.

Zack shifted his weight. "Maybe I shouldn't leave you here alone."

"I'll be fine." I turned and faced the street. "It's okay, Ralph!" I waved and glanced at Zack. "You, on the other hand, might want to watch yourself."

"You sure? I can stay, if you want."

Ralph spun the hatchet around faster with a scowl on his face, the silver of the blade flashing in the moonlight again as he stared Zack down.

"I'm good. Really," I reassured Zack.

Ralph pointed at his eyes with his index and middle finger, turning his hand to aim the same gesture at Zack before heading back toward his house. Darkness returned when he turned off his porch light.

"You should probably go," I said. "He's pretty protective for a neighbor. And he's gun happy...even though his aim sucks."

"And he's got a permit?"

"Ehhh...doubtful."

Once Zack was certain Ralph was out of view, his attention turned back toward me again with his inhibitions absent. "Where were we?"

"You were going home." I glanced toward his truck.

My momentary lapse in being alert was long enough for him to execute his next move. He lifted my chin with his curled index finger as he brushed my hair out of my face and leaned in, closing in on most of the remaining distance between us. "You know, I could stare at those eyes all night long and into the next morning."

Before my brain could process what was happening and I could protest, his lips captured mine. As his kiss demanded more with the soft tip of his tongue, all I could think about was Adam. Sweeping the dark hair out of his face with my fingers. Breaking down the anger behind his eyes. Somehow turning that scowl into a smile. Wondering what his lips tasted like. Zack did nothing for me. His warm hands cupped my face when I tried to back up, and I think he interpreted it as a game of playing hard to get.

His tongue probed at my lips again, and I pulled away more firmly. "I should go."

"You sure?" His tone was both velvet and edged with steel. "We could head back to my place."

The world swayed a little and so did my judgment. Damn

144

the alcohol. My mouth opened, but I bit my tongue. "No. I'm sure."

He stroked my cheek with his thumb. "Until Tuesday?"

Shit. I'd forgotten about the party. Whether I liked it or not, I was stuck seeing Zachary Main again. "Sure. Tuesday."

"Sweet dreams."

"'Night."

I watched Zack walk back to the driver side of his truck without breaking eye contact with me. My heart pounded in my chest, impatiently waiting until I saw him take off down the street. The tension released from my shoulders. *Finally!* I could breathe again.

Still on edge, I walked back to the mother-in-law house, showered off Fill & Spill stink, and got ready for bed while my ears rang. It could've been from the loud music, or it could've been from my brain's inability to shut down. I felt too sick to care about much that happened that night, but I had a feeling I'd have regrets the next day.

* * *

The following morning, I woke up with a monstrous headache and the fuzzy hint of dairy-tinged alcohol in my mouth. I smacked my lips and frowned. And then I remembered Zack. The aftertaste his kiss left in my mind was far worse than the alcohol I'd drank.

I rubbed my eyes. "Why, Blue?"

After a quick shower and beating myself up over every word from the prior night in my head, I got dressed in clothing deemed professional and headed toward the house. My mother stood in the kitchen, her figure distorted through the rain-covered window. I wasn't ready to deal with confronting her yet with my hangover in tow, so I started to walk down to The Lean, Mean, Coffee Bean for a post-drunken stupor remedy. For once, Ralph wasn't in sight as I took off down the street.

When I walked in the door of the café, I saw Zack sitting at a table for two, reading the sports page of the local newspaper.

My plan to sneak in and back out undetected went belly

up when he glimpsed me over the top of the sports section. "Hey, you."

"Don't you ever go home?" I asked, shuffling past him and toward the end of the line.

"I'm glad you're here." He stood up and trailed after me. "I need to talk to you."

"Great. Me too," I replied. Thank goodness. A weight had been taken off my shoulders. We were on the same page and could admit our kiss was a mistake. Better yet, we could move on with our lives, never to discuss it again.

"Listen, it's about the party tomorrow," he said.

Yes! Things were looking up, and he was about to break off our date! Maybe I wasn't cursed after all!

I breathed a sigh of relief. "Good. I'm really glad you brought it up. I shouldn't be going with—"

"I had to change the venue," he cut me off.

"Change the venue? Wait. I thought the party was to show off the remodel you'd done on your house."

"It was. And don't get me wrong. I was stoked to display all of the modifications I made since last year."

"But?"

"I had an unexpected visitor last night who stunk up my plans."

The only visitor I could think of might be Ms. Endless Legs. "So, why the change?"

"It's kind of embarrassing. One of the construction guys, who I employ, didn't cover up a hole in the crawl space before he left to go home. Long story short, a skunk got in the house and marked his territory. It's a foul mess in there. I'm not sure Steele Falls has enough tomato juice to help. Exterminator said it's an easy fix, but it'll take a few days. With the party being tomorrow? I don't have that kind of time on my hands."

"That does stink."

"Literally. It wasn't what I expected to go home to last night. That's for sure."

His tone left me wondering if it was a dig at me for not asking him to stay the night.

My defenses with him were raising like walls of a fortress.

But with his next statement, they were threatening to falter again.

"Anyway, you remember Adam, right?"

"Yes?" I squeaked, trying to keep my tone sound from sounding as unsure as possible.

"So, the party's going to be at his house. That guy's bailing me out big time here. He's pretty reclusive when it comes to anyone coming over, but it's too late for me to reschedule with the caterer."

I nodded and pretended to fix my hair.

Zack continued, "It'll be perfect though. On the beach. The weather should hold up before the storm rolls through in a couple of days. Plus, I told him it'd be mostly outdoors, so no one would track sand inside."

"So, Adam's house?"

"Is that an issue?" He furrowed his brow.

Was he fucking kidding? The last place I wanted to be was near where Adam Rockwell lived. I mean, I knew I had drunken visions of what it'd be like to kiss him the night before, but it was a moment of weakness. A lapse in judgment because of the alcohol. I was back to being sober. Straight and narrow. Besides, with my luck his place would be booby-trapped, I'd be thrown into some hole in the floor, and I'd never be seen again. "No, not a problem," I lied.

"Ahhhhh. I get it now." Zack nodded.

"Y...you do?"

"Sure. You don't know where he lives. Don't worry, I'll pick you up. It'll be great. We can go for a walk on the beach when the festivities die down."

Even Zack used the word "die" when he talked about Adam. If that wasn't foreshadowing, I didn't know what was.

"We can bring a blanket and a bottle of wine," he continued. "I know this romantic little spot."

"Yeah. Sounds great."

He looked at his watch. "It's getting late, and I've got to go. Work meeting. I'll see you tomorrow." With a quick peck on the cheek, he headed toward the door.

What happened, I wondered to myself. The kiss on the

cheek almost felt more personal than when his tongue tried to climb down my throat the night before. He paused near a mirror at the doorway and adjusted his tie.

Tie.

Ty.

Oh, no.

I glanced at the clock as I placed my order for ginger tea with a side of dry toast. My heart stuttered. "Shit!" I only had fifteen minutes to get across town for my meeting with Ty.

I hurried out the door and raced across town with a pounding headache, a hot cup of tea, glancing at my watch every thirty seconds, all while trying to find some way to slow time down. It was the epitome of multi-tasking.

* * *

Twelve minutes later, I scuttled up the pathway to Brennan Construction and took a fraction of a second to admire the massive building in my sweaty splendor. There were three minutes to spare until nine o'clock. When I'd left Steele Falls, the company was taking off, the main office a small portable. Times had changed though. My uncle's eye for detail and the risks he took with architectural design made him one of the most sought-after outfits in the area. His name was associated with a handful of celebrities, and I'd read a few articles in magazines about his jobs being in high demand.

I walked through the front doors and up to a Cherrywood reception desk where a redheaded woman talked on a cordless headset. Her name read 'Rita' in black bold font on a simple gold tag. She held up her index finger toward me as she continued her phone conversation. "No, Mr. Brennan is currently unavailable." A nod. "Yes, I'll tell him you called, and I'll send the email immediately." She pushed a button on her headset to end the call.

Looking up at me, she asked, "How can I help you?"

I rocked back on my heels. "I'm here to see Ty Brennan."

Rita clicked her tongue against the roof of her mouth as she tapped a "no soliciting" sign five times with the tip of an ink pen. "That's so cute, sweetie." Her expression was condescending. "We're not interested in buying your cookies. Why don't you try the gym across the street? Those ladies are always stuffing their faces in the parking lot before and after aerobics class."

"I'm twenty-three, and I'm not here to sell you anything," I replied, fighting the glare on my face.

Rita looked at me and folded her hands with a sugar-coated smile. "Well, I assure you we're not interested in your organized religion, whatever it may be."

"Well, I *assure you* I'm not interested in hearing your judgmental assumptions."

"Aren't you a little spitfire?" Rita huffed. "I'm certain Mr. Brennan is too busy for your funny business. Should I call security or can you find your way to the exit all by yourself like a big girl?"

"That's not necessary."

"Well, then shoo." Rita made a motion, dismissing me with her hand before she removed her headset.

I remained still.

"Look, his schedule is full this week. Maybe if you call back later today," she paused, skimming a calendar with a pointy red fingernail, "I can land you a five-minute meeting with him three weeks from Tuesday. He's a very busy man."

I leaned across the slick surface of the desk, bracing either side with my palms. "Tell him his niece is here," I whispered. "He'll know what it means."

"Niece?" Rita's face paled from freckled and rosy red to pallid white. "You're..." her voice trailed off.

"Blue Brennan? I am. Now, if you'd call Ty and tell him his bible-thumping macaroon-selling niece is here, I'd greatly appreciate it. If you're lucky, I'll say a prayer for you tonight while I'm brushing cookie crumbs off my pillow."

With shaky fingers, Rita jabbed a series of buttons on her phone. "Mr. Brennan?" her voice squeaked. "Blue is here to see you." A pause. "Yes, sir. I'll send her right up."

I crossed my arms. "Well?"

"Elevator bank, third floor, office at the end of the

corridor."

"Thanks." I turned and headed down the hall.

"Oh! And Ms. Brennan?" Rita called out after me.

I stopped and turned around.

"Can we keep this whole cookie religion conversation between us?" She batted her eyes.

"Of course. We'll keep it between the three of us."

"Three of us?" Rita looked confused.

"Sure thing. You, me, and the big guy upstairs." I pointed at the ceiling with my index finger. "I'll let you figure out whether I'm talking about Ty or God."

Rita's face blanched and her jaw dropped as I walked away.

The elevator was at the end of the hall, a current pop song playing softly in the background as the cabled box whirred, sending me upward. If anything, my uncle was trendy. No dated classical music was in earshot.

With clammy hands, I knocked three times.

"Come in," a deep, male voice said.

Be cool. Sell yourself.

I opened the door and saw my uncle on a phone call with his hand cupped over the speaker.

"I'll be a minute."

I walked in and surveyed my surroundings. It was comfortable, the polar opposite of Price's frigid office. Plush carpeting. Warm colors. Stylish artwork. Concrete walls. Rounded light fixtures. I sat down on an oversized bench chair and patiently waited for him to finish his phone call.

Thirty seconds later, the receiver met the cradle with a defining click.

"Blue!" Ty's face lit up once he'd exited work mode. Pushing back from his desk, he stood up and walked over, motioning for me to give him a hug. The smell of spicy cologne and black coffee was calming and lingered in his wake. I studied my uncle, who was a spitting image of my father, as I'd been told. Tall. Thin. Dark-colored hair, styled with a generous amount of gel. His white button-up shirt was crisp, accented with a blue tie and matching suspenders. A complementing jacket was draped over the back of his office chair that matched his trendy, denim slacks. All of it suited him. "How are things?" he asked.

"They're...okay."

"God, Tom just died." He shook his head. "I'm sorry. That was a stupid question and insensitive."

"No, really. It's all right," I assured him.

"I'm still floored you're here. In Steele Falls of all places. And my condolences to hear about why you're back. The circumstances of your visit suck."

Tom was a topic I didn't want to discuss, so I decided to be blunt. "I'm looking for a job." There they were—all of my cards laid out in a row.

His eyes lit up with a hint of laughter behind them. "You don't waste any time, do you? I like that."

My face reddened.

"So, does that mean you're coming back to Steele Falls permanently? That's great news for your—"

"No!" My exclamation was louder than I'd intended. "I mean, do you have any positions that can be handled remotely. Computer work? Personal assistant? Accounting? I'll take anything."

He looked thoughtful as he stroked the goatee on his chin. "What kind of experience do you have? Are you currently employed?"

"I...uhhh...got laid off." I averted my eyes. "Friday. Just a bad time of year, I guess."

"That's too bad. Where from?"

"A company called Jensen & Jensen."

"Hmmm. I know how rough layoffs can be in this industry. Haven't heard of Jensen & Jensen. Are they a big outfit?"

"You could say they're a big deal in...construction." In my eyes, it wasn't a total lie. I thought about Tony and his many penile procedures as I carefully formed my words. "They've done some unimaginable projects over the past few years and have experienced significant...growth. Definite trendsetters that don't like to be caught with their...pants down. Not afraid to take risks when things get...hard."

He leaned back in his chair. "What was your role within the company?"

"Paper pushing mostly. There were a few projects I worked on consistently outside the office." I thought back to my half-drawer at Cash's condo.

Office work for a plastic surgeon and for a construction company could translate easily. Yeah, even I wasn't convinced. I hoped my uncle wouldn't do a whole lot of digging behind who they were. Maybe since we were family, he'd take my word at face value, realize what a great addition I'd be to his company, and the rest would be history. Easy peasy!

"And you left on good terms without complications or issues? I can't stand office drama."

"I was told my letter of recommendation would arrive in the mail next week." I beamed.

He leaned back in his chair and templed his index fingers as he looked deep in thought. "I might have an idea for a trial run." He shook his head. "No. I can't. You're here for a funeral. Elana'd have my hide if she knew we were having this conversation right now. She may be my sister-in-law, well, ex-sister-in-law, sort of ex-sister-in-law...whatever we're calling her these days. Either way, she packs a wallop."

"Trust me, I know how she is, and nothing's changed there. I've been out of touch with everyone in the family for the most part." I sat up straighter and made a motion as if I were locking my lips. "She doesn't have to know we met today."

"Are you sure you're up to transition jobs so quickly? Don't you need some time to process? Standard bereavement leave is two weeks when it comes to immediate family passing away."

I thought about my step-father. Nothing felt immediate with him then and never had in the past. "Tom and I weren't tight. I can compartmentalize my emotions, and I can make this work. The situation going on back home isn't a dynamic of my capabilities."

"I do like that answer. But if you and Tom weren't close, then why are you here?" he asked. "In Steele Falls, I mean."

I opened my mouth and shut it twice while the question

resonated inside me. Part of me was starting to wonder the same damn thing myself. The money aspect was still relevant, but it felt more trivial the longer I stuck around. "I—"

He cut me off before I had time to invent another lie. "I'll tell you what. There's a job I've been mulling over for the past few months. Honestly, I wasn't sure who'd be suited to handle it internally, and I haven't made the time to work on it. But I'm willing to give you a shot if a few of the project managers agree you have the necessary experience."

I smiled, the tension melting out of my shoulders. "Thank you! You have no idea how much this means to me."

"Meet me here for a business dinner at five tonight. I'll drive over with you to meet with a couple of the people involved. If it's a good fit, we'll give it a shot. No promises until they weigh in though."

I clasped my hands together. "You won't regret this. I swear."

Little did I know, I would be the one doing the regretting.

twelve

I practically skipped on my way back to the house. If I wasn't hungover, maybe a cartwheel or two would've been possible. The past few days' worth of crap had almost been forgotten, and then my phone rang. An unknown local number flashed on the screen. I clicked the green button. "Hello?"

"Blue? Blue Brennan?" a raspy voice asked.

I stopped on the sidewalk. "Yes, that's me."

"This is Eddie Miller...from Fast Eddie's. You forgot to give me your number before you skedaddled out of here on Friday, but I found it scribbled on some paperwork in your glove compartment. I'm a regular gumshoe!"

"Eddie!" My euphoria from the meeting with Ty still hadn't subsided, so I didn't even bring up the topic he was a few days late in contacting me. "How are you?"

"I'm good." He paused. "A lot better than your car."

Suddenly, my cloud nine mood plummeted and my feet were firmly planted back on the ground as I trudged up the porch to the house. Words like overhaul, lemon, and cracked cylinder were what stuck out most from our conversation. And the price to have it fixed left me reeling. If I didn't know better, dollar signs were spinning behind my eyes like a slot machine refusing to pay out. It was far more than I'd expected, and it'd likely have been more cost-effective to buy a new car. But I didn't have an established job for the financing.

After telling Eddie I needed to think about what I wanted him to do, I opened the front door with a heavy heart. Praying the day would look up, I locked it behind me and hoped for a few minutes alone.

My wish was short-lived.

"Blue, come to the kitchen. Now," my mother's voice sounded through the house, and it sliced the air like a hot knife through butter.

I walked down the hall, my mood already soured from the talk with Eddie. Listening to whatever bullshit Elana was about to unload on me left me on the verge of snapping. "What? I haven't written anything for the funeral yet, and I don't need to be chastised for it."

Her eyes were cold and emotionless, but the redness spanning her cheeks and her folded arms told another story. A total paradox. It was poker face, level expert.

In turn, I crossed my arms. Mockery was certain to make the situation better. Okay, maybe not.

"Care to tell me what the hell is going on around here?" Her entire body shook with rage.

"What are you up in arms about now?" I asked. "I've done what you wanted and stayed out of your hair. Just like old times."

"Are you trying to destroy my chances at being re-elected?" Her upper lip twitched as she spoke. "Would that make you happy?"

"No?" My unintended lilt formed the response into a question.

"When were you going to tell me? Did you think you'd be able to hide it forever? What you've gone and done is a big deal, missy."

Oh, no. She'd broken out the M-word. Shit was about to get real. "Find. Out. What? Why do people around here have to act so fucking cryptic about everything?" I asked through bared teeth, my voice rising and my tone hardening. "It's like one of those artsy movies. Everyone watches and pretends to get it, but no one really understands what's happening."

She walked over to the counter and yanked opened a drawer, the contents all sliding to the front from the force. Rifling through the junk, she slammed items on the counter. Tape measure. Ball of string. Stapler. Old cell phone charger.

All of them seemed pretty common for a crap drawer. Finally, she gripped a white stick and thrust it in my direction. That was the mystery item that didn't belong. "Here. Since you think I'm stupid."

"Are we playing board games now? Was it Elana Meyers in the kitchen with a white piece of plastic?" I asked.

"Take it." She waved it my direction and forced it into my hand. "You know damn well what that is. You two bonded with a golden shower not too long ago."

I looked down at the object resting against my palm. My brain told me it was one thing, but my eyes refused to acknowledge it. A square window was on one end with a prominent plus sign on it. The other showed a bright blue company logo fading into hot pink that read, "Possibly Pregnant?"

Fuck. My. Life.

I tried to hide my shock, but my own poker face had been rusty since arriving in Steele Falls. "I don't know what you're so upset about." I offered it back to her. "It's not mine."

"If it's not yours, who does it belong to? Finn isn't here, and I doubt he'd even know what to do with a..." She scrunched her eyes shut for a moment before continuing. "Daveigh isn't dumb enough to get herself knocked up and leave the evidence in the garbage can. So, that leaves—"

"Wait, did you call me dumb..." My eyes flicked up at my mom and I could see Daveigh, who'd entered the room sometime during the conversation. She stared at me from behind Elana with tears welling in her eyes. Lower lip trembling, my little sister silently mouthed the word, "Please?"

If there were ever a time in my life to protect Daveigh, it was then. I shut my eyes and remained quiet while every curse word in the book flitted through my mind.

Damn it.

"Okay, you're right. I'm pregnant." I smacked the countertop with my hand. "And I did it out of spite so I could ruin your chances at winning the election. That's all I could think about the entire time he fucked me six ways to Sunday. Happy now?"

"Hardly. And you can drop your load of sarcasm at the door. Since someone else has already dropped theirs in your vagina." She narrowed her eyes. "Who's the father?"

The father. Double shit. I had no baby daddy lined up for the story's next chapter.

"It's no one you know," I lied, fumbling for a name. The next sentence flew out of my mouth faster than one of Cash's cock sneezes. "He's a plastic surgeon." *Really, Blue? You couldn't do better than Cash?*

"Great. Not even a 'real doctor'." She used air quotes as she let her hands fall, her palms slapping her outer thighs. "How could you be so stupid? The media—"

"He went to medical school for eight years. Cash is a real doctor."

"Blue, plastic surgeons don't save lives. They inject with Botox and suck fat off asses. They sculpt noses and make people into who they aren't. That's hardly worth commending with a degree, let alone a paycheck."

"And being a politician is worthy of applause?" I never thought I'd see the day where I'd be defending Cash, but there I stood. I glanced toward the window to check the weather. Maybe hell had frozen over.

She bumped the drawer closed with her hip. "So, when's the wedding?"

Hold up, home slice! Marriage? My eyes bulged. Why did the conversation have to take a detour out in left field? "No to a wedding, Mom. We broke up." Okay, so there was some truth.

Her jaw dropped. "So, you're going to do what exactly? Raise this child alone? On your salary?"

"By the way, it gets better," I lowered my voice to a whisper and narrowed my eyes. "Not only did I get laid, but I got laid off."

She rubbed her temples with her fingertips. "Oh, for the love of everything Holy. I'm going to have to up my blood pressure medication over this."

"A wedding doesn't solve problems. You should know that from when you married that fuckwad father of mine. The only reason you did it was because you were knocked up with me!"

I'd pushed the envelope.

Her teeth bared. I watched her choke on the toxic words she wanted to spew at me. I wasn't certain why she didn't follow through.

"What? You don't think I can do it on my own? I'll figure things out." For a moment, I almost wanted to take it on as a personal challenge to prove her wrong. I'd forgotten I wasn't actually pregnant.

"I don't think you understand how much work it takes to raise a kid," she said. "You lose sleep, you lose freedom, you lose—"

I couldn't help but laugh. "Are you shitting me right now?"

"Blue." Daveigh touched my arm. "Don't."

I couldn't hold back. It was the straw that broke the pseudo-pregnant woman's back. "For all the times you were too busy with the election to handle your own children? I may have well as been Daveigh and Finn's parent." I began counting tasks off on my fingers. "I did the cooking, the cleaning, helped with their homework before I did my own. I tucked them in and read them bedtime stories every damn night! What did you do? That's right. Came home late at night after campaign meetings and went to bed, only to do the same damn thing the next damn day. Wash. Rinse. Repeat. It was as if we didn't even exist."

She gripped the top of a dining room chair, her knuckles whitening.

Daveigh pleaded. "Let it go."

"No, 'Veigh. I've bit my tongue for too long." I turned my attention from my sister back to my mother. "If you spent half the time worrying about your kids as you do about how the media portrays you, maybe we wouldn't be such a fucking dysfunctional family. You were a wife and a parent to nothing but your political status."

She recoiled, as if I'd shot her in the chest, and it was the biggest stance I'd ever taken against her.

"Look at us, Mom. Take a good look around. Do you know

of any other family who goes through what we did growing up?" I stood my ground and awaited her response. Waited for the pain. Waited for the anger. It had to come at some point.

But it didn't. Poker face remained engaged.

Something ticked inside me at that very second. It was a mirror effect, and I hated that it took an altercation with my mother to learn something about myself. In our heated words, I understood that I'd become her. Over the past two years, I'd learned how to bury my feelings. Being absent from all of it numbed the pain that I fought so hard to evade. I didn't know how to deal with any of it now that I was back. All I could do was deflect.

"What's it gonna take to get some emotion out of you?" I yelled.

She still didn't acknowledge a word of what I said. She merely swallowed, straightened out her blouse, and then stilled. "The plans for the funeral have changed. You're to read a scripture verse. I don't need some pregnant, hormonal, twenty-something year old bumbling her way through a speech I haven't approved. And don't go advertising this error you made to the town. I still have to figure out a way put a positive spin on it."

"Well, Elana, it'll make you happy to know I'll be leaving in a couple of days, so you'll never have to worry about this baby." I cradled my abdomen. "But I'm pretty sure the town of Steele Falls doesn't give a rip whether the mayor's daughter is pregnant. Enjoy not knowing your grandchild."

The corners of her mouth drooped farther into a frown before she went to speak, but I didn't care about what she had to say.

"Trust me. I've got this just fine on my own." I cut her off and headed toward the door, narrowing my eyes at Daveigh. My voice rumbled through my chest, "You owe me. More than you've ever owed me in your entire life."

The look on her face was filled with a mixture of thirty-five percent panic, thirty-five percent regret, and thirty percent indecision.

I slammed the front door behind me, letting the screen

door slap shut as an echo. How the hell was I going to get myself out of my situation? I had no clue.

I sat down on the porch swing and pushed back, locking my knees to brace the seat in place. Anger pulsed in my veins, and I didn't even feel the cold as it whipped through my sweater. A few minutes later, Daveigh closed the door quietly behind her.

My little sister stood in front of me, looking guilty as hell.

"Well, I could really use a drink right now, which seems to be the common theme to this visit," I said. "But I'm pretty sure the eyes and ears of the town will turn me in to the momster police if I make one wrong move with an imaginary baby hiding in my uterus. So, thanks for that," I said.

Daveigh remained silent as she shifted her weight.

I looked up at her and cocked my head to the side. "Talk to me. Tell me what's going on. I'm your sister."

"Just because you're my sister, doesn't mean you're my friend," she mumbled.

"What happened to us? We used to tell each other everything. Pregnant? That's a huge secret to keep hidden."

"Everything changed when you left. It was so different." Her voice hitched. "Where were you when I needed you?"

"'Veigh...'"

"Damn it, Blue. Don't give me that look, like I failed you. I'm pregnant; I didn't commit a crime I need to fess up about. I'm sorry I got you involved in all this." She blotted her eyes with a tissue. "I peed on a dozen sticks before I believed it was true. Trust me, I bought every last one the dollar store had. The one Mommy found had fallen behind the vanity, and I didn't notice it when I took the others to the dumpster behind the coffee stand last week. I thought I buried it deep enough in the bathroom trash. Didn't know she examined every fucking wad of dryer lint and piece of dental floss before she took it out."

"Why didn't you tell me on the phone Friday?" I asked.

She let a laugh out through her nose. "Do you really think you'd have come to Steele Falls if you knew beforehand? Be honest. It wouldn't have swayed your decision a damn bit."

I tried to answer her, and I thought about flinging her

comment back about the horse tranquilizers she'd made earlier, but I genuinely didn't know what to say. Would I have come to support my sister or would I have chalked it up to more of her hysterics and swept it all under the rug?

My voice was timid, "I don't know what I would've done."

"Kinda what I expected you to say," she replied before blowing a wisp of hair out of her face.

I leaned back farther into the porch swing before lifting my feet. "Who's the father?"

"Who do you think?"

My eyes widened. "Please tell me you didn't go back for one last pump and dump with Gene. Is there going to be a mini Rent-A-Cop running around here in a handful of months?" I wrinkled my nose.

"It's not Gene's."

"Bean...Wesley?" I asked.

She nodded.

"I guess you guys are more serious than I thought. How far along?" I asked.

"A couple of months. First ultrasound was last week." She lifted her shirt to expose the nearly non-existent swell of her belly above her unbuttoned jeans. "I'm so bloated, I can't wear any of my cute stuff. My pants don't fit. I can't color my hair. Food makes me wanna barf. Whoever said it got it wrong. Pregnant life blows. It doesn't glow."

"Is that," I glanced down at her stomach, "why you quit working at the coffee stand?"

"No one will want to see this in the coming months." She motioned to her frame. "Well, I take that back. There are a few creeps who want to see a pregnant chick in a G-string and pasties, but they gross me out. I mean, Cindi did it and worked right up until her water broke. Made a shit ton of tips too. So gross." She sat down next to me on the porch swing. "There's no way I'm serving drinks with tiger stripes that look like a road map across my stomach and thighs."

Serving drinks. A light clicked on in my head and my eyes bulged. "And you had alcohol the other night at The Fill & Spill? And last night too?" I flicked her ear. "What were you thinking?"

She held up a hand to shield herself from me. "I didn't drink."

"Um. So, was it your body double holding that beer when you came back from talking on the phone?"

"It was apple juice. I'm not stupid, Blue. But I'm not ready to tell anyone about this yet, so I'm doing everything I can to hide it. Mommy especially needs to be kept in the dark. With the whole funeral thing? The whole politics thing?"

I looked at my sister and pitied her. What should've been an exciting series of moments in her life was being made into a time of shame and regret. She needed someone to lean against. A rock. There was no doubt Beanbag was taking on that role, but I could tell she ached for another female to be involved and sympathize with her. It sure as hell wasn't going to be Elana considering what went down in the house. How would she take it when she found out it was really her golden child? I didn't envy Daveigh one bit.

"So, what happens now? You stay with Beanbag?"

"Yes. Maybe. I don't know. He's keeps bringing up a wedding. I mean, he's the most loyal guy I've ever been with. But that's not a reason to get married. And what if he's better off without me?"

"That's the hormones talking. I've known that guy for a long time, longer than you have. He doesn't take that kind of stuff lightly."

"And what if he leaves like your dad left Mommy? And like you left us? That'd destroy me, Blue. I don't want to become..." She glanced toward the house. Tears welled in her eyes as she looked at me for guidance. "Maybe being alone is best, and I can save myself the pain by ending it now. What do you think?"

Her fears struck home with me in so many ways, even though our situations were worlds apart. She wanted my opinion. In turn, I wanted to shake some sense into her. I wanted to hug her and say everything would be okay. I wanted to reveal my own secrets for her to relate to. So damn bad. But I was terrified and couldn't bring myself to do it. All I could do was ask her the one question I was too afraid to ask myself because it would break me. "How does he make you feel?"

Without hesitation, she sniffled. "I love him."

"And what about the baby?"

"I dunno. He's excited. It's so annoying; he helicopters around me like I'm made of glass and I'm going to shatter if someone looks at me wrong. That's why we've been arguing. The secretive phone calls. And add Mommy's attitude on top of it all..."

I let out a slow breath through my nose. "'Veigh, you're an adult. You don't need the momster's permission to give birth. You don't even live under her roof anymore. I'll tell you what though—you need to tell her the truth. Before she finds out on her own. She'll figure it out when I'm baby-free in a handful of months and you're the size of a house."

"I know," she said. "I just wish...everything was different."

I wrapped my arm around her as she rested her head on my shoulder. "You and me both, kid."

Like every other day in Steele Falls, that one contained elements I couldn't have predicted. For a few hours, I sat there and held my little sister while neither of us spoke a word. Our silence was the most honest conversation we'd had since I'd arrived.

* * *

Later that afternoon, I ransacked my closet, pulling out a black-and-red floral maxi skirt that grazed the floor and a fitted black camisole. Strappy sandals and a sheer kimono with crimson accents completed the look. I freshened up my makeup, a rarity in my world, and tamed my mess of curls.

Fortunately, the house was empty when I was ready to head over to Brennan Construction, which meant no further reprimand from the momster. Lucy had picked up Daveigh for dinner twenty minutes prior, and my sister was kind enough to let me borrow her car for the night.

The drive was quick, and the closer I got, the more my stomach tied itself in complicated knots. I pulled up five minutes early and wiped my sweaty palms on my skirt before heading inside. The lobby was quiet, Rita, the nosy receptionist, had already left for the day.

Ty was walking by the front desk at a brisk pace with a couple of file folders as I headed toward the waiting area. "Hey, Blue. I'll be with you in a few minutes. Last minute fire to put out. Not literally, thank goodness." He thumbed halfway through the papers. "Go down the hall to the break room and I'll meet you in there. Second door on the left. Bottled water's in the fridge and the coffee's still on. No guarantees it isn't mud though."

I headed down the quiet hallway, plush carpet underfoot. The music was absent, and the lights buzzed overhead. The break room was empty. I grabbed a miniature bottle of water from the fridge, cracking the lid as I absentmindedly looked at the bulletin board of notices. State laws, minimum wage posters, a suggestion box with a half-used tablet of paper, and a whiteboard of sketches caught my eye.

I wasn't paying attention when someone walked in behind me. "Are you fucking kidding me?" the voice was masculine and annoyed.

Slowly, I turned around and saw the face I was hoping to never encounter again.

"Adam Rockwell," I replied. "What are you doing here?"

He looked down at his dust-coated tee-shirt and mud-stained jeans. "Well, if I don't work here, it'd be weird to walk in looking like this."

"Sarcastic much?"

"What? Sorry. Can't hear you." Adam cupped his hands under the running faucet at the stainless sink and splashed water on his face.

I leaned against the fridge. "It's like you're stalking me or something."

"You're the one who walked in here. And now you have a problem with where I work? Is there a secret list of Blue-approved companies I should know about? Please, tell me where I can buy a copy for my bookshelf."

I gritted my teeth. "It's my uncle's company, and you know it. The last name is a dead giveaway."

"A lot doesn't get past you, does it?" he asked. "So, what's the issue, blue eyes?"

"Don't you see the irony? And don't call me that."

Crystal clear droplets dripped from Adam's chin and stubble, distracting me. He offered another hate-filled stare that he'd become an expert at. "Please. Explain the issue and tell me how it's ironic."

An elongated silence filled the air as both of us refused to back down. Where? Where was my uncle and why was it taking him so long to come back?

"The issue is," I paused, "you're working in construction. The way you act, it seems like destruction is more your speed."

"Are you talking about what happened at the bar? If memory serves right, *you're* the one who spilled the beer on *me*, and *you're* also the one who went digging up *my* past. Forgiving you isn't a requirement of your sad attempt at a truce."

I glared at him.

"And not that you give two shits about it, but a lot of companies aren't willing to take a chance on a guy like me who—"

Just then, the door opened and Ty walked back into the room. "Great! I see you two have met. There's some good news and some bad news. Blue Brennan, this is my project lead, Adam Rockwell. Adam, this is my niece, Blue. She might be coming to work for Brennan Construction."

"Project...lead?" I felt the color drain from my face.

Adam's eyes looked as if they'd pop out of his head. "Her? Work here?"

Fabulous.

"From afar. Working from way afar," I corrected Ty.

"This is a hands-on and high-pressure company. Reliability is important," Adam said. "Remote positions rarely work out. What makes you think you can handle it from miles away? Would you remain in contact on a consistent basis or would you slack off and disappear before your shift ends?"

"Guys." Ty looked at each of us as if he were watching a tennis match. "I said I had good and bad news."

I let out a deep breath, not knowing what could possibly

be worse. The plague? Growing a third eye? Finding out Santa wasn't real? "And the bad news?"

His attention turned toward Adam. "The bad news is I had an issue come up with that Gervais strip mall I've been working on. It means I'll be about an hour late, but the good news is I'm sending you two over to The Oasis to get started. Discuss the project and see if it's of interest to Blue. Tell Lyle to put it on my tab."

Adam's face blanched as he stumbled over his words. "What about Stephan? Shouldn't he be there? His input would be far more—"

"Sonia has the stomach flu, and they have six-week old twins. You two can wing it until I get there. Like I said, it shouldn't be more than an hour."

I let out a long, audible breath and pursed my lips. Being alone in a restaurant with a guy who looked like he wanted to destroy me with every fiber of his being sounded less than appealing.

"I guess we don't have any choice," I mumbled. "Let's go get this over with."

"Finally. Something we can agree on." Adam grabbed his jacket off a coat hook on the back of the door.

I reluctantly followed him toward the door.

Adam stopped abruptly. "Hey, Ty?"

My uncle turned around. "What's up?"

"Why don't we go to Mario's instead? It's right down the street from the office. Besides, the wait time at The Oasis is always about two years long. It makes more sense."

I clutched the strap to my tote bag tightly. "I don't think—"

"You don't think what?" Adam asked.

"I don't think the setting is suited for a business dinner. That's all." I huffed.

"Well, I think it's a great idea," Ty replied, pulling his cell phone from his pocket to answer a call.

"I'm sure you have GPS and can find the restaurant on your own." Adam smirked and headed toward the exit. "See you there, Blue."

I closed my eyes, trying to maintain my composure.

* * *

Mario's was a five-minute drive from Ty's office, and I beat Adam there. I sat in Daveigh's car for a few minutes and chewed my lip before mustering enough bravery to get out and lock the door.

"It's one dinner," I whispered to myself as I wiped my hands on my skirt.

Memories flitted through my mind as I walked across the parking lot. The same gravel-coated pavement with faded stall lines and giant street lamps. The same quiet street and giant bushes surrounded the small building. The same distant crash of the ocean waves.

As I approached the entrance, Adam appeared from around the side of the building where overflow parking spaces were located. He didn't acknowledge my presence as he walked ten feet behind me.

My nostalgia of the restaurant didn't go unnoticed, and I was sure every contradicting emotion I felt was spelled out on my face in bold Sharpie marker. I tugged on the brass door handle; it felt heavier than I remembered. A significant click gave way when I pulled harder. The wave of warmth that washed over me used to be inviting and comforting during my eight-hour shifts. It'd morphed to crushing and debilitating.

I could've drawn the layout from memory down to the minor details. Faded brickwork surrounded the tunnel-shaped hallway from the entrance to the hosting station. The smell of garlic, olive oil, and fresh bread filled the air, bringing back unwanted flickers of the past. I swallowed down the lump in my throat.

A wicker basket sat in the corner, displaying a graveyard of lost children's toys. Each was heavily worn from love while they waited for their devastated owner to come back. I immediately recognized a floppy rabbit on the left; it'd been in the same spot since my last trip to Mario's.

Antiquated license plates had been made into artwork. Their age was showcased with rusty edges while a row of vintage soda bottles jutted against the lip of a counter. Red-

and-white labels were each staged perfectly, facing forward. Strings of garlic and dried chili peppers adorned the vertical support beams, giving distraction from their flaky, green paint. All of the pieces were present, completing a jigsaw puzzle of my past. It was like I'd never quit working there, reiterating time had stopped.

A young waitress walked around the corner with a bounce in her step and vibrant pink streaks in her pale blonde hair. She wore jeans and a baseball t-shirt. I wondered if the tops were still as scratchy as I remembered. Her nametag read Lyndsie in simple red font on a white background. "Two tonight?" she asked with a southern accent.

"For now, y...yes," I said, my voice hoarse as I took in more of the surroundings.

"Y'all want a table or booth?" she asked.

"Booth," Adam replied without hesitation.

For a moment, I'd forgotten he was there.

Lyndsie led us to a booth along a wall where fake vines of pale ivy clung to the brick, intertwining their way along the top of a makeshift cable car. Tiny lights twinkled along the top in red-and-green, their hues enriched against the dark ceiling. Chandeliers with checkered maroon-and-cream-colored glass hung from above.

"Is this okay?" Lyndsie asked.

"It's fine," I mumbled under my breath.

"Actually," Adam nodded toward the next booth down, "could we sit there?"

Lyndsie gave him a questioning look.

"Lighting's better." Adam flashed me a fake smile and gestured to a file folder in his hand. "Work meeting."

"Well, of course." Lyndsie nodded. With one swoop, she gathered the menus and moved them to the next table over along with a pitcher of water before disappearing into the kitchen.

I stood, frozen. "Are you kidding me right now?"

Adam sat down on the worn cushion of the bench-style seating. "If I'm joking, Lyndsie's not going to be very happy about the whole table switch thing. Is this a problem for you?"

"Nope." I ground my teeth and threw my bag down on the seat.

Adam's smile was smug.

"Of all the restaurants in town, why so fucking persistent about Mario's?" I shivered and sank against the bench across from him, the familiar ambience doing little to console me.

"Why wouldn't I suggest my favorite restaurant? I have dinner here. Every Tuesday."

"Every Tuesday." I sighed, elongating both words. "Don't lie to me, Adam."

"You seem standoffish. Do you not trust me?" He took a swig of water from a cheap plastic cup, a ring of condensation left behind on the table. "I'm not lying."

"You hate Italian food. You made it blatantly clear at the bar last night," I replied.

"I didn't say I came here for the food."

Knots tightened in my stomach, my appetite gone. "Then, I don't get it."

"Call it punishment," he muttered, his focus turning to the faded menu.

"So, you come here, a restaurant that exclusively serves Italian food, because you don't like fettuccine and manicotti? Makes total sense."

His eyes locked with mine. "No, Blue. I come here for the memories."

Shit.

I felt the corners of my mouth droop as silence took a firm hold at our table.

Soft country music played in the background and it didn't fit the mood. At all. Something angry and intense, like heavy metal, felt more appropriate.

"Maybe I shouldn't be doing this," I said, pushing the napkin-wrapped silverware setting away from me. "Dinner. It was a mistake."

Lyndsie had suddenly appeared again, interrupting us. "Can I get y'all some drinks?"

From where she stood, I was trapped between her and the wall. My only escape route was under or over the table.

Both would cause a scene and neither seemed like a good idea. It left one fact remaining. A single dinner with Adam was a situation I'd need to endure. "Just the water," I replied.

"Cola, please." Adam said. "Oh, and can I get some crayons?"

"Sure...thing." Lyndsie shook her head slowly as she walked away.

Awkward silence was quickly trumping words.

"So, do you want to talk about the details of the job?" My eyes flicked down toward the folder on the table.

"Not yet," Adam replied. "Be patient, blue eyes. I want to order first."

I drummed my index finger on the table and let out a deep breath. "I asked you to not call me that." There was no denying it'd be a long evening.

A few minutes later Lyndsie returned with our drinks. "Would y'all like to hear our dinner special?"

"No," I said as Adam interjected simultaneously, negating my answer.

"Would you quit prolonging this?" I glared at him.

"Come on. I'd love to hear about the amazing special this place has to offer." Adam leaned back and stretched out his arms on either side of him, resting his elbows on the top of the shoulder-high bench cushion, his hands left dangling, relaxed. "We owe it to Mario's best waitress here."

"Ummm...well," Lyndsie shifted her weight, uncomfortable, "we've got a seasonal pumpkin pasta with fennel, sausage, and toasted hazelnuts. It's pretty rad."

"That sounds interesting." Adam adjusted his posture and folded his hands before flashing me a glance. "Now, what would you say about the mood of the pumpkin when you were in the kitchen?"

"The mood?" She blinked with confusion.

"Yeah, the mood. Does it look trustworthy? It's not one of those white, ghost pumpkins that might disappear when you're least expecting it to, is it?"

"I don't know?" Lyndsie furrowed her brow. "It's a squash."

"Would you stop!" I snapped. "You're embarrassing me."

"What? I want to make sure I can expect my dinner won't take off on me. It's a valid question."

It was my breaking point, and I'd had enough. I wasn't proud of that moment, but I decided to stoop to Adam's level. Our poor waitress would be the victim. "Speaking of trust, how's the lasagna, Lyndsie? It's supposed to be a comfort food, right?"

"I guess?" Lyndsie said.

"Would you say it's consoling?" I narrowed my eyes at Adam. "Maybe even understanding in a horrible situation, even?"

"So, should I give y'all a few more minutes to look at the menu?" Lyndsie bit her lip, and it was clear she wanted to pass us off to the waiter across the way.

"I'll make this easy. We'll both have the lasagna. No doubt it's perfect." I smiled sweetly and handed her both our menus.

"And could I still get those crayons? Maybe a kid's menu to draw on?" Adam shouted after her as she walked away.

"She's gonna spit in our food, you know."

Adam glared at me. "By the way, I hate lasagna."

"Good." I took a drink of my water and crunched an ice cube. "Are we going to talk about this job yet or what?" I asked. "Pretty sure Ty isn't going to be impressed with how you've treated me so far."

"How *you've* been treated? If that's not the pot calling the kettle black, I don't know what is." Adam looked away. "Maybe I should order some Jack for this soda."

Lyndsie headed toward us with a small box of crayons and an oversized kid's menu with cartoon noodles on the front of it. I didn't stare, but I was pretty sure she tiptoed until she reached our booth. Then, she tossed it all on the table as she practically ran off.

"Perfect!" Adam's eyes lit up as he ignored me, immediately opening the little cardboard box, spilling four miniature crayons onto the table. It was clear he was about to be lost in his doodle. I fiddled with my straw wrapper, twisting it into the tightest coil possible.

He continued to ignore me.

I blew a lock of hair out of my face. "Seriously?"

"Seriously what?" He didn't look up from the scrawl of blue crayon across the paper.

"You're going to sit there and do a dot-to-dot puzzle or a maze instead of talking to me?"

He let out a laugh through his nose. "You suddenly want to talk? That's new."

"Would you knock it off and act your age for once?" Immediately, I regretted the words as I clamped my hand over my mouth. The combination of syllables was a low blow and I knew it.

"Act my age?" His grip tightened on the crayon as it broke in half. Rage flooded his face, and he swallowed hard. "Go to hell."

My heart thudded as I watched Adam stand up.

He tossed the two pieces of blue crayon on the table and crumpled up the paper menu he'd been scribbling on without breaking eye contact with me. "Don't do that, damn it. I hate it when you do that."

I shrugged my shoulders and gave him a questioning look. "What?"

"That thing with your face."

"What? When I exist? Where the hell do you think you're going, anyway?" I snapped.

"The bar." He pushed the sleeves of his worn leather jacket up his arms and stood up. "You know, to act my age and have a fucking beer. God knows I need one after being around you."

"Way to run away, Rockwell," I muttered.

He leaned over and braced his hands on the table, his face inches from mine. "Listen to what I'm about to say and you listen good. Don't even try to pin this on me or say a damn word about me turning my back on you. I'm not the one who walked out on us two years ago. You are. Live with it."

Thirteen

I was floored. "You wanna talk about low blows? I'm not the one who picked this restaurant, let alone the booth where you first told me—"

"Are y'all playing musical chairs or what?" Lyndsie interrupted.

"I'm not hungry anymore." Adam stormed toward the exit.

"Wait until Alex hears about this. Worst third day at a new job ever," Lyndsie muttered as she set down the two plates and the bill on the table in front of me before walking away. "I don't get paid enough to deal with these crazies."

I was left sitting alone with enough lasagna to feed a small army and bread with so much garlic, vampires wouldn't come within a ten-mile radius of me. Looking down at the table with hot tears stinging my eyes, I reached for the paper and straightened out the menu with shaky fingers to study what he'd been working on. The colors were a mottled blur until I blinked, sending teardrops cascading down my cheeks. Adam Rockwell was the only man I knew who could take four restaurant crayons and draw a piece of artwork that rivaled one belonging on the wall of a museum. The one everyone wanted. The one that gave a glimpse inside someone's broken soul. The one that made sense. Just like him. The one I'd thrown away.

"What have I done?" I whispered as I gripped the sketch. A series of puzzle pieces that weren't quite connected illustrated a beach scene—a familiar beach scene. Suddenly, the room was too big, too small, and too hot as I took in the symbolism. I needed to breathe.

With clammy hands, I reached into my pocket and pulled out two wadded twenty dollar bills. With zero fucks left to give, I threw them on the table, slipping the check in my bag. Ty could reimburse me later.

I took off toward the front of the restaurant, determined to catch up with Adam. Words jumbled in my head as I tried to formulate coherent thoughts to speak my peace, to explain my actions, but logic was lost. Two years of pent up feelings surged through me. On most days, I wouldn't allow myself to think about the past, and I definitely didn't let myself relive a single moment I'd spent with Adam. Every time a memory tried to take hold, I'd shove it away and replace it with projects at Jensen & Jensen, Cash's SHAT-worthy antics, or anything else that could hold my attention until the sentiment subsided. It was hard work, and I was exhausted from the amount of time I'd invested in forgetting about him.

The rest of the world was unimportant as I shouldered my way through the double doors. A cool blast of evening air socked me in the face, but it wasn't enough to take the edge off the rage I felt from within.

I skidded to a halt on the sidewalk where I could see center stage. A streetlight illuminated a triangular-shaped beam downward, the honey-tinted color accenting where Adam stood. He flicked a lighter with shaky hands, an incomplete spark repeatedly emitting from the top. Ginger-footedly, I made my way toward his truck, almost afraid that by sneaking up on him, I'd scare him off.

"Come on," he muttered under his breath with the cigarette pinned gingerly between his lips. The frustration behind his voice was almost tangible. After a few more tries, he succeeded at lighting the tip. Adam leaned back against the truck and bent his left knee, resting the sole of his shoe against the door. His eyes closed before he swallowed hard, tipping his head back against the window to let out a thin stream of smoke.

From where I stood behind a van, he couldn't see me. Even from across the parking lot, I could sense a lot. The pain on his face was raw and evident as I studied his eyes. It was the same expression from when I'd first talked to him on the beach. It had taken so long for me to gain his trust. Not much had physically changed about Adam Rockwell in the two years I'd been gone, but I'd spent so much time pushing everything about him out of my mind, I'd forgotten to remember the little things. The way he pushed his shaggy hair out of his face when it needed a trim and he was nervous. The way I could feel his pain without even being near, wishing there was a way I could kiss it all away from him and make it better. The way his mouth would curl into a half-smile when he was teasing me. The way he stared at me as if I were the only person who mattered on the planet.

Quit it, Blue.

I slowed to a stop in front of him. "I thought you quit smoking."

"Not that I have to answer to you, but I did. Until tonight." He took a long drag. "Celebrating three years smoke-free with a cigarette that's just as old seems appropriate. I quit the day I asked for your phone number, and here I am with a Riverdale in my hand. Tastes like ass, but so did the idea of spending one more minute with you in that restaurant."

"Glad I have such an effect on you," I said, trailing a circular pattern in the gravel with the toe of my tennis shoe.

"Don't go flattering yourself, Brennan." The cigarette dangled from his lips. "Here."

I looked down at the folder he held out to me. "What am I supposed to do with this?"

"Take it." Adam nudged the stack of papers forward an inch farther with a jolt of agitation. "You can still read, right? Figure out what you want to do." He took another drag. "Ty texted to say he's not coming. Gervais still isn't resolved because of another zoning issue. I'm going home."

"Whoa. He gave you directive to go over all of this with me." I shook my head as I flipped through the pages full of foreign numbers, shorthand, and sketches. "Don't leave me high and dry."

"Leave you high and dry? Do you hear yourself right now?" His smile was condescending. "Two years ago, you left me 'high and dry' in this God-forsaken town," his voice intensified and there was no doubt the entire parking lot could hear him, "without a fucking word!"

I recoiled. "It was complicated and I needed room to breathe after—"

"Room to breathe and abandoning someone you're supposedly in love..." He cleared his throat. "They are two different things. There's no sugar-coating it. We were in the crossfire of a fucked-up situation, and I'm not discounting that a damn bit, but you sure as hell live up to your name."

I furrowed my brow. "What's that supposed to mean?"

"You were my oxygen, and I suffocated when you left. For months, I couldn't breathe when you took off; air was like a cage. It's been two God damned years, Blue. I don't think you understand that. Two years. With nothing." He dropped the butt to the gravel and ground it with the sole of his shoe. "Think about it. I didn't know if you were dead, alive, or what the fuck happened. All I knew was the girl who I'd planned on having a future with took off on me. There was nowhere to turn except sit down and wonder what the hell I did wrong because last time I checked, calling what we had 'happy'? That was an understatement."

Every word he spoke stung like lemon juice in a million paper cuts, but I absorbed all of it, every last ounce of pain he'd offered to me.

"And then you come waltzing back into town like it's a normal Saturday night?" He paused. "You have nothing to say? Unbelievable."

I closed my eyes and tilted my head down.

"Let all that sink in for a minute. Maybe two years even. Then, you'll know what it's like." I watched him climb into the driver's seat of his truck and rev the engine.

A blaze of boldness took hold of me. "Adam, wait!"

He gunned the engine again and motioned toward his ear as if he couldn't hear me.

"Please?" I squeaked.

Gravel spun out behind his tires as his pickup took off down the street.

There was no chance for a response. No opportunity for a rebuttal. No break in the conversation for an explanation. His exit echoed within me more loudly than any argument could.

I was left alone in the parking lot of Mario's with nothing to contend with but my thoughts and Adam's words. Once he was out of sight, I started the walk to Daveigh's car. Trying to hold back my emotions left me losing the tug of war battle. Hot tears spilled down my cheeks, blurring my vision. The dam was about to burst. I was tired of fighting. Tired of holding myself together. Tired of shoving away everything that'd been so important to me. I had trouble catching my breath through the sobs as I stopped under the eave of the building and covered my face with my hands. Two years of feelings were trying to pour out of me at once. The realization of how much I'd fucked up was the scariest part of all, and I dreaded sorting through the memories, one by one.

* * *

Roughly Two Years Ago

It was fall, my favorite time of year. I ran over to the window, watching the leaves as they fluttered to the ground. Every time I saw them, it was like the first time. Rich hues of auburn, gold, and crimson littered the grass. The sky was a dreary gray backdrop to the setting, and rain dumped from the sky. Washington weather. It always left me feeling giddy, like a small child on a snow day. That was the best way I could explain it.

"Do you know what's only two days away?" I smiled, looking over my shoulder. "Guess."

Adam walked up behind me and slid his arms around my waist from behind. I could feel the blanket of comforting warmth radiate off his skin as he turned me around. In only a way he could, he held me tight and made me feel safe. I inhaled deeply, the scent of his aftershave making my stomach do somersaults. Every damn time.

I looked up at him with a smile spreading across my face, impatiently awaiting his answer.

He looked thoughtful as the corners of his lips curled upward. "Full moon?"

"Nope. I'll give you one more shot." I snuggled up closer to him, a sigh escaping me.

He was my addiction.

He was my sanctuary.

He was my protection.

Nothing could ever change that. I was certain of it.

"I know! The annual chili cook-off! Pancake breakfast? Am I getting closer?"

"That's cheating with an extra guess and a question. Strike two. I'll give you a hint." I walked him backward until he was pressed against the wall, a sly grin spanning my face.

"What are you doing?" His voice grew husky.

"You'll see." I pushed myself up onto my toes and let my mouth graze his lips.

Adam's arms tightened around me as the kiss deepened, my tongue gently teasing his. "I like your hints. Can I get a dozen more?"

With heavy-lidded eyes, I took a step back, lacing my fingers through his. "In two days, the election will be over, one hundred and eighty days will have passed, and we'll be able to stop hiding. Let's work on our idea to escape this hellhole. Where do you want to go first? Stay nearby or drive?"

"Slow down, blue eyes. You sure you're ready to tell the world you're dating a felon, let alone run off with one?"

"Yes. Not yes, but one thousand percent yes," I said. "Are you having second thoughts?"

"No, but plans need to be in place. My grandfather's house..."

"I'll scream it from the rooftops, if you want me to. Besides, I told you from day one I wasn't interested in hiding our relationship. That was all your crazy idea. And saying you're a 'felon' makes it sound way worse than it actually is."

"Well, first off, it was Elana's demand. Second of all, everyone in Steele Falls cares about gossip, not the truth. Third, with the election and your family, I didn't want to be responsible for anything the media slings—"

A knock sounded at the door.

I jumped back and tugged at my rumpled shirt. "Shit. Is it five o'clock already? That's Madelyn. Do I look like we had sex?"

Adam smiled and kissed my nose. "You're cute when you're flustered. You know that?"

"That's a yes, isn't it?" I ran my fingers through my hair, trying to tame the curls as my shoulders slumped. "It is."

"You look fine," he reassured me.

"You know I hate that word," I said. It's like saying something is barely acceptable.

He looked into my eyes and twirled me around once. "You look amazing, beautiful, and like you had sex. Is that better?"

I playfully smacked him on the shoulder and looked at my face in the mirror. Hair disheveled. Cheeks rosy. Lips swollen. Satisfied expression on my face. He was right. And there was no time to hide what I considered to be obvious.

Adam slid his feet into the worn pair of tennis shoes near the bed and shrugged his way into a thermal sweatshirt. "I'll see you later tonight," he said with a slight smile before opening the back window. "Love you."

"Love you too." I nodded as he gave me a chaste kiss before climbing out, shutting it behind him.

The knocking sounded again.

"Just a sec!" I let out a deep breath and I headed toward the door, taking a few moments to compose myself. With a deep breath, I pulled on the handle with a smile affixed to my face. "Hey, Mads."

"Hi," she replied, adjusting the tote bag on her shoulder. "Let me in. It's raining harder than a cow pissing on a flat rock out here."

"Now, that's a visual I could've gone through life without." I glanced back at the window, a wave of sadness washing over me that Adam was gone and out in the bad weather because of me.

Madelyn took off her rain jacket and draped it on the back of a chair before she eyed my shirt. "You know, they make irons, right? Unless you're trying to start a new trend. And if so, don't." Her long blonde hair clung to her shoulders from the relentless rain, yet it was still the color of lustrous glass. "Since it's my turn to buy, I brought Mario's. They had a half-off special on lasagna tonight, and I don't get paid for another week. So, Italian we get." She flopped down on the loveseat and started unloading cardboard boxes from her sequined tote bag. "What's new?"

"Not much." I unhinged a clamshell container full of salad and popped a crouton in my mouth. "Just been trying to hide out with the whole election thing coming up. The usual."

"Has your momster been that bad?" She offered me a pained look with bright green eyes.

I shook my head. "Always. What about you? Did you hear back from that college you've been waiting on?"

"Not yet. They technically have until tomorrow to reply." She absentmindedly poked at a pool of grease on top of her dinner. "Oh! Do you know who I saw when I was waiting for you to answer the door?"

I raised an eyebrow. "Please tell me it wasn't the campaign caravan. I can't deal with any more—"

"Not even close. Adam Rockwell was walking down your street."

"Nice," I said, thumbing my way through a magazine at breakneck speed, not taking time to look at the articles.

She arched an eyebrow. "Do you always read fashion mags upside-down?"

"Huh?" I blinked and focused on the words below, realizing she was right. "Out of it today, I guess. Sorry." I flopped the fashion magazine closed and tossed it in a basket next to the TV.

"What do you think of him? Is he seeing anyone?" Madelyn looked down at her reflection in the glass of the coffee table and applied a layer of lip balm.

"Who?" I asked.

"Duh. Adam. I mean, I know he's a little older and all. But who cares, right?"

I blinked quickly. "How would I know who he dates?"

"I dunno." She shrugged before taking a bite of lasagna.

"He's always so withdrawn and keeps to himself. It's mysterious. Plus, he's got that tall, dark, and handsome thing going for him. Thought maybe you'd heard something around town."

"Around town?" I felt my heartrate speed up. "Is there something I should know about?"

"Man, you're acting weird tonight. Relax." She giggled and started the process of braiding her hair. "He's...he's fucking hot. I mean, you're not interested, right? I thought I saw him checking you out last week when we were down at the beach. Maybe I was wrong."

"No!" I blurted. Suddenly, my heart was as heavy as the lump of pasta sitting in my stomach. As happy as I was Adam was mine, no one knew. And that killed me. It broke my heart Mads didn't know what was going on in my life. We'd told each other everything since we were kids. "Nope. Not interested."

"So, you'd be cool if I asked him to dinner? Like on a date?"

I hesitated for a few seconds and bit my lip. Forcing that smile onto my face was one of the hardest things I'd ever done. "S....sure. Doesn't matter to me." The words were bitter as they crossed my tongue.

"Good." She studied my expression and then grinned. "Maybe I'll get up the courage to talk to him when I'm back home in a few days."

"Fantastic," I replied, jamming a massive bite of salad into my mouth to keep myself from saying anything I'd regret.

"I'm probably wasting my time." She undid the braid, dissatisfied. "He's not going to be into someone like me."

"Come on, Mads," I replied. "What guy wouldn't want to date you? You're perfect. Smart. Funny. Thoughtful. Plus, you have that cutesy blonde hair, green eyed, freckled look. And those years of soccer practice left you with an athlete's figure. Guys around here go bananas for that kind of stuff."

Wait a minute. What am I doing? Was I actually encouraging her to ask out my boyfriend? *Abort! Abort!* I needed more salad to occupy my mouth.

"Hey!" Her eyes lit up. "Maybe we could double. You and my little brother could—"

"Huh-huh. No way," I immediately cut her off. "You're my best friend, and I love you to the moon and back, Mads. But I have to draw the line somewhere. That's like incest. Not happening. Ever."

"Fine." She closed her box of lasagna. "So, I've been thinking about cutting my hair into a bob. You know, something drastic. What do you think..."

Her lips moved, but I didn't hear what she said. Thankfully, the topic of Adam Rockwell had been dropped. At least for the time being.

Life was getting complicated, and each day seemed to have more enormous hurdles for us to clear. I had to find a way to tell Madelyn about my relationship with Adam, but there hadn't been a good time. Okay. There had been plenty of opportunities. Probably hundreds. But I was a chicken shit. With what I knew, I needed to protect him by any means possible, even if that meant keeping my best friend in the dark.

The rest of the night fit our standard hangout protocol. It entailed hours of watching old movies on the freebie channel, laughing at inside jokes, attempts at amateur manicures, and my downing a couple of bottles of wine. Madelyn was slightly younger than me, and miss straight and narrow always turned down the booze since she wasn't twenty-one yet.

At ten o'clock, the second movie had ended and so had the rainstorm.

"I should get going." Madelyn yawned. "I've got a headache, and I have to work tomorrow."

"Want some ibuprofen?" I reached into a cupboard.

"No!" she exclaimed and then calmed her tone. "I mean, I'm good. Call you tomorrow?"

"Sounds good." I wiped down the counter with a wet paper towel where a blob of lasagna had landed earlier in the evening. "Drive safe."

"Always." Madelyn slung her tote bag on her shoulder as she closed the door.

I continued cleaning up the mess of paper plates and wine bottles when I heard a tapping at the back window.

Butterflies flitted in my stomach as I dropped the paper

towel and darted across the room. As always, it took mega-force to jam the warped window upward with the heels of my hand. "You're soaked." I looked at the dark-colored shirt clinging to his frame while he crawled through the window. "Wasn't this thing light gray when you left?" I tugged on the sleeve.

"I think so." His teeth chattered as I peeled it off him, letting the weighted material drop into a soggy pile on the floor. "It's kind of hard to avoid the raindrops on foot. Two more car-free days to go."

"And you're freezing."

"I'll bet you could warm me up." His icy fingertips trembled as they greeted my face, leaning down for a kiss. Adam's cool lips met mine, and I fell into his embrace. As he pulled back, his coy smile took hold of my heart. "See? With your help, the chill will be gone in no time."

He grabbed a spare shirt from the bottom dresser drawer along with a pair of his athletic pants. Our relationship had been kept so hidden, we'd both started stashing clothes at each other's houses to avoid extra trips out in public.

"We need to talk about something." I fought to focus on my words and not on Adam's abdominal muscles.

He grabbed a breadstick from the foil bag on the table and took a bite. "About what?"

"Please put a shirt on. I can't concentrate with you standing here half-naked."

"Why not?" He smiled, flexing with his biceps in an overdramatic pose.

"I dunno." I blushed and glimpsed his tattooed arms. "It makes me want to do stuff to you."

He waggled his eyebrows. "Ooh! What kind of stuff? Kinky stuff?"

"Stop!" I covered my eyes with my hands. "Not looking at you. Otherwise, I'm going to get distracted again. And this is important."

He laughed. "Fine. I'm decent. You can look now."

"If I've told you once, I've told you a million times, you're more than decent." Peeking through the gaps between my fingers, I lowered my hands to my sides. "Thank you." I let out a deep sigh of relief.

"What's up, blue eyes? You look worried."

I chewed my lip. "I think Mads has a thing for you."

"A thing?" he replied. "What kind of thing?"

"A romantic thing. She likes you."

He swallowed the mouthful of bread with a pained look on his face. "Blue..."

I spoke quickly, like ripping a bandage off a hairy arm. "Heads up, she's planning to ask you on a date after she gets back from some vacation next week. We need to find a way to tell her about us before this all backfires."

"Tell me about it." He rubbed his face. "Maybe it's because we only have two more days to go and victory is on the horizon, but I swear this relationship is getting harder to keep quiet by the minute. Fortunately, you're worth every second of the struggle."

Heat crept into my cheeks while I fiddled with a stray string on my shirt. "She asked if I was interested in you."

He got quiet and the mood shifted from playful to serious. "What did you tell her?"

"I was on the spot. Of course, I told her 'no'."

A flicker of pain showed behind his eyes and it was like I'd been sucker-punched in the stomach. He was the one person who I vowed to never hurt. He'd been dealt enough of that in his life, and I'd deemed it my job to not let it happen again.

"Adam," I touched his arm and swallowed the lump in my throat, "the lie burned like hell, but I had to protect you...us. This asinine six-month thing is almost over. I can't risk losing either—"

"Shhh..." Adam wrapped his arms around me. "You don't have to justify anything, and I'm not going anywhere."

"I know. But I feel..."

"You feel what?" Adam lifted me up and I instinctively wound my legs around his waist, his hands cupping my ass before he engaged me in a deep kiss. "Tell me what you're so afraid of."

I braced my hands against his pectorals and moaned. "I don't remember."

"Good," he whispered. He slid one hand under my shirt, his flat palm inching its way up stomach, the coldness making me flinch. His grip around my waist tightened with the other. It was a reassurance he'd never let go. Our kiss only broke long enough to let the annoyance of fabric pass between us before my tongue sought his out again.

"God, I want you," he murmured as he fumbled with the clasp on my bra one-handedly.

A knock and a click caused my eyes to open.

The front door creaked and we froze mid-kiss, mid-half-nakedness, and mid-passion.

"Hey, I forgot my rain jacket, and I'm not talking about condoms...Blue?" It was the ultimate let down, both figuratively and literally. Madelyn's hands dropped to her sides, her tote bag landed on the floor, and her jaw fell. The color drained from her face, her expression crushed.

"Mads, this isn't what it looks like." I squirmed from Adam's grip and scooped up my shirt from the floor. The damn thing was inside out with one sleeve wound through the head hole, so diving my way into it wasn't nearly as graceful as I'd hoped.

"Do you have him on speed dial or something? You couldn't wait long enough for me to get turned down before you swooped in?"

"You don't understand. It's complicated," I replied.

"It's only complicated if you make it complicated. Some friend. Not interested, my ass." She snatched up her belongings and bolted out the door.

"Fuck." I grabbed my tennis shoes, jamming my feet in without bothering to unlace them first. "I'm sorry, Adam. I need to talk to her."

"I get it," he said. "I'll stay here. You go."

"Madelyn! Wait!" I yelled as I raced through the open doorway, leaving Adam in my wake.

For hours that night, I looked for her all over Steele Falls and into the outskirts of Ocean Shores. I continued my search until the sun began to rise the next morning before I finally gave up.

She wasn't at home.

She wasn't at either of the local parks.

She wasn't drowning her sorrows in ice cream at Chilly Philly's.

She wasn't driving down the 101.

Regret flooded my stomach, and I threw up half-digested lasagna on the sidewalk twice. I could have avoided the entire situation unfolding by telling her the truth, but I didn't.

Over the next three days, I sent thirty-seven texts—none of them ever marked as read. I also phoned her fifty-two times—each call immediately sending me to her peppy voicemail greeting until the mailbox was full of messages from me. It was borderline stalking, but I was desperate. Begging her to talk to me. Begging her to yell at me. Begging for anything. Any type of attention I could get, I wanted it. Scratch that. I needed it. Needed to know she was okay. Instead, I was left disappointed because we never spoke again.

Fourteen

The drive home from Mario's was a blur I didn't remember. Standing in the entryway of the mother-in-law house with the door wide open was difficult as I tried to let my walls down. My fingers quaked as I lightly touched the brass handle Madelyn gripped when she walked in on us that night. The sharp pangs of disappointment and bitter betrayal she experienced were nearly palpable if I closed my eyes.

Across the room, there was complex history between Adam and I, so many emotions swirling together in an invisible cloud of desire and lust. And that was one night out of many— the memories took my breath away.

I could almost see us in our past fiery embrace.

I could almost taste the whisper of his soft kiss on my lips.

I could almost hear the sound of my pulse racing when I caught him staring at me.

I could almost feel the echo of his hands claiming my body.

I could almost smell the comfort his aftershave gave me.

But "almost" wasn't enough. Every sense failed at giving me absolution if it ever existed.

That situation haunted me like no other. But all of it was only a tainted memory, a ghost. None of it was real and never could be again. All I was left with was lack of closure and a sense of inescapable loneliness. And for the rest of my life, those demons would be shackled to me without a skeleton key. It was my own damn fault, and I'd earned that punishment.

I took a deep breath and closed the door behind me, resting my back against the heavy wood paneling. It was fortunate I was separated from the rest of the house. With heaving sobs escaping my chest, I let myself sink to the floor, my cheek pressed to the cold linoleum. The wails were relentless and took hold until there were no more tears left to shed.

* * *

The next day, I woke up to the sound of my phone vibrating on the night stand, dancing its way toward the edge. I fumbled for it with one eye open, waiting for the red numbers on the alarm clock to come into focus. Three minutes after eight o'clock. My uncle's name popped up on the screen of my cell with a text message.

Ty

Reply to this when you have a chance. No rush.

I drummed my fingers against the itchy comforter, wondering if I should respond immediately to express interest or if that would make me look too desperate. I bit my lip. Maybe waiting an hour would be better. Ehhh. Desperation won the battle while my fingers flew across the keys.

Ty

What's up?

Sorry I had to bail last night. I talked to Adam this morning. Are you available to come in and chat? I'd rather have this conversation in person instead of over text.

My heart lurched in my chest as the prior evening came flooding back and smacked me in the face with brute force. It was over. Adam ratted me out and provided Ty with his unsavory opinion, sealing my fate on not having a job at Brennan Construction.

Reluctantly, I replied.

Ty

Sure. Does 10am work?

Sounds good. Don't bother getting dressed up. Jeans are fine. What I have to say won't take long.

Okay.

See you then.

There it sat. My future employment opportunity was about to be flushed down the toilet like a giant wad of toilet paper, and it took less than two minutes of text messaging with Ty and one fucked up dinner with Adam Rockwell. I was left to anticipate scolding and disappointment for another hour and fifty-five minutes. Make that fifty-four minutes. No matter how I spun it, confidence in my uncle's wording was absent. Especially after I saw the look on Adam's face when he sped off from Mario's. Nothing good could come from it.

I thought back to our heated words, fully-aware my temper had gotten the best of me. It wasn't pretty. Storming out of the restaurant was a newfound skill that probably wouldn't make it onto my résumé. As much as I didn't want to admit it, I could've swayed the evening with Adam in a different direction, but I didn't. I beat myself up, asking why. Maybe it was self-sabotage.

I walked into the bathroom and flinched when I saw my reflection in the mirror. One of my Brennan traits had reared its ugly head. Post-ugly cry face. Anytime I had a really good sob, I looked like hell the next day. My cheeks were blotchy and pink, eyes swollen and reduced to puffy, red-rimmed slits.

Outside of wearing a brown paper bag over my head, there was little that could be done to remedy my face before the meeting. Hopefully, my uncle wouldn't be frightened into making a Ty-shaped hole in the wall.

Absentmindedly, I went through the motions of taking a long shower before throwing on my favorite sweatshirt and faded jeans. It was the polar opposite of what I'd worn the night before, but if Ty was fine with casual, that's what he was gonna get. Fuck it. I wasn't about to dress up to get shut down. My Chucks were still near the front door along with a graveyard of wadded tissues I wasn't ready to clean up. I grabbed a strawberry protein bar from my suitcase and pinned my hair up into a messy bun before beginning my walk toward the construction company.

"Blue!" Ralph called out, jogging to catch up to me. He had a book tucked under his arm.

"Ralph, I'm in a hurry." I tried to brush him off by avoiding eye contact, even though the dark sunglasses took care of that.

He skidded to a stop in front of me. "This'll only take a second."

He was old. I tried to be polite and hear him out.

"Can you help with this?" He extended the book toward me. A yellow sticky note was on the front.

"I can't find these two words in here," he continued through his thick accent. "This dictionary is both useless and broken. That Merriam-Webster is a fool."

I looked down at the sticky note. Written in shaky pencil were the words "perfusely" and "misterious".

"Ralph—"

"Also," he tapped the cover with his index finger, "the history of pheasants isn't in here."

I closed my eyes and with as much patience as I could muster, I explained the difference between an encyclopedia and a dictionary. Additionally, I suggested a spelling lesson.

The look on his face told me he didn't believe I knew what I was talking about. "Okay. I'll ask someone else. You go."

"Oh! Here." He handed me a plastic bag he held in his other hand.

"What's this?" I asked.

"Plastic containers. From meals you'd sent over for me. I'm returning them."

"The meals I sent?" My eyes got wide as I peeked inside the bag. The clear plastic still had bits of food clumped into the corners, now olive green and fuzzy.

Ralph's wife had passed years prior, and he lived alone, his daughter out of state. On Sunday nights, I'd task Daveigh with taking him leftovers.

"And I thank you," he said.

"You're welcome? Ralph, I've been gone for nearly two years," I replied.

"Better late than never, right?" He nodded once and walked back toward his driveway.

I headed around the side of the house and opened the trash can to throw in the bag of plastic dishes before I left. "Gross."

I took a deep breath as I headed down the sidewalk. The air was both calm and still with the faint smell of rain lingering on the horizon. It reminded me of what happened before a big storm hit Steele Falls, and Zack's words echoed in my head about the weather changing. Zack. The party. It was already Tuesday. *Damn it.*

I'd finished my near-flavorless breakfast that had the consistency of soggy cardboard by the time I walked up to the entrance of Brennan Construction. Absentmindedly, I took off my sunglasses, like I would before walking inside any building. The front doors closed behind me and was greeted by Rita, the wonder receptionist. At that moment, I wasn't sure which of them left a worse taste in my mouth.

"Blue!" A fake grin manifested on Rita's face as she perched a pair of rectangular-shaped reading glasses on her round face. "It's so nice to see you again. Can I get you a cup of coffee or a cheese Danish from the break room? Made them myself." She scrunched her nose and focused on my eyes. "Dear God, honey. What happened? You look awful. Did someone die?"

Evidently, I still looked like shit. "Actually, someone did

die. The mayor's husband. My step-father. Do you not keep up on town gossip?" I shot her a glare. She didn't need to know Tom wasn't the reason for yesterday's tears. "No thanks on the coffee or the pastry though," I replied, unwilling to return her phony smile. "Any other awkward questions you care to ask while I'm standing here? Wanna know what color my underwear are or how many men I've slept with? Maybe you're wondering if the curtains match the carpet."

Rita blinked rapidly. "I..."

I sighed, knowing I'd taken it a smidge too far. "Just let Ty know I'm here, please."

"I'll call him while you're on your way up." She dialed on a phone and glanced at me with concern spanning her face three times before nodding for me to continue through the double doors.

As I exited the elevator on the second floor and walked toward Ty's office, I froze when someone rounded the corner at the end of the hall. Adam was headed in the opposite direction, bee-lining toward me while on his cell phone. He hadn't seen me yet, his secondary focus on spinning a ring of keys in his hand. My watch indicated it was too late to turn around and run the other way. Two minutes until ten o'clock. I could either be a coward and bolt for the nearby stairwell or be on time for my meeting. Hello, big girl pants. We meet again. Guess that blueberry muffin of Cash's wouldn't have hurt my waistline after all.

My heart thudded in my chest as I tried to remain inconspicuous. It'd be a difficult feat considering we were the only two in the corridor. My goal was to be transparent while rushing by him. *Be cool. Be casual. Walk. Maybe he won't notice.* Unfortunately, I failed and didn't go undetected.

For a brief moment, his eyes locked with mine and his pace slowed, but I couldn't pinpoint what his questioning expression conveyed. Horror? Pity? Curiosity? Maybe it was all three and he'd mastered the fine art of how to SHAT on me like Cash used to too.

"Fuck off, Rockwell," I replied as I blasted past him with a hitch in my voice. Twice more, I glanced over my shoulder and he'd stopped in the hall with his head cocked to the side, watching me walk away.

When I was outside of Ty's office and out of sight from any other Brennan Construction employees, I pulled the pair of oversized sunglasses from my tote bag again. After I put them on, I checked my reflection in the glass of a painting before knocking on the door. Much better.

"Come in," Ty said.

I opened the door and walked inside, closing it quietly behind me, the bottom abutting the plush carpeting.

Like last time, my uncle welcomed me with open arms paired with a hug and a warm smile. It had to be a consolation prize before he unleashed the bad news. Could've won the trip to Tahiti, but instead Blue gets the booby prize. Score. "Have a seat." He glanced at my eyewear for a few seconds, but didn't question it.

There was another knock on the door as I set my bag on the floor and did what I was asked.

"Sorry," Ty said to me with a sigh. "Come on in."

The door opened and I craned my neck, immediately wishing I hadn't.

Adam walked in, holding a stack of papers in one hand and his cell phone in the other. I was so concerned with passing him in the hallway, I hadn't noticed he wasn't in his muddy work gear like he had been the day prior. Instead, he was clean-shaven, his hair styled with just enough gel. I scanned him from head to toe. A powder blue-and-white striped button-up shirt. Dark slacks. Black shiny dress shoes. I'd forgotten how well he cleaned up.

"What's up, Adam?" Ty asked. "I thought you were meeting with Calvin this morning?"

"I am. He pushed it back to noon."

"Sounds like Calvin. So, what's up?" Ty asked again.

Adam cleared his throat. "Um. Can you sign off on these modifications for Gervais? I just got off the phone with him, and I think we finally reached an agreement."

"You don't need my signature on those. I trust your judgment more than—"

"I'd feel better if you reviewed them," his eyes flicked to me, "and knowing everything was all right."

I averted my eyes even though I knew he couldn't see them through the tinted lenses.

Ty gestured toward me. "Does it have to be done now? I'm in the middle of a meeting."

"It can't wait. I told him I'd call him back in five with a final." Adam handed the stack of paperwork to Ty. "He's about to board a plane at SeaTac, and we both know impatience is that man's greatest strength."

"Yeah, I know." The room was silent as my uncle let out a sigh before scanning the documents.

"What's with the sunglasses?" Adam looked at me and crossed his arms. "You're indoors, and it's November."

"Migraine." I repositioned them. "Must be the lighting."

"Uh huh. Makes perfect sense," he replied, scrutinizing my expression as I tried to keep my cheeks from tingling.

"Everything appears to be in order, as I suspected. Call Phil and tell him we're good to go."

"Will do," Adam said as he grabbed the papers from Ty, flashing me one last glance before he walked toward the door.

Ty remained silent until it clicked shut, indicating we were alone. "I want to talk about what happened last night."

I swallowed. "I can explain all of that. It wasn't my best representation, and I'd like to apologize—"

"Apologize? For what?" Ty furrowed his brow. "Adam loved you. Maybe those weren't his exact words, but he said he believes you'd be an asset."

Are you sure he didn't say "ass" instead of asset?

"So, I'm offering you the job," he continued, yammering about pay, benefits, a schedule, policies, and vacation time. All of them were important points I should've taken detailed note of, but I couldn't stop replaying the dinner at Mario's in my head.

"So...what do you think? Are you on board?"

"Seriously? That's it? No second interview, calls to references, or anything?" I blinked, wondering if Adam remembered the same evening I did. *Good thing you weren't there last night, Uncle Ty.*

"Look. You said you have experience from being with that other outfit. Plus, anyone who puts up with the rescheduling hurdles I put you through and no-show employees for an on-the-clock dinner meeting? You took it in stride. The position can be performed remotely, so I'll have IT set up your virtual office and supply you with a laptop before you head out of town. When do you leave?"

Out of town. I'd almost forgotten about my old life in Sacramento. "Leave." I blinked. "I haven't decided yet. The funeral's tomorrow. Fast Eddie still has my car."

"Keep me posted when you figure it all out," Ty said as his phone rang. He pushed a button to ship it to voicemail.

"I don't know what to say." What I should've said was I didn't have any experience and I needed an immeasurable amount of on the job training in a twenty-four-hour period. Instead, I kept my mouth shut and decided to swim instead of sink.

"Well, hopefully you accept." Ty laughed. "That's why we're here, isn't it?"

"Yes. Sorry." I got up and hugged him. "I totally accept. Thank you for this. I mean it."

"My pleasure. Now, not to run you off, but I have a meeting in fifteen minutes. My people will call your people." He smiled and gathered a few file folders, along with his travel mug.

"Of course." I grabbed my tote bag and headed for the door after saying goodbye. On my way out, I didn't even throw any snarky comments in Rita's direction. For that, I deserved a gold star and a cookie.

Much like the walk home from the Lean, Mean, Coffee Bean a few days prior, I practically floated back to the house. A burden had been lifted from my shoulders instead of a new one weighing me down. Something had actually gone in my favor. A new job would be a new beginning for me. I could feel it.

When I arrived back at the house, a yellow taxi was in the driveway, the back driver-side door hanging wide open. A man wearing a pea coat, red plaid scarf, jeans, and loafers gestured and laughed with the cab driver through the open window, a rolling suitcase next to him. I watched him pass a wad of bills before turning his attention to me. A wide smile spread across his face.

My feet began to take off at a rapid pace before I even realized it happened.

"Blue!" he exclaimed with open arms.

I fell into Finn's embrace and held him tight. "You're here!"

"Well, a last-minute flight from around the world cost a pretty penny, and despite two layovers and one missed connection, it was meant to be."

I looked up at him, blinking back hot tears.

"Let me look at you, pretty girl." He twirled me around in a circle. "Just as radiant as the last time I saw you. Wait. Have you been crying?"

"I—" The door on the other side of the cab unexpectedly opened and caught my attention. It didn't add up.

An unfamiliar male got out of the back seat on the passenger side, his eyes locking with mine for a brief moment before he looked away. I drank in his appearance as he ran his fingers through his hair. It was long enough to showcase the tips of nutmeg-colored curls with hints of topaz, matching the irises of his eyes. It was the perfect complement to his golden-brown skin and his manicured goatee. He wore a buttoned trench coat, jeans, and trendy tennis shoes. The gravel crunched under his feet as he walked around to the side of the car where I stood. Quietly, he unloaded his luggage from the trunk.

"Big sister," Finn toward the man next to me, "I'd like you to meet someone."

"Hi. I'm Blue," I said, extending my hand toward his.

His accent was far thicker than Finn's. "It's a pleasure. I've heard a lot about you. The eyes live up to the name."

Finn smiled. "This is my boyfriend, Scott."

My hand tightened around Scott's and I continued to pump it for a few seconds too long before letting go at the unexpected news.

"Boyfriend?" I murmured to Finn through the side of my

mouth. "Can I talk to you for a sec?"

"Sure." Finn turned toward Scott and lowered his voice. "Give me a minute with her."

"We won't be long," I replied.

Finn led me to the edge of the driveway. "What's up?"

"What do you mean 'what's up?' You're..."

"You can say it. The word won't bite. I'm gay." He paused, seriousness behind his dark blue eyes. "Is that an issue for you? Because if it is—"

"No. I just...you didn't tell me."

"Why would I?" He laughed. "We haven't spoken for two years until the other day. Besides, do you blast from the rooftops that you're hetero?" he asked.

"No. I mean..."

"It's the same thing."

"Finn, that's not where I'm going with this. I don't care if you're gay, straight, or somewhere in-between. You could prefer the company of llamas and I wouldn't judge you." I paused. "Okay, maybe not llamas. Their teeth creep me out, and they do that weird spitting thing. But that's not what I'm trying to say. You have my unwavering support; you know that. I...don't feel like I know you anymore. So much time has gone by..." I replied with a twinge of sadness in my voice.

"Well, you stopped taking my calls much like Mom did—"

"Wait. Don't compare me to the momster. I avoided everyone because..."

"Because why?" He cocked his head to the side. "Why did you leave us all behind?"

My mouth opened, but I suddenly didn't know how to consolidate everything into one single sentence without unraveling at the seams. It took three solid attempts before the lump in my throat let me speak without risking tears. "Because I had my own shit I didn't know how to handle."

"We all have our hang-ups. Look at me. I let her," he glanced toward the house, "pay for my college tuition, and I know perfectly well she does it to keep me away from Steele Falls. The last time she and I spoke, she called me a 'black mark' on her pristine election record. How's that for unconditional love? But I'm not innocent either. I couldn't afford college abroad, so I allow her to buy me off."

"But I was afraid if I revisited..."

"If you revisited what?" He nudged me with his elbow. "The dive bar? The coffee shop? What?"

"Wait a sec," I said as a lightbulb went off over my head at the word 'revisited'. "Don't you have finals right now?"

"No." His brow furrowed. "I took a semester off because I needed a break. Why?"

"And Mom knows?"

"Of course, she knows. She's the one footing my tuition bill."

"And this," I nodded toward Scott, "is why mom...isn't talking to you. Don't you realize the election is right around the corner?"

"Don't go diving too far into the rabbit hole, Blue. I don't. It's not worth it. And you'll never find your way back out."

The momster's words echoed throughout my head.

"Finn's not coming home. He has finals to study for, and with what I have to pay for his tuition. Just no."

It wasn't that he had exams. Not telling him about Tom was intentionally done to keep him far away from the public eye.

"I'm an adult now. You don't have to protect me anymore." Finn studied my face. "If Mom and I don't see eye-to-eye on my life, I really couldn't care less. I'm here to pay my respects, not to reconcile."

"But you brought Scott? Here. Did you forget the momster lives in there?" I pointed to the house. "That's like offering a blood sacrifice to an angry god. She'll season him with her anxiety meds and eat him for breakfast with her bare hands."

"Safety in numbers. Remember?" He winked at me before flashing Scott a quick glance. "He's my support as much as you are."

"Finn, don't downplay this. She didn't even tell you your own dad died, so she could protect her image. Doesn't that piss you off? What kind of fucked up move is that?"

"Of course, it makes me angry..."

"She's paying to hide you nearly five thousand miles away. You're her kid. All of this is bullshit, and I've had enough." I stormed toward the porch, glancing at the carport. My mother's SUV was parked underneath it, which meant she was in the house. I'd hit my breaking point. "Bullshit." I hurried up the steps, the third from the bottom groaning as usual. The screen door nearly came off its hinges as I yanked it open. "Bullshit! Bullshit! Bullshit!"

"Blue! Don't!" Finn trailed after me up the steps. "It's a waste—"

I let the door slam behind me. "Mom! Where are you?"

Elana appeared in the doorway to the kitchen with a frown on her face. "What on earth are you screaming about now? Can't you see I'm on an important call?" she hissed as she cupped her hand over the speaker of the corded phone stretched across the kitchen.

She'd pushed me too far with her attitude, her condescension, and all of her actions. I marched over to where she stood, ripped the phone from her hand, and put it up to my ear. "Harold, she's busy and will have to call you later." With a forceful slam, I hung up the receiver, the ringer inside dinging. "There."

"Who the hell do you think you are?" she seethed.

I wasn't given the opportunity to volley an answer. Someone else did it on my behalf.

"Hello, Mother," Finn's voice sounded as he walked in behind me, draping his coat over his arm. Scott wasn't in view, which was probably for the best.

Elana's face blanched and she let out a slow breath through her mouth, her hands shaking. Fear filled her eyes, but it wasn't the kind of panic where you're scared of *someone*. It was the type of fear when you're afraid of someone finding out about *something*. "Finn. You're here. In Steele Falls. How..."

I crossed my arms. "I might've forgotten to mention I told Finn about Tom. Figured he had the right to know since you didn't have a big enough set of balls to do it yourself."

She narrowed her eyes at me. "You did what?"

I walked past her on the way back to the front door. "Oh!

199

And maybe you could work on not being such a judgmental bitch if you're given the chance to meet Scott," I muttered as I walked back out onto the porch.

"Blue! Don't you dare walk out of this house right now!" she shouted.

"Mom, this isn't about Blue. It's..." Finn's voice trailed off after the door closed.

Scott was seated on the porch swing with his hands deep in his pockets as he stared out at the ocean.

I sat down next to him and tucked my knees up under my chin. "Sorry if you heard any of or all of that. Not the warmest of welcomes."

"It's all right." He offered a half-smile. "No worse than what I endured back home in London with my family."

"Yeah, well the momster's a special kind of crazy."

"That special kind of crazy, as you call it, isn't confined to Steele Falls. Here's some perspective." He crossed one ankle over his knee. "When I came out at sixteen, my dad got trashed, and he beat the shit out of me in front of my mom. That stunt landed me in the hospital with a busted nose, two broken ribs, a collapsed lung, and the number of stitches was humiliating. Before he took off, he spat on my face told me I needed to figure out how to fix my 'problem' before I could talk to him again. And that's what started two years of me living on the streets. What Finn's got going on in there right now isn't trivial, but he needs to be the one to establish boundaries with her. Your 'momster' doesn't scare me."

"That's rough. I'm sorry," I replied.

"Don't be. I'm not. The lesson I learned was real family isn't defined by blood. I haven't spoken to my parents since."

I glanced up at the front door, wishing I'd left it open. The sounds of Finn's voice mingled with the momster's, and they were escalating. Even with straining, the words were still too muffled to make out. "Where are you staying?"

"I think Finn said it's called the Wave Inn."

"He's got good taste. It has incredible views of the ocean, and—"

"I think you have a visitor." Scott nodded toward the

driveway where Zack leaned against his truck, holding a single red rose.

I let out a deep breath through my nose and closed my eyes.

"Not a suitor of yours?" Scott raised an eyebrow.

"No, he's here for me," I replied. "Didn't realize how late it was already."

"You don't look very happy about seeing him."

"Jury's still out on this one." I stood up.

"Oh, one of those." Scott laughed. "Good luck."

"You gonna be okay waiting here for Finn?"

"I'll try not to let Elana season me with too much Xanax before she devours me." He smiled. "You go."

"Tell Finn I'll be back later."

"Will do."

I scuttled down the porch steps to where Zack stood and glanced down at my sweatshirt. "Sorry. I didn't realize it was so late. I'm not even remotely dressed for—"

He held the flower out to me as his eyes flicked up at Scott. "Shhh. There's no dress code for the party. Besides, you look gorgeous."

"Thanks." I wrinkled my nose. "But I'm allergic to those."

He gave me a half-smile as he tossed it over his head, the single flower landing in the bed of his truck. "Noted for future instances of bringing you gifts. You don't have a chocolate allergy, do you?"

"Only when it sticks to my hips." I laughed.

"The box with the bow on the console is approved then," he replied. "And Ralph hasn't shot me yet. So, it's turning out to be a good day. Maybe we should leave the flower as a present for him?"

"Don't push your luck if you want to keep both of your kneecaps," I said.

"So, who's that on the porch?" he asked before closing the passenger door.

I glanced up at Scott watching us. I felt bad for him. Listening to Finn and my mom argue couldn't be fun. "That's my brother's..."

For a brief second, I stumbled. Did I piss off my mom and call him Finn's boyfriend this close to the election? There'd be no going back after that. Finn wasn't keeping Scott a secret, and my loyalties aligned with my brother. "That's my brother's boyfriend."

The tension released from Zack's shoulders. "Good."

The drive over to Adam's was full of Zack telling me about every spectacular and mundane detail of his life, leaving no room for me to reply. Occasionally, I'd give a smile and a nod. It was clear he was impressed with his own laundry list of accomplishments; maybe he should've been dating himself. He'd been mentioned in numerous financial magazines, climbed Mount Rainier, played guitar in front of five hundred people. Blah. Blah. Blah. The list went on and on. And on. With the amount of information being socked at me, I wondered if there'd be a quiz later. Hopefully not. I was only half-listening.

When we arrived, there were multiple cars parked on the makeshift lot Adam and I had created using driftwood as a perimeter when we'd first started dating. By then, I'd tuned out most of the words Zack said. Future quiz failed.

I got out of the truck and looked up at the house. It looked the same as I remembered. Another round of history fought to take hold, but I shooed it away. My feet took some convincing, hesitating at the property line. The cedar shakes on the side of the house were worn with age, battered by years of salty air. A thin blanket of sand coated the sparse grass. None of that had changed.

If I thought coming back to Steele Falls was difficult, visiting Adam's house brought it to a whole new level.

"Are you okay?" Zack grabbed my hand. "You look like you saw a ghost."

"It's nothing. Just a big day with the funeral tomorrow and all," I lied.

"It's tomorrow? I keep forgetting that's the whole reason you came to town in the first place." He scrolled through his phone with his thumb. "Damn. I can't go. I have a meeting in Aberdeen I can't reschedule."

"It's okay. Funerals aren't fun anyway," I reassured him.

Deep down, I was relieved Zack wouldn't be there.

"Come on then." He squeezed my hand. "We can go say hi to everyone and then I'll take you out back to the beach. Adam has this great patch of sand with this huge chunk of driftwood near the far end of his property line."

I swallowed and closed my eyes, thinking of the initials carved deeply into the wood and the pocketknife in my tote bag that was used to make it. "Uh huh. Sounds great."

He led me into the house, practically having to pull me along. A handful of people were in the kitchen, congregating around a table full of fancy appetizers. Rock music blasted in the background. Another small group was in front of the fireplace overlooking the ocean out back. If anything, Adam's house was nothing short of spectacular, and he'd done a considerable number of updates in the past two years.

"The Main event has arrived!" Zack said, lifting his hand up high, his fingers still intertwined with mine.

Everyone within earshot cheered.

I leaned up toward him and whispered, "Did you announce your presence with your last name and call yourself the Main event?"

"Sure did." He winked. "Clever, huh?"

I let out a nervous chuckle, unimpressed.

"Hey!" Lucy said as she appeared from the kitchen to give me a hug with a beer in-hand. "How are you?" It was as if the other night never even happened.

"Good?" I replied.

"Daveigh said she's running late. Sounds like Finn's in town and something dramatic happened earlier? Know any details about it? I wouldn't mind banging that brother of yours if he's available..."

I shook my head no as I saw Adam across the room. Lucy and Zack were suddenly unimportant. His eyes locked with mine as he dumped a bag of chips in a near-empty bowl.

Zack put his arm around my waist, his fingertips curling under the bottom of my sweatshirt, greeting the small of my back again. It felt too intimate as I tried to wriggle away. "Come here for a second," he said.

"Where are we going?"

"It's polite to greet the host." He led me across the room to where Adam stood, crumpling the bag with more force than necessary.

Zack shook Adam's hand and clapped his shoulder twice. "Thanks for bailing me out on this party. I owe you one. Next year, no skunks."

Adam nodded and scanned the room.

Awkward.

The air was thick with tension. "Are you two still not over what happened the other night?" Zack grabbed a bottle of beer from the cooler and handed it to me.

"Like oil and water." I twisted the top off and took a swig.

Zack sighed and turned toward Adam. "Do me a favor. Go out back. Take five minutes to get to know her. And forget about that whole damn beer mess. It was an accident. You've been a real ass."

"I don't think that's a good idea." My eyes bulged at the idea of another encounter alone with Adam. "He's made it clear..."

"Crystal. Clear," he corrected me. "And why are you pushing this, Zack? It's evident she's your date. You babysit her."

"Quit being a tool. I like this girl." Zack elbowed Adam, his voice borderline begging, "C'mon, man. You're my best friend. Believe it or not, it's important to me that you get along with her."

Adam lowered his voice. "Haven't I already done enough by hosting this party for you?"

Zack gave him a disapproving look. "If the roles were reversed—"

"The roles would never be reversed. That's the thing," Adam said as he tried to walk away.

Zack crossed his arms and moved in front of him.

"You're not going to let this go, are you?" Adam huffed. "Fine. Whatever. Let's get this over with."

"I knew you'd see it my way," Zack replied.

Adam stormed out onto the back porch, slamming the

door shut behind him.

"Go on," Zack said. "I know as soon as he spends a few minutes with you, he'll agree you're amazing. Don't be too amazing though." He laughed. "What am I saying? I'm confident enough to know you're going home with me tonight."

"I think maybe I should go back to check on Finn." I tried to hide my scowl. "He just got here from..."

"Don't make me bust out the coffee quips again." Zack's dimples appeared.

My shoulders slumped. There was no other easy exit. Without speaking, I walked out to the back porch and closed the door behind me, the gentle click announcing my presence. A few people were out in the yard smoking cigars, and three people were heading toward the beach underneath the moonlit sky with a volleyball in tow. Adam and I were officially alone.

I sat down on the top step as far from him as possible. "Hey," I said, tucking a stray lock of hair behind my ear.

He looked out at the ocean and offered a simple nod.

"I'm not sure why Zack is pushing this so hard," I continued.

"Beats me." Adam took a drink of his beer. "There are far better ways I could be spending my time."

"You didn't have to do that, you know," I replied.

He set the bottle down and folded his arms atop his knees. "Do what?"

"Recommend me for the job."

"I'd hardly call it recommending you. I merely said—"

"And I'm saying thank you." I looked at him. "Let me know if I need to explain what that phrase means, like I did with the handshake. The proper response is 'you're welcome'."

Silence.

"Why did you do it?" I asked. "You had every opportunity to throw me under the bus."

Adam ran his fingers through his hair before pulling a cigarette and a lighter from his pocket. "Honestly, I have no fucking clue. It's not like you deserve it. And you're not qualified."

"All true statements."

He laughed out his nose and set the red-and-gold labeled pack of cigarettes on the step where his feet rested. "And what's stupid is I only need to smoke these damn things when you're around."

I started to stand up. "Then, maybe I should go inside and distance—"

"Wanna hear what pisses me off?" He leaned back and lit the cigarette.

"Here we go." I sighed and sat back down.

"First of all, I'm calling bullshit on your headache excuse this morning. You don't get migraines. That was the classic Blue Brennan post-crying face. I remember it well."

"So?"

He looked at me before taking a drag. "Second of all, why the waterworks show?"

"Why do you care?"

"I don't," he replied. "I quit caring a long time ago."

"This conversation is going nowhere." I rubbed my temples.

He grabbed for his frosty beer bottle before standing up, the rickety boards of the warped porch creaking beneath him as he leaned against the railing. "Do you have any idea how many nights I've looked up at that starry sky and wondered if you were doing the same?"

I gulped. "Adam—"

"278."

My lungs stopped working. Shit. He had an actual number. And it was a doozy.

"You look surprised." He glanced at me before taking a swig. "Two hundred and fucking seventy-eight. And then...I stopped. Want to know why?"

What felt like years passed before I was able to whisper my response. "Why?"

"I decided to stop punishing myself, wondering what I'd done wrong to make you leave."

"Please." I shook my head, questioning whether I needed to start smoking. "Don't make this harder..."

"No one knew, Blue. No one knew about us being together.

I actually started to wonder if I were crazy, and I dreamed up our entire relationship, so you don't get to talk about making things harder. You have no right."

I tucked my hands up into the sleeves of my sweatshirt. "What I have a right to do isn't a factor in this equation. We were the product of an unfortunate situation." I paused and furrowed my brow in thought. "No, wait. The unfortunate situation was a product of us?"

Adam rubbed his face with his hands. "God, don't make this into some complicated math problem. You and I were the product of us falling in love. You. Me. It was that simple. One plus one equaled two. And that entire 'equation' of us, as you so eloquently put it," he frowned and used air quotes, "started long before what happened to—"

"Don't," my voice wavered. "Don't say her name out loud."

"It's Madelyn! Say it! You have to face what happened sooner or later!" he yelled. "When are you going to come to grips with that?"

"Damn it, Adam. She died!" Tears spilled down my cheeks. "Nothing you or I do can fix that!"

Fifteen

Adam fought to swallow his emotions. "Don't you think I know that? That I'm reminded every day when I drive by your old house, when I speed up past the cemetery and can't even look out my damn window because I know she's buried there? Don't you think it haunts me every time I see her parents at the grocery store? Stop me anytime now. I can go on all night."

I mashed the heels of my hands against my eyes. "Why do you think I left Steele Falls in the first place? I couldn't handle knowing we were responsible for her death. Being surrounded by memories of her..."

"We weren't at fault for what happened to—"

"You're right." I pursed my lips. "*We* weren't. But *I* was. I couldn't stay and live with that. It was too hard."

Adam quieted. "Too hard. So, that reinforces what I suspected all along. You left because of me too."

"That's not—"

"Fucking bullshit!" Adam yelled as he threw the beer bottle at the sidewalk, the brown glass smashing into countless glittering shards.

A grouping of people near the fence took notice and turned their attention toward us. After a few seconds of our silence, they trickled back into their conversation.

Adam lowered his voice and his nostrils flared. "Why do you think I didn't leave after you went MIA? There was an invisible ball and chain around my ankle. Part of me waited to see if you'd come back. To see if it was all some kind of mistake

208

I didn't understand. I may have stayed, but I eventually moved on." He stood up. "But at least I know," he motioned between the two of us, "this meant nothing. What we had was a joke, and I was the punchline."

His words cut deep into my heart. "That's not true, and you know it." The tears began to tumble and my lower lip quivered. "All of it was so fucking complicated. You're not being fair."

"Fair? Do you really want to talk about what's fair?" He sighed. "And there you go with the crying again. Quit trying to be the victim. Let me give you the condensed soup version of what happened. Once upon a time, you were my happily never after. That's it. Past tense. Were." He flicked the cigarette butt to the pathway at the bottom of the steps and blew a stream of smoke out his nose.

I fiddled with a pebble wedged in the bottom of my shoe, unsure of what to say.

He adjusted his posture. "I can only imagine the shit show that funeral will turn out to be tomorrow. Tis the season for your mom to be in the spotlight. She probably hired circus performers, some outrageously-priced pop singer, and a balloon artist."

"Yeah, I guess we'll find out."

He pulled out another cigarette with quaking fingers, but he didn't bother lighting it before he looked at me. "Correction. You'll find out."

"You're not going?" I sniffled, my eyes widening.

He laughed. "Why would I go? To pay my respects? Shed a tear? It'd be a waste of time. Tom Meyers and I didn't see eye-to-eye on anything. He deserves to rot in Hell."

"But the entire town will be there. Won't it be weird if you're the only one not going? I mean, besides Zack."

"Zack. That's right." He let out another laugh, this time through his nose. "You should know by now I don't care what anyone thinks about me around here. So, what'd be 'weird' is if I went. Good luck with tomorrow, with Zack, and with the rest of your life." Adam patted me on the knee twice, stood up, and walked back inside without looking back, the door clicking shut behind him.

I felt alone, in so many ways.

* * *

Roughly Two Years Ago

I snapped to attention and jumped to my feet. The knock on the door left me hopeful for a fraction of a second, like a dog waiting for the mailman. Maybe it was Madelyn, and she came to talk to me. I was willing to apologize, beg, or get down on my hands and knees for the chance to explain. I'd take any of it over the eerie silence that loomed for the past three days with her ignoring me.

When I yanked on the door handle, I didn't mean to look disappointed, but I knew I did a horrible job of hiding it.

"Hey, beautiful," Adam said with a soft smile. "I brought you some dinner." He held up a brown paper bag with the Mario's logo on it. "No one's home, so I figured it was safe to use the front door. Can I come in?"

I moved to allow him enough space to walk through before closing it again. "That was sweet, but I'm really not hungry."

"Come on. I'll bet you haven't left this place in three days, and you won't take any of my calls. I figured if I just showed up, maybe you'd let me in on account you love me." He set the bag down on the counter and took his coat off. "When was the last time you ate?"

I looked up at the ceiling and rubbed the back of my neck. "I don't know. Two days ago? Maybe? Can't remember for sure. Everything's been such a blur since..."

"You need to eat something. Please? For me?" He handed me a container and a fork while flashing the pleading look he knew I was a sucker for. "Everyone at work's wondering where you're at. You can't call out sick forever."

I slumped my shoulders in defeat, and my stomach growled to voice its own opinion. Plus, it was so damn difficult to turn him down. Everything about Adam had an effect on me. I sat on the couch and he joined me a couple of minutes later while I picked at a cheese bubble on top of the lasagna. Even with a growling belly, my appetite was non-existent, but I jammed a floppy noodle into my mouth. All of it reminded me of Madelyn. After four bites of what should've been flavorful lasagna that suddenly tasted like cardboard to me, I couldn't stomach more and wondered if I could even keep that much down.

I pushed the box away on the coffee table and settled back into the couch, resting my head on his shoulder. "I miss her."

He ran his fingers through my hair and kissed the top of my head. "I know you do."

"It's been three days. Why won't she talk to me?"

The hairs raised on the back of my neck. Adam's posture was more rigid than usual and his knee did a weird, nervous, bouncing thing. It was a mannerism I'd only witnessed on two other occasions since knowing him. "What's wrong?" I asked. "Something's not right."

He puffed out his cheeks and let out a breath. "We need to talk."

I'm not sure what caused it. Perhaps it was his tone. Maybe it was because I knew Adam inside and out, and I could sense when anything was wrong with him. But a switch inside of me clicked, and I went cold, frigid. Looking back, I think it might've been when the fortress started to skyrocket around my heart. A thick layer of panic and dread had replaced the heady peacefulness Adam brought me. Nothing good ever came from the 'we need to talk' line. Even I was smart enough to know that. "About what?" I asked, my pulse taking off at a rapid rate.

"Sit up and look at me."

Reluctantly, I turned until I faced Adam on the couch. Since he'd walked through the door, I hadn't taken the time to notice the dark circles cradling his eyes. They were also bloodshot and puffy. Terror crept into my stomach with spindly fingers, threatening to return the little bit of food I was able to coax into it.

He grabbed my hands and rubbed my knuckles with his warm fingertips. "You know how much I adore you, right?"

"Are you breaking up with me?" I blurted.

"No. God, no." He shook his head, closing his eyes for a brief moment before focusing on me again. "I love you and promise I'm not going anywhere."

"Then why do you look like you're about to cry?" I asked. "What are you holding back?"

He opened his mouth but had trouble finding the words for longer than what felt necessary.

"Say it. You're scaring me." I sat up straighter and tried to pull my hands away, but he wouldn't let me.

"I was scheduled to close last night. And when I left Mario's, there were a few cops in the parking lot. They didn't know I was listening."

I stilled. "Did my mom find some way to have you arrested after—"

"No, it's nothing like that," he cut me off. "Baby, I'm sorry. This is so hard. I don't want to be the one to tell you, but I feel like it has to come from me."

"Sorry for what? Did you do something illegal?"

He shook his head left and right. "The cops were talking about a crime scene they were working on. A local one."

I furrowed my brow. "And?"

"Blue," a single tear slid down Adam's cheek and his breathing hitched, "Madelyn committed suicide. She swallowed a bunch of pills, and she was found next to her dad's gun. The EMTs...they tried," he took a breath, "they tried to save her, but it was already too late by the time they got there."

"No." My response was instant and cold because his words were asinine.

His lower lip trembled as he stared into my eyes.

Then, everything took a complete turn. The next sentences spilled from me so quickly, I wasn't sure whether I took a breath. "No...no. You're wrong. She was here, with me, three days ago. In this living room." I pulled my hand away from his and slapped my palm against the cushion of the couch. "She sat right here and...and we read magazines and we ate dinner and we laughed and we gave each other manicures and..." I looked down at the botched nail polish job she'd given me.

"Baby, slow down." Adam cradled my face in his hands.

"No." I shook my head in disbelief. "It has to be someone else. She wouldn't do that. Madelyn wasn't depressed; she was happy." My eyes welled. "I know it...I know her."

"It was Madelyn," his voice was cautious in an attempt to not upset me further, which was impossible. "They were talking about her parents by name, saying how her dad was on a leave of absence from the police force, and even said her brother's—"

"No!" I screamed louder. My lungs suddenly couldn't get enough oxygen and I hyperventilated. "You're wrong!"

"I'm so, so sorry."

I don't recall a lot of what happened next, but I do remember trying to shove Adam away from me as hard as I could. However, he wouldn't let me. Regardless of how many foul sobs escaped me that sounded like a wild animal dying and how much I fought him off with balled-up fists, he wrapped his arms around me tighter and didn't let go. My mouth continued to gape open, and my shoulders heaved. Fractions of agonizing moans and cries were all I could muster, none of it coherent.

Adam was my rock, the one person who'd seen me at my worst and at my best. Nothing fazed that man or deterred him from loving me unconditionally. That night, he'd seen me at one of my lowest points. As much as I fought his embrace, all he did was love me more, whisper repeatedly how sorry he was, and tell me how he wanted to take away my pain while tears of his own spilled down his face. It was everything I needed in that moment, but didn't feel like I deserved.

All of his attempts at consoling me were like raindrops bouncing off a tin roof as he spoke. None of his tender, comforting words soaked into me. Not one. I was impenetrable. As he cradled me in his arms and rocked me, part of me withered and died. What started as an innocent and passionate love affair between Adam and I had once blossomed, flourishing into something beautiful. But in an instant, it had been tainted and turned into something dark and unthinkable, its season ending. Withered. If Madelyn were truly dead, I was the puppet responsible for her pulling the imaginary trigger while she committed the actual act herself. The look on her face three days prior would be one etched in my head forever.

The next afternoon, I packed a few belongings and left Steele Falls without telling a soul, vowing to never look back on the sleepy town again.

* * *

Zack opened the back door and poked his head out. "Is everything okay out here? Adam came in about thirty minutes ago, and I thought you were behind him. Then, I couldn't find you."

"Everything's fine." I wiped my eyes.

He closed the door behind him and sat down next to me on the porch steps. "What's wrong?"

"I don't want to talk about it right now." I forced a lopsided smile. "Call it another bad night."

"Wanna go for a walk?" Zack rubbed my knee. "It might help."

Truth be told, nothing would make me feel better. I didn't want to go wander the beach with Zack, and I didn't want to participate in his feel-better remedy. With my luck, it'd involve some combination of skinny-dipping in the ocean and a roofie cocktail to get me in the sack. For damn sure, I didn't want to revisit that piece of driftwood where Adam and I had carved our initials. And I definitely didn't want to listen to more of Zack's lame stories about his life's accomplishments. Every fiber of my being fought being alone with him, but I found myself acquiescing because it'd be a distraction and distance from Adam.

"Sure," I replied.

He stood up and tugged me to my feet, toward him, a little harder than I anticipated. His face was mere inches from mine, the heat of his body radiating against my skin. My personal bubble threatened to burst. "Zack..." I pulled back.

"I can help you forget about what's bothering you." His

214

voice lowered to a whisper, "You just have to let me..." He brushed my hair out of my face. "We can get out of here and find some place quiet."

"You can't leave. It's your party. Besides, I'm not...." I struggled to find an emergency exit strategy from being pinned in the corner. "There's a lot going on with me right now. The funeral's tomorrow and I leave for Sacramento soon. It's all catching up with me."

"You sure you and Adam weren't yelling earlier?" Zack eyed the broken glass on the ground. "He didn't hurt you, did he?"

My jaw fell. "No. He would never..." I stopped myself before I said too much. "You know, it's getting kinda cold out here. Maybe a walk isn't the best idea." I started to head up the porch stairs. "Plus, I need to use the bathroom."

"Blue?" Zack asked.

"Yeah?" I replied absentmindedly.

"Don't you need me to show you where the bathroom is?"

Shit. As far as Zack knew, I'd never been to Adam's house. Being anywhere alone with him inside asked for trouble. "I... heard someone else earlier mention where it's at. I'm good."

"All right." Zack flashed me a smile, appeased with my lie before he walked away and dove into conversation with a group of men near the driveway.

I went inside and wove my way through the crowd to the bathroom, which was thankfully available, and locked the door behind me.

I looked around. Silence took hold with the exception of fresh-falling rain hitting the roof. So much for an outdoor party. Pristine blue plaid towels matched the rugs and the shower curtains I remembered. They were a surprise I'd picked out after he remodeled the space, a project that took two months and was laced with pitfalls along the way.

A large, clay soap dish rested between the back corner of the counter and the lip of the sink. The pale blue and white swirls of paint reminded me of Steele Falls' sky overlooking the ocean in the spring. I gingerly traced over a minor fissure that had woven its way around the dish, almost perfectly segregating the fused pieces into two halves. Bubbles of superglue had adhered it back together again, the edges not quite aligned to perfection. The hardened glaze was cold, and I held my breath before turning it over in my hand. The lusterless surface on the bottom revealed a faint message.

> *Adam,*
> *To the world, you may only be one person,*
> *But to me, you're the world.*
> *A & F,*
> *Blue*

I rubbed my fingertips against my palms, almost able to feel the cool, wet clay still in my hands when I'd molded it at the pottery shop downtown. Always and forever, no more.

A knock at the door caused me to jump, nearly dropping the dish. I fumbled and caught it before it slid from my fingers and set it back in its spot, perfectly angled. "Just a sec!" I shouted, my heart pounding in my chest.

I went through the motions of washing my hands, so it wouldn't appear unusual when I left the bathroom with no water ran in the sink. Rumors I was shooting up were the last scenario I wanted to deal with on top of everything else.

I opened the door and Beanbag leaned against the wall in the hall with his hands buried in his pockets.

"Oh. It's you." The pep dwindled from his face.

"Always a pleasure to see you too, Beanbag," I replied.

"It's still Wesley. Want me to write it out on a piece of paper so you can practice saying it? I know two syllables can be difficult to remember."

"I'll pass."

"And as reassurance, I'm not stalking you. Just really have to take a leak."

"Right." I glanced down the hall.

"I think your boyfriend is in the kitchen."

"Adam is not..." I stopped myself.

"Whoa." Beanbag raised an eyebrow, confusion spanning

his face. "Who said anything about Adam? I thought you came with Zack?"

"That's what I said," I spoke quickly and averted my eyes. "Zack."

"Must be my mistake then." He blinked. "Maybe you've been saying Wesley all this time too, and I've developed hearing loss since you arrived."

"Enjoy your piss." I shoved past him and heard the door slam shut behind me a few seconds later.

The kitchen was less crowded than earlier, the party slowly dying down. I grabbed a cracker from the table and crunched it in half. Zack approached one of the men he'd been drinking with at the bar the first night I met him. He multi-tasked, continuing to glance at Lucy across the room as she bent over in front of the cooler.

Lucy glanced at him over her shoulder and smirked before giving her ass a shimmy.

"Hey, Wade," Zack said as he shook his friend's hand, clamping his other hand on his shoulder with a firm squeeze. He faced the counter, unaware of my presence.

I lingered in the background and munched on another cracker, eavesdropping on their conversation.

"So, what is it with you and that girl you showed up with tonight? I thought you were gonna hook up with Heather the other night at The Fill & Spill? That long blonde hair and those legs? Perfection." Wade let out a long, low whistle.

"Oh, don't think I didn't close the deal. Heather and I took our party of two back to my place and hit the hot tub. God, that girl can bend in ways you wouldn't believe. Like a fuckin' pretzel."

"Damn, man. I swear, you're some kind of chick whisperer."

Zack laughed. "It's a gift."

"Seriously though. If you could bang someone like Heather Miller, why bother with an average Jane Doe like Blue Brennan?"

Zack gave Wade a knowing look. "Come on. Think about it. She's the mayor's daughter. That minor detail could do wonders for Main Enterprises exploding even farther. The connections Elana Meyers has is endless with as long as she's been in office. I'd be stupid to not slip that ace up my sleeve." He elbowed Wade. "Don't get me wrong, Blue's definitely no Heather. Not even close. It'll take some definite work on my end to try and make her that kind of eye candy." He began counting on his fingers. "Replace her wardrobe, send her to the spa for an overhaul, sign her up to the gym so she can drop ten pounds, and a steady diet of celery sticks could have her flawless eventually. In the meantime, my black book is full of women, waiting to keep me satisfied."

"Can't wait to see this next project of yours unfold." Wade laughed. "You slay me, bro."

Flawless eventually. I crushed the remaining piece of cracker in my hand, a shower of crumbs falling to the floor. Those two words burned into me like a branding iron, and rage bubbled beneath the surface of my skin. *Flawless eventually.* It was the same phrase Cash used on me days ago.

I closed my eyes and took a breath to regain my composure, but it was already miles gone, a blip on the horizon. Seeing red, I walked over to Zack and tapped him on the shoulder.

Zack lowered his voice, waving away who stood behind him, "But between you and me, I've just about got her eating out of the palm of my hand now. She's all emotional and shit with that funeral tomorrow. I have to amp up the charm a little more, and fucking her will be easier than getting laid by Lucy, the cum dumpster. Blue Brennan will be screaming my name in no time."

He turned and looked at me, surprise spelled out on his face. "Oh! Hey."

I smiled sweetly and batted my eyes. "Hey, yourself. Missed you."

"See what I mean?" Zack looked at Wade and grinned.

"I'll leave you guys alone." Wade smirked and turned to walk away.

"You don't have to go." I gripped his arm to stop him. "Plus, I think you should hear this too." The smile on my face turned to a vicious frown as I bared my teeth and turned my attention to Zack. What I wanted to say next didn't require words. I looked into his gray eyes and cocked my hand back, delivering a powerful slap across his face.

His head whipped to the side from the blow, the sound loud enough to draw the attention of every other person in the kitchen, including those trailing in from the rain. "What was that for?" He touched his cheek, a red handprint immediately appearing.

I tilted my head to the side and licked my lips. "I think my delivery could use some work, but it'll be flawless...eventually. Right?" I patted him on the arm. "Goodbye, Zack."

The room remained silent and all eyes were on me as I walked through the kitchen toward the front door, hurrying down the steps and into the pouring rain. Cold droplets pelted me in the face, and the wind had intensified, pushing me along as I headed down the sandy road toward town.

"Hey!" a voice shouted behind me, mildly muffled by the weather.

I increased my speed and wrapped my arms around myself tighter. "Go away!"

"For Christ's sake, wait up!"

I turned around and saw Adam jogging to catch up to me. Rain dripped from his hair down his face, dark tendrils plastered to his forehead. "What was that all about?"

"What?" I crossed my arms.

"Come on, Blue. You deck a guy in my kitchen and then take off into the night like a bat out of hell?"

"Not decked. Slapped."

"Semantics," he replied. "What the fuck happened back there?"

"I thought you stopped caring? He's a dick. Isn't that reason enough?"

"He's Zack. Of course, he's a dick. Anyone who can see and hear knows that."

"Well, he says you're his best friend. Great choice."

"Not that you have a say in who I hang out with, but I never said he was mine. I don't do best friends anymore." His face reddened. "In bed or at all. Not worth it."

SARAH JAYNE CARR

I placed my hands on my hips. "Then, why's it still there?"

Adam looked confused. "What? The red mark? You hit Zack pretty hard, and—"

"Not that." I paused. "The stuff in the bathroom. The rugs. The shower curtain. The soap dish with the inscription. Why haven't you gotten rid of it?"

"I didn't know you'd be dissecting my bathroom like an eighth-grade science project." Adam rubbed the back of his neck. "Did you go through the medicine cabinet too?"

"It's hard to not notice if you have eyes. Kinda like Zack being a dick."

Adam sighed. "Blue, don't read into what you saw. It's just stuff."

"No! It's *stuff* that's tied to me! Intimately!"

His voice rose an octave. "Not that I have to explain, but it's holed up in a spare bathroom that's never used unless my *dick*," he used air quotes, "of a friend, not best friend, mind you, hosts a party at my house because his got skunked! Outside of cleaning it up for tonight, that door hasn't been opened in who knows how long!"

I rubbed my face. "Forget it. I have to go prepare to face one of the hardest days of my life."

"No one likes funerals."

I deadpanned him. "That's not why I'm dreading tomorrow, and you know it." With no more fight left to give, I turned and walked away. "You're still the only one who knows."

Sixteen

The next day, I woke up soaked in cold sweat with my heart pounding. A nightmare jolted me awake where I tried to tread water while being tossed around the Pacific Ocean. Frigid water numbed my limbs, and I couldn't keep my head above the turbulent surface. Coughing. Choking. Gasping for air.

A fleet of boats overflowing with orange life vests surrounded me, the townspeople of Steele Falls on board each one. Yet, every familiar face and even strangers watched me suffer with a blank expression on their faces. No one would help. A massive tidal wave crashed over me, shoving me downward, a flurry of miniature bubbles blinding me from knowing which way was up. Weightlessness took hold, and I sank into the abyss of the ocean while a final rush of icy water greeted my lungs. Burning. Indescribable pain. I was too exhausted to fight back, and my body went limp.

It was so vivid, I could almost feel the salt on my skin as I rubbed my thumb against the pads of my fingers.

I rolled over and looked out the window. The rain had stopped, but a gray sky still loomed overhead, telling me more was on the way. Thick branches of the near-leafless trees bent in the strong breeze, and the gate slammed against the fence, not properly locked from the last visitor. It looked both cold and uncomfortable to be standing outside. Perfect weather and tone for a funeral. I checked my cell phone and there was a series of texts from my sister, sent fifteen minutes ago.

'Veigh

I left my spare keys on the counter for you.
I'll give you a ride back home if you need it.

Meeting with the executor is scheduled
for eleven. Office building across from the
cemetery. Suite C.

Mommy and I are leaving now. Finn will
meet us there. See you soon. xoxo

I tossed the phone back on the nightstand without sending a response. So much had happened in the few days since I arrived in Steele Falls, it seemed like weeks. Yet, the day of the funeral had snuck up so fast.

I went to the closet and stood there for about ten minutes, indecisive. Nausea filled me and my hands felt clammy. Remaining hidden and non-existent was my goal. After much debate, I pulled out a fitted charcoal-colored sweater and a black, floor-length skirt. Picking out clothing and pulling the hangers from the rack made everything more real. Escape was still possible. It wasn't too late to run. But I questioned whether it'd do me any good. I used to think it would, but I wasn't so sure anymore.

The heaviness of the day took hold, which gave me unwanted time to reflect. I pinned my hair up in bobby pins and allowed a few loose tendrils of curls to frame my face. With little makeup on, I looked at myself in the mirror, seeing a younger version of me in my eyes. A less guarded girl. A free-spirited girl. A girl who knew how to laugh and love. "Where did she go?" I touched my lips. That girl was in there somewhere, and I vowed to find her again.

* * *

I arrived at the single-story building across from the cemetery five minutes early. The exterior was aged and faded, empty planter boxes lining the walkway. I parallel-parked Daveigh's car in the last empty slot on the street and stared head-on at one of the moments I was most afraid of. It took a few attempts to convince myself to get out and head up the walkway, but I finally prevailed. *One foot in front of the other.* The double doors were unlocked, the lobby eerily quiet and dim as I walked inside. A deep breath. The smell of stale coffee and the feeling of sadness swilled together, both cloying in the back of my throat. Suite C was on the right at the end of the hall.

I knocked three times.

"Come in," a male voice bellowed.

I opened the door and saw an older man seated behind a baroque desk. His stature domineered, but a glint of compassion behind his eyes reminded me of a squishy teddy bear. His head was both bald and shiny, glossy against the fluorescent lighting overhead. A substantial amount of facial hair cradled his chin, appearing to have slid down from atop his scalp. "You must be Blue," he said.

I nodded and shut the door behind me. "Sorry, I'm late."

"You're not late. Two minutes early, according to my clock." He perched a pair of bifocals on his face. "Have a seat. My name is Douglas Crenshaw, but we have two employees and a service dog named Doug around here, so everyone calls me Crenshaw."

I looked around. The walls were drenched in rich tones of deep brown and forest green. Elana and Daveigh were seated side-by-side across the room on an oversized leather couch near a lit gas fireplace. Finn sat as far from them as possible on a loveseat with an ankle resting on his opposing knee. I opted to occupy the empty cushion next to my brother.

"Hey," he said with a half-smile, scooting over.

"Hi," I replied quietly. "Did I miss anything?"

"Not yet."

"Is this everyone you want present, Elana?" Crenshaw asked.

My mother straightened her posture and tightened her gloved grip around a tissue. She wore her usual skirt-blouse-and-jacket combo, this time in black. A matching 40's pillbox hat donned her head with netting covering her face. "Yes."

Crenshaw shuffled a stack of papers on his desk. "Now, I'm not only the executor of Tom's will and his lawyer, but I was his friend for a few decades. With that said, I'll be honest. This matter has been more complicated than most that've passed by my desk. Main reason being a majority of his money being in his sister's name. A sibling holding money over a spouse isn't a common occurrence. But then again, the term 'spouse' doesn't directly apply here."

My mother cringed, her personal business being put on display like a caged animal in a zoo. "May I see the will?" she asked before pursing her lips together.

"No, Elana," Crenshaw said flatly. "That's not necessary."

She blinked rapidly in surprise of being turned down. "Why—"

"Tom was very cut and dry on what was to be assigned where. Of course, the house and any items inside belong to you, along with all vehicles and your joint bank ventures. However, Tom did have the separate account I mentioned, in Julie's name, and he was very specific about it."

Crenshaw fiddled with the combination lock on a safe behind his desk. I looked at the simple clock on the wall, a massive white circle with bold black numbers. The second hand lazily made its way around in a complete revolution twice while the room remained silent; at least it wasn't stuck on 39. Sweat trickled down my back in the overheated space, a reminder that I wanted to run far and run fast. Funeral time was set to start in a little over an hour. All I had to do was get through the day, and it'd all be over with for good.

Crenshaw stood up from his crouched position. His knees cracked like a bowl of rice cereal, giving away his age. He hobbled around to the front of his desk with a stack of thin yellow envelopes in his hand. "In my experience, I recommend waiting to open these later, in private. There's no doubt today will be tolling on each of you, both mentally and emotionally. Nothing in here will change whether you open them now or tomorrow. However, there is only one chance to pay your respects at the funeral. Daveigh."

224

My sister reached out with shaky fingers and accepted the first envelope. "Thank you."

"Elana." He extended the second to my mother.

Her only response of gratitude was a slight head nod as she dabbed at her eyes with a fresh tissue.

Next, Crenshaw walked over to where Finn and I were seated. "Blue." He handed the third envelope to me. Unlike everyone else's, a second envelope was paper-clipped to the back of the yellow one.

I took the envelopes from him and tried to split them apart. "One of these must be yours, Finn."

"No," Crenshaw said, placing his warm palm atop my hand. "Both of those are for you. "This one is Finn's." He handed a final envelope to my brother.

I looked up at him. "I don't understand. Why am I the only one with two?"

"I'm merely the messenger on Tom's behalf." He glanced at Elana. "I'll leave you and your children to talk for a few minutes."

I fingered over the sealed envelopes in my hand, the handwriting reading 'Blue' unfamiliar to me. The paper felt heavy in my palm, and I was suddenly unsure whether I wanted to know what was inside. *The money's the whole reason you came back to Steele Falls. Isn't it?*

My thoughts were interrupted by the sound of paper ripping as my mother hastily tore the edge of her envelope. "Five thousand dollars?" she scoffed "That's it? From a seasoned stock investor?"

Daveigh opened her envelope and peered inside. "Same," she replied before tucking it into her purse. With tears in her eyes, she looked up at the ceiling. "Thanks, Daddy."

Without opening his, Finn held his envelope against the lighting and nodded before slipping it in his inside jacket pocket.

Suddenly, two pairs of eyes were on me—Elana's and Daveigh's. "What?"

"Well, aren't you going to open yours?" my sister asked.

My mother sported her classic poker face. Not surprising.

Opening the envelope in front of everyone felt wrong to me, but the two of them waited with bated breath.

"Like Crenshaw said, I think I'd rather wait until I'm alone later—"

"For Pete's sake, Blue. Quit dragging this out, and open the damn thing." Elana pointed at the envelope on my lap.

Finn gave me a nudge. "It's your choice, but the sooner you look, the sooner it's over with. Safety in numbers. Remember?"

I closed my eyes and wondered if he were right. Maybe getting it over with would be like ripping off a bandage. The unknown wouldn't be looming over my head for the rest of the day—one hurdle cleared. My hands shook as I slid my index finger under the seal of the larger of the two envelopes, making a neat tear. I pulled the document out and froze.

"Blue, you're really pale. What's wrong?" Finn whispered.

"It's nothing." I folded the piece of paper as small as possible, hoping to bury it for eternity. "Everything's fine," I said, shoving both envelopes in my jacket pocket.

"What is it? We're all family here." Daveigh walked over to where I sat and gave me a hug. Before I realized what happened, she'd reached into my pocket and pulled the larger envelope out.

"What are you? A child?" I swatted at her, reaching for it, but she'd darted out of the way. "Don't, 'Veigh. Please."

"Oh, come on. Don't make a big deal about it. I'm sure..." She let out a whistle as she peered inside. "What the hell?"

Elana huffed as she pinched the bridge of her nose. "What now?"

"Blue's total." Daveigh looked up at me. "It's for five million dollars."

"Let me see that," my mother snapped, storming across the room to snatch the envelope from Daveigh's hand. Her line of vision darted around every inch of the piece of paper. Front and back. "There has to be some mistake."

As if on cue, Crenshaw entered the room and quietly closed the door behind him. "Are there any questions or do you need a few more minutes before you head over to the cemetery?"

My mother opened her mouth and then closed it again before dropping the envelope onto my lap. "No. No questions at this time. Thank you."

"All right. Funds will be dispersed when..."

The rest of Crenshaw's words were lost on me. I fought to stay in the present while he said his goodbyes to each of us. In a single file line and in silence, the four of us left the office and walked out toward the parking lot.

Much like letting go of a forced smile, I wasn't sure what facial expression was appropriate. Tom had left me a ridiculous sum of money, and the rest of my family was left to wonder why. No one could tell them but me. *Damn him.* The whole scenario made me want to throw up. "I'll meet you across the street in a minute," I said to Finn.

"You sure? I can wait." His eyes flicked up toward Elana.

"Trust me, I don't mind. It'd be a welcome excuse."

I nodded and swallowed. "I'm sure. You go."

"Okay." He gave me a quick hug paired with a look of concern before he trailed after them.

I stood near the breezeway linking two buildings and waited until they were out of sight before I fished the second envelope from my jacket. Fortunately, Daveigh missed that one when she pickpocketed me. It, too, had my name written on the front in shaky, blue ink. I pulled out the piece of paper and unfolded it. Tom's handwriting was unmistakable.

> *Blue,*
> *I want to take a moment of your time to...*

Eleven words. Eleven words were enough, perhaps too many. I stopped reading. You want to take a moment of my time, Tom? A moment? Last time I checked, that was indicative of "one". Singular. What you took from me was well beyond that. The first six words alone were enough to make me vomit my breakfast on the sidewalk, and they caused my knees to knock together. I didn't need to read the rest of the letter to know it was filled with crap. Tears stung my eyes and I tore it to shreds, refusing to stop until the pieces were each the size of confetti. I wanted no chance of it ever being put back together by anyone. My life was better off without any additional words or advice Tom Meyers had to offer.

I took the handful of paper bits and threw them in a nearby garbage can, a pathetic attempt at the closure I'd never obtain. A few stray pieces caught the wind and danced into the parking lot. "Good riddance," I muttered as I thrust my hands in my pockets before heading across the street to the cemetery.

The rusty, wrought iron gates were wide open, spiked tops aimed toward the heavens. My shoes clicked against the cobblestone pathway as I made my way toward a gathering of people with more joining. The space wasn't nearly as crowded as I thought it'd be. Saving grace. Maybe I could go through with the service, after all.

I saw my mother, Daveigh, and Finn in the distance as I my eyes scanned the gently rolling hills. A sea of gray tombstones punctuated the lush green grass. My hands were sweaty as fear pulsed through my veins.

Finn spotted me and changed directions, closing in on the distance between us with his brow furrowed. "Is everything okay? I'm worried about you."

"I'm good. Promise." I blinked rapidly.

He let out a deep breath. "Okay, but don't think I'm going to let this go. You're still the worst liar in the world."

I gave him a quick hug. "I know."

"Come on. We need to find our seats soon. It's about to start."

I let Finn lead me over the crest of the hill. Just when I thought I'd dug deep enough to find my courage, my feet forced me to a screeching halt. "Holy shit." What I thought was initially a small grouping of people, revealed a surprise.

"I know," Finn replied. "Big turn out."

"I mean, I thought the whole town would come, but I really didn't think there'd be this many...how many towns came?" My eyes honed in on where a sea of people continued to flock to where my mother stood. Camera men. Two local news crew. An entertainment channel spokesperson. Adam was right. It was going to be a circus, and I regretted my decision to attend.

Finn leaned over and whispered into my ear, "For everything being okay, you sure are hanging onto my arm similar to how politicians cling to corruption."

I stifled my giggle at his attempt to lighten the mood.

"There's a smile. You gonna be all right for a few minutes? I need to find Scott before the shit show starts."

I nodded. "Go. Save him."

Finn headed down the hill and turned around, walking backward as he spoke, "The director said rows one and two are reserved for immediate family."

"Got it." I took a breath and walked toward the dramatic setup. Seats with rounded tops were positioned in long rows, each draped in a white dressing and adorned with a single calla lily. Oversized silver-and-black bows countered the long, green stems. A blood red runner with flecks of gold glitter split the seating area into left and right hemispheres. It was the ostentatious path to where Tom's coffin rested. Open casket. *Why?* No one had mentioned there'd be a viewing before the service. Until that point, seeing my step-father again hadn't crossed my mind. I watched people stop to peer at him, stare at him, talk to him. An up-close and personal goodbye wasn't going to happen by me. It took everything I had to convince my feet that walking forward to my seat was the correct action to take.

I kept my head down and hurried to the front row, trying to draw little attention to myself. From the corner of my eye, I saw my mother soaking up the attention from a continuous line of people. She even smiled a few times. People hugged her, consoled her, and patted her on the shoulder. It was the SHAT-combo's distant cousin; she ate it up. For believing a short while ago we were so similar, it seemed like such a polar opposite.

A few minutes later, everyone was seated, and the classical music dwindled. The service was about to begin. In the second row, Finn and Scott were to my left, along with Daveigh and Beanbag. My mother was in front of us, seated alone, without her children by her side.

A brunette woman wearing a black clergy robe with a bold cross stitched on either side approached the lectern. She adjusted the microphone and stared out at the sea of faces. "Today, we meet here, in Steele Falls, to pay tribute and honor the life of Tom Meyers. Also, we're here to comfort those he was close to who've been saddened by his unexpected death."

Daveigh quietly sniffled, dabbing at her eyes with a tissue. I was frozen, memories pouring through me like a sieve; I felt like I was drowning and alone. Like last night's bad dream came true.

The clergywoman continued, "Tom was a spiritual person. It's appropriate his celebration of life reflect him for what he was: A kindhearted and gentle family man who adored his wife and three children. Each of you will likely remember today differently, but I hope you can recall it as a special moment where you shared time and fond memories with the ones you care about."

You bet I'll remember today differently. There was no way she'd know any better, but her words made me sick as I dug my fingernails into the palms of my hands, fighting to maintain my stoic expression.

I saw my mother glance back at me from the corner of her eye and frown. She closed in on the distance between us as much as she could. "The least you could do is show some remorse for your dead father. Eyes are upon us," she hissed.

"Step-father," I mumbled under my breath.

"You're lucky we're in public or else I'd slap you." Her stare was ferocious. "I don't care if you called him the Pope, a unicorn, or Santa Claus. That man was relevant in your life since you were a child."

I closed my eyes and smirked, afraid to open them again. "Relevant." That was one fact she had right. Parents were supposed to be significant, and mine were. Just not in the way I'd hoped. I bit my lip, using the pain to chain me in the present.

Unexpectedly, the empty wooden chair to my right shifted and creaked as someone sat down next to me. I opened my eyes and turned my attention to who it was, caught off guard.

"Sorry, I'm late," Adam murmured, facing forward. He was dressed in a classic black suit, and he smelled like a combination of pine trees and rain.

My stomach lurched. There was no opportunity for me to combat the tears threatening the corners of my eyes. "You said you weren't—"

"I'm not letting you sit here on your own, Blue. No one should have to..." His voice trailed off as he pursed his lips.

"You don't have to do this, you know."

He didn't modify his posture, his Adam's apple bobbing in his throat when he swallowed hard. "I know."

My ears piqued at the sound of the clergywoman mentioning my name, bringing my focus back to the funeral. "Despite their individual struggles with the situation, I've been told each of Tom's children would like to come up and say a few words. Blue?"

I glanced at Adam with a blank expression, almost seeking direction.

"Now, it's my turn to use your words." His face had never been so serious. "You don't have to do this, you know."

I couldn't muster more than a faint whisper, "But I think I do." It took three tries of my brain communicating for my feet to move before they finally complied. Each step was an undertaking as I made my way up the three stairs. The top half of the coffin was propped open, and I was able to see Tom's face. His oversized nose. His receding hairline. His pockmarked complexion. His beady eyes behind closed lids. I was thankful they were shut. Seeing the foggy windows to his soul would've pushed me over the edge. The clergywoman patted me on the shoulder and nodded her encouragement before moving out of the way.

Countless eyes and ears awaited my words. I cleared my throat, their murmurs quieting. A camera snapped a series of rapid shots from the left, and I jumped. It felt wrong knowing the event was being documented down to the most minute detail. Even worse, I was under the magnifying glass.

Adrenaline tingled my tongue, and I glanced at Adam while pulling a crumpled piece of paper from my pocket. He nodded slowly. I wasn't sure if he blinked, his eyes remaining fixated on me. Even after two years of no contact and a few days of heated arguments, he was my reassurance and my security when I'd needed him most.

Focus.

My breath echoed in my ears as I fought for the courage to speak. "The Lord is my shepherd; I shall not want." The words were barely legible as the paper moved in my hands. "He maketh me to lie down in green pastures; He leadeth me beside the still waters."

Focus.

A flicker of memory took hold, an ember. It was one I'd kept locked up for so long. I prayed it wouldn't catch fire and ignite. "He restoreth my soul; He leadeth me," I paused as a single tear slid down my cheek, "in the paths of righteousness for His name's sake."

My voice squeaked. "Yea, though I walk through the valley of the shadow of death, I will fear no evil."

Focus.

I swallowed that last word hard as debilitating anxiety set in, and I wondered if the people seated in front of me knew. Knew my secret. I was certain everyone's eyes scrutinized me for the truth.

Focus.

"For Thou art with me; Thy rod and Thy staff, they comfort..."

I knew there was no comfort. It was ripped away long ago. I looked up, unable to go on without crumbling. My mother watched me, her lips pressed into the thinnest, tightest line possible.

"I'm sorry." I bolted down the steps near the lectern and sprinted across the grass toward a grouping of trees in the distance. The folded piece of paper with my words was lost and forgotten. One of the thick trunks concealed me from the crowd, and I leaned against the rough bark to keep from falling. It was useless. My knees buckled and I sank to the ground, burying my face in my hands.

"Blue?" Adam's voice was laced with concern as I heard his footsteps become louder.

I felt him kneel next to me, but I couldn't uncover my

eyes. My only response was in shaking my head left and right.

Adam didn't ask if I was okay; he already knew the answer. I wasn't. That was the first time I'd acknowledged it. Tears streamed down my cheeks as my shoulders heaved, an overdue cry of pained relief escaping my chest. His arms encompassed my frame while he held me tight. I didn't care about the rest of the funeral. I didn't care about my mother's future reprimand. I didn't care about the five million dollars. So much emotion fought to pour out of me at once, all I could do was let go.

"Slow down. Breathe." He rested his chin on top of my head. "Let it out."

I'm not sure how long I sat there with the shelter of his arms wrapped around me. He didn't pressure me with a slew of questions or rush me to go back to the funeral. He didn't shush me from crying or tell me a cliché 'everything will be all right'. He held me, and that was what I needed. Damn him for always knowing what I *needed*. A little while later, maybe two minutes, maybe twenty, my sobs had subdued into a pattern of hitched breathing and hiccups.

"Are you going to tell her?" He helped me to my feet.

"No, the past is buried." My eyes flicked over to the casket. "Or it's about to be. Let's just go back, so I can put this God-awful day behind me."

He opened his mouth to say something and then closed it. "Okay."

By the time we arrived at the burial site, the funeral had ended. People were congregating in small clusters. I was surrounded by the monotony of black clothing and solemn faces while they quietly spoke amongst one another. A few looked at me as I passed by, but I kept my head down.

My mother spotted me from fifty feet away and bee-lined to where I stood. Daveigh and Finn weren't in sight. So much for safety in numbers. Alone with the momster. My lucky day.

"I'm pleasantly surprised with your presentation," she said. "The tears were a nice touch. It's likely the only positive attribute from you being impregnated by that useless plastic surgeon."

Adam's eyed my stomach, a flicker of disappointment on his face. "Cash got you pregnant?"

The unsavory lie was too difficult to purge, so I answered with a nod.

"Christ," Adam muttered.

"I'll explain later," I hissed at him.

"Spare me the details on how it happened. I got the gist of the birds and the bees talk long ago."

"Not now."

Elana's eyes flicked over to Adam, acknowledging him with a lethal glare. "Her choice in who she spread her legs for could've been worse, I suppose."

It was the lowest of blows.

As always, the world revolved around my mother. Her image. Her wishes. Her victories. She didn't ask how I was doing or if I were okay. Hell, she was under the impression I was pregnant, and...nothing. I bit my tongue from saying something I'd regret later on.

The topic quickly curved back to the one I dreaded.

"I still don't understand why Tom left you significantly more money than the rest of us. Ridiculous." She spoke with certainty. "Those extra zeros have to be a hellacious mistake."

"Extra zeros?" Adam asked, confused.

"I don't know why." A few loose locks of hair shielded my face, and I was grateful for that. If there were a way for me to sink into the graveyard, I'd have already been six feet under with the rest of the corpses.

"Well, there had to be a reason or someone should be fired for screwing up royally. He wouldn't give you four million, nine hundred and ninety-five thousand dollars more than his own wife." She clicked her tongue against the roof of her mouth in dissatisfaction. As if I were a fly tangled in a spider web, my mother waited for the most opportune moment to strike and sink her fangs in.

"What's she talking about?" Adam asked.

"I already said I don't know." I stomped my foot. "Can we drop this? Please?"

My mother crossed her arms. "No. I don't want to drop it.

Think back, Blue. Hard."

I remained still, flashes of memories wrapping around my ribcage like gangly fingers taking hold of my soul. Gripping. Tearing. Puncturing. Shredding. Breathing was difficult as I tried to pace filling and emptying my lungs.

"C'mon. Let's get out of here," Adam murmured, nudging my elbow. "Don't let her badger you like this."

I looked around at the throng of people wallowing in post-funeral conversation; few had left. Escaping through the maze felt impossible. Drowning. Sinking. Suffocating. Just like my nightmare.

"Use your brain," she pressed on. "There has to be a semblance of a clue in there somewhere."

Adam was right. I should've left. It would've been best for everyone. Little did my mother know, my mind was the most terrifying place of all, history hidden under lock and key. The pressure of being at Tom's funeral on top of holding my silence over the years was too much to bear. Like a twig, I finally snapped. "I have no fucking clue. Maybe it's hush money. Maybe it's remorse money." My voice escalated to a yell, "Maybe it's because your asshole of a husband tried to rape me!" I clamped my hand over my mouth.

There was no going back. Elana Meyers had her answer.

Seventeen

Our surroundings tanked to instant silence, people stealing an occasional glance our way to determine what the commotion was about. Elana flashed them a forced smile and a half-wave.

Her attention turned toward me, her breathing slowing as she squinted. "What did you say?"

Adam touched my elbow. "Come on. Let's go."

"No." I stood my ground. "Not this time. I'm tired of running from it."

She grabbed my wrist, her fingers like frosty ice against my skin. "What. Did. You. Say?"

"Why do you think Tom was up so late that night? Cleaning his gun? I don't think so." I laughed through my nose as tears glistened in my eyes. "You really believed in those bullshit lies of his, didn't you? Couldn't you see the fear on my face? Hear him slurring? Smell the alcohol? Feel the tension? Are you that out of touch with reality?"

"We're leaving," my mother commanded. "Your attempt at making a mockery of this service can be dealt with back home, not in public."

"No, it can't and it won't. I don't want to talk about this. Not with you. Not ever." I shook free from her grip. "Besides, you've got a reception to attend as a widow, which should be beneficial for your upcoming election. Enjoy."

"You listen here," she spoke through bared teeth. "You are coming with me right now."

Adam stepped between us. "No offense, Mrs. Meyers, but

I don't think she wants to go with you."

"That's cute. The beach-dwelling rodent wants to intervene?" Her laughter had a serrated edge to it. "Please, enlighten me with what you have to say."

Adam balled his fists at his sides repeatedly, his arms shaking.

She jutted her chin upward in an attempt to look down at him from eight inches below his towering frame. "See? The felon can't even carry an intelligent conversation, let alone a reputable job without the help of a joke like Ty. Just who do you think you are, anyway?"

Adam's expression was stone cold. "I'm the only person who knows every disgusting word of what happened. Why do you think I got that felony DUI? It took hearing five words of what that fuckwad husband of yours was doing before I burned rubber across town. What did *you* do?" He shook his head slowly. "That's right. You went back to bed, a few feet away from what went on with your daughter. All because you had a 'meeting in the morning with that tool, Harold, as you'd put it."

Her complexion turned ashy.

"Did my decision to drink and drive backfire? Yes." The muscles in Adam's jaw clenched. "For her, I'd have lost it all. Even risked life in prison to stop that shit bag."

* * *

Roughly Two Years
and A Little Over Six Months Ago

"The momster's gonna kill me." I angled the key in the moonlight while squinting one eye. My fingers were numb from the sea air, and guiding the key into the hole was like threading a needle in the dark. It was three in the morning, and I'd missed curfew. Again. There were few rules the Brennan/Meyers kids had to abide by, but being late was a doozy. Even as a young adult. That night, intelligence wasn't in my favor, and I'd stayed out at the bonfire for too long with Madelyn. It was my own fault. I forgot to leave my bedroom window open a fraction of an inch so I could scale the trellis and sneak in undetected.

I opened the door and crept inside, carefully crossing over the floorboard that creaked as loudly as the third porch step. It was pitch black and the heavily cinnamon-scented air was stagnant. Fortunately, I knew the layout with my eyes closed. So, so close to being off the hook.

That night went differently than I envisioned though. The lights flicked on, and I froze mid-step, half-expecting to see my mother wearing curlers and her floral bathrobe with the thick lace on the borders. Thinking back, the feminine colors did little to soften her resting bitch face. But it wasn't her who waited for me.

"Well, look what the tide washed in," Tom slurred. "I've been waiting to see if you'd show your face before sunrise."

I turned my head, waiting to focus from the drastic change in lighting. My stepfather sat there with bloodshot eyes, a rosy red nose, and dots of sweat beading his brow. His white tank top was yellowed around the neckline with sweat stains, puffs of gray, scraggly hair curling over the top of it. A near-empty bottle of vodka sat next to him on the table as his latest drinking companion—alongside his pistol.

As the years went on throughout my childhood, the liquor cabinet had become a swift, revolving door for every type of alcohol imaginable. I called it the "no bottle left behind" act. Every time the cupboard was fully stocked, he'd walk through the door a short while later with three more brown bags to refill what he'd polish off that night and the next. Throw in the gun rack perched next to it, and things were bound to get messy, if not lethal. I almost had enough money saved up to skip town, but knowing Daveigh and Finn still lived at home held me back. Someone had to protect them from the alcohol-induced yelling. The post-gambling loss rages. The drunken swings at inanimate objects.

"Oh. Hey, Tom." I glanced at the cuckoo clock and cringed. Yep, it was still a little after three, and I had no justifiable excuse. "I guess I lost track of time tonight. Sorry."

He motioned to the chair across from him with the top of the bottle. "Have a seat."

Sitting around with my drunken stepfather on any night wasn't on my bucket list. A lie needed to manifest. Fast. "Work scheduled me at nine this morning, so I should head up to bed." I stifled a fake yawn.

"Come on. No one should have to drink alone." His beady eyes had trouble focusing, and I knew "no" wasn't going to be an acceptable answer.

"Um. Okay," I said slowly as I walked over to the table and sat down, knowing the repercussion from my mother would be worse if I argued. Her highness was a beast if awakened from her beauty rest.

He poured a sloppy shot, the clear liquid sloshing over the side before he downed it, slamming the glass onto the table. The staccato sound punctuated the silence. "Man, that's good stuff. So, how was your night?"

"It was...good." I jammed my hands in the pockets of my hoodie.

"Good is...good," he stretched out the words awkwardly before refilling the glass, nudging it across the table to where I sat. "Have one."

Goosebumps inched up my spine and tiptoed down my arms. "I...I'm not twenty-one yet. I can't."

"Can't or won't?" He rolled his eyes and made a raspberry sound with his mouth. "I've seen you down at The Fpill & Sill," he corrected himself with a chuckle, "Fill & Spill with your friends and your fake license. Don't bullshit a bullshitter."

It was a new level of drunk, even for Tom. There was no doubt his liver was permanently pickled. When I'd forgotten to lock my bedroom window the last time, I'd snuck in through the front door and found him passed out, face-down on the kitchen floor. Stepping over his unconscious body was my preferred version of him.

He pushed away from the table, shoving his chair backward in a grandiose gesture. The feet noisily scooted across the floor. His arm swung forward and knocked over the capped bottle, causing the glass to rattle as it rolled across the tabletop. Silence loomed again as Tom stumbled until he stood behind me. "Drink up."

I didn't dare turn around. The silence was thick. Suddenly, I'd become very aware we were the only two in the room, and the hairs on the back of my neck raised. My eyes remained on that shot glass, panic captivating me from looking up. The worn Las Vegas emblem in red and yellow was my only focus. "No. If she finds out, she'll..." I tried to stand up, but his hands forcefully pushed down on my shoulders until I was seated again.

Trapped.

He leaned over me from behind, bracing either side of the table with his hands. A whiff of stale vodka struck my nose at the same time his hot breath hit my ear. "No one has to know except for us."

Terror paralyzed my limbs. We were no longer talking about a simple shot. The conversation had taken a turn I couldn't have anticipated. "Tom..."

"Come on. We're not blood-related. That makes what's about to happen so, so right." His right hand left the lip of the table and his palm met my thigh, fingers splayed wide as they moved toward the zipper on my jeans, fumbling for the pull tab. "We both know you want this."

My heart zoomed in my chest, my arms refusing to function. Fear ruled me as I fought to catch my breath. I tried to determine if there were a way I could be misconstruing his actions. Any remote possibility at all. It had to be a mistake. My brain didn't want to believe what was actually happening. Was his hand really on me? It was unchartered, revolting, vile territory. "Tom, please."

"Yeah. Beg," he whispered as the entirety of his tongue greeted the side of my neck, licking upward like a starving man taking charge of a melting ice cream cone. "I like that."

My lip quivered and nausea filled my stomach. "Stop."

The argument as to why I didn't fight back was strong. And if you hadn't lived it, you wouldn't understand. If I made the wrong move, he'd snap into one of his famous rages. I was accustomed to Tom's everyday hostility and knew how to deal with that. The swearing. The wall punches. The threats. Differentiating factors that night included his intentions and a

.45 lying on the table. Those were major game changers.

I'd spoken too soon about the pistol. His left hand reached for the gun, and he dragged it across the table, the sound of metal scraping across the wood drawing out the moment before he spun it in his hand three times, nearly dropping the piece twice. It was no longer sitting idle, another dynamic in not retaliating.

Blood whooshed in my ears, potent adrenaline surging through my veins. I wondered how much longer it'd take before he killed me, whether it was on accident or on purpose. Every fiber of my being told me both to scream and not to.

"You sure you don't want that drink before we have a little fun?" He raised the gun until the cold muzzle was pressed against my jaw, my head forced upward to look at the popcorn texture on the ceiling. A click. He'd cocked it. "Anticipation feels good, doesn't it? I'll bet your panties are nice and wet," he said.

Much to my surprise, I was still alive. But my options were narrowing. Would he actually pull the trigger? Could he go through with it if I shot down his advances? Pun intended. With my hands already in my pockets, I gripped my cell phone tight in a last-ditch effort, my fingers feeling around for the number two key. Madelyn. She was awake. Her dad was a cop, and they only lived one street over. He would help me. I held it down for three seconds and let go, praying the call would connect. I just hoped she'd answer and could hear the intention behind my words.

"Take your hands off me. I don't want this, Tom," I swallowed, enunciating carefully.

"Shhhh...you don't want to wake your brother and sister, do you? How would this look to them?" He brushed my hair out of my face before dragging the barrel of the gun down toward my zippered cleavage. "Your mouth says, 'no', but your eyes are moaning, 'Tom, yes'." His hand greeted my crotch, rubbing, grabbing, squeezing. Jeans and underwear were the only layers separating him from violating me further. "Try to deny it. Beg me for your life, Blue. I want to hear you say I'm in control."

Fuck. That's what it was all about. Control. My mother

held all of it and Tom was left with nothing. It'd been that way for years. So, he drove the evening toward what would hurt Elana most, giving him the satisfaction and attention he'd craved.

"You're drunk and you don't know what you're saying. Put the gun down," I pleaded with fear in my voice. "Get off me."

He laughed. "I get it. So, that good for nothing delinquent down at the beach is good enough for you to fuck, but I'm not?" He grabbed my breast and twisted hard, causing me to yelp in pain.

A surge of bravery took hold, and I knew what was about to happen if I didn't save myself. With a growl, I shoved him away and forced myself to my feet, but he was bigger and stronger. Halfway between sitting and standing, he'd managed to lift me up and contort my body, slamming me down against the table. Hard. Stars exploded behind my eyes as my skull connected with the surface. I struggled against his hands as he pawed angrily at my clothes. One of his meaty thighs was pinned between mine and my hands were suddenly restrained over my head. Both were firm reminders I wasn't going anywhere. I'd been forced into a ninety-degree angle with my back flat against the glossy wood.

The metallic sound of his belt buckle unfastening with one hand repulsed me while his other squeezed both of my wrists together. His grip was so tight, I was positive the bones would break. Looming over me, a sinister smile spanned his face as he unbuttoned my jeans while I squirmed, exhausting myself. His firm erection was pressed against my leg, and tears spilled down my face.

"Let me show you what a real man can do with his—"

One of the doors opened upstairs. "What on earth is going on down there? It sounds like a bar fight."

In a sense, she was right.

The stairs creaked.

Tom jumped into a nearby chair and grabbed a handkerchief from his pocket, turning his focus to polishing the gun. "Nothing, Elana. Cleaning my .45. Go back to bed."

I scrambled off the table and backed away toward the door, my heart thumping wildly.

My mother's frame appeared, her eyes squinting into the brightly-lit room. "Blue? Why are you up? It's nearly four in the morning."

"I..." I glanced at Tom. "I was just leaving. Got up early. Work. In an hour. Big catering thing."

"Weren't you wearing those clothes yesterday?" She scanned me from head to toe.

I looked down and answered quickly, "Nope."

"I thought I heard someone breaking in, so I came down to check it out," Tom mumbled, shooting me a dirty look. "Turns out, it was Blue *baiting me.*"

I knew his words held more than one meaning, and I was one hundred percent certain I'd never given him any inclination I was interested. Tom sickened me and had for as long as I could remember. Avoiding him had always been paramount, not enticing him.

"Well, keep it down." Elana frowned before she slogged back up the stairs. "Some of us have a useless meeting with that tool, Harold, in the morning we need to be rested for."

That was my chance. I used the next three-second window to my advantage and bolted for the front door, my hands shaking so hard as I worked the lock and the handle. Without looking back, I leapt into my car, and peeled out of the driveway. Freedom, but not really. Half a mile down the road, I pulled over and grabbed my cell phone from my pocket.

Regret filled me when I looked at the screen. I'd been so stupid.

"Damn it." My heart sank at my mistake. What I thought was a call to Madelyn, wasn't after all. Not by far. While fumbling for the speed dial in my pocket, I accidentally called my boyfriend—number three, not number two. The line to Adam had been disconnected after ten minutes. That meant he'd heard everything. It also meant a death sentence for Tom. With quaking fingers, I tried calling him five times with no answer.

"No. No!" For the next hour, I rested my head on the

steering wheel and cried, unsure of where to go or who to turn to. I no longer wanted Madelyn's father's help...or anyone's for that matter. All I wanted was to forget that night happened.

Home was no longer a comfort. It wasn't always perfect, not by any means. But over twenty years of safety and security of living there had been destroyed in a single ten-minute exchange. The next day, I moved out to the mother-in-law house, vowing to never step foot in the same room as my stepfather again. That was an oath I'd kept.

* * *

Blinking brought me back to the present. I was in the passenger seat of Adam's truck as we passed by The Lean, Mean Coffee Bean with no recollection of how I got there.

"You're quieter than I remember," he said.

"A lot to think about, I guess."

"I'll bet. A baby's a game changer."

"Huh?" I said.

"You're pregnant. And frankly, I'm disappointed."

"You are?" Butterflies flitted in my stomach, a feeling I hadn't experienced in a long time.

"How could I not be? You know better than to get shitfaced at the bar, and—"

"Oh, that. I'm not really pregnant," I cut him off.

He shook his head, stealing a glance my way. "Don't lie to me about this."

"I'm not lying. Daveigh's the one who's knocked up, and I had to cover for her. If you want, I'll piss on a stick for you right now."

"As appealing as that sounds on a Wednesday, I'll pass," he said.

"I'm serious. Stop at the dollar store. I'll prove it."

He looked at me as he slowed at a stop light. "So, you're not...Cash didn't..."

"Hell no," I replied quickly. From the corner of my eye, I swore Adam let out a sigh of relief.

I let a few minutes tick by before I spoke again. "Did you

really beat the shit out of Tom in The Fill & Spill parking lot?"

He closed his eyes for a brief moment at a stop sign. "Blue, I don't want to dredge up ancient history. Can't we let some things go?"

"Sure, but this isn't one of them." I adjusted my position in the seat until I faced him. "Did you, or didn't you?"

He let out a sigh as he pulled into the momster's driveway, putting the truck in park. A full minute passed by, but his line of vision remained straight ahead. "It was about a month after you took off, and I was in a bad place mentally. I'd just quit Mario's and started working for your uncle. A truck with a delivery of windows t-boned a Mercedes on Third and Olive. The delivery guy had a suspended license. Ultimately, I was responsible because I'd charged that job out to him. Long story short, it was a rookie mistake. To top it off, my girlfriend left town. I had nothing going for me."

I clung to the blow of his words and kept my mouth shut.

"I went into the bar after work and ordered a steak, which I never got around to eating. Oh. And a beer. Maybe a couple of beers. Probably closer to a dozen. I'd lost count. History including a DUI said to not drink, but I didn't listen. With the house so close, I decided to walk it off and come back for the truck in the morning. Al was managing that night; he wouldn't care if I was parked there overnight.

"At some point, I needed a smoke and stumbled toward the door, but I couldn't find my cigarettes. The damn pack was in my hand the whole time, which tells you how much I'd already drank. As the front door shut behind me, I fumbled in my pocket for a lighter. That's when I ran into someone.

"I slurred an apology to whoever it was and made a move to keep walking. But it was his response that caught my attention, sending me over the edge." He paused. "It was about you and it was so vulgar, I won't even repeat what he said. It only took a second for the rage to choke me, and I lost it. I grabbed him by the lapels of his jacket and slammed him up against a nearby truck, my face inches from his. You should've seen the fear in his eyes.

"He asked what the fuck I was doing, but I didn't answer

with words. Instead, I shook him hard, slamming him against that truck over and over again. I couldn't hold back, Blue. I tried. I swear, I tried.

"And it got worse. He smirked and said you were a better lay than his wife. Said if you were good enough for me, you were good enough..." he shut his eyes, "good enough for him.

"Then, I started wailing on his face until he was a bloody mess. Three times? Four times? Five times? Who knows? I couldn't stop. Cartilage cracked. A tooth flew out of his mouth. Blood poured down his chin. He sobbed and shielded himself from my hits, recoiling like a coward. And that was when I delivered the fatal blow. But it was with words instead of my fists. With my teeth bared, I told him I had what happened with you on tape. That was the moment he knew *I knew*."

I wound my arms around myself and scrunched my eyes shut.

"It was a lie, but you should've seen the look on his face. Like he stared at the Grim Reaper himself. That was when Harold came running out of The Fill & Spill to see what happened, asking if he should call the cops to have me arrested." Adam paused. "I was thankful for that. Otherwise, I might've killed him.

"And Tom just lay on the ground, frozen, eyes wide as dinner plates while he looked at me. He told Harold it wasn't necessary and he called what happened that night in the parking lot nothing more than a 'misunderstanding'."

Adam let a laugh out through his nose. "Some misunderstanding. My hand was broken in two places, and it swelled up like a balloon. I thought beating the shit out of him would make me feel better and lessen the pain of losing you. But it didn't. And that's when I realized it."

"Realized what?" I asked.

"That you weren't coming back. That I needed to pull my shit together. If I didn't do something, Tom Meyers wouldn't live."

"Yeah, well Daveigh saw the whole thing happen. She thinks you made him into a punching bag for a good time."

"That's because you never told her the truth, but that's

beside the point. We've come full circle to me not caring about what anyone around here thinks about me. Remember? Anyway, I should get going." He rubbed the perimeter of the steering wheel with his palm.

Silence.

"Do...you want to come in?" I asked, fiddling with the hem of my jacket.

He hesitated and shook his head. "Ehhhh...that's probably not the best idea. Your family will be back eventually. It was already awkward enough at the funeral with your mom."

I nodded and blinked before opening the door. "Yeah. No, you're right. I just...really don't want to be alone right now. Maybe I can get...or I could ask...Never mind." I was at a loss. There was no one left for me to call. "Thanks for the ride home."

"Hold on." Adam looked at me and let out a slow breath before pulling the keys from the ignition. "I'll hang out for a few minutes. That's it."

A little flicker of something inside my chest smiled. Relief. Familiarity. Comfort. It was a feeling I hadn't experienced in two years. He followed me around the side of the house. No one was home, and Ralph's driveway was empty.

"Everything looks the same back here." Adam surveyed the ground on the pathway to the backyard.

"Nothing changes if..." I stopped myself from finishing the saying.

I unlocked the door to the house out back and walked inside, taking my coat off, hanging it on the rack. The lack of footsteps behind me caused me to turn around. "Are you coming in?"

Adam stood in the doorway, not stepping past the welcome mat. I could tell what he felt by his labored breathing and vacant stare. It was my same reaction when I'd arrived.

"I know. It's kinda like opening a time capsule, isn't it? Everything's hermetically sealed. Like the clock stopped."

"Yeah, except years have passed." He rubbed the back of his neck. "It's strange."

I changed the subject to something more comfortable.

"So, can I get you some coffee or water? I don't have the fridge stocked with anything else."

"Coffee." He yawned as he sat down on the sofa. "Please. Hold the sugar."

I closed my eyes and braced the counter, remembering back to when he'd finish off the line by saying, "You're sweet enough for both of us."

But he didn't say it that time. It caused that glimmer of relief, comfort, and familiarity I felt in my chest to fizzle.

With my back to Adam, I went through the motions of making a packet of instant coffee I'd picked up at The Lean, Mean, Coffee Bean. Tea had always been my preference, but I was exhausted and needed an infusion of caffeine. If the tea had expired, I didn't want to know what two-year-old coffee tasted like. The room was too quiet, and I knew neither of us knew what to say or how to act around each other. Adam and I had two speeds: arguing and being in love. There wasn't an in-between.

"Can I say something and not have you interrupt?" I asked.

"Shoot." He slouched on the couch and folded his hands over his stomach.

I tapped the counter with the heel of my fist, fighting for the nerve to speak. "Adam, I'm sorry," I bit my lip, "for so many reasons. Everything. I don't know where to start. When Madelyn...I didn't know how to cope. I'd lost her, and if I lost you...I got scared and took off on the one person who mattered and ruined it all. I figured it out. If I left you first, that meant you'd never be able to leave me. That soap dish didn't lie. It may have cracked and been put back together, but you were my world. Just like that," I snapped my fingers, "I broke us, and I don't blame you if you spend the rest of your life hating me."

He didn't reply.

"I guess what I'm trying to say is I'm just as lost as I was when...I mean...what I'm trying to say is..." I turned around and disappointment flooded me. That spark I mentioned had fully extinguished, not even a whisper of smoke remaining.

The front door was wide open, and Adam was gone.

Eighteen

I'm not sure how long I sat on that uncomfortable couch with the door open. Chilly wind whipped through, pushing the creaking oak back until the handle rhythmically bumped the wall behind it, but I couldn't bring myself to get up and close it. I was numb to the core. From the outside in due to the cold and from the inside out due to Adam.

I knew what I felt was minimal in comparison to what I'd done to him. So fucking inconsequential. However, it still stung. A lot. Perspective sucked.

At six-thirty that night, my phone jingled, jarring me from my daze.

'Veigh

We're down at The Fill & Spill. Wanna come?

Who's 'we'?

Me. Wesley. Finn. Scott. Lucy said she might show.

I don't think so.

Come on. You're going to leave me for Sacramento soon. Please?

I slouched on the couch and groaned, knowing she was

right. I could either have a pity party alone or I could suck it up and have a drink with my sister and brother before we all parted ways again. With Finn in college and Daveigh pregnant, I didn't know when we'd have another opportunity to be together. Maybe never. No one got along with the momster, so she wasn't a binding tie. Reluctantly, I stood up and got ready to head to the bar.

* * *

The Fill & Spill was half-empty that night when I walked in. Lucy was across the way, deeply engrossed in conversation with Santi. It wasn't long before she noticed me. She flashed one of those annoying, dainty waves where she wiggled all of her fingers. It made me want to slap her. A few minutes later, Daveigh walked out of the bathroom and spotted me immediately, like a heat-seeking missile. She marched over to where I stood near the doorway. "Hey, can I talk to you for a minute?"

"What now?" I sighed. "I thought you wanted me to come have a drink with you guys. Or was that some kind of trap?"

Her lips tightened, the corners turning into a bleak frown as she placed her hands on her hips. "Didn't I warn you about hanging around with Adam Rockwell? I saw you two at the funeral together. Surprised he had the balls to show up."

"Well, that answers my question about your invitation being a trap." I draped my jacket over my arm. "You warned me. But you forget I'm an adult."

"Blue..."

"'Veigh, you got knocked up by a guy named Beanbag. And don't forget you used to date a Rent-A-Cop more than twice your age. Or should we talk about how you're too afraid to tell 'Mommy' about the bun you're baking? Tell me which part of what I said makes you an expert on giving out relationship advice?"

She closed her eyes and took a breath. "I know I haven't always made the best decisions. But Adam's bad news. I can feel it."

"I think what you're feeling are those pregnancy hormones again. Go eat some dill pickles and ice cream."

She narrowed her eyes. "Don't try to be cute. He's still bad news, no matter how you try to spin this."

"Would you stop saying 'bad news'? What if he's not? What if you're wrong about him, and you don't know the whole story?"

Her eyes widened. "Shit! What if he's using you for the money?"

"Slow it down and put away your detective kit, super sleuther. He's not like that."

"Well, speaking of money, what happened with Crenshaw today?"

"Hard limit." I scanned the crowd. "Not talking about it."

"You come in here defending Adam Rockwell after I told you what he did to Daddy, and you don't want to talk about the giant lump of money he left you? Give me something to work with here."

"Not now, Daveigh." I rubbed my temples. "Maybe not ever."

"We're all owed an explanation. I don't get it. Trust me when I say money isn't my motivation here. I don't care whether Daddy left me a nickel or five million dollars. All I want to know is why?"

"I don't owe anyone anything. Look, I can't..." I shook my head, solidifying my decision to keep my mouth shut. "I can't say it without destroying lives. Can't you accept that and be blissfully ignorant?"

"No. What did I ever do to shut you out?"

"It's not what *you* did." I looked her in the eyes while tears pricked at mine, hoping that would be enough of an answer to appease her. Why couldn't she read between the lines? I felt like an angry beehive, and Daveigh was the curious kid holding a stick. Poking at me wasn't a good idea.

Her voice grew louder. "You're like talking to one of those magic eight balls sometimes. No real answers are—"

Beanbag walked up and halted our escalating conversation by stepping between us. "Is everything okay with you two?"

"Couldn't be better," I replied, my tone laced with sarcasm. I glanced toward Santi before walking away. "I need a beer or an IV of beer. A trough of beer. A beer of beer. Whatever."

"Blue!" Daveigh shouted after me. "Would you listen to me?"

I didn't look back as I headed up to the bar, realizing Adam sat next to the only open space nearest the door. *Just my luck.* I slunk down on the empty stool and remained quiet for a minute before I spoke. My voice was low. "Your coffee's likely cold by now."

He winced. "I know...I'm sorry..."

"Don't apologize. It's no big deal." Fighting the bitterness in my voice was an epic fail.

He glanced at me. "Standing in that room, remembering the past, listening to you give some clunky speech, tripping over sentences about apologies, and that damn soap dish...I..."

The door to the bar jingled to interrupt. Zack walked in with Heather Miller attached to his arm. I watched him lean over and whisper something in her ear before she threw her head back in loud, chirpy laughter.

Exactly what I need to top off my night.

He scanned the room, his eyes stumbling when he saw me. Without words, he guided Heather to the only empty table in the bar—a two-top next to Daveigh and Beanbag.

"This trip gets better and better," I mumbled.

As I looked away, I caught a glimpse of Daveigh. Her eyes did a double take when she saw who I was seated next to. She jabbed her index finger in my direction and whispered something to Beanbag before standing up. Anger and frustration flooded her face while she bounced over to where I sat. "Hey, Blue. Why don't you come sit with us?"

"Excuse me? Did you forget about the argument we had?" I motioned between our bodies. "That was you involved, right?"

"Yeah," her eyes flicked over to Adam and back at me again, "but I'd really like it if *you* hung out with us."

Maybe my response was out of spite. Maybe it was out of annoyance. "Sure." I smiled sweetly. "Come on, Adam."

Daveigh stuck out her lower lip. "Bummer. There aren't

enough seats for both..."

"It's okay. We can share," I replied, tugging Adam across the room toward the table. "C'mon."

"What's going on with you?" he hissed. "I don't want to hang out with—"

"I've had a real shitty day, Rockwell. Humor me and sit for a few minutes," I commanded.

Adam puffed out his cheeks and sank into the only available chair.

I began introductions, "Finn, you remember Adam, right? And this is Finn's boyfriend, Scott."

Adam nodded at my brother. "It's been a while. Long since before you left for college." His focus turned toward Scott, shaking his hand. "Nice to meet you."

"You sure everything's okay between you and your sister?" Beanbag asked Daveigh quietly.

My lip-reading skills were on point that night.

She slammed her purse on the table. "I swear to God, Wesley! If you don't stop treating me like I'm going to break, I'm going to flip my shit."

"Hormonal much?" I muttered.

One of the TVs behind the bar caught my attention, and it was like history repeating itself. "Hold on. I want to see what this is all about," I replied.

The rest of the table fell into a conversation about a football game on an opposing screen, and I'd lost interest. An oversized image panned to Cash and Price Jensen in a follow up interview. Like last time, Price did all the talking while Cash sat there with a wide grin on his face.

Fortunately, the chairs nearest to me had been vacated by my brother and Scott who'd gone up to the bar for a refill. I sank down into the seat and set my tote bag on the floor without breaking eye contact with the screen.

Adam's eyes trailed to the television and I could sense his mood darkening while he focused on their faces. "What is it about that asshole that captivates you so much?" he murmured to me. "You can tell by the way he looks and talks. Is it his inflated ego or the fact he's a dick? Both qualities are charming."

I froze. There was no answer to his question that wouldn't ship me into a frenzy of tears. The air stifled my lungs as I took short, choppy breaths. Ignoring him was the simplest solution, but he made it damn near impossible.

"What is it," he leaned closer, closing in on the distance between his mouth and my ear, "that draws you to Cash?"

The vibration from his voice sent a tingle through my core. I had no argument. Every word he spoke about my ex-boss and ex-arrangement was accurate. Yet my actions over the past two years left each syllable difficult to hear because they told a different story.

"Well?"

Santi broke up the tense moment long enough to deliver more drinks to the table. This time, he set an entire bottle of whiskey in front of Adam. "Owner said you looked like you needed this."

Adam didn't acknowledge the gesture of alcohol, his attention still fixated on me.

"I..." I shuddered. Heat radiated through Adam's shirt as he leaned over my shoulder, my fingertips begging to reach over and trace the worn flannel. Holding back was like asking two magnets to not connect. He was close. Too unbearably close.

A hint of spearmint lingered in the air when he spoke again. "Tell me, Blue. Tell me right now. What's so amazing about him? Give me a real answer and I'll walk out that door right now, never questioning you again. I want the truth."

"The truth?" Tears stung my eyes and I couldn't bring my voice above a whisper. "Cash's an asshole." The lump in my throat grew tenfold. "Being with him was intentional. A constant, shitty reminder I didn't deserve better. He's the opposite of everything I had, I wanted, and I needed in you. Does hearing that make you happy?"

I turned in my seat until I faced away from him, blinking rapidly. "Please, everyone. Let's hear your opinions on Cash. I'm sure each of you has one."

Adam grabbed two legs of my chair and yanked, adjusting it to where I'd have no choice but to listen to the mounting rumble of his voice. "You suddenly want my two cents on Cash Jensen? That's doubtful." Adam poured a shot of whiskey and threw it back, grimacing before he set the glass on the table.

Lucy snickered, honing in on our dialogue. "Funny, Adam. I see what you did there. Cash. Cents."

I kicked her under the table. "Don't encourage him."

Lucy looked confused. "What? It was funny?"

I stood up. "I need to pee."

"No, you don't." Adam grabbed my arm to stop me. "In fact, I'll bet there are a lot of topics you don't want my opinion about."

"Like what?" I spat.

He stood up, looming over me until our bodies nearly touched. The smell of alcohol on his breath rivaled the anger stirring behind his eyes. "Walk away, Blue. Get out of here. I don't think you want to hear everything I have to say."

"Try me," I replied hoarsely.

He sat back down and counted on his fingers, his voice intensifying, "First off, let's talk about their names. Who the hell names their kids Price and Cash? Let me guess, they have an aunt and uncle named Rich and Penny?" Adam laughed.

"Penny's his sister, and Richard prefers to be called Dick!" I retorted without thinking.

"I'll bet he does." Adam snorted.

Damn it. I'd made it worse.

"Oh, shit!" Lucy hooted and smacked the table with the palm of her hand. "It's hilarious because it's true."

"Look." I rubbed my face and grabbed my tote bag. "I've had enough of this whole pick on Blue event I didn't sign up for. It's been great, but I'm leaving now."

Without another word, I stormed toward the exit and let the door slam shut behind me. I tried to put in the effort of being with my siblings one last time, but I'd somehow fucked that up too. Maybe I was meant to be a loner. Isolation wouldn't be judgmental. A blast of wind socked me in the face while I walked to the far corner of the building. The ground welcomed me as I sat down, the cold, wet pavement seeping through my jeans. None of it mattered. I drew my knees up under my chin and wrapped my arms around my knees. The harsh reality of the evening being abysmal took hold as it fought the constant, constricting ache in my chest.

A few minutes later, the door to The Fill & Spill opened, a momentary burst of loud music, laughter, and honey-tinted lights escaping before it creaked shut again. Without looking, I knew who stood twenty feet away and closed in on the distance between us.

"What do you want now?" I grumbled.

Adam sat down next to me on the cement with a groan. "Penny for your thoughts?"

"Ha-ha. No more Cash jokes tonight. Please?"

Elongated quiet permeated the air.

He let out a deep breath. "Fair enough. Truce?"

With defeat saturating me, I waited for the punchline, the smirk, or the asshole remark. But they didn't happen. Only an outstretched hand was present. "What are you doing?"

"Someone once told me, it's called a handshake. They're commonly used in greeting or to finalize an agreement." He paused before finishing what were once my words to him. "I thought it could be a fresh start."

I bit my lip and hesitated, shaking my head. "I don't think we—"

"Got it." He pulled back abruptly, his tone icing over. "Message received, loud and clear. You know, I've got no damn idea how to read you anymore."

"I know." My eyes shut before I braved extending a sweaty hand. Each second felt like eternity while my heart begged me to run. Fast. I'd promised myself to never be in a position to be hurt again. But there I sat, the fortress beginning to fracture and splinter.

His palm met mine gingerly and I flinched. Adam's touch was more painful than I imagined. Flashes and flickers of past filled my head; I couldn't breathe.

"Tell me what you're thinking. Let me in," he said.

"I don't remember how."

* * *

Roughly Two Years
⁕⁻and A Little Over Six Months Ago⁻⁕

"Fuckity fuck. Fuck. Fuck. Fuck." I closed the heavy door to the house and braced myself against it. My heart thudded in my throat as I tried to swallow it back down, nearly choking on the damn thing. *Calm down, Blue. Everything will be fine.* The pep talk didn't last more than two seconds before panic mode set in again. "Mom?" I shouted.

Nothing.

"Shit." I paced the darkened living room, thoughts bouncing through my head like a pinball machine. It was my fault, and I needed to find a solution. Fast. The problem was I couldn't do it on my own. My hands were sweaty as I rubbed them on the back of my jeans; I felt sick. *How could this happen?*

"Well, it's about time. We're late. You need to wear the navy Versace dress with the Gucci heels," a stern voice sounded from the top of the stairs.

The shiver began when I heard her descending the steps. As always, the icy sensation started at the base of my spine and clambered up to my neck, rendering me unable to breathe in a normal pattern. I was about to enter the lion's den. The momster appeared, wearing a sensible, black pencil skirt, matching heels, and a white button-up blouse. A single strand of pearls completed her bland outfit. Her chestnut hair was cut into a dated bob, not a strand out of place. It did nothing to combat her valleys of frown lines or soften her expression.

Often, I'd wondered what it'd be like to have a normal mother. One who wasn't obsessed with politics. One who cared about her kids' interests. One who knew how to cook without burning water. One who didn't pay off the high school principal to handle fudging test scores, ensuring 4.0 GPAs.

"Blue," her shoulders wilted as she brushed imaginary dust off mine, "why aren't you dressed appropriately? Flannel is for lumberjacks."

"I like this shirt." I glanced down at the red plaid pattern.

She lifted one of my limp curls with one hand and tilted

my chin upward with the other. "You need an appointment at the salon, yesterday. And a full makeover isn't a bad idea either. We have an image to uphold."

"No, you have an image to uphold." I swatted her hand away. "Mom, we need to talk."

She fished around in her purse until she found a tube of frosty pink lipstick. It was less than fascinating to watch her apply layer after layer of the pasty mess. "Can't it wait? You know I have a luncheon with the head of the education board today. A luncheon that you're supposed to attend as my devoted daughter."

"I need your help."

She slid the top on the lipstick slowly until it clicked. "With what? You know this is a busy time of year with the election approaching."

"There's this guy I've been seeing for a while now, and—"

"Dear God. Are you pregnant? My ratings can't handle a teen being knocked up, let alone the abortion I'd have to pay—"

"Mom! No!"

"Did he rape you? Rob you? Hit you?"

"No, no, and no."

She set the tube down on the table. "Then, it can wait."

"I really don't think this can."

She huffed. "What? What is the pressing issue then?"

I took a deep breath. "He was arrested and—"

"What?" she shrieked. "Do you know the ramifications this could have on whether I win or not?"

"This isn't about you."

"Who is worth damaging my reputation?"

I was quiet.

She arched an eyebrow, awaiting an answer.

"Adam Rockwell," I replied quietly.

She scrunched her nose. "That...that deviant who lives in the shack on the beach?"

"Come off it. He's not a deviant, and it's not a shack. That house was left to him by his grandfather when he died."

"I don't want you hanging around that hoodlum or his dilapidated house. Rumor has it his parents disowned him. I can only imagine what foul behaviors of his warranted that type of banishment."

I felt anger simmering in my veins. "He emancipated himself when he was sixteen because his dad beat the shit out of him on a weekly basis and his mom preferred heroin to feeding her kid. His parents didn't even show up at the court hearing."

"My tax dollars hard at work again in some way, I'm sure." She rolled her eyes and crossed her arms. "And he was arrested for what?"

"DUI," I muttered.

"A DUI? That's a felony!" Her eyes bulged as she threw her arms in the air. "My opponent will have a flipping heyday if he knows you had any involvement..." She froze. "Does anyone else know about this...blip in your judgment?"

"It's not a blip, but you're close. It rhymes. Relationship. You can say the R-word. It won't bite."

"Oh, no it doesn't. Not my daughter."

"It does. And no, no one knows. We both work at Mario's, and we didn't want it to get weird with the rules on employees dating."

"Good."

"What's 'good' about this? They're holding him. He's going to be given a year in prison. You know how strict the rules are around here. Can't you pull some strings?"

Her laughter was condescending. "Me? Pull strings? It's a waste. He could've killed someone."

Little did she know it was my life in danger that night, no one else's.

I gritted my teeth. "Was what he did right? No. But he did it to protect me. In turn, I need you to protect him."

"He protected you from what? Alcoholics Anonymous?"

I swallowed. It was time to take the lion head-on with my bare hands, but I'd chickened out as quickly as I'd attained my courage. "When your..." I couldn't finish the sentence, telling her about what Tom did to me. It was too difficult to relive. Saying the words out loud would make it real all over again.

"Look." Her expression was stern. "The election is

months away..."

"Fuck the election, Elana! That's all you ever talk about, I swear. It's more important than Daveigh or Finn. Or even me."

The conversation didn't sway; the most important topic was still evident in her eyes. "Is that what it's going to take to make your tantrum go away and for you to go get dressed? This lunch is important, and I'm running out of time for your shenanigans!"

"You tell me," I replied. "You have friends in high places, and I need help."

I'd never used my mom's location on the political ladder as leverage, until that moment. But I was willing to do whatever it took to keep Adam safe.

Her glare was toxic as she looked at her watch. "You're really not going to let this go, are you?"

I locked eyes with hers and shook my head left and right.

She pinched the bridge of her nose. "I'll see what I can do, but you're not going to see or talk to that trash receptacle again. And if I even catch you breathing his name before the election? I'll be sure he's given the harshest sentence possible. With no soap-on-a-rope available. Don't forget I can make it happen. Judge Bledsoe and I are close friends."

* * *

When I tried to pull back, Adam's grip firmed while his thumb caressed the top of my hand. "Blue..."

It was too much. I yanked away. "Your turn. What are you thinking about?" my voice hitched as I fought to change the subject with glassy tears in my eyes.

He leaned against the wall, tilting his head back against the worn brick. "Part of me is anxiously counting down the days until you leave Steele Falls again."

I sucked my lower lip into my mouth for a few seconds. "And the other part?"

He took his time in turning to look at me. "The other part of me knows if I don't fight for—"

Tires squealing.

Engine revving.

Black and red blur whizzing.

Car door slamming.

"Blue?" a familiar voice sounded from across the street in the vacant gravel lot. Something about the situation didn't make sense. The masculine voice I knew didn't match the sleepy town. And then it dawned on me.

Fuck my life.

I looked at who stood outside an ostentatious red-and-black Ferrari, my fears confirmed. He set the alarm before leaving it behind. "Shit," I muttered, watching in horror. *This isn't happening.*

"Blue? Are you hurt?" he called out. "Are you okay? Is this guy hurting you?"

"What are you doing here?" I blurted as Cash hurried across the street.

"Unfuckingbelievable," Adam said.

"Are you okay?" He rushed over to me. "You look pale, but I guess that's normal."

"I'm fine." I stood up, brushing off the back of my pants with my hands. "Why are you here?"

"The card." He furrowed his brow. "Remember?"

"What card?" I asked. "Have you been taste testing the office pharmacy cabinet again?"

"My credit card. You said if anyone used it, it was a sign you needed help. You know, the garden gnome thing? The flamethrowers?"

"I didn't use your...Oh, God." My eyes scrunched shut, and I thought back to when I asked Daveigh to use my card to pay the tab the other night. She wouldn't have paid attention and must've grabbed the wrong one. I quickly fished it out of my tote bag and thrust it in his direction. "Here, Cash. I'll pay you back. It was a misunderstanding—"

Cash looked down at Adam. "I'm sorry. We haven't met. Cash Jensen."

"The famous Cash." Adam snorted, crossing his ankles. "Perfect."

The fireball of Adam's sarcasm sailed right over Cash's

head. "You've heard of me? Not surprising. I'm a big deal in the plastic surgery world."

"That must be it," Adam's tone remained cold.

Cash extended his hand. "I'm Blue's better half, her old balls and chain, her *boyfriend*."

"You're not my...I...I..."

Adam nodded and forced a fake smile accompanied with a knowing nod. "That reaffirms a lot, actually."

Cash's focus turned to me. "I booked a room down the street at the Wave Inn. Come stay with me." He glanced at his crotch. "Mini Cash will be excited to see you."

"What's he talking about?" Adam asked.

"Mini Cash? It's the nickname we call my—"

"It's not what you think," I cut Cash off. "We broke—"

"Oh! I almost forgot!" Cash snapped his fingers. "I swung by the sex shop and picked up the stuff I asked you to buy. I figured it'd save some time. Gotta clean the cobwebs of the 'ol womb room." His focus turned toward Adam. "It's been a few days, if you know what I mean."

"Wait. You two are still sleeping together?" Adam asked me under his breath. "Seems like an important detail to omit."

I wanted to disappear as I tipped my head up toward the sky and groaned.

"Your lack of words says it all." Adam patted the knee of my jeans. "Go. Be with your boyfriend. He can console you since *I'm sure you don't want to be alone right now*."

Nothing could've made the evening worse, or so I thought.

Wrong.

Seconds later, the door to The Fill & Spill burst open and Lucy stumbled out, her hands clamped over her mouth while she dry-heaved. It looked like a scene out of a movie. Her entire body made a crazed, jerky movement as if it were being exorcised from toe to head. She vomited, a stream and a splatter pouring over Adam's jeans and onto the cement. The harsh smell of margarita and stomach acid instantly flooded the air. "I am so, so sorry, Adam." She sank to her hands and knees to puke again. "No more tequila for me. Ever. It's a bottle of Satan's piss."

"Well, this evening has been sobering in more ways than one," Adam said as he stood up and frowned at the chunky clumps dripping down his pant leg. "It was nice to meet you, Cash." He turned toward me. "Blue. Take care."

"Adam, wait..." I called out as he briskly walked away. "Please!" But there were no words to bandage what happened. All I could do was watch and hope he'd look back at me, giving me a fraction of hope he cared. But he didn't slow down.

"You coming to help launch the meat missile?" Cash hiked his thumb over his shoulder toward his car.

I turned to him and closed my eyes, trying to stay calm. "You should go back to California. I've got a lot to deal with here."

"Blue..."

"Please." I tried to walk away, but he grabbed my upper arm firmly.

"Wait," he said.

"Believe me, you've caused enough damage." Nausea sloshed in my gut, knowing those were the same words Adam doled to me on my first night back in Steele Falls.

"Just...let me talk to you for a minute," Cash said.

"Haven't you spoken your piece already?" I glanced down the street, but Adam was already out of view. "I tried to break up with you back—"

He let go of my arm, his voice soft. Different. "What's it going to take?"

My face was warm with rage. "What's what going to take?"

"Blue, I'm a plastic surgeon. And I'm a damn good one."

"And not the least bit narcissistic." I rolled my eyes.

"All it took was two seconds of me watching you from across the parking lot."

I opened my mouth, but he cut me off.

"Let me finish," Cash said. "Please."

I pursed my lips.

"All it took was two seconds of watching you from across the street to see what makes you tick." His eyes flicked up and toward the beach. "And it's whoever just walked away."

I looked at him and narrowed my eyes.

"Don't get upset at me for calling you out on the truth."

"I—"

"I fix people for a living. Everything they don't like about themselves—I improve. You're the one person I haven't been able to repair, and that's been so aggravating."

I placed my hands on my hips. "I'm not broken."

"Don't lie to yourself. Do you think this is the real me?" He gestured toward his face. "That I can be this much of an ass?"

"Um. Yes."

"C'mon. I'm not arguing that I don't have my dick moments. I'm a guy."

Silence.

"Blue, think about it. I sang *Mambo Number Five* while we were having sex. I've mentioned your weight countless times and used every sleazy sex euphemism I know. Who does that?" He let out a breath through his nose. "Look. For a long time now, I've wondered what it'll take to get real emotion out of you. Fuck. I've tried everything imaginable. Treated you like shit. Forced myself to be a minute man in the bedroom. I even pressured Price to lay you off from Jensen & Jensen. All of it was to try to get you to crack. And I finally saw a little bit of that happen tonight...but it wasn't for me."

My shoulders wilted slowly.

"I wanted to see the emotion that lives behind those gorgeous blue eyes. My cock maneuvers were amped up to the max to get a rise out of you. I honestly don't know what more I could have done. None of it worked."

I opened my mouth and was cut off yet again.

"Do you know why I hired you?"

"My D-cup twins?" I replied, looking down at my chest.

"No." He laughed. "Don't get me wrong. You've got a great rack, but that's not why I brought you on at Jensen & Jensen. I saw a flicker of something in you I hadn't seen in a long time. It was innocent and beautiful and genuine. You were someone who didn't care about my money and didn't want lipo done on them for dirt cheap. You didn't want any part of my place in the Sacramento spotlight. And I wanted to get to know that person."

My jaw fell and he held a finger to my lips.

"But these walls of yours have been impossible to scale. After a while, it became an obsession to break you down and figure you out. I failed."

I looked down at the ground.

He tilted my chin upward. "I thought I loved you, but tonight I realized I was wrong. I was in love with a concept— fixing a broken heart. And for whatever the reason, you craved the negativity I created. I wanted to repair you so badly, but I didn't know how. And then," he glanced toward the beach, "I saw the answer. He was here less than two minutes ago. For what it's worth? I'm sorry I got you canned. I can talk to Price and tell him everything if you want to come back."

I was speechless. Cash was the last person I expected to teach me a lesson, especially one that was so pivotal about myself. Every word he spoke struck home in the worst way.

"I don't think I can ever go back." I blinked, unsure if I meant go back to Sacramento or to the person who I'd been for the past two years. Hell, maybe I meant both. "Everything we had was fake. For both of us."

"I get it. You know where to find me if you ever change your mind and want to get to know the real Cash." He looked down at me and cupped my face in his warm hands before giving me a chaste kiss on the forehead. "Bye, Blue."

Much like Adam, he began to walk away, vanishing while leaving with an echoing numbness of his own.

"Cash, wait!" I called out, emotion choking my voice.

He stopped and turned around, a glimmer of hope spelled out on his face. "Yeah?"

My voice hitched and my nose burned, knowing it was likely the last time I'd ever see or speak to him again. "Do me a favor? Look after Otis?"

There was a hint of disappointment behind his eyes. "Who? The old guy in the parking garage?"

I nodded.

"Who do you think bought him the sleeping bag?" He gave me a last of his signature winks before turning to leave.

This time, I didn't stop him.

That was my first glimpse of the real Cash, and it hurt watching him walk away. How could a stranger be so important and so irrelevant to me at the same time? I was left standing alone on the sidewalk with heavy thoughts. He was right. I'd made myself unattainable by keeping everyone at bay. Friends. Neighbors. Men. Family. As he sped off in his Ferrari, he didn't look my direction.

An even bigger question had reared its ugly head in the wake of his speech. What happened to the real Blue? I'd bottled her up the moment I'd left Steele Falls. Trying to pour all of me out in the past few days? It hurt so damn bad.

Tears burned my eyes over Cash's departure as I stood alone. So much time was wasted, both of us doing a complex dance of chasing and avoiding ghosts for nearly a year. It was up to interpretation as to who led and who followed. But none of that mattered. Not anymore. He'd been brought into my life for one reason: to teach me how to let go.

Once again, perspective sucked big, hairy balls. I needed to evict Cash from my thoughts. There was someone I needed to talk to, and he was due all of my attention. With determination fueling me as I stood outside the door of The Fill & Spill, I buttoned my jacket and prepared to tackle one of my most intimidating demons.

As I was about to take my first steps toward clearing that hurdle, the door of bar flung open again and a bulky frame collided into mine, knocking me to the ground.

"Shit. I'm so sorry." And then his tone changed when he glanced down at me lying on the sidewalk. "Oh...it's you."

"Yeah, well thanks for the informal plow down." Bits of rock had embedded themselves in my palms. My flesh stung, but it didn't combat the fear pouring through my veins. Instead of hunting down my demon, he'd found me instead.

No one could make the next move except for me.

"Beanbag." I choked back tears. *Don't be a sissy and run, Blue. Prove you can do this.* With every ounce of courage I had,

I pushed myself to my feet and looked him in the eyes. "I'm ready to talk."

Nineteen

"You...want to talk right now?" He looked around to see if there was anyone else nearby. "To me?"

I lowered my gaze to the ground and nodded. "Uh huh."

"Are you sure you realize what you're asking?"

I shook my head no and yes as I stood up, brushing bits of dirt from my palms. "I mean, yes. I'm sure. And no, I'm not running. Not anymore."

His eyes sparkled with tears. "Don't fucking play games with me right now, Blue Brennan. My heart can't take it."

I made the motion of drawing an X across my chest with my index finger. "I know. Promise."

What I did to Beanbag in the past wasn't fair. In fact, it was downright brutal and spineless. Everything I had coming was warranted. Forgiveness wasn't in the cards, and I wasn't going to ask him for it. Ever. All I could do was make an attempt to right my wrong, two years too late, and hope for some sense of peace—for both our sakes.

"How do I know I can believe you?" His face was unreadable. "You're about to crawl through Hell."

I wrapped my arms around myself to keep from unraveling at the seams. "Even if it makes me bleed, I need to face what happened. Please?"

After studying my face, he nodded. "We should probably go somewhere private."

"What about 'Veigh?" I hiked my thumb over my shoulder.

"What about her? Your sister is blissfully unaware of the

268

anchor I've carried around, and I'm not about to tell her now. Especially when she's hopped up on baby hormones. This is between you and me."

"But isn't she waiting for you?"

"Daveigh's taking Lucy home once she stops greeting her guts. Plus, I have to stop by Eddie's on the way home, so I drove myself."

"If you need to go..."

"Huh uh. I've waited too long for this. Walking away isn't an option on my end," his voice wavered. "Holding this in is killing me, and I can't let go until..." He closed his eyes, stopping himself from crying.

I nodded in the direction of The Lean, Mean, Coffee Bean across the street. "Coffee shop? Eddie can't be all wrong."

"Not secluded enough. How about the park?"

I nodded and walked beside him for two blocks, the only sound our shoes connecting with the pavement. A thick layer of fog settled in the farther we went. Wisps of sheer white blanketed the grass, blade by blade. My teeth chattered as I fought off the shiver. Silently, I wondered how much was from the weather and how much was from trepidation.

Beanbag sat down on one of the tire swings and stared at the ocean. "You know, this was one of her favorite places."

Anyone mentioning her felt like a dagger piercing my heart. But when Beanbag did it? It cut deeper than ever. "I remember."

"When my sister..." He pushed out a deep breath. "When Madelyn took that monster pill cocktail..."

I fought back the urge to throw up with my hand clamped over my mouth.

"You knew about the OD, right? And the gun?" He looked alarmed.

I nodded, my voice unsteady. "It hurts. Hearing you say her name..."

He dug the toes of his shoes into the thick layer of sand beneath the swing and looked up at me. "Maybe we should start at the beginning. What do you know about that night?"

I sat down on the lowest platform of the big toy. "Not a

lot. She was angry with me."

"So, you know the how but not the why." He stopped the swing from moving.

"It was because of me."

There was a hint of argument behind his voice. "Being upset with you had nothing to do with what she did."

I lowered my head in shame. "Right."

"Jesus, Blue. Is that what you've thought for the past two years? She didn't kill herself because of any fight you two may have had."

"Don't soften the blow for me. It won't work."

"She didn't and I'm not. Madelyn didn't tell any of us why until after, but she did a damn good job of hiding it."

My heart skipped a beat in my chest. "Hiding what?"

"I have something for you." He reached into his back pocket and pulled out his worn leather wallet. Inside was a plain, white envelope that'd been folded into quarters. The edges were discolored and bent with age.

"What's that?" I frowned, flashbacks of Tom's unwanted envelopes whispering for my attention.

He held it out to me. "Take it. Please. I can't carry this fucking thing around for you anymore. It's too heavy."

Fear ruled me.

"I'm begging." Two tears tumbled down his cheeks.

Holding my breath, I took the envelope from him and set it on my lap, afraid holding it would heighten the sting in my chest. With the pad of my index finger, I traced over the bubbly letters that spelled my name on the front. Madelyn's writing. I'd have known it anywhere. "What am I supposed do now?"

His response was simple. "Read it."

Reality took a firm hold. Once I opened that envelope, my life would be forever changed. "What if I'm not ready for her words?"

"Come on." He motioned for me to follow him over to a nearby picnic table where he sat down across from me. "If you need to stop, put it away. I'm not here to judge you or pressure you into finishing it. It took me damn near a week to get through mine, and every last sentence shredded me from skin to soul."

My eyes flicked up at him. "Wait. She left one of these for you too?"

"I assume it's similar; I didn't open yours." He counted on his fingers. "There was one for you, one for my mom and dad, and one for me. That was it."

He reached across the table and gave my hand a gentle squeeze, compassion behind his eyes. "If you want me to stay while you read it, I will. You can lean on me when the pain's too much to bear."

"No!" My tone was snappish. I waited for him to rescind the offer before setting the envelope down, but it didn't happen. "I won't ask you to do that. You've already dealt..." I shook my head. The gesture was too much.

"Blue, you're not asking. I'm offering. No one," he pressed his thumb down on the paper, pinning it to the table, "should be alone if what's in that letter is anything like what was in mine. I was by myself when I learned the truth, and it damn near broke me.

"When I found her body, the letters were clutched in her hand. Blue slack lips. Wide open eyes. A bullet hole. No evidence of breathing. But her grip? It looked so tight, I thought a piece of her hung on in there, and I could somehow win her back. But I was wrong. Madelyn spent a ridiculous amount of time piecing all of this together. I wish...she'd have invested those moments telling us instead, you know?"

"You were the one who found her?"

The weight of the conversation hit me like a ton of bricks, my body feeling like a deflated balloon. I couldn't fathom the grief wracking his heart in losing a sibling. If Finn or Daveigh had died, unable to cope with...I don't know what I would've done. And to top it off, the idea of not getting to say goodbye made me physically ill. But wasn't I just as guilty? I'd done the same thing by cutting ties with Daveigh and Finn? And Adam. Internally, I fell apart.

He nodded. "When I found her, it took three tries to call 911. My hands, they wouldn't work." He wiped his nose with his sleeve.

"Beanbag..."

He blinked, two more symmetrical tears falling down his face. "You can only outrun so much, but you can't outrun what lives inside you."

I touched the sealed edge of the envelope. It was time. My finger slid under the edge, breaking the seal before I pulled out three full-length pieces of paper. The front and backs were saturated from top to bottom with words.

The handwriting was in neat pink ink. Over time, I'd allowed myself to forget she'd only written in that color. Every i was dotted with a perfect star and each period had been replaced with a tiny heart. Signature Madelyn.

I straightened out the deep creases and looked up at Beanbag, who gave me a nod of encouragement. His eyes didn't falter toward the paper. Instead, they remained fixated on me.

Holding my breath, I internally counted to three before I dove into what would be one of the hardest ventures of my life.

Blue,
If you're reading this, you already know.
Before you ask aloud or give this piece of paper any judgmental looks, my decision was made three days ago. It was 100% mine. I want you to understand that before you continue reading. Let that concept sink in. No one else knew what I went through or what I'd decided, not even you. It wasn't your cross to bear, so I sheltered you from my truth.
Are people gossiping and calling me selfish? Probably. Are they whispering I'm a chicken? Likely. In my opinion, it's selfish for me to continue living, and I'd be a chicken to not carry out my plan. So, to those who call me greedy or weak, I'm raising my final glass with zero fucks to give. Their opinions don't matter because I'm finally going to be free from the burden of this body. Free. That single word sends a steady stream of tears down my face. They've been near-constant lately as I prepare my goodbyes, but they're laced with a combination of salty terror and sweet joy.
Three days ago, I received a phone call from White Pines. You know, it says something when your cancer doctor is

number six on speed dial. The sickening dread in my gut was immediate when I saw his name blinking on the caller ID. My hands began to sweat and shake while my heart pounded up into my throat. It reminded me of that same feeling we both got before riding the big roller coaster at the fair back when we were kids. Remember? God, I'm going to miss that.

It took four rings before I had enough courage to answer. Four rings. And they were doozies. Each one felt like a lifetime as I stared at the screen. Part of me thought if I didn't answer, I wouldn't have to acknowledge what he had to say. Pretty stupid, huh? Either way, I was wrong. My truth awaited, and I needed to face it head-on. Three words were all I needed to hear before I crumbled to my knees in the parking lot of The Lean, Mean, Coffee Bean. I probably looked like an idiot, but I challenge anyone to hear "inoperable brain tumor" and continue functioning. Thinking back, I think those were the only three words I remember hearing. The rest? I processed them, but it was hazy. "Aggressive" was mentioned and it felt like a knife in my chest. "Stage four" was another ugly combo. That was the one that made me dry heave the most. The real kicker was "only a few months". That phrase was the worst, and it made me numb. Kinda like my body tried to protect my brain. Ironic since my brain had been the one attacking me. The bottom line was recovery had been yanked off the table like a cheap optical illusion at a magic show.

At first, I didn't know how to describe what I felt most. Was it anger? Denial? Regret? Sadness? Looking back, it was all of those and more, but it was like my emotions were jumbled into a giant blender. It was an unpleasant feelings smoothie, and I had a tough time choking it down.

What really hit me was when I realized I was only a few days from touring that expensive college I told you about. My parents, they were so excited someone in the family was finally going to a four-year school. Even if I took time off after high school. And they were willing to pay the tuition. Beanbag sure wasn't interested in furthering his education. Here's a secret I didn't tell anyone—my dad took on a second job outside of the police force to help pay for it. He gave up his spare time doing something he hated. And he did it for me to succeed at something I loved. To me, it was the ultimate sacrifice.

But my prognosis had been dealt to me like a losing hand of poker. I couldn't go to school. Hell, I didn't even know if I'd get to go to my upcoming dentist appointment or see the next horror movie release with you at the Cineplex. There was one fact I was certain of: I couldn't leave my family with the burden this disease would leave them. It wasn't even an option. The new insurance policy I was covered under, the first one on my own as an adult, wouldn't pay for what they considered my "pre-existing condition". I couldn't bear my parents watching me die a slow, painful death while confined to a sterile hospital bed – almost as if I'd somehow let them down. Discussing a DNR or whether or not to terminate life support, if it came down to it, wasn't a decision I wanted them to endure.

I've seen people die from cancer as I've endured this nightmare.

I've seen the way their bodies starve and deteriorate.

I've seen their skin become translucent, lighting up a map of purple and blue veins.

I've seen their mouths go lax, gaping open as they gasp for precious mouthfuls of air.

I've seen their hair in disheveled disarray when before they'd never allow a lock to be out of place.

I've seen way they become incoherent and confused, like a terrified child unsure of what's to come.

I've seen them look up at the corner of the room, as if someone is patiently waiting for them to take their last breath and give up the fight.

I've heard them moan, as if they're a prisoner in their own body, trying desperately to communicate, failing.

I've heard the death rattle when the end is near, a sound I wouldn't wish on anyone to hear.

There's a nervous energy that skitters along your skin

*when someone you know is about to pass away. You're
helpless, unable to focus as you continue to wait for the
exact moment it happens. The deafening silence causes
your ears to ring and your mind to race while you're on
high alert.*

*I can't give anyone those memories about me...at my
expense. I can't, Blue.*

*Questions flooded my mind constantly. Why me? Why was
I chosen to be broken and unfixable? What did I do wrong
to deserve this? And then it hit me. I have the capability
to fix it! I took the most difficult problem and decided to
make it into a simple answer. I'm ripping the bandage
off quickly to end it all. No long hospital stays or hospice
services equating to astronomical bills. No drawn-out
death. Thanks to confidentiality laws, no one knows my
situation except for Dr. Ritchie and me—my parents think
their daughter is healthy as a horse. And I'm determined
for it to stay that way up until the end before I become sick
enough for them to figure it out. Now, it's my turn to make
my own ultimate sacrifice. And that gives me a sense of
peace.*

*It's sad my future had been snuffed by a single five-minute
phone call. I'd never go to college. Never get married.
Never have children, grandchildren, or be that creepy old
lady with thirty cats we'd joked about. I'd never see what
I'd look like with white hair and wrinkles. I'd never get
to grow old and reminisce with you about our pasts. My
life had veered off the main path with a dead end on the
horizon, and someone is stepping on the accelerator. Hard.
The headaches are worsening by the day now, and it's
taking everything I have to fake normalcy while I eat meals
of specifically-measured pills. Periodic episodes of blurred
vision and multiple, daily trips to vomit have become my
new routine. Anxiety that someone will find out the truth
consumes me day and night. I'm so tired. This disease has
stolen enough from me, and it's time I take matters into
my own hands. Once and for all.*

There's something I need you to know though, and if it's

the only piece of information you take away from this letter,
I want it to be this: Don't ever question whether my actions
were a reflection of yours. Did you read what I wrote? If
you need to take a minute and digest that thought, do it.
This letter isn't going anywhere. Even though I'm not, my
words will be waiting for you to return. I'm serious. **Don't**
ever question whether my actions were a reflection of
yours. *They weren't. It was all a matter of poor timing.*

She knew me all too well. For a brief moment, I closed
my eyes, clenching them shut as giant sobs overtook me. My
shoulders heaved. The smothering guilt that overtook me for
years, the tremendous weight on my shoulders...she gave me
permission to let it all go. Her words were too painful to take
in all at once, but I knew I had to continue reading. I owed
Madelyn that much.

I'm not sure if you know this, but Adam came to see me
the night after I left your place and saw...you two...well, you
know. Anger and betrayal didn't begin to describe what
I felt. But after thinking about it, I realized the hostility
was misdirected because of other issues in my life, issues
neither he nor you knew about. He was so patient and
composed, saying he'd wait until I was ready to talk. It
took me two hours to let my stubbornness subside. We had
a long chat on the front porch. He'd come to defend you,
asking me if I hated anyone...to hate him instead of you.
And then with the purest look in his eyes...he told me he
was in love with you. I was dumbfounded.
It all seems so trivial now. I'm sorry I blew up at you that
night. Looking back, there was a better way to have gone
about it, a more constructive way, but I've been so fucking
emotional. That was one of my better days—health-wise,
and I was so excited to see you. Cancer or not, there's no
excuse. I'm sorry. About so many things. Mostly, I'm sorry
our last conversation ever was a string of damaging words.
What I don't understand is why you didn't tell me about
you two? For so many months you kept it quiet? Impressive,

my friend. I probably asked Adam a dozen times to tell me why no one knew; I might've even resorted to begging at one point. If I learned one thing that night, it's that Adam Rockwell is loyal as hell to you. P.S. He never budged and told me why your relationship was kept a secret. For that, I'm so curious, but at the same time it makes me admire him even more. You're in love. Planning on leaving Steele Falls together. It's like some kind of romantic fairy tale. Oh, how I wish you would've trusted me with that information. Would I have been a little green with envy? It'd be a lie to say no. But would I have been ecstatic for my best friend? Hell yes. Either way, I'm sure whatever the reason, it's a valid one.

Would the truth have changed my decision to end my life before it had a chance to end me? Not a damn bit.

I want you to be happy, Blue Ann Brennan. I want you to experience all of the things I won't be able to. Whether you get married or not, have children, grandchildren, or become that creepy old lady with thirty cats, or whatever else life throws your way. And don't you doubt I'll be watching over you as you do all of it, cheering my best friend on. It just won't be from the confines of this broken body. We've been inseparable since we were in elementary school, so don't think I'm bailing on you. I'm not; I promise. And trust that I'll find a way to let you know I'm around. Whether your happiness is with Adam or if it isn't, I want you to enjoy every second of this life. It's the only one you get. And speaking of life, I can tell you one thing without a doubt—that boyfriend you've been hiding from the world? He adores the fuck out of you. You should see the way his eyes lit up when we talked. He got this goofy smile like a little kid at Christmas every time your name came up. It was cute, and it was honest, and it was...one of the most genuine moments I've witnessed. For once in my life, I wish I'd have experienced a love of that magnitude, but it wasn't meant for me. Do me a favor and don't let that kind of love go. Hang onto it tight.

What was one of the last things you told me? Do you

remember? The words may have been laced with resentment at the time, but I think it's important to turn them into a positive message now. When I walked into that room unexpectedly, you told me, "You don't understand. It's complicated." I replied and told you, "It's only complicated if you make it complicated."
That's my two cents. Whatever you do, don't make it complicated. *You'll know when the time comes how to implement that advice into your life.*

"Fuck." I lowered the letter and wiped away my tears, the weight of the papers excruciating. I fingered over the indentations on the stationery from her handwriting as I desperately tried to connect with her, hoping for a sign of her presence, but I felt lonelier than ever. With a deep breath, I swallowed and gripped it tight as I punished myself with the ending.

Most of all, I'm sorry I can't say a proper goodbye. I wish I could've hugged you one last time. Kissed you on the cheek. Told you I love you and that I couldn't have asked for a better best friend. You deserve so much more than what I gave you, but I couldn't bear to see the look of disappointment in your eyes if you found out what I was about to do. I don't want you to remember me as someone to pity; I want you to remember me as Madelyn.

XOXO <u>ALWAYS</u>,
Mads

So many emotions filled me. Anger. Denial. Regret. Sadness. All of them were jumbled into that giant blender of feelings she'd mentioned. She was right...about so many things. I both hated and loved her for that. But mostly, I hated me.

Everything had come full circle again on that heinous carousel. Time had been wasted, and I'd thrown so much of it away. I thought back over the last two years of how I ran away from the past. It was time I could've been using to make

Madelyn proud. Time. I'd taken for granted the one thing she didn't have. Was she watching over me? Could I honestly say she'd have been pleased with what I'd done in life? I didn't think so.

"Wesley." I rubbed my lips together. "I am so, so sorry. I'm sorry I left things the way I did."

He smirked. "That's the first time you've used my real name."

I forced a lopsided smile. "Yeah. Well, don't go thinking it'll become some habit."

"And I know you're sorry," he replied. "I am too. You're not really a heartless bitch."

"And you're not really the poster child for gonorrhea."

He gave me a quizzical look.

"Never mind."

A buzzing sound interrupted us. Beanbag reached into his pocket and pulled out his cell phone, scanning the screen. "Gah." He rubbed his eyes with the heels of his hands. "That's Eddie. I need to get going. The old man worries if someone's thirty seconds late. Watches too many of those late-night crime shows. You gonna be okay? I can bail on him if you need me to."

I nodded and did my best to smile. "Go. I'll be all right. Eventually."

"Thank you for tonight. I know it wasn't easy, but I feel like I can start to heal now." He gave my hand a squeeze and stood up from the picnic table. I watched him walk away, turning back once. "Don't be a stranger, Blue. I mean that. If not for me, for 'Veigh. She's going to need you." With one last glance, he jogged toward the direction of his truck in The Fill & Spill parking lot.

I sat there and breathed in wet Washington air, letting it soak into me along with the words I'd read. There was so much I wanted to tell Madelyn. More than anything, I wished I could've told her how important she was to me and how much I love...

Love.

I stood up. There was somewhere I needed to go, and the time dictated on my watch didn't matter. Fate tapped me on the shoulder harder and harder as the evening went on, and all I'd done was ignore it. Enough was enough.

twenty

I knocked on the door as breathing became difficult, each second heightening the tension in the air. My feet begged me to run while my mind negated the action. It was now or never. I chose now.

Something caught my eye while I waited. On the newly-redone porch, two glimmers of copper caught my eye. There was no doubt I looked like an idiot as I sank down to my hands and knees with my face three inches above the ground. My fingers traced over the two pennies pushed into the once-wet cement. The porch light illuminated the detailed etching that reflected a four-digit number. One conveyed Adam's birth year and the other his grandfather's, the man who'd built the house. The gesture hit home a little closer to me as I thought of the letter I'd read. Two cents. Madelyn.

That is my two cents. Whatever you do, don't make it complicated. *You'll know when the time comes how to implement that advice into your life.*

It was my sign.

Don't worry, Mads. I'm not gonna fuck it up again.

Reality reined me back in with the sound of massive waves crashing on the beach in the background, wind whistling through the air. I shivered and stood up, pulling my hands inside the cuffs on my coat. My fingertips were both numb and thrumming with adrenaline. I knocked louder, this time with the heel of my hand.

About a minute later, the door opened, the room dark. Adam's hair was damp and disheveled as he squinted at the brightly-lit porch. A pair of gray sweatpants hung low on his hips, drawing my attention to his shirtless torso.

"Hi." I shifted my weight from one foot to the other.

His shoulders slumped in defeat. "What do you want? It's almost midnight."

The right words continued to fail me. "Hi."

You said 'hi' twice? Really, Blue? That's the best you could come up with?

"I think you already established that." His expression turned from questioning to irritated as he started to shut the door a few inches. "Well, this was fun, but I'm sure Cash is waiting with his cobweb treatment—"

"Help me." A lump formed in my throat while I tried to speak, my cold fingers aching to touch him. I kept my fists inside my sleeves to keep temptation at bay. Being in his presence felt as necessary as breathing. My face burned and my pulse pounded with the memory of last time he'd kissed me. It'd been so long.

"Help you what?" He crossed his arms and leaned against the frame of the doorway.

Holding back was no longer possible. The dam of emotions I'd reserved for Adam was finally bursting as tears flowed down my cheeks. My tone was timid while my heart swelled up into my throat. "Help me remember what I've fought so hard to forget?"

"Go home and get some rest, Blue. You're drunk."

"I'm not." I wiped my nose with my sleeve. "I swear."

He studied me for what felt like eternity before opening the door farther, stepping back to allow me inside before he closed it behind us. "What do you want me to say?" he asked. With the click of a table lamp, the room brightened to a dim shade of buttermilk.

"I'm here," I replied. "In Podunk Steele Falls."

"So what?" Adam slammed his hand against the tiled surface of a baker's rack near the front door, the table lamp jumping a few inches and its shade knocked off kilter. "Tell me!" he yelled. "What is so fucking terrible about being back in Steele Falls again. Family shit? The thing between Daveigh and

Beanbag? Your mom being the frigid snow queen with an entire iceberg wedged up her ass? Or is it not about family? Maybe it's because the fling with you and Zack didn't work out?"

I fidgeted with the zipper on my jacket because I couldn't bear to look at him. It hurt too much. "No. None of those."

"Then what has you walking up to my door at midnight saying 'hi' twice while sounding like you should be awarded with a gold star for coming back?"

"It's you." I scrunched my eyes shut, hoping the tighter they were closed, the pain would lessen. It didn't work.

"Me?" He paused. "Why?"

Expressing myself was harder than I expected. A fresh trail of emotion took hold. "You made me feel again."

Adam let a laugh out through his nose and shook his head. "Well, I guess I'm the biggest asshole out of everyone around here then."

"That's not what I'm trying to say."

"Then, spit it out already!"

"Listen. On Friday, I thought I was coming back for Tom's funeral and to collect my part of the inheritance. But I was wrong. So fucking wrong. I was homesick," I looked at the floor and drew a deep breath before looking up at him, "for you."

He crossed his arms, his face giving me zero reaction.

"Don't do that." I stomped my foot.

"What?" he asked.

"That look. The poker face."

His voice intensified. "Like the one you've been giving everyone else around here since you arrived?"

As if to balance the teeter totter, my voice took on a decrescendo. "You look like you're disappointed. Like I'm the worst person on the planet."

Silence.

And there was the truth without him having to say it. The simplicity of shaking his head back and forth slowly with a stoic expression said what he thought of me.

I didn't know what to do, so I stood there and waited, feeling both raw and exposed. My walls were already crumbling into rubble. I didn't know how to stop it if I wanted to. The quiet was a million shades of awkward and uncomfortable, but I deserved every painstaking moment.

Adam ran his fingers through his hair and stormed across the living room without a word.

"That's it? You're walking away from me?" I threw my arms up in the air.

"No, I'm not stooping to your level. But I feel like this conversation requires beer," he replied.

"Great." Some of the tension released from my shoulders. "I could use one."

"Not for you. For me."

"Didn't you hear me, Adam? I have feelings for you. I'm still in love..."

He cringed and hesitated in the doorway to the kitchen before continuing. A few seconds later, the fridge door opened and then slammed shut before he thundered past me, a breeze in his wake and his hands empty.

"What now?" I asked.

He reappeared with a bottle of bourbon and a shot glass, slamming them both down on the coffee table. The smile on his face was fueled with disparagement and had nothing to do with humor. "You broke out the L-word. Beer isn't strong enough for what I've got to say to you."

I watched him unscrew the lid and pour of shot of golden brown liquid, filling the glass to the brim. "So, let's talk about you and me, formerly known as 'us'. I want to make sure I get this right. You're still in love," he downed it and frowned as he formed the last two words, "with me."

"I know. It sounds crazy, but—"

"No. No, no." He chuckled as he immediately poured another. "Crazy would be running out on a relationship when you're supposedly in love. Crazy would be changing your phone number and not telling anyone where you'd gone. Crazy would be showing up two years later and acting like nothing happened! But you wouldn't be an expert on any of that. Right?"

I took a deep breath. "I never meant—"

"Fuck. That." He spat the words like venom before he

took a swig directly from the bottle. "You're telling me you accidentally penned me a one-lined note saying you were leaving, you slipped and put your foot on the accelerator to take off in your car, and you forgot your way back to Steele Falls because someone jacked your trail of breadcrumbs? I'm calling bullshit, Blue. Bull. Fucking. Shit. Christ, did you even look back when you hightailed it out of here?"

My voice went up an octave and I felt my chest heave. "I'm so sorry I hurt you."

He poured another shot and left it on the table as he blinked quickly. "Well, take comfort in knowing you couldn't break what was already broken."

My eyes filled with fresh tears. Those words stung worse than any others he'd slung at me. Knowing I'd broken a promise I'd made to never hurt him destroyed me. And there I was, lumped with everyone else who'd betrayed him. No number of apologies was going to cut it.

"Were you trying to make me jealous? This whole thing with Zack? And Cash? I don't get it." He made a circular gesture with his middle finger. "It's like you're a revolving door of dipshits. Why are you here again? Do I fit the dipshit bill? Maybe I didn't get the memo."

"But I'm not. A revolving door, I mean."

He screwed the lid on the bottle of bourbon. "The truth will hunt you down, Blue. Sooner or later."

I looked up at the ceiling and let my head loll to the right with a groan. "I already told you, the thing with Cash was a mistake. A big, massive, stupid, stupid, meaningless fuck up of a mistake. And you probably wouldn't believe what happened with him if I told you. The thing with Zack...wasn't even a thing. I don't know how it snowballed, but I wasn't interested in him from day one."

"Well, bravo. You did a damn good job of putting on a show for Steele Falls then. If you want me to lie, sugar-coat the past, and tell you everything's okay, you've come to the wrong place. That's all we seem to do. The wrong place at the wrong time. Just like when..."

"Just like what?"

He tightened his lips. "When you stopped caring."

"You think..." I clenched my jaw. "If I stopped caring..." With shaking hands, I yanked the zipper on my tote bag open, pulling items out by the fistful and stacking them on the table. "For fuck's sake. Why don't I ever clean this thing out?" By then, I was rummaging elbows-deep with both hands.

Adam stood up with an annoyed look on his face. "Are you done yet?"

"Hold on." I shot him a glare. My wallet, keys, and lip balm were all on display, quickly followed by a package of tissues and my cell phone. "Damn it," I muttered, dumping the entire bag upside down. Coins made a tinking sound on the tabletop before they rolled off and onto the floor. Sunglasses. Pens. Pocketknife. The mints from the redheaded chick at The Fill & Spill. A tampon. And then I finally saw it. A small, violet embroidered pouch was the last item to fall onto the pile. "Aha!"

Adam rubbed his face with his hands. "Purple's not really my color."

"Calm down for a sec." I picked it up and unfastened the snap, dumping small pieces of metal into my hand, held together by a dainty silver chain. With one finger, I spread them out until they were all face up.

The smug look slid off Adam's face when he looked down at my hand.

"If I didn't care," I paused, "then why the hell would I still be carrying these around?"

A tear fell from my face, exploding when it hit the bracelet resting against my palm.

The shiny puzzle pieces glinted under the light. Adam had given me one charm for each month we'd been together. I'd worn the piece of jewelry religiously during the course of our relationship. When I left Steele Falls, I'd taken it off, burying the memory deep into a small bag in my purse. Throwing it away would've broken my heart, and I knew I wasn't ready to part with the memory. Looking back, I'd never let go.

"I don't know what you want me to say." Adam fought to regain his composure. "It's late and you're here, trying to what? Resurrect memories from two years ago? I don't buy it."

"What's not to buy?" A new lump formed in my throat.

"If what we had," he motioned between our bodies with his index finger, "meant what you say it did, you'd have never left in the first place."

I growled. "I hate..."

"Say it!" He paced the room twice and stopped to brace both sides of the splintered doorway tight. "Does it feel good to hate me? To not even be able to look in my damn eyes for more than a few seconds after what *you* did? Once upon a time, you used to be my ending. Instead, you ended me, Blue Brennan."

"I thought I made it clear with my declaration when I got here, but maybe you didn't hear me! I don't hate you. I hate this. This situation. And I ended you? You said I couldn't break what was already broken!"

"Yeah, well you're not the only one who can lie to yourself," he muttered before downing the full glass on the table.

"I'm done with all that. Like you said, the truth found me." I sank down into a chair. The clock on the wall ticked endlessly before I had the courage to bring up the next topic. "You went to talk to her...to see Madelyn." I grimaced. It was the first time I'd said her full name out loud since I'd left two years ago. "Why didn't you tell me?"

"At the time, I figured it'd have made things worse." He shrugged. "Then, you left, so it didn't matter. Looking back, none of it mattered."

"How can you say that?"

"How can I not?" he asked matter-of-factly. "You weren't here for her funeral. You weren't here to see her ashes scattered, and I'm willing to bet money you don't know where they were spread. You didn't have to see her parents in town, red-eyed and sobbing, clinging to each other like the other would fall down at a moment's notice. You were a fixture in their lives too, and you disappeared. Just like that." He snapped his fingers. "They were forced to mourn the loss of two children, all at once."

I took the scolding. "I know," I said.

"No, I don't think you do," he continued.

"Don't what?"

"Know what kind of impact you had around here. Until you, I didn't believe in me. And that had to change when you took off. Everyone you left in your wake had to adapt."

"Adapt? You want to talk about change?" My lips trembled. "I left behind everything I knew, including my heart. Went somewhere foreign and uncomfortable. Surrounded myself with a job and a boss and an apartment I hated." I wiped my eyes. "My best friend died two years ago, and until tonight I thought it was my fault. I was sure she killed herself, ended her life because of me. That's heavy, inescapable weight to carry around. For that, I deserved to suffer, so I destroyed the one incredible, amazing, and important thing I had in my life...before I lost him too. Figured it'd hurt less if I ended it first, but I was wrong. I was scared, Adam. Fucking terrified. Don't you get that?" My shoulders slumped. "Look at me! I lost everything, including myself."

Adam sat down on the couch and didn't speak.

The tears were unstoppable. "I'm telling you how I feel, damn it. Opening up for the first time since I left, to the only person I want to, and all I get is a blank stare?"

"This is the first real talk we've had in two years. It doesn't make sense. You've been slammed shut like Fort Knox. What's the sudden change?"

The conversation was more difficult to endure than I thought it'd be, and it lived up to being one of the toughest of my life. With defeat coursing through me, I uttered one simple word. "You."

He nodded slowly twice, his face giving me no indication of what ran through his mind. The thorny silence was unbearable. At least when we fought, I knew what he was thinking.

"Maybe coming here was a mistake, and I should leave. Sorry to have bothered you."

Adam watched me stand up and grab my bag, scooping my belongings into it with my forearm before heading for the exit. The door handle was cold as I gripped it and turned. While I yanked back, there was a jolt of resistance as Adam's palm slammed it shut again.

"What?" I looked up at him. "Do you want to reprimand

me some more?"

"Stop."

"Do you want to make me feel even worse than I already do? Go 'head." My eyes welled. "Take your best shot. It should be easy."

He looked down at me with caramel-colored eyes, his face close enough to where I could hear his breathing and smell the strong scent of bourbon on his breath. There was honesty and sincerity behind his voice. "You're my hurricane, and you've caused nothing but devastation. You don't understand what it's like to fall for you. 'Fucking terrified' summed it up best. I'm scared to want you, to love and lose you all over again." He cleared his throat. "That's why I have to say goodbye."

Hearing those seven words felt like seven bullets exploding in my chest, annihilating my heart in one final and deadly blow. It was too late. I was too late. Too late to touch him. Too late to kiss him. Too late to cradle his heart and too late to help heal his pain. All of it was impossible because of me.

He reached for the doorknob. I'd lost the fight. Even after I put it all out there in front of him, he'd made up his mind. I wanted to keep trying to convince him otherwise, but I couldn't. It was time for me to let go of Adam Rockwell—for good. With my heart full of melancholy and justifiable ache, I waited to for the door to open, cuing my exit.

But nothing happened.

The switch on the handle clicked as he secured the lock. "I have to say goodbye," he repeated, "to the fear and take a risk. Do you still want my help?"

I blinked and furrowed my brow in confusion.

His hand was firm on my shoulder, giving me a familiar sense of security as he turned me around. Adam tilted my chin upward with his thumb and index finger. Lethal calmness resided behind his eyes. "When you got here, you asked me a question. Do you still want me to help you remember what you've tried to forget?"

My pulse answered for me while my fingers reached up to trace the shape of his face.

"What are you doing?" His voice was husky.

"Trying to make every minute with you last longer," I whispered.

"Damn it." He closed his eyes. "If you're not sure about this, one hundred percent, tell me to stop. Right now. I can't..."

"Don't stop," I replied. This time I said the two words, it was different than when I said them to Cash. They were spoken in a single sentence, with absolution and without reluctance.

"What would you say if I tried to kiss you right now?" He leaned down, his lips hovering above mine, teasing before they pulled back slightly.

My heart pounded in anticipation. "Nothing."

"Nothing? Not a word?"

"I wouldn't be able to say anything because I'd be too busy kissing you back."

I heard the deadbolt lock as he trailed his other hand up my arm, his fingertips tugging at the elastic collar of my shirt as he moved behind me. "Do you remember how I used to start out by kissing you here?" His lips nuzzled my shoulder, making their way up to my collarbone and back down again. There wasn't a sense of urgency. It was like every inch of flesh needed his attention and we had eternity. "And the way my hands used to twist your hair up tight, so I could graze your neck with my lips." He followed suit with the motion, tugging my wavy curls gently to the right, giving him better access while he ran the tip of his tongue along my skin until he greeted my ear lobe.

I closed my eyes and leaned back into him, my pulse quickening and a flurry of goosebumps exploding down my arms. Like a drug, I was addicted to his touch. All it took was one hit and I'd fallen back under his spell.

"And do you recall how—"

I spun around and pushed myself up onto my toes, wrapping my arms around his neck, my face inches from his. "I think I'm starting to remember."

Urgency triumphed. His mouth crashed down on mine like two magnets connecting undeniably. The kiss deepened and I fell into his embrace, skimming my fingertips down his chest as his hands slid around the small of my back with his fingers splayed wide. The heat and pressure of his body caused me to shudder. My tote bag dropped to the floor, forgotten.

He rested his forehead against mine. "I've been just as lost as you...until Saturday night when you walked through the doors of The Fill & Spill." With the coy smile I remembered so well and a gaze that never left mine, Adam grabbed my hands in his and led me across the kitchen floor, through the doorway of the living room, and toward the bedroom.

Darkness prevailed with the exception of moonlight shining through the floor-to-ceiling panels of glass. Everything was tinted in deep shades of grays and blues from the shadows, but there was still enough light to see the hunger behind Adam's eyes.

"I've waited so long for this." The strong, hardness of his lips on mine was unexpected, almost possessive.

I moaned into him as my body responded by sending a tingle from my core that exploded throughout my chest. "Adam..." I whispered.

"Shhhh..." He looked into my eyes and reached down to lift my sweater over my head in one fluid motion. His eyes raked over my body, and I witnessed new contentment on his face. Adam took a step toward me and reached for my hands, lifting them to his mouth. He planted a gentle kiss on each of my knuckles before teasing his fingers up my arms, across my shoulders, and between the valley of my breasts. The pads of his thumbs and his palms slowed as they caressed over the pebbled peaks through my bra.

My breath hitched through parted lips, need roiling through me. I wanted to beg him to hurry. Yet, I also never wanted the moment to end. With trembling fingers, I explored the solid muscles of his upper arms until my hands met the abrasive stubble on his face, and I leaned up to kiss him again.

Our mouths met with savage intensity, my knees weakening when I granted his tongue access. The desire burning between us was a scorching heat that could fuse metal. Adam's arms tightened around me in a raw act of control as he fumbled with the clasp on the back of my bra, the cool air swirling around my breasts as it hit the floor.

My sky-high walls had been destroyed, and my defenses demolished by the intensity of his next kiss while the rest of the world disappeared. My actions were as forceful and eager as I hooked my index fingers over the waistband of his sweat pants. "Off." I panted. Two years of pent up sexual frustration were trying to explode from me all at once.

"Patience," he replied. As if I weighed nothing, Adam lifted me up and carried me over to the bed, letting me fall a few inches onto the mattress. I yipped and let out a giggle before he settled on top of me, the moment turning serious again. Words weren't necessary. He brushed my hair out of my face with one hand, his eyes locked on mine while his flattened palm inched its way down my stomach and beneath my jeans. Gentle fingertips stroked my lace underwear in slow, deliberate circles before he nudged the material to the side.

I arched my back against him as two fingers slid inside me. It'd been so long since I'd had sex, good sex that didn't require a vibrator. It wouldn't take me long, even with just his hand. A throaty moan slipped through my lips as his speed increased. "If you don't slow down, the moment's going to be over before it begins."

"What's your rush? We've got all night for an encore." He nipped at my lower lip.

I drank in the fiery desire of his touch, left intoxicated as his lips trailed down my body toward my breasts. His mouth paid careful attention to nip and suck each marble-hard nipple before he continued to litter kisses toward my stomach.

I begged for more while lust crept through my veins.

Adam unbuttoned my jeans and I lifted my hips to assist him in helping pull them free, along with my underwear. He maintained eye contact and a slight grin, planting a kiss on my knee. Four more followed along my inner thigh as he bumped my legs apart with his nose, his eyes seeking permission.

"Please?" I tipped my head back against the pillow and gripped a fistful of sheets while his warm mouth greeted me with eager need. My body squirmed and arched at the force his tongue brought, my ability to speak in complete sentences absent. "Up here. Now. Please?" I gasped, desperately needing more.

"I'm not going to argue with a naked woman in my bed." Adam wriggled free from his sweat pants, rubbing his nose along my body. "Promise me you won't disappear in the middle of the night?"

The corners of my mouth lifted into a soft smile. "I promise. Wanna shake on it?"

"I think we've passed the handshake stage." With a grin of his own, Adam's mouth claimed mine again as my body fought to rise and meet his. His frame moved on top of mine, settling between my legs as I welcomed him.

Our bodies found a perfect tempo, as if no time had passed. Even with our flesh pressed together as one, I ached for more. Needed it. Wanted it. Craved it. Long, relinquishing whimpers escaped me while his hips rocked fast and hard against me, my back arching against the mattress. Adam's hand gripped the headboard as I wound my legs around him. Our passion skyrocketed while our bodies threatened to ignite together.

"Adam!" I clenched my eyes shut, my thoughts fragmented. I was close.

"Let go, Blue. Surrender everything to me. Everything you've held back," he breathed into my ear.

With command in his voice, it was enough to send me over the edge. Heat rippled under my skin. I cried out and shattered into a million, shimmering stars.

Like a domino effect, Adam followed suit and trailed my climax with one of his own. His body tensed, riding out his orgasm with a satisfied groan before settling next to me in the bed, his arms wound around me tight.

A sense of peace filled me, and I'd have been content if he never let go.

"Was I able to help you remember?" His fingertips trailed over my skin.

"Mmmhmmm." I sighed dreamily with contented exhaustion. "All of it."

That night would be remembered for many reasons, but one resonated above all others. Adam Rockwell may have filled a handful of moments with fiery, physical desire, but more importantly he managed to heal my irreparable, broken soul.

Twenty-One

L ater that morning, Adam woke up first. His nose nuzzled against my neck with a throaty growl while his hands roamed my body. The scent of his skin was enough to send butterflies flitting through my stomach, let alone memories of the night before.

"What are you doing?" I mumbled, fighting off the growing smile on my face.

"Waking you up. I want to go somewhere."

I opened one eye to squint at the digital numbers on the clock. "It's seven in the morning. We didn't go to sleep until almost four."

"The annual pancake breakfast is today." He planted his lips on my temple, creating a path of kisses down to the corner of my mouth. "We're going."

I'd forgotten the pancake breakfast happened rain or shine, regardless of what day of the week the date fell on. Businesses shut down in the morning for the event like the Queen of England came to visit. "It's a pile of carbs topped with more carbs. Sounds like a sure-fire path to the world of diabetes." I rubbed a patch of the comforter next to me. "Wouldn't you rather stay here and burn off some calories?"

"Tempting. And we'll have plenty of time for our own workout today. These are the best pancakes of the year, and I'm hungry." He drew circles around my bellybutton with his fingertip. "Besides, I have other plans too."

"Like what?"

"I'm," he tugged me to a sitting up position, "taking you,

Blue Brennan, on a date. That storm's rolling in, so we need to get going."

I felt the smile tug at the corners of my mouth. "A date? Seriously?"

"Yep. Now, up and at 'em, beautiful." He gave me a chaste kiss on the forehead before leaving the room. "Clothes are on the end of the bed!" he yelled from the hallway.

A faded pair of my jeans and my fuzzy, pink hoodie sat on top of the rumpled comforter. The material was as soft as I remembered when I'd left it at his house more than two years ago. My eyes burned and I lost myself in thought, realizing he'd hung onto it. He'd hung onto me.

"Hey." He rapped on the open door with a concerned look on his face. "What's wrong?"

I jolted. "Nothing. It's stupid."

He walked over to me and cupped my chin in his hand, tilting upward. "What's stupid?"

"I'm afraid this isn't real. Like it's all a dream or something." I set the shirt down.

"Well," he sank down onto the bed and wrapped his warm arms around me, "if it is, I don't want to wake up. You know what? Maybe we have a little extra time before breakfast, after all. Join me in the shower? Purely in the name of conserving water, of course."

I giggled at his attempted distraction. "For the sake of the environment, how can I say no?"

He kissed the top of my head. "That's my girl."

Those three medicating words were all I needed.

He was my addiction again.

He was my sanctuary again.

He was my protection again.

Everything was going to be all right.

* * *

After two toe-curling orgasms up against the shower wall, we arrived at a park, three quarters of a mile down the beach from Adam's house. Worn picnic tables were arranged in a few clusters, the last two still being positioned into place by four large men. Small hunks of driftwood pinned down the checkered red-and-white tablecloths in order to combat the unpredictable wind gusts. My watch confirmed it was still early; most of the town hadn't arrived yet.

"See? The smart people are home sleeping," I said.

He looked at me with a serious expression. "I've lost two years with you. This person is smart enough to not give up another minute while you're in town. C'mon."

In town. My stomach dropped at the thought of leaving Steele Falls behind, of leaving Adam behind.

The sky was a gloomy shade of gray, a much drearier hue on the distant horizon. Calm waves lapped at the shore, making a therapeutic and rhythmic suction sound while they filtered through the sand. Ebb and flow. The water dictated a calm before the storm, and it was supposed to be the worst in over twenty years. I broke my spellbound gaze from the beach and latched back onto reality.

Adam tugged at my fingers, leading me toward the end of the short buffet line. "I'm starving."

"Hey! Rockwell!" a voice called out from behind us.

I immediately cringed.

"Shit," Adam muttered.

"See?" I tried to let go of his hand to avoid the impending confrontation, but Adam's grip tightened. "We could've been back at your place, still in the shower. Instead, someone needed carbs…"

Zack walked up to us, his steely eyes locked on mine. "Funeral's over. Thought you'd have left town by now."

"Sorry to disappoint you." I glanced down at my shoes. "Yep. Still here."

Zack did a double take at our interlaced fingers and raised an eyebrow. "What the hell is this?"

Adam sighed. "Okay. So, here's what—"

"This goes against the code. Haven't you heard of bros before hoes?" Zack cut him off. "Did you see the way she assaulted me at your place?"

"It's not like that." Adam cleared his throat, redness

tinging his cheeks.

"Why bother? Fucking cocktease doesn't put out anyway," Zack muttered.

Adam's jaw clenched as he bit back his anger. "I'm only going to say this once: don't go there."

"What's with you, man?" Zack asked. "You hated her the other night."

"Remember, a long time ago, when I told you about the girl who wrecked me?"

"That whole reason you wouldn't let me set you up with Sabina, Christine, Karmin, Hazel, Lainy, Autumn, or those Swedish gymnast twins?" Zack counted on his fingers. "Jesus, Lucy's been practically begging you to test her humidity for months now. Why settle for," he glanced toward me and jutted his chin upward, "this?"

I opened my mouth to reply, but Adam squeezed my hand hard to stop me.

"I don't dip my pen in shared Steele Falls ink. And you didn't answer me. Do you remember me talking about her?"

"Dude, you were so fucked up that night." Zack crossed his arms, chuckling in memory.

Adam sighed. "You do remember though?"

"Yeah, you told me about Satan. So?"

"You called me Satan?" I exclaimed. "For fuck's sake, Adam!"

"Wait. You're..." Zack's index finger waggled back and forth between Adam and I. "You two have a history?"

Adam raised our handhold a few inches. "Zack, meet Blue, my..."

I could tell he didn't know what to call me and pink flooded my cheeks again.

Adam let out a long breath through his nose. "Look, none of this was intended to hurt or mislead you. A long time ago, Blue and I were in—"

Zack rolled his eyes. "Don't say love, man. Whatever you do, don't be like some sappy greeting card and say 'love'."

"Love," Adam cemented.

"Can I talk to you for a minute?" Zack asked Adam.

"Alone?"

Adam puffed out his cheeks and rolled his head until he faced me. "I'll be back."

I nodded and watched the two men walk away, gesturing at one another in the distance while Zack shook his head disapprovingly.

I sat down on a piece of driftwood, wondering why Adam wanted to take me to a town-wide event instead of being alone. Zack's reaction to finding out the truth was less than stellar. With the crowd beginning to grow, we were bound to run in to other people we knew before we could escape.

My body lurched. Someone had clamped onto me from behind. "Hey!"

I glanced over my shoulder. "Hi, 'Veigh." *Here we go.*

"You didn't come home last night. After you stormed out of The Fill & Spill, I thought maybe you left town without saying goodbye or something."

"Yeah. Or something." My eyes flicked up at Adam's handsome figure as he headed back next to where I stood. I couldn't help but smile.

Daveigh's loving expression frosted over when she noticed. "Is the 'bad news' the 'or something'?"

"Are you two speaking in some weird sister language?" Adam murmured out the side of his mouth.

I stood my ground, Daveigh and I in an epic stare down. "So, what if it is?"

"You've hung out with this guy for what? Five days. And all you do is fight. Don't you listen to a word I say? You're getting in way over your head."

"Well, when you know, you know." I slipped my arms around Adam's waist.

"When you know, you know what?" Daveigh replayed the words in her head. "Wait. Okay, now I'm confused."

"I'll explain it all later when—"

"Shut up! I'm so jelly!" Lucy bounced over. "Did you hook up with the untouchable Steele Falls bachelor?" She crossed her arms and examined my face. "You did! You brought an al dente noodle to your spaghetti house! I can see it in your eyes."

"I..."

Lucy put her hand up for a high five. "Way to prove me wrong about the vaginal funeral, Brennan. Color me impressed."

Adam shot me a curious look and a half-chuckle.

"Don't ask. Please?" I averted my eyes and leaned up toward his ear. "Can we get out of here? Now?"

He nodded toward Zack stewing in the distance. "I think that's a good idea."

"'Veigh, I'll call you later. Promise!" I shouted over my shoulder.

She didn't look amused.

Adam and I made our way through the line. We grabbed two paper plates, pancakes, sausages, plastic forks, and bottled water before heading toward his truck.

"You haven't said much. Are you upset I didn't tell Daveigh about us? You know, how we have a history?" I asked. "You came right out with it to Zack."

He continued to walk. "You'll tell her when you're ready."

Ouch.

"It's not that I'm not ready."

"Okay," he said.

I grabbed his bicep and forced him to stop. "Look at me."

"Blue, I'm fine. You don't have to explain. I get it. We were under wraps then, and we're under wraps—"

"No, I don't think you get it at all. I'm not hiding this. When I tell 'Veigh about our history, I'll have to tell her about Tom too. It'll knock over the giant pedestal she held him on."

It made sense. We'd spent our relationship hidden, every aspect locked up behind closed doors. Not because we wanted to, but because we had to. He'd brought me out to a public event, in Steele Falls, because nothing forced us to stay a secret. He wanted a first. For us. I felt awful.

His expression softened. "Don't overwhelm yourself with family. Let today be about you and me. Please?"

I nodded in agreement. "So, where are we going?" I ripped off a piece of pancake and popped it in my mouth, chewing, frowning. Suddenly, I remembered why I quit eating them in years past. They had the consistency of bubble gum and the flavor of old frying oil. "That's terrible." I spat the doughy wad into a cluster of tall grass. "You like these?"

"Sure do." He ripped off a large piece with his mouth and flashed me a wink. "And to answer your first question, it's a surprise."

* * *

Late that morning, we pulled off the highway between two horribly mangled pieces of twisted guardrail. The gap opened to a dirt road funneling to a trailhead. Familiar trees loomed, their oversized branches creating a tunnel effect over the roadway. Aside from Adam's truck, the small parking lot was empty. It was a literal memory lane.

"Remember this place?" He killed the engine.

"I think I forgot to remember it until now." I hopped out of the truck and looked around, breathing deeply. The scent of fresh pine trees permeated the frigid air. Even in near-freezing temperatures, all of it brought back the warmest memories.

Adam grabbed my hand and we walked along the gravel-covered trail, talking about what we'd been through during our absence from one another. There were no awkward moments. There were no lulls. It was like we'd picked up where we left off. Puffs of steam left our mouths in miniature clouds as we trudged along, every lush color and vibrant hue sending me back in time. The footpath was one of our hideouts and always vacant. It was our spot, somewhere no one could find us.

One hundred yards ahead, there was a wide, circular opening surrounded by giant fir trees. In the middle, an enormous, misshapen boulder created a fork in the path.

I scaled the angular side of it, my hands recalling the location of the footholds and crannies so vividly, like I'd last been there yesterday. My frame settled back onto a flat piece of the stone. It was the perfect spot to look up at the sky through the mess of tangled branches overhead. Threatening clouds moved swiftly, leaving few blips of bluish sky exposed. "This exact spot used to be one of my favorite places."

"Mine too." Adam laid down next to me and propped

himself up on his side. "But I haven't been back since you left. I couldn't do it."

I studied his face as he brushed my cheek with his thumb, his lips touching mine like a whisper. When he leaned back against the rock, I rested my head on his chest, staring off into the trees.

"And I told you that old Zen proverb," his voice rumbled as he patted the boulder. "Obstacles don't block the path—they are the path."

I closed my eyes. "I forgot about that too."

"Do you know why I brought you here?" he asked.

I turned my head so I could see his face. "To reenact our first kiss? For the record, it was pretty spot-on."

"No, that's not why." He shook his head. "This rock is where I realized you were the first person to look at me for who I was, instead of trusting the rumors around town. Without knowing it, you'd taken away my pain. For once, someone believed in me, and that felt incredible. But all of that reassurance vanished the moment you left. The proverb I'd lived by became bullshit to me. You'd gone from being my path to being my obstacle."

I felt my heart sink. "Adam, I'm sorry."

"I know," he replied quietly. "And I'm not saying any of this for another apology."

I tucked my hair behind my ears. "When I got back, hurting you was easier."

"Easier than what?" He chuckled. "Sneezing with your eyes open?"

"Hurting you was easier," I paused, "than admitting I was the one who ruined what we had."

"I guess hurting you was easier for me too." He wrapped his arms around me in a tight embrace, many minutes passing by while he simply held me. "C'mon. I want to take you somewhere else."

* * *

"We're here," he said, pulling into a parking lot in town.

I blinked back to reality. "Mario's? But we had the best pancakes this morning, and I'm so full." I rubbed my stomach and rolled my eyes. "How will I possibly find room for lunch?"

"Humor me," he replied. "Let's go."

Adam walked around to my side of the truck and opened the door to help me out, guiding me toward the entrance with a gentle touch to my low back. Just like last time, nostalgia hit me with blunt force when we walked inside.

The smell of fresh bread.

The warm ambience.

The sensation of it being home.

It was Thursday and the lunch rush had already subsided. Outside of a woman at the salad bar contemplating two types of lettuce, the restaurant was nearly void of customers. Everyone was probably still in a pancake coma.

"Can I help you?" Lyndsie asked as she absentmindedly stacked a pile of glossy menus that'd slid catawampus across the counter.

"Two, please." Adam laced his fingers through mine.

"Great. I'll show you to a..." She looked up at us, her mouth making a perfect circle in surprise. "Oh, no. No, no, no. Not on my shift. Huh-uh."

Adam laughed. "She and I have met our quota of arguing."

Lyndsie gave us both the stink eye and aimed the point of a cap-less ink pen in my direction. "If you two try to play musical chairs even once today, I'm gonna..."

"We'll behave. We promise," Adam said with a laugh.

"All right." Lyndsie didn't look convinced or amused while she led us over to the same booth we'd sat at a few days prior. Instead of sitting across from me, Adam slid across the bench next to me and rested his hand on my knee.

"Do you two need a minute to look at the menu or should I poll any vegetables in the kitchen first?" Lyndsie's irritation was disclosed when she set two glasses of water down harder than necessary.

"We'll share the lasagna," Adam said.

"Uh huh." Lyndsie scooped the menus off the table and walked back to the kitchen.

"What do you think her problem is?" he asked innocently.

I sipped my water. "My money's still betting on her spitting in our food."

"We'll live in blissful ignorance and never know."

I slouched into the worn cushion of the booth and let out a long breath. "I don't want to go back to California."

"Then don't go," he murmured in my ear as he rubbed my thigh. "Stay in Steele Falls. With me."

I rested my head on his shoulder, medicating myself in his warmth.

"Do you know why I brought you here?" he asked.

I smiled. "Because you love Italian food and are coming to grips with your torrid love affair for lasagna?"

He shook his head left and right. "Not even close."

My tone took a serious turn. "Because this spot is the first place where you told me you loved me?"

"No, but you're getting warmer. That same night was the first time I realized you were my home. I envisioned us fifty, sixty years from then, gray and wrinkled. Sitting here for an early bird, senior citizen, discounted dinner. There was nothing I was surer of than that being our future. And then you left. My heart shattered, but I still loved you with each jagged piece. And I hated myself for that. For a long time."

I blinked and looked away.

"I already told you, this date isn't meant to make you sad. I need to get this off my chest. I've had two years, Blue. Two years to form words on how I felt with no one to express them to. You've got to understand that."

"No. I get it," I replied. "And I deserve it."

"It's not about deserving anything." He scooted closer to me. "I—"

Lyndsie interrupted with a plate of lasagna and two forks. "Need anything else? Crayons? Want me to pick a tune on the jukebox for musical chairs?"

"I think we're set," he said.

I poked at the lasagna, having trouble finding my appetite. Adam and I spent the rest of lunch continuing our game of catch up, but I didn't remember a lot of what he said. I was too busy digesting every word he spoke before our food arrived.

Twenty-two

66 **T**here's one more place I want to take you," he said when he pulled into his driveway. Adam walked around to my side of the truck and opened the door for me again. "Mystery awaits." He grabbed my hand and helped me out.

The wind was more powerful down at the beach than it was in town, waves crashing loudly against the shore. There wasn't a soul in sight. Hostile gray clouds fought to blanket the sky, combating the veil of autumn darkness. The storm had officially arrived.

Adam's house was nearly dark when we went inside. A lamp illuminated the corner of the living room, its shade still off-kilter from the night before. "I want to show you something." He led me to the small enclosed deck he'd built off the back of the kitchen. With a flick of the lock, he slid the glass door open along its corresponding runner.

"What's this?" I looked around.

A pile of throw pillows was situated on an oversized beanbag chair to the left with a couple of fluffy blankets folded neatly next to it. He walked around with a box of matches and lit a cluster of pillar candles. White wine chilled in a small cooler of ice next to two glasses.

"You put this together for me?" I asked.

He gestured with an empty hand. "Sit."

I sank down into the cushion and spun the bottle of wine so I could see the label. Feminine gold lettering curled impressively over a matte black background. "Cannon Bay. You remembered my favorite."

He picked up a corkscrew. "Do you know why I brought you here?"

"This deck is where we had sex for the first time," I replied.

"While that's true, it's not why." He smirked and sat down next to me. "I spent 278 nights sitting here, wondering if you were thinking about me. That was a lonely road, Blue. My home," he motioned between us, "had to be rebuilt."

I stroked thick fringe on the edge of a fleece blanket. "Working construction is more fitting for you than I originally thought."

"I racked my brain for anything rational. Did I hit her? Did I cheat on her? Did I lie to her? I even wondered if I pressured you after the whole thing with...We didn't have sex for two months after that. I was patient until you were ready again. But every question I asked myself...the answers were all a resounding 'no'."

I hung my head. "You should've known better. It had nothing to do with you."

"Except for everything." He dug it into the cork and spun the point deep into it, the firm tug resulting in a blunt pop.

The starless sky caught my attention. "Do you think Madelyn's looking down here? And she's finally happy now?"

Adam set down the corkscrew on the table and looked thoughtful. "I believe she's at peace, and she wants you to be happy. I don't doubt that for a second."

I drew my knees to my chest, my nose burning as I fought back tears.

"But this date is about us. Can you grab that tin for me?" He nodded toward a lidless canister on the ground.

I picked it up and looked at the faded label advertising a local coffee brand. "What's this for?" A large pile of miniature folded papers rattled against the bottom when I jostled it. If I had to guess, there were over one hundred of them inside.

"Something I found on Pinterest after you fell asleep last night. We're going to watch the storm, drink wine, and play a game."

"Wait. You've been hanging out on Pinterest?" I raised an eyebrow.

"I'm secure enough in my masculinity to ignore the look on your face right now." Resting his forearms on his knees, he looked into my eyes. "I want us to know each other again." He motioned for me to reach into the tin. "No peeking. Just pick and read it out loud."

Reluctantly, I scrunched my eyes shut and fished for one, unfolding it while he poured two glasses of wine. The typewritten font said, "What's your favorite movie?"

"It hasn't changed." He smiled.

I giggled. "Still *Dirty Dancing*, huh?"

"It's a classic! But if anyone else asks, I'll deny it and say Gladiator or Fight Club." He reached in the tin and grabbed a piece of paper, opening it carefully. "What's your most embarrassing moment in the past year?"

"Really? You get an easy movie question and I get this?" I covered my face. "Do I have to?"

"Hey, I don't make the rules."

I peeked through my fingers and shot him a glare.

"Okay, so maybe I made these rules. But, it's what the game gods want." Adam flashed me the half-smile I couldn't resist. "Come on. It's probably not that bad."

Without being able to look at him, I told the story of Trixie Taylor's erotica in Lucy's e-reader at the coffee shop.

Adam exploded with laughter until tears rolled down his face.

"It's not funny!" I socked him in the arm playfully and reached into the tin, pausing. "Do you know how hard it is to walk in there after everyone's heard purse porn?"

He bit his lip to stifle his chuckle. "No doubt."

I didn't bother reading the words as I looked up at him. "How many people have you dated since I left?"

His brow furrowed. "That's not one of the questions I printed out."

I shrugged my shoulders. "Game gods want what they want."

He pursed his lips.

"Hey, if you don't want to play." I made a move, pretending I'd stand up.

"Sit back down, spoilsport," he jested.

I settled back into my seat with my wine.

"Four," he replied.

The number stung. It shouldn't have. I had no right to feel a pang of jealousy, especially with Cash under my belt. The thought of Adam being with anyone else bothered me more than I realized it would.

"None of them lasted more than one or two dates though," he continued. "The shoes were too large to fill. Go again." He nodded toward the tin. "Your cheat question didn't count."

"What's your first memory?" I'd made the mistake of reading it aloud before thinking. My mouth slipped into a distinct frown as I crumpled the latest paper. "You don't have to answer that. I'll pick a different one."

He touched my arm to stop me. After a considerable wait, he spoke. "It was Christmas, and I was four. My family didn't do the normal holiday stuff. No tree. No stockings. No presents. No Santa. The only reason I knew it was December 25th was because my grandpa came over with a new green bike, complete with a giant, red bow. Training wheels. Neon-colored beads on the spokes. I'd never seen anything like it." Adam smiled fleetingly, and then it fell from his face. "After he left, my mom called the neighbor who lived in the apartment above us, a fellow heroin junkie. There was a knock at the door, and an exchange was made. Christmas lost its appeal after that."

My heart sank. "Wait. She traded your bike for drugs?"

"Sure did." Adam nodded, taking a drink from his wine glass. "Merry Christmas, huh?"

"Why didn't you tell me that story before?" I asked. Adam's first memory was a terrible one.

"I wrote off that part of my life, a long time ago." He reached for a question and unfolded it. "If you could be a superhero, what would your power be?"

I bit my lip in contemplative thought. "Can I have two?"

"Game gods vote yes."

"I'd be able to heal." I fingered over the etching on the

wine glass. "And go back in time to fix what I broke." I forced out a deep breath to ward off the tears and leaned in for another piece of paper. "If you could have anything right now, what would it be?"

He looked into my eyes, his head barely moving left and right. "She's sitting next to me."

That moment was heavier than most. More and more each day, I wondered what I'd done to deserve him and why I'd ever left in the first place. Blue Brennan was a fool. I set down my glass and stood up, using the scenery outside as a distraction.

A flicker of fear spanned his face. "Are you leaving?"

"No." I broke my gaze from the ocean as a bolt of lightning flashed and thunder boomed overhead. My heart overflowed with emotion, ready to burst. It was a sensation that'd been foreign to me for so long. It was all-consuming. I crossed my arms at the waist and lifted the fuzzy, pink sweatshirt over my head slowly. "I'm going to fix what I broke. Superpowers may not be involved, but I won't stop until I succeed. 278 nights will be repaired, one at a time."

"That's a tall order." A smile lifted at the corners of his mouth. "How are you going to do that?"

"Do you trust me?" I walked over and sat down in front of him, sliding my hands up the material of his jeans before unfastening the button.

He didn't answer immediately. The apprehension behind his eyes was undeniable, and it killed me to know I'd ever given him any sense of doubt. Reluctantly, he offered me a faint nod. "I'm trying."

"It's my turn for a while. Let me be the one to try."

His eyes locked with mine as I unzipped his jeans and hooked my fingers over the waist, tugging lightly.

He lifted his hips a few inches while I pulled his pants and boxers free.

With a devious smile, I pushed myself to my knees. His sharp intake of breath was followed by a low moan when I took action with my mouth. Adam's body tensed. I went deeper, his hand wound through my hair while his hips responded to my movements. It might've taken the rest of my life, but I was determined to right my wrongs.

Another boom of thunder and flash of lightning commenced, causing the lights to flicker and then extinguish. It didn't matter. Adam and I didn't need electricity for what I'd planned.

The rest of that night was spent on the deck during the severe rainstorm, my focus on ensuring he erased the number 278 from his memory. For good.

* * *

The next morning, I felt a gentle kiss on my forehead. Somehow, I'd ended up in Adam's bed without knowing how I got there. Wind gusts wailed as they whipped the house, the siding groaning from the force.

"Hang out here today," he whispered. "That storm's still violent."

"What about you?" I mumbled with one unopened eye. "Stay?"

"Don't tempt me. I doubt Ty would approve of me lying in bed with his niece all day." He planted a kiss on my nose. "I'll be back before six."

"Okay," I said dreamily, sleep fighting to conquer me again.

A few minutes later, I heard the engine of his truck start, and my eyes half-opened, fixating on the battery-operated clock. *What time is it?* 7:56 a.m. His wallet rested on the nightstand.

"Shit." I threw on his sweat pants and a nearby shirt, dashing outside. "Wait! You left your..." his truck disappeared over the hill while I waved it high over my head, "wallet."

I wrapped my arms around myself to ward off the cold, a forceful gust of icy wind bullying me along to the front door.

I flopped down on the couch and dialed Adam's cell.

After three rings, the line opened.

"Miss me already?" he asked.

"That's beside the point. You forgot your wallet."

"Great," he said. "I'm already late. Should've left twenty minutes ago, but I was distracted by a beautiful woman in my bed." A sigh. "I'll survive without it."

"You sure you don't need me to bring it to you?" I asked.

"No. I don't want you driving around in this wind. Besides, the brakes are nearly shot on the old rust-bucket in the driveway," he replied. "But, I'm going to say something before we hang up. I love—"

"No! Not now," I exclaimed. "Don't finish that phrase."

There was hollowness behind his voice. "Why not?"

"Not until you're here tonight. I want it to be in-person."

He let out a sigh. "But..."

"Please? It's important to me."

"Fine. You know, I forgot how stubborn you are."

"You're welcome," I said smugly. "See you tonight?"

"Nothing can keep me away," he replied before hanging up.

The call ended at the same time the power returned. I settled back against the couch, wondering how I'd occupy myself all day. It was night two of 278. There was planning to be done.

I grabbed my cell phone and ran a few Google searches. Success. I dialed a local number and waited for someone to pick up.

"Beachside Bikes, Joey speaking," a young voice said.

"Hi, Joey. I'm looking for a bicycle for my...boyfriend," I said. "It has to be green, and I need a giant, red bow for it."

A pause. "We got in the latest RacerRide late last week. I think it's the only green model we've got in stock right now. Will that work?"

The limited availability on my credit card tapped me on the shoulder, but I quickly waved away responsibility. I could figure it out later, and there was zero temptation to cash in the five million from Tom. "Sold. Oh! And do you have any of those neon-colored bead things for the spokes?"

"Yeah. We've got 'em. They're usually for kids bikes though."

"Doesn't matter. I'll take those too." Adam's first memory

would be rectified yet.

"Great. Do you want me to hold it?" he asked. "I'd need a deposit since it's the only one we've got in stock."

I thought to my lack of a car. "Is there any way you can deliver? I'm local and can pay in full over the phone."

"Not in this weather." He laughed. "If it can wait until tomorrow, I can have someone drop it off in the morning after we open."

I smiled. "That's perfect. Thank you."

After finalizing the transaction, I set my cell on the table, impressed with my handiwork. *One task down, a million to go.* While I was in the shower, another idea came to me. Adam planned an important and meaningful date. One I'd never forget. It was time I did the same for him. I got dressed, pinned my hair up in a sloppy bun, and headed into the kitchen.

I spent a ridiculous amount of time rifling through the cupboards, most of them only half or a quarter-full. Adam was the epitome of a bachelor. Every recipe I tried was missing two or three ingredients. Not helpful and a fail. I scoured the pantry for something romantic. Anything. Ramen noodles. Instant rice. A loaf of bread. Spaghetti in a can. "Gross." I scrunched my nose, none of them worthy of saying, "I love you". And then I saw it. Score! A box of cheap brownie mix. Chocolate equated to love, right?

I listened to music and danced around the kitchen while the rain slapped against the windows. Droplets raced down the glass, competing against one another. The wind screamed like a banshee and the lights flickered as I cracked the last two eggs from the carton and added oil to a mixing bowl. One last step. I needed to measure out three tablespoons of water.

"Hmmm...if I were a measuring spoon, where would I be?" I fumbled through drawer after cupboard after shelf on the wraparound island, searching. The contents of a deep drawer abutting a stool at the breakfast bar made me forget about the measuring spoon. Inside, I saw a shoebox.

Even though I was certain no one else was home, I ridiculously looked around the room. *Don't do it, Blue.* But curiosity got the best of me and I lifted the lid to peek inside.

My lungs stopped working. A small velvet box.

* * *

→ Roughly A Little Over Two Years Ago ←

It was an early autumn evening when we walked through downtown Aberdeen. The city was far enough away from Steele Falls where Adam and I could be in public without the wrath of the momster. All of the sleepy shops were closing up for the night, owners bringing in their sandwich board signs and antique furniture from the sidewalk. Each of us held an ice cream cone in our hands from the old soda shop on Third Avenue.

Adam slowed in front of a massive glass window of a jewelry store. "Let's go in here."

I glanced at some of the price tags through the glass. So many commas and zeroes. Massive diamond solitaires spun slowly on a charcoal-colored display. Gaudy bracelets glinted with sapphires, emeralds, and rubies under the fluorescent lighting. There was nothing in the ritzy store Adam could afford on his income from Mario's. And none of it was my simple style. The situation needed to diffuse. Fast.

"I don't think so," I replied. Giving Adam any ideas about going into debt on my behalf wasn't on my agenda.

He looked hurt. "Why not?"

I scrambled for a reason, not wanting to offend him. "It's three minutes until they close. I'm sure the old woman with the severe bun and the scowl at the counter wants to go home. We'll go in next time."

"Fine." He smirked, throwing away the paper from his ice cream cone in a nearby trash can.

I smiled and wiped my hands with a napkin. "What's the goofy look for?"

"So, someday," he interlaced his fingers with mine, "when I propose, what kind of ring do you want?"

I bit my lip, my heart thumping wildly at the thought of Adam speculating about our future. "Doesn't asking me defeat the purpose? It's supposed to be a surprise, something you pick out."

"Help a clueless guy out here." He jabbed me playfully in the ribs. "Otherwise, you might end up with a piece of heart-shaped jewelry you hate."

"Stop!" I giggled. "Seriously. You could make me a ring out of tin foil and I'd be happy because it's from you."

He gave me the look that he wasn't going to let up until I gave him a real response.

I linked my arm through his as we walked along. "If you need a hint, go with non-traditional and simple. But in all honesty, all I want is your heart."

* * *

I set the velvet clamshell aside without opening it.

A piece of paper was folded up in the shoebox. Again, I was nosy. My hands shook as I unfolded the thick sheet of watercolor paper, a detailed sketch of a puzzle piece inside. A charcoal-colored silhouette of a man and a woman in an embrace with explosions of pastel sunset in the background saturated the paper, AJR jotted at the bottom. It was dated with what would've been our anniversary. Adam Jacob Rockwell. I thought back to the bracelet of puzzle charms in my tote bag.

I scrunched my eyes shut and reached for the box twice, telling myself not to do it. But I had to know. My lungs stopped as I looked inside and stared at the ring, perching it between my thumb and index finger. The black metal of the band contrasted against a simple round sapphire set in the middle. What made it worse was knowing it was the right size before I even slid it onto my finger. A perfect fit.

All of it was too much, and emotion filled me from toe to head. I took the ring off and put it back in the box. Opening it felt like it belonged to someone else, in a different life, as if it weren't intended for me. But it had been, once upon a time. The piece of jewelry was everything I'd asked for, but I deserved none of it. All I'd done was throw away the moment before it ever happened.

A crumpled piece of typing paper was nestled in the opposite corner of the box. You'd have thought I'd learned my lesson, but I kept diving deeper. The world around me stilled as I scoured the words, letting them soak in one-by-one.

Okay, Rockwell. This is your last-minute pep talk. It's game day. Take a deep breath. Six months is officially up <u>at six o'clock tonight</u>, and you're meeting her at seven. It's taken you two months to put this proposal together. Don't fuck it up. This is what you want. I know you're scared of rejection, but if you don't ask her now, someone else will later.
Blue fixed your heart.
Blue believed in you.
Blue made you realize there are things in life worth fighting for.
Blue showed you...

I clenched my jaw and wadded the paper back into its respective ball once again, unable finish reading it. It wasn't fair. I was none of those things he'd written. All I'd done was broken him, let him down, and showed him the people you care about most will fail you.

I tossed the box down on the floor and screamed, cradling my head in my hands. "How did everything that should've been perfect get so fucked up?"

After my mini-tantrum, I looked at the box lying on its side. One more piece of paper was neatly folded into quarters that I hadn't noticed before. "Might as well finish the pain off." My heart ached as I unfolded it, afraid of what it said. Doodles of more puzzle pieces, faces, nature scenery, and stars decorated the margins. Random words had been scratched out and replaced throughout.

Blue,
The past six months of our relationship have challenged ~~me~~ us in ways I didn't know possible. And what was supposed to break us apart has made us stronger. We were forced to

*hide, ~~and I don't want to~~ can't do it anymore. You've taught
me about loyalty, trust, and honesty. I don't know what I
did to deserve you ~~in this life~~, but I'm not about to let go.
My world was gray, empty, and lifeless before you came
into it. You've awakened something in me and shown me
what it's like to feel again.*
*It may not be the piece of tin foil you wanted, but you said
the important part was giving you my heart.*
Blue Ann Brennan, will you marry me?

I wasn't sure which was harder to read: Adam's proposal
he'd written to me—the one that should've happened three
hours after I left town. Or the pep talk he'd written for himself.
His words were so loving, so pure. And then I'd gone and
tainted the whole damn thing.

Knowing he was destroyed without me—before it even
happened.

Knowing he was alone—when I hadn't even left yet.

Knowing his heart was broken—when I was the one
responsible for keeping it safe.

I'm not sure how long I sat on the floor and stared at that
box. I'm not even sure I blinked while the sea of tears blurred
my vision.

Silence became too much. I needed some kind of sound to
combat the thoughts racing through my head. Voices. Talking.
Music wasn't cutting it. To distract myself, I turned on channel
four and watched the news. Cathy McPhee provided a grim
update on the storm. It wasn't letting up and the meteorologists
underestimated its power as it converged with another system
off the coast. The screen panned to a familiar commercial
with Gonorrhea Guy. I flipped the TV off before he spoke his
signature line.

Making all of my screws up better for Adam was going
to be harder than I anticipated. All I could do was show him
I was everything he thought I once was. Prove to him I was
worthy. The clock read five until six. At any moment, the front
door would open and we could pick up where we left off. I was
giddy, like a little kid waiting for Christmas.

Forcing the contents from my head, I put away the box and busied myself with making dinner. My options were limited as I used the opener to empty an off-brand can of chili into a pot. A few minutes later, I covered the bowls with foil and placed them on the table. It might not have been gourmet, but I didn't care. All that mattered was who'd be sitting across from me. Candles lit. Wine poured. Napkins folded—in the fancy way we'd learned at Mario's. I smiled at the effort I'd put into it. I was finally home.

At 6:07, he still wasn't back.

At 6:33, I tried to call his cell. No answer.

At 7:11, my mind began to play tricks, causing me to wonder if he'd been stringing me along as some kind of vicious payback. I felt sick.

At 7:29, my cell phone rang and vibrated across the counter. I dove for it, finally feeling a sense of relief. Until I saw the name on the screen. Daveigh.

"Crap," I muttered, realizing I'd forgotten to call her after promising I would. Glancing out the window at the empty driveway, I decided to chance it. If I had to, I'd cut the conversation short when Adam arrived.

I pushed the button, waiting for the latest reprimand. "Hey, 'Veigh."

"Blue, are you watching the news?" she asked.

"No. Why?" I straightened the cockeyed spoon at the place setting in front of me.

"Don't turn it on, but I think you should sit down for what I'm about to tell you."

An icy feeling settled into my chest. "Why?"

Silence.

I couldn't breathe. "What is it? Is it Finn? Are you okay? The baby?"

"One of Ty's work trucks got into an accident off the 101, and his cell phone is off. No one knows what's happening. You should go to the hospital."

twenty-three

The rest of her words were a choppy mess while I raced around the room. Every last syllable.

Massive head-on collision.

Water on the roadway.

Semi-truck driver fell asleep at the wheel.

Impact at 70 miles per hour.

Loss of control.

Adam's work truck careening over the side of a cliff.

I quickly blew out the candles and grabbed my jacket before fumbling through a stack of papers and knickknacks on the counter. "Where are they?" A jingling sound chimed as I located his spare keys under a stack of mail. Like old times.

Every second felt like hours and I moved in slow-motion. Dense rain fell while ferocious gusts of wind pummeled me sideways. In all of my years as a Steele Falls resident, I'd never experienced a storm of that magnitude. Puddles splashed and the wet earth squished as my feet connected with the ground on my way to his old pickup truck. Icy water soaked through my shoes and socks, numbing my toes instantly. I didn't care. It took three tries to greet the ignition with the key. With blunt force, I slammed the gear shifter in reverse, fishtailing down the road like a race car driver.

My thumb tapped the steering wheel nervously while my stomach tied itself in endless knots. The hospital was thirty minutes away, and my mind was left to reel. Concentrating was near impossible. Visibility was poor as rain battered the windshield, the wipers barely able to keep up with the blurry smears of water on the glass.

All I could think about was getting to the hospital. The fastest route. Not knowing what was going on was the worst, and I wasn't sure if I wanted to cry, scream, or climb out of my own skin. Most of the drive along the side streets was intense as the air whipped through the trees, bullying the truck to the right. I struggled to stay in the lane, the muscles in my forearms clenched tight. The street lights made it difficult to see the faded lines on the road, which didn't help my cause.

I pushed the pedal harder, the odometer hovering at almost sixty miles an hour when I shouldn't have been exceeding twenty-five. Logic told me it wasn't safe and I risked getting pulled over, but my heart spoke louder, telling me to hurry. "Why is it taking me so long to get there?" In the back of my mind, I wondered if it was how Adam felt as he raced to me the night he got the DUI.

One flicker of that flashback was all it took to disrupt my focus from what I approached. Flashing lights. Flares. A blur of red, white, and blue blips. It was barely enough to illuminate what the surroundings because of the brightness. I'd taken too long pull back into the present and focus on what was happening in front of me. With a desperate plea, I jammed my foot on the brake. Nothing happened and my heart thudded.

"No. I don't want you out driving around in this wind. Besides, the brakes are nearly shot on the rust-bucket in the driveway," he replied. "But, I'm going to say something before we hang up. I love—"

A terrified sob emitted from my mouth. I pushed both feet on the brake time and time again, mashing it into the floor with everything I had. The needle had only slowed to fifty-six, and that was because I wasn't touching the accelerator. The mishap ahead between two smaller cars at the bottom of the massive hill on First and Olive was becoming alarmingly close.

Panic set in.

The truck started its the descent, gaining speed quickly. It hydroplaned where the ground leveled out halfway down before angling downward again. I screamed and spun the steering wheel to the right, desperately trying to avoid the oncoming accident. Instead, I was about to create one of my own. I screamed as the truck turned sideways, the severe movement causing it to flip on its side and roll down the remainder of the hill. It felt as if I were in a washing machine, the spin cycle out of control. My head smashed into the driver's side window, rainbow-colored bursts exploding behind my eyes. Metal crunched and scraped along the pavement, a sound so deafening as the truck folded around me. It finally slowed, resting on its top while a power pole fell toward the window, resulting in one tumultuous thud and more glass crunching. I fought to open my eyes. What looked like fireworks exploded outside the window. A jolt zapped me and my body tensed. White-hot, searing pain took hold of my mind, body, and soul, ending in an inhuman scream. Everything went black.

* * *

My eyes were so heavy, thoughts like cotton candy swirling inside my head. None of them connected. Tired. "Adam?" I mouthed. Forcing my eyes to open, I focused on my surroundings. Everything smelled medicinal and sharp in my nose. I stood in a hospital room, a dark-haired girl lying lifeless in the bed nearby. Machines clicked and beeped around her, all of them unfamiliar to me. Fuzzy. *Who is she?* Her face was swollen beyond recognition. A black eye. Two lacerations above her forehead. Countless burns and abrasions. A long trickle of blackened blood had dried near each of her ears. Three fingernails were missing.

I watched as a flurry of nurses and doctors scurried around the room, directing others, like an orchestrated tornado before they left again. It made me wonder what happened. What could put her in such a dire situation? Clothing had been cut from her body, and a jagged piece of metal impaled her left bicep. Her skin was abnormally pale in the few patches that weren't a searing red. Seizing. Shaking.

"Help her!" I screamed. "Can't someone hear me?" But nothing happened. No one reacted to the sound of my voice.

Someone needed to fix her. Fast. I made my way into the hall where a woman stood. She looked like someone I once knew, but I couldn't remember her name.

"Do you know who I am or what my last name is?" she demanded. "I want to see my daughter right now."

A nurse remained calm as she spoke in hushed tones. "Elana, we're doing everything we can for her, but she's sustained serious injuries. You're best suited to stay in the waiting room until we have an update."

Elana! That was her name. The momster. What was she doing in the hospital? Was it Daveigh? The baby?

My mom threw her arms up in the air as she demanded to be heard.

A younger woman rushed over and wrapped an arm around Elana's shoulder, leading her down the hall to an open seating area. *Thank God! Daveigh appeared to be okay. Shit. Was it Finn?*

I'd never seen so much emotion, outside of anger, on the momster's face before. Her lips trembled while her eyes glistened with tears.

"Oh, God." Elana raised her hand to her mouth as she sank onto a chair. "They don't know she's pregnant. The baby." She forced herself to her feet. "I have to tell the doctors."

What baby? There's another baby?

Terror flooded Daveigh's face as she grabbed Elana's arm to stop her. "Mommy, don't."

"Now isn't the time." She yanked her arm away. "This is important."

"Blue's not pregnant." Daveigh looked down at the floor and my heart ached as I watched, unable to help explain or console them.

"What do you mean? Of course, she is. I found the test."

"No, Mommy. The test isn't Blue's. It's mine." Her face contorted into pained shame.

"You? Wait." Elana blinked and shook her head. "Why wouldn't you..."

"Because you scare me," Daveigh replied, tears streaming down her face. "All of us are terrified of you. Blue said she was pregnant, so I wouldn't have to deal with your reaction."

Elana swallowed hard. "I'll be back."

"Didn't you hear what I said. Blue isn't the one who's pregnant!" Daveigh sobbed.

The momster approach the nurse's station, determination on her face. "I want to speak to the head of the hospital. Right now."

Like sun breaking through the clouds, a fog lifted. It may have taken me longer than anyone else, but I realized who laid on the hospital bed down the hall.

It was me.

* * *

I walked down a corridor, hurrying to locate my mom. After four tries, I finally found her. She sat on a leather couch, wringing her hands. Like always, she wore a sensible knee-length skirt and blazer.

"Sorry to keep you waiting, Elana. It's been chaotic around here, and we're understaffed. What can I do for you?" The name placard on her desk read: "Andrea Marks – Dean of Medicine."

"My daughter—"

"I'll stop you right there. You know I'm not at liberty to discuss the condition of patients who are over the age of eighteen without consent, medical release, or a POA. Do you have any of those with you?"

"No, but..." Elana straightened out her skirt. "Look, I know she has massive injuries, broken bones, lacerations, and a punctured lung. She was electrocuted and the truck was struck by lightning, which Dr. Kline already told me."

"Then you already know far more than you should." Andrea tightened her lips. "And perhaps I should have a chat with Dr. Kline to revisit our confidentiality policies."

My mother's voice intensified. "What I do know is the condition of this hospital is under scrutiny. Its future is uncertain if something doesn't happen soon in regard to cash flow. It doesn't take a crystal ball to illustrate that. I've seen the reports."

The head of the hospital folded her hands on her desk

and looked at my mother. "Did you come here to tell me the fate of the building or did you want something else?"

"Save. My daughter."

She let out a deep breath and placed the cap back on the pen she held. "There are HIPAA rules, and I shouldn't even be discussing this with you right now." She got up to ensure the door was fully closed. "Blue underwent a lot of stress during the accident. Her heart is considerably weak."

"How...weak?"

"With her laundry list of injuries, it isn't functioning properly without the support of the machines she's hooked up to."

My mother covered her mouth with a shaky hand, her eyes closing. "Well, the answer is clear as day to me. Find her a new one."

The Dean of Medicine rubbed her temples. "It's not that simple, Elana. Human hearts aren't available in a vending machine for $1 apiece in the nurse's station. There are rules. A transplant list. Strict protocols. Paperwork. Regions across the United States. Whoever fits the criteria and is at the top of that list is eligible and has first option."

"This is my daughter here, Andrea. Do something."

"I understand that, but my hands are tied. This is a hospital, not a negotiating board to prove how far up the political ladder you're sitting."

"What if I told you I had access to money? Five million dollars. A sum like that'd do wonders for your uncompensated care program and would ensure you more time to try and save your beloved hospital. Jesus, keep it for yourself. I'll never know."

Andrea hesitated.

"Your job is on the line next quarter. We both know there isn't another care center in the area, and no one can get in or out of this town with this storm. It's been two days. Bridges are unsafe. Parts of the highway have eroded into the ocean. Cell services are sketchy. And helicoptering a heart out of Steele Falls is going to be risky as hell in weather like this. No one's going to take that on. The road to Aberdeen and the 101 are washed out in multiple places. It's all over the news."

"It's not ethical. Twenty people die each day waiting for a vital organ."

My mother stood up and jabbed a finger toward the window. "Who gives a flying fuck about God damned ethics? Come on! Someone has to be close to kicking the bucket around here!"

Another round of thunder and lightning sounded outside, illuminating the room briefly. The dark shadows mingling with the brevity in bright lighting made my mother look like the Devil herself.

Andrea lowered her voice. "There have been eight traffic accidents in Steele Falls from this storm. Two are minor, three are severe, and three are critical."

"And?" my mother asked.

"One of the critical ones, a John Doe, recently underwent a test on his brain stem reflexes. There's no indication of higher brain function. The patient is currently undergoing a formal brain-death eval with a second physician. It's not looking good."

"Is that patient a donor...and a match to Blue?" My mother looked hopeful.

Andrea chuckled at Elana's stupidity. "We don't have confirmation on his name yet, whether he's a donor or not, or whether he's going to make it. Don't get your hopes up. You've got a better chance of being struck by...sorry. Bad comparison considering the circumstances."

My mother winced.

"Besides, to start there's blood testing, HLA typing, and cross-match testing that have to occur. And that's saying the results for the brain eval prove the patient won't survive. He has to be a donor. Once the heart is removed, it has to be examined to determine whether it's healthy enough. There are so many legalities and complications with what you're asking me to consider..."

My mother sat there, still.

"Immunosuppressants haven't been administered. She hasn't undergone the required physical, emotional, or psychological testing. Discussing this is asinine."

"How do you want her to undergo some of those tests? That's what's asinine." My mother gestured toward the hallway. "How is that even possible when she's unconscious!"

"Do you have any idea how much paperwork goes into this? The number of forms that need signatures? And the required approvals? Decisions like this are well aren't my jurisdiction and—"

"I have no doubt you have the appropriate connections."

"And the forms?"

"Forge them."

"I could face jail time. Forgery is illegal, Elana."

My mother nudged a pen across Andrea's desk slowly. "It isn't if you're not caught."

Everything went dark again.

* * *

I woke up and my eyes felt like they were coated with sand. Yet, it oddly didn't hurt. Nothing did. The world was blurry and I was so tired. It was a momentary attempt. Keeping them open was impossibly exhausting.

I didn't know the time.

I didn't know the day.

I didn't know the setting.

Wires and beeping machines surrounded me. Everything else was a thick, heavy blanket of nothingness.

In the distance, I could hear Daveigh's voice and then a hand gripped mine. "Blue?" My sister's voice was soft.

I tried to open my mouth, but realized there something keeping me from doing it. There was a tube in my throat. Speaking was impossible. *What's wrong with me?*

"Can she hear us, Dr. Lee?" Daveigh asked.

A male voice replied, "No. The sedatives we use are strong, and she won't come to until they wear off."

"Don't try to talk," Daveigh shushed me anyway, although under the impression I couldn't hear a word she said. "You were in a bad accident."

I felt panic creeping through my veins. *Wasn't it all a*

dream? Please, let it have been a dream.

"It's going to be okay though," Daveigh's voice wavered as she sniffled. "I promise. You won't be able to talk for a little while because of the breathing machine. You've been sedated and in a coma for a while."

Another voice sounded. One that was familiar and stern. "When will she be able to go home?" It was the momster.

"There are still too many extenuating factors to speculate," Dr. Lee said. "Heterotopic procedures aren't commonly performed."

Heterotopic? What did that mean?

"You can't give me an estimate?" my mother demanded.

Dr. Lee's voice remained calm. "She's not a car that underwent a simple oil change. Her heart was heavily damaged in the accident. And it was a one in a million shot everything aligned with the transplant. I don't think you understand that." He paused. "You should consider yourself one lucky woman."

Aligned? What was wrong with my heart?

"It still baffles me," Daveigh said. "I can't believe the surgeon took a second heart and placed it on top of hers. The vessels and chambers can all connect? It's crazy."

What is she talking about?

Then, there was another voice I recognized. Finn. "What's a damn miracle is one of the top cardiac surgeons works in this hospital." The emotion in his voice intensified, "I'm going to change my flight. I can't leave her in this condition. What if..."

Somber silence filled the air.

A pager beeped and Dr. Lee spoke, "That's my cue, they need me in the OR. If you two need anything, they can help you at the nurse's station down the hall."

"Thank you," Daveigh paused, "for everything."

The door clicked shut.

Next, my mother spoke again. "It's almost three, and I have a teleconference scheduled with Harold in five minutes. If she wakes up, don't tell her about what happened to Adam."

Wait. What's wrong with Adam? I'm so confused, and everything's hazy.

"And don't you dare mention a word about the surgeon

using his heart in the transplant to save her life. She'll thank me for the strings I pulled someday."

Adam? Adam who? Not my Adam. No! No, no, no!

My head tried to loll to the right and left. It couldn't be.

I heard them wrong. He wouldn't leave. He wouldn't do that to me. He's a fighter! Keep fighting for me. For us!

My chest clenched, the sudden onset of pain tremendous.

Adam! Don't you dare check out on me! Not now. Not after finding you again. After everything we've...

An endless beep sounded as the door burst open, the sound of many footsteps scurrying around. "Quick! She's crashing!"

Twenty-Four

Twenty-Five

Twenty-Six

Twenty-Seven

Twenty-Eight

They say time heals all wounds, but that's a lie. All it does is draw out the pain. The most heart-wrenching goodbyes are the unexpected ones. There's no chance to prepare. There's no opportunity to reconcile. There's no risk taken, to make the most of every moment beforehand. Everything stops abruptly and turns into a flawlessly dark vortex of nothingness. Nothing to cling to. Nothing to grasp. Falling into endless sorrow. Grief, it had no expiration date. My repaired heart was broken, each breath in my lungs an agonizing undertaking, but no one else could fathom what the frigidity felt like.

For me, time had stopped. There would be no more beginnings and no more endings. All that remained was being lumped uselessly somewhere in the middle—left behind to simply exist.

Adam lied to me. *"Nothing can keep me away," he replied before hanging up.* But something did keep him from me, and it wasn't fair. Those words played on repeat in my head like a broken record.

My hospital stay was a blur. How much time ticked by? Days. Weeks. I still wasn't sure, and I didn't ask. More honestly, I didn't care. Tests. X-rays. Scans. Poking. Prodding. I was numb to the core from all of it. Fucking irrevocably numb. I'd become a zombie, but the ironic part was the heart in my chest continued to beat.

At first, I thought it was a nightmare. Somehow, Adam would rub his face against my cheek and run his hands over my body to wake me up. I'd be able to feel the beat of his heart when I rested my head on his chest, and everything would be okay. Except it wouldn't be.

I was already awake.

I was already devastated.

All because I was already able to feel the beat of his heart. Every damn thud. Yet, he was nowhere nearby.

* * *

For weeks, I'd stayed with Daveigh while I recovered—for lack of a better word. But there was no recovering from what I'd undergone. Finn stayed as long as he could, dragging his heels until he was satisfied with the doctor's prognosis. The moment his flight took off, my heart broke all over again. Much like when I was with Cash, I was still the loser. There was no trophy in sight.

I'd lost everything. Every damn thing.

Not allowed to leave.

Not allowed to drive.

Not allowed to go for a walk alone.

Not allowed to have a private moment to myself.

Not allowed to love and be loved in return.

After too many rounds of pleading and begging for days on end, Daveigh gave in and acquiesced to the one favor I wanted. It would both break and destroy, but it was what I needed. For me.

An hour later, she drove her car up alongside Adam's house and pulled the keys from the ignition. The driftwood perimeter we constructed was still there. The porch he'd built looked the same. The glittering glass from the smashed beer bottle sparkled on the ground. His ghost was everywhere. In the walls. Beneath my feet. Tangled into the air.

My breath hitched when I saw a green bicycle on the porch with neon spokes on the wheels. A giant, red bow made it impossibly perfect, yet it'd already been rendered useless. "I need to go in alone." I stared at the tag dangling on the string, affixed to the shiny handlebars. It'd remain forever new. My heart shattered all over again in that isolated moment.

"Blue, I don't think going in by yourself is a good idea." She reached over the console and touched my arm.

"Give," I closed my eyes, "me a few minutes. Please?"

Reluctantly, my sister nodded. "I'll wait on the steps, but if you don't come out in five, I'm coming in."

My body was still considerably weak, Daveigh taking it upon herself to act as my crutch up to the porch. I pulled the spare set of keys from my pocket and unlocked the door. Silence had never been so loud as when I walked into that house. Utter stillness. The chili I'd heated was wrapped up on the table. Glasses of wine remained full. Brownies uneaten. A romantic dinner awaited that would never come to be. Everything was the same, except for one gaping, cavernous hole in my life.

Acidic guilt flooded my veins with every beat of Adam's heart. I was sickened by all of it. My mother had connections at the local bank. The money I'd received from the inheritance was gifted to someone at the hospital, used to buy my life and sell Adam's—regardless of his prognosis. I didn't want any of Tom's guilt-laced money. Not a God damned penny. Yet, the fact remained it was thievery in so many fucked up ways.

With shaky steps, I walked across the room and sat on the floor. Summoning enough bravery to pull out the shoebox and lifting the lid sent tears to my eyes. Fully intact. I'm not sure why I expected otherwise. My chest threatened to explode as I pulled out the velvet box and shakily slid the ring on my finger. The band was cold as I rubbed it with my thumb, knowing Adam once touched it. The bond I ached, longed, and hoped for was absent.

I stood up and walked over to the kitchen table, trailing my fingers over the foil on one of the bowls. A surge of anger rushed through me before I could try to counter it. I screamed, and picked up the bowl, lobbing it at the wall with the little strength I had. Jagged pieces of ceramic fell to the floor while a splatter of dark-colored chili marked the wall in an abstract explosion.

Daveigh hurried into the room and skidded to a halt when she saw me.

I stared at the blobs of beans and meat dripping down the

wall, unable to make my limbs move. With trembling lips and more tears threatening to spill, I whispered, "I'm so sorry."

"I'll take care of that." She ushered me into a chair. "Sit down."

It seemed like such a short while ago that I'd giddily waited for Adam to arrive home to sweep me into his arms in only the way he could, kiss me in only the way he could, and love me in only the way he could. I'd be left hollow and unfulfilled for any of that love, craving it, needing it. Being let down.

Love.

But... I do want to say something before we hang up, and it needs to be now. I love—"

"No! Not now," I exclaimed. *"Don't say it."*

I heard the hollowness behind his voice. "Why?"

"Not until you're here tonight. In person."

He let out a sigh. "But..."

"Please? Tonight."

"Fine. You know, I forgot about how stubborn you are."

"You're welcome," I sang with a smile. *"See you tonight."*

I'd lost out on the chance to say I loved him. Adam was the only man who'd ever captured my heart, and I couldn't tell him. Why was I so stupid? He died never hearing those three little words come from my mouth after two years of blanketing silence and doubt. Maybe, if we'd continued the conversation on the phone, or if I'd have caught up to him with his wallet, or if I'd have begged a little harder for him to stay home, the few seconds would've made a difference in whether he survived. Instead, I'd be left wondering an endless number of "what ifs".

My addiction was dead.

My sanctuary was dead.

My protection was dead.

If you think death is painful, try living.

I looked at the door, half-expecting it to open and for him to walk in. But it didn't happen and I knew I'd be left disappointed every time my heart, his heart slipped up and forgot he wasn't coming back. It was too much.

I pushed myself to my feet and shuffled into the bathroom.

My palms met the sides of the sink, and I angrily stared at the soap dish. The doctors told me to not get worked up. Stay calm. But how could I? Looking at my reflection in the mirror, my injuries still hadn't fully healed. I touched my cheek, wincing at the pain—both external and internal.

With shaking hands, I unbuttoned my shirt, studying the massive black stitches spanning the area under my sternum and down between my breasts. My breath hitched while I fingered over the surrounding flesh, unable to comprehend Adam being so close to me, yet so far away.

I tilted my head toward the ceiling and a piece of paper caught my eye, affixed to the top of the mirror with a piece of cellophane tape. Tugging it free felt like it signified the end of something, something I had to come to grips with. My eyes brimmed as I unfolded it. It was a series of cartoon letters formed from puzzle pieces written in simple black ink.

You've always held my heart

As always, he'd initialed and dated the piece of artwork on the bottom. He'd left it the day he died, but he had no idea how poignant those words would be mere hours later. I couldn't handle standing in the bathroom anymore.

Like the mother-in-law house, I punished myself by walking through each room to revisit the memories.

Where we'd argued at the table.

Where we'd played that silly question game.

Where we'd had sex on his bed.

Emotional exhaustion far exceeded the physical. I crawled onto the rumpled sheets and sobbed, clutching his pillow, his scent still irrefutably present.

Daveigh walked in the room a few minutes later and sat down next to me. Her frame made the mattress sink a few inches as she stroked my hair. "I wish I could take away your pain."

I rested my head on her lap and let the tears freely fall as my shoulders heaved. No more holding back. It was finally time I told Daveigh the entire story. She needed to know everything about Adam and Tom, to get it off my chest, once and for all.

Twenty-Nine

⁕⁕ Roughly Eight Months Later ⁕⁕

I sat outside on the porch, rubbing the two pennies embedded in the cement. It was my daily ritual. Even though the property was technically mine, I still couldn't call it my own. It seemed like I did a disservice to say those words aloud. After Ty learned about everything that'd happened and formalities surrounding Adam's death were finalized, he'd put in an offer on the house. In turn, a bidding war ensued with Zachary Main. It was a final dig at me. Ty Brennan won, and the house was put in my name. The beyond-generous gesture took a long time for me to accept. I felt like I lived inside a shrine, afraid to move anything, afraid to touch anything. Terror consumed me it would erase his memory. But at the same time, I couldn't bring myself to leave it behind either.

I wrapped my hands around a cup of tea and wound a blanket around my frame. *So cold lately.* I'd been in Steele Falls a full year at that point, only going back to Sacramento with Daveigh and Wesley to pack up my apartment and Catzilla. I never looked back.

Cancer and suicide stole Madelyn from me, two constituents outside my control. Even though Adam's truck accident wasn't my fault, I felt like my own fear and stupidity were catalysts in his death.

Over the past few months, Cash reached out, saying he missed me, asking if I'd ever thought about reconciling with him. Every message from CREAM went ignored on my phone. He didn't know about the accident, the heart transplant, or about Adam's death. If he did, I had a feeling he'd show up in his flashy Ferrari. There wasn't a procedure in any of his medical books that could fix me, even if he wanted to. Not this time.

Daveigh came by almost daily, half the time with Wesley and the baby in tow. Those were my least favorite visits. I could see the pity residing behind his eyes in knowing I'd lost two loves. First Mads and then Adam. Everyone walked on eggshells around me, not knowing how to act or what to say. Hell, I didn't know how to keep myself from falling apart either. I'd been dealt the worst hand of cards imaginable, and death sounded like a welcome invitation.

I looked at my watch and grimaced at the idea of socializing. The week before, I promised Daveigh I'd go over to the momster's house to visit the baby, my niece—Mireille Faith. The namesake was my sister's way of making peace with the way she'd treated Adam, especially after she'd found out everything that'd really happened. Mireille means miracle, and it was a tribute to Adam—that I'd survived because of him.

When I arrived, I was thirty-five minutes early. No one was home, so I sat down on the porch. On most days, I wanted to be alone. Isolation welcomed me with open arms, and I didn't have to fake normalcy. I didn't have to listen to anyone pretend to care about how I was doing or what I felt.

I still hadn't spoken to the momster since the accident, despite her numerous attempts to reconcile. Since I'd been discharged, she'd put more effort in connecting with me than she ever did over twenty plus years. Texts. Emails. Phone calls. Visits. All of them went ignored. In fact, that moment was the first time I'd stepped foot on her property since October. That weekend, she was out of town though. A romantic getaway with her new husband—Harold. I didn't attend the wedding, give them my blessing, or buy them a toaster. As far as I was concerned, she was dead to me. The bridge between her and I had burned into a blackened pile of ash. And there was no repairing that. It was her fault I was left alone. I'd have rather died alongside Adam than to survive alone.

I'd become a hermit, a recluse. It was like being back in Sacramento again. Afraid of letting anyone in. Afraid of being hurt. And my walls were sky high. They were never coming back down. Every beat in my chest was a cruel tease, an ironic taunt, and a malicious reminder of what could never be again. There was no fixing me. In repairing my heart, I'd become eternally broken.

I sat on the porch bench with my knees drawn up to my chest when I heard someone walking up the gravel driveway. Looking out, I saw Ralph. He had a brown paper bag tucked under his arm. Much like the momster, I hadn't seen him since last fall either.

"I'm not in the mood right now," I said.

"Here." He held a bag out to me and gave it a firm shake. I didn't move.

He reached into the sack and pulled out what appeared to be a greasy sandwich wrapped in thin, white paper.

"What's that?" I crinkled my nose in disgust.

"The man at the deli called it a gut cleaner," he replied.

My stomach flip-flopped its negative opinion. "I'm not hungry."

"You need your strength." He nodded toward the sandwich.

The smell of old lunchmeat filled the air, making my stomach churn. "Strength for what?"

"Come on." He motioned for me to follow him.

"Ralph, please...I'm supposed to meet Daveigh and Wesley."

"They'll wait for you. Besides, we won't be long." The look on his little, old, wrinkled face told me he wasn't going to take no for an answer.

My heart wasn't into arguing, or anything for that matter. I slumped my shoulders and followed him over to his house and crossed my arms in the driveway.

"Get in." He motioned to his sports car.

"Why? Where are we going?"

"Humor an old man," he said. "Come."

After five more minutes of debating, he'd won. I sat in his car, and he drove down Main Street. Loud, classical music blared.

"Are you going to tell me where we're going yet?" My voice competed against the sound of robust cellos.

"The cemetery," he said, looking straight ahead.

"Whoa. Hold the bus." My mouth hung open. "Stop."

He gave me the knowing look once more before zooming off at a green light.

"I can't go there," I said. "It's too soon."

He slowed at a stop sign. "I want to talk to you."

"This isn't going to be like the time you wanted to talk to me about virgins and picking apples, is it?"

He looked contemplative for a moment. "Ah! No, not like that."

"Like the time you talked about planting 'seeds' with the hand gestures?"

"Blue," Ralph looked at me, "It's nearing a year for you. My wife died five years ago. The first time is always the hardest. You'll never be able to open up again until you gain closure."

"I'm not looking for any openings or closings." My tone was sour. I hated every word of our conversation. *Who does he think he is?* The last thing I needed was to let go. I needed the opposite—to hold on for as long as possible so I wouldn't fall to my knees.

He gave me a third round of the knowing look. This time, it was without words.

I spent a few minutes wondering if what he did could be considered abduction. It was hard to concentrate with a lukewarm gut cleaner on my lap though.

The rest of the drive to the cemetery was impossibly long, and I got lost in thought. There were so many times I thought I saw Adam in the house. In the bedroom. In the kitchen. At the front door. I thought I heard him call out my name when I sat on the beach. I was certain I smelled his aftershave as a breeze drifted through the window on a spring night. In a sense, it was like he was always with me. Going to the cemetery would solidify he was gone. The only part of him remaining was still beating inside my chest—and I wasn't ready to face that.

I stared out the window with my arms folded around my waist, trying to somehow hold myself together. It had become a daily chore, and I was exhausted, wondering when it'd ever end. But I continued to wake up day after day, an ongoing disappointment.

The entrance to the cemetery was lined with the black wrought iron gates I remembered from Tom's funeral, the tops of each spire a point, reminding me the people who were buried didn't actually rest below. "Turn around. I don't think I can do this," I said.

Ralph parked the car in an empty space near the cobblestone pathway. "You can. And you will." He gave my arm a squeeze of reassurance before he got out. "Do you know why?"

"Why?"

His smile was both soft and sincere. "Because he'd want you to. Much like Carol would want me to."

Those five words shipped tears to my eyes. Would Adam want to see me? Would he know I was there? There were so many unknowns, and they would remain unknowns. That was one of the hardest parts. No matter what Ralph said, real closure was unattainable.

I looked at him and blinked quickly.

"I'll be over there if you need me." He gestured to a cluster of tombstones on the left of the path.

I stood there and watched Ralph walk away until he was out of sight, his red jacket shrinking until it was a tiny dot. It was time for my own journey to begin. "Obstacles don't block the path—they are the path," I whispered to myself.

Shaky step after step, I walked toward the weeping willow tree where I'd been told Adam's grave rested, the wispy branches blowing in the wind overhead. A gray tombstone sat beneath, the grass in front of it still not fully thick and lush.

Without words, I collapsed to my knees in front of it, covering my face with my hands. Knowing his body was only six feet away was agonizing. But he wasn't there anymore; he wasn't sleeping. I couldn't touch him and my fingers pined for that. All that was left was his shell surrounded by wood and a stupid gray slab with his name. Seeing the words on his tombstone ripped open the invisible wounds that threatened to burst over the months. The lettering was still sharp and new on the edges as I pressed against it with the pads of my index fingers.

Adam Jacob Rockwell
You touched our lives
for the briefest of moments,
but you'll be with us forever

I fingered over the scar through my shirt at the double meaning. A part of Adam would always be with me.

"Hi," I said, wiping my nose. The one simple word gave me a pang of sadness as I thought back to the night I showed up on his doorstep.

In some stupid way, I expected there to be a response. A sign. Something. Anything. There wasn't.

"I'm sorry it's taken me so long to visit. 278 days to be exact." Pathetically, I'd kept count on a calendar, as if I were counting toward some cataclysmic event, unknowing when it'd arrive. "Ironic, huh? You've been my hardest goodbye, and I couldn't bring myself to come..."

Part of me felt stupid talking to his grave. There was no point. No one was going to tell me everything would be okay. And if they did, it'd be nothing more than a bloated lie.

I leaned back against the grave marker. "It seems like all I was ever good at was fucking up and trying to apologize. I'm sorry I ever left in the first place. I'm sorry I made you sad. I'm sorry I lived while you died. I'm sorry I didn't let you say I love you on the phone that day. You know what?" I paused. "I love you too." I hiccupped, the emotion taking hold in my throat. "None of this is fair. None of it's fucking fair! This wasn't part of the plan. Our plan." I punched at the ground with my fist over and over, my knuckles meeting the cold earth. "We were supposed to grow old together. Have babies together. Laugh and cry together. Have senior citizen dinners at Mario's. When will the missing you stop? Because this," I rubbed my face, "fucking hurts. So bad. There's nothing left. I'm empty."

My bawling caused a flock of nearby birds to take flight. I

was sorry, for so many things. I didn't know where I started or ended anymore. Hell, I didn't know which way was up half the time. Every task, simple or difficult, was a mountain, much like the boulder on the trail. And then I realized that must've been how Adam felt for those 278 days before he'd let me go. But I wasn't brave enough or strong enough or resilient enough for any of that.

Losing him is what showed me his worth. History was cruel in its repetition. "We had a good run, right? Maybe a love like ours was too perfect to exist. It seemed like the world was against it all along." I sighed. "God, what I'd give to hear your voice, even one last time." My fingers ran over the sparse blades of grass. "Remember when we walked in front of that jewelry store in Aberdeen and you asked me what kind of engagement ring I wanted? I told you I didn't care what it looked like; I only wanted your heart." I sniffled and gestured to his grave, my words a garbled mess, "I didn't mean I wanted it like this."

Leaning back, I rested my head against the cool stone for a few moments, feeling more uncomfortable than usual, almost prickly. I brushed the sensation off and chalked it up to the emotion invested in my visit. Besides, who wouldn't get the heebie-jeebies while sitting in a cemetery? But a foreign tightness in my chest took hold. Breathing became harder, like my lungs had holes in them. Staying calm was impossible as anxiety filled me. Only it didn't feel like panic anymore. It was different. My vocal chords refused to work. A pathetic squeak. So much coldness poured through my limbs while my heart took off like a racehorse in my chest. Next, tunnel vision arrived simultaneously when my body went limp. The cold ground did little to embrace my face as it struck the dirt with a heavy smack. So nauseated. So dizzy. So shaky. So much pain. Something wasn't right. My mouth gaped open and shut, and I felt like a fish out of water.

Ralph shouted from across the cemetery as his blurry figure scurried to where I lay on the damp earth. Everything looked hazy and I smiled. Letting go had never felt so good. It was the first sense of relief I'd experienced in 278 days, and my own day one was finally being repaired. The pain drained from me, exiting through my fingertips and toes. It made me feel weightless. A paradox. Because at the same time, it'd become harder to move my limbs and everything felt so, so cold and chokingly heavy.

"Blue! Blue! Can you hear me?" Ralph patted at my cheek, but I couldn't feel his touch. "Blue!"

For a moment, I fought to focus on him, but releasing everything was peaceful. Almost heavenly. I could barely make out the words he spoke through his thick accent while he called 911. Something about blue lips and struggling to breathe. I didn't care. My ability to comprehend what he said was dwindling. With a round of CPR compressions as he talked himself through the motions, the world brightened for a brief moment before it dimmed again. Ralph's voice quieted into a dull echo as his demands for me to stay awake became more incoherent.

A final beat. And then the most beautiful, wonderful nothingness took hold. It was both comforting and consoling for one reason: I wasn't afraid anymore. That moment was when I saw him. Patiently, he waited for me under the willow tree with an outstretched hand, the half-smile I couldn't resist, and those caramel-colored eyes.

He would always be my addiction.

He would always be my sanctuary.

He would always be my protection.

Steele Falls was a small town in Washington State, flavorlessly sandwiched in a cranny between Hoquiam and Ocean Shores. It was nothing shy of bland. Some argued you'd miss the city if you blinked. If you asked me, I didn't miss it at all. Not a damn bit.

Children grew up there, dreaming of ways to get out of the sleepy and dilapidated city. Adults longed to retire there. Either way, few stuck around the aged tourist trap for long. Hurry up and get out or hurry up and arrive to die.

I was one of the escapists, the lucky ones. Leaving meant I was finally home.

the End

Acknowledgments

This book ruined me. It ripped and tore into my soul in ways I couldn't have imagined. There were times I had to put it away because I couldn't handle the content. I'm not a sappy writer. Ask anyone I know. Love stories aren't my niche. But this story? It was different. The characters were raw, passionate, and vivid to me. Each one had complicated issues and skeletons tumbling from their closets. When I thought I knew someone's secrets? WHAM. Another twist revealed, devastating me all over again. As always, I fell hard for the cast within the pages, but this emotional roller coaster was an entirely different ride than what I'm used to.

With that said...

Thank you to **Clint. Every day, you put up with my updates on my word count, my chattering about the people who live inside my head, and my inconsistent bedtimes. It's a wonder you haven't had me committed yet. XXXOOO!!!

Thank you to **Lyndsie. You've been my sounding board and my plot hole filler. Although we sometimes write at the speed of a turtle running through peanut butter, we have tiny humans thwarting our writing plans, and we have mountains of laundry piling up, you've still been my daily confidant. As my partner in crime, we've egged each other's word counts onward and upward. You've helped poke and prod at me to get this book finished, whether you've realized it or not.

Thank you to **Michelle. For wrangling the Kraken, and sometimes the Nugget, so I could sling words. The many escapes to the coffee shop were beyond appreciated.

Thank you to **Fray. Your artwork for this book was on point, and there's no one else I'd have trusted my book baby with. Not only are you an inspiration who makes me want to be a better writer, but you are also a phenomenal and talented artist—and a loyal friend. Never question any of that.

Thank you to **Wonder. Your generosity over the years, endless creativity, and vision for writing music is incomprehensively beautiful. Your ability to sock me in the gut with all the feels by pouring any string of words into song is something I'll treasure forever. Heck, you could probably make a grocery list sound incredible in song.

Thank you to my publisher. **Sarah Davis Brandon, you've always believed in me even when I didn't. Crushing Hearts & Black Butterfly is my home and my family.

Thank you to **Sabina. You harbor my writing secrets, entertain my many book snippets, applaud my word count updates, endure my writing rants, and you are my cheerleader. A giant pond may separate us physically, but you are still, and will always be, my sister at heart.

Thank you to **Christine. Had you not written Three Days of Rain and destroyed me for weeks (let's face it, I still haven't recovered fully), I wouldn't have been inspired to make an attempt at annihilating your robotic heart.

Thank you to **Trixie Taylor for allowing me to use a snippet of her story within the pages, even though I think Blue was mortified.

Thank you to **Elizabeth Anne Lance for swashbuckling these pages with her red pen and making this baby shine like a star.

Thank you to my **readers. Your endless and unwavering support makes writing stories my passion. I hope you enjoy reading Blue as much as I loved writing it.

**Without any one of you being involved, this book wouldn't be what it turned out to be—one of the most meaningful tales I've written yet.

xoxo

Playlist

Steele Falls – Wonder
Snuff – Slipknot
Trust in Me –Mr. Fijiwiji, Holly Drummond, & Direct
Drifting – Nathan Ball
Wake Up Call – Theory of a Deadman
Eventually Silence – Tuvaband
Even in Death – Evanescence
Rainy Days – Life On Planet 9
Goodbye – Life On Planet 9
Break Your Plans – The Fray
Don't Give Up On Me – RIVVRS
I Want To Know What Love Is – Foreigner
Where's My Love? – SYML
Hurts Like Hell – Fleurie
If I Be Wrong – Wolf Larsen
Scars – Boy Epic
Up Down – Boy Epic
Tell Me You Love Me – Boy Epic
These Are The Lies – The Cab
How Do You Say Goodbye? – The Engineers
Oceans – Seafret
Killing Me To Love You – Vancouver Sleep Clinic
Come Back For Me – Jaymes Young
Barely Breathing – Ghost Loft
Without You – Oh Wonder
Dark Bloom – Amber Run
I Found – Amber Run
White Lie – Amber Run
No Answers – Amber Run
Fickle Game – Amber Run
You And I – PVRIS
Winter – PVRIS
The Wreck – Delta Spirit
Seven – Revis
Even If It Hurts – Sam Tinnesz

When The Truth Hunts You Down – Sam Tinnesz
Don't Close Your Eyes – Sam Tinnesz
Hold On For Your Life – Sam Tinnesz
I Still Wait For You – XYLO
Closer – Cape Cub
You Should Be Here – Cole Swindell
Our July In The Rain – He Is We
Modern Flame – Emmit Fenn (Feat. Yuna)
How To Disappear Completely – Ane Brun
Every Moment – Dead Times
Don't Hold Me – Sandro Cavazza
Losing You – Aquilo
Sorry – Aquilo
Human – Aquilo
Gone – Michl
Almost Over – Hedley
Drown Pt. II – Squid the Whale
Love Again – Hedley
When You Can't Sleep At Night – Of Mice & Men
Before I Cave In – Too Close to Touch
I Don't Want to Lose You – Aaron Krause

Also By the Author

About the Author

Sarah Jayne Carr is a novelist who can be found most evenings with a cup of tea in-hand and her imagination tormenting many characters. When away from the computer, part of her mind is always brainstorming her next story, and she tries to keep writing utensils within reach. If paper isn't nearby, she may scribble on the nearest person's forehead.

She wrote stories as a child, but became more serious about her passion during her twenties. In her spare time, she likes to read, draw, splash in mud puddles, smell bookstores, and eat Honeycrisp apples.

Sarah Jayne has participated in eight NaNoWriMos and has mentored others through the program. Due to her dedication to National Novel Writing Month, she has made many friends through an amazing writing group.
Since August of 2012, Sarah Jayne has proudly been a part of Crushing Hearts and Black Butterfly Publishing. To date, she has multiple stories published within her JackRabbit7 series, and her Grim Reaper novel is a work in progress with Vamptasy Publishing.

Born and raised in Washington State, Sarah Jayne still resides in the area. Her life is richly filled with her supportive, and swashbuckling, husband, and their golden Nugget / Barracuda.

Made in the USA
San Bernardino, CA
20 April 2018